T.E. BAKUTIS
RISE OF A MANOR LORD

Book two

aethonbooks.com

RISE OF A MANOR LORD 2
©2024 TE BAKUTIS

This book is protected under the copyright laws of the United States of America. No part of this publication may be reproduced, stored in a retrieval system, or transmitted, in any form or by any means, without the prior permission in writing of the publisher, nor be otherwise circulated in any form of binding or cover other than that in which it is published and without a similar condition including this condition being imposed on the subsequent purchaser. Any reproduction or unauthorized use of the material or artwork contained herein is prohibited without the express written permission of the authors.

Aethon Books supports the right to free expression and the value of copyright. The purpose of copyright is to encourage writers and artists to produce the creative works that enrich our culture.

The scanning, uploading, and distribution of this book without permission is a theft of the author's intellectual property. If you would like to use material from the book (other than for review purposes), please contact editor@aethonbooks.com. Thank you for your support of the author's rights.

Aethon Books
www.aethonbooks.com

Interior print and eBook formatting by Josh Hayes. Artwork provided by Francel Garrotte.

Published by Aethon Books LLC.

Aethon Books is not responsible for websites (or their content) that are not owned by the publisher.

This book is a work of fiction. Names, characters, places, and incidents are the product of the author's imagination or are used fictitiously. Any resemblance to actual events, locales, or persons, living or dead is coincidental.

All rights reserved.

ALSO IN SERIES

The Rise of a Manor Lord 1

The Rise of a Manor Lord 2

The Rise of a Manor Lord 3

North Lincolnshire
Council
www.northlincs.gov.uk

Library items can be renewed online 24/7, you will need your library card number and PIN.

Avoid library overdue charges by signing up to receive email preoverdue reminders.

To find out more about North Lincolnshire Library and Information Services, visit www.northlincs.gov.uk/libraries

www.northlincs.gov.uk/librarycatalogue

1
I AM NOT A CAMEL

Sitting by a warm fire with warm soup and his unusually cheery battle maid, Drake was more content than he had been for quite some time. Around him, the camp was full of tents, and his people were still settling in for the night. Everyone else was done with dinner, and he was too. Yet there was no reason not to sit here a little longer.

"We really should go inside, lord," Emily said. "You're going to catch an arrow."

"Just a little longer." Drake looked to the clear night sky. "It's been a rough few weeks. Let me enjoy this peace and quiet before it all goes to shit again."

In the past month he'd been summoned against his will to a fantasy world, almost ritually sacrificed, inherited a massive Victorian manor in the middle of some freaky silver woods, gained the loyalty of five powerful battle maids and dozens of others, met a hot manor lord named Sky Skybreak, and saved an adorable little girl from bandits.

He'd also brought his butler Samuel back from the dead, saved his battle maid Valentia from being executed for a crime she didn't commit, learned he could absorb the rarities of others, and finally stopped turning into a wererat. Also, he could regenerate now.

These were good things. Good accomplishments. And ahead waited the capital, and a cabal where he would finally find out why they'd summoned all nine manor lords on such short notice. He was finally going to attend his first cabal.

But first, he decided, he wanted to see his brand-new crossbow.

He stood. "Hey, Emily, want to see something cool?"

She hopped to her feet. "Always, lord."

Drake led her to the wagons and hailed the first servant he saw, a clean-shaven, dark-skinned man wearing plain, workmanlike clothes. "Hey there."

The man turned around, went wide-eyed, and snapped to attention. "Lord Gloomwood! How may I serve?"

"Just need to find something. Where's my crossbow?"

"Your crossbow, lord?"

"Big metal thing that spits bolts at people. Might have a zarovian carved on it?"

"Oh!" The man nodded. "Yes, lord, I believe we have that... this way." He hurried off. Drake followed in amusement with Emily practically on his heels.

The man reached the back of a wagon, yanked a sheet aside, and then reached into the wagon. With a wince and a grunt, he carefully pulled out what might be the most beautiful goddamn weapon Drake had ever seen. It was a crossbow... but *what* a crossbow!

The fine wooden stock was black wood, the same as the manor, and drank up the light. The stock dived down where the barrel on a gun would have started, and above it but slightly detached, in place of a barrel, was a four-sided mechanism loaded with bolts.

That part of the weapon was gunmetal gorgeous, and Lydia had been right. There was a metal dragon's mouth on the end of the stock. Goktul had gone absolutely nuts with this thing.

As the man cautiously handed him the weapon, Drake instinctively grabbed the middle of the stock behind the trigger with one hand and the front of the stock with the other. This weapon was as heavy as he'd expect, but that only reassured him he should respect it. He lifted it sideways to examine the way the bolts worked.

The weapon was already loaded with four bolts, and while he wasn't sure transporting it loaded was advisable, it was too late to complain. The "limbs" that held the bow strings on each of the four sides weren't as wide as on a typical crossbow, only a little wider than the bolt itself. Stretched out and cocked, the thick bowstrings looked more like two parallel lines than wide Vs.

Remembering both his classes on rifle ownership and trigger discipline, Drake faced well away from anyone with the weapon still held low. He then hefted the crossbow and rested the back of the stock against his right shoulder, holding the front of the stock with his left hand. This brought the rotating metal mechanism with the four bolts to about eye level.

There were no sights—perhaps there hadn't been a place to attach one with everything else going on—but the way he could brace this weapon against his shoulder made him feel comfortable eyeballing most shots. This was closer to a rifle than a medieval crossbow.

Which was fucking perfect for Drake.

He assumed all he had to do was pull the trigger and the barrel would spin, like a revolver, to ready the next bolt for release. As he eased the weapon back down and tilted it, he even spotted a lever near the trigger that was obviously a safety or lock of some sort.

This was a weapon worthy of a manor lord. Better yet, Drake could fire it four times without having to reload. He cautiously lowered his weapon to a rest position, glanced at Emily, and smiled. "I'm going to call it Magnum."

"Ooooooh." Emily grinned. "Is that a powerful name from your realm?"

"It was Dirty Harry's weapon of choice."

"Lord?" Lydia asked. She'd approached as he played with his new murder weapon.

Drake glanced at her and kept his new weapon pointed at the ground. "What's up?"

"I cannot find Anna."

The fact that Lydia didn't bother to disguise the worry in her voice immediately dampened his enthusiasm for his new crossbow. Emily stiffened at his side. Drake took a quick look around the camp and told himself not to panic.

Little kids played hide-and-seek all the time. Maybe she was playing hide-and-seek right now. "And the others?" he asked. "Anyone seen her?"

"She was seen, lord, many times after we began to set up camp. She assisted in those preparations, and multiple people commented on how helpful and cheerful she was. Yet while many have seen her, I cannot find any who saw her after we entered your tent." She smoothed down her apron. "I cannot find her anywhere."

Drake looked around the camp again to see no adorable blond-headed children in sight. "Well, let's go look for the little scamp. I'll give her a talking to about running off." He pondered lugging Magnum around the camp with him, but he decided not to. Not with Anna missing.

He looked to his servant. "Name?"

"Hugo, lord."

"I won't forget it. Put this weapon in my tent, would you? I'll be right back."

He handed the magnificent weapon off to Hugo and left with Lydia and Emily to search the camp, even though he knew Lydia had already done that far better than he would. What he needed was time to think. Anna wouldn't just leave, so... had someone taken her?

How could anyone abduct Anna from their camp? There were

people all over, zarovians standing guard just beyond that, and Sachi. Sachi should have smelled anyone who tried to abduct Anna, unless there were so many smells here she couldn't distinguish between them.

Drake looked to Lydia. "Where's Sachi?"

"This way, lord." Lydia set off into the darkness. "She said she would be right back."

Drake considered running back to his tent to grab Magnum, but he still carried his trusty club and also had Lydia and Emily to protect him. He'd be fine. As they rushed out of the camp at not quite a jog, the reddest zarovian Drake had ever seen ran after them carrying a club and a shield. Cresh must have ordered the zarovian to stick with Drake at all times.

The zarovian had to rush to catch up. When he did so, Drake glanced his way. "Name?"

"Thak." The bright red zarovian bared rows of white teeth. "I hit things."

"That's great. I need things hit." He glanced at Lydia. "How far up was Sachi?"

"I don't know exactly, lord," Lydia said. "She last told me she planned to scout ahead but would be back in a few moments."

They continued until they were almost beyond the range of the large cooking fire back at their camp. Drake was just considering going back for reinforcements when Emily pointed.

"She's there, lord." Emily pointed at a dense cluster of grass and bushes. "In there."

Emily could see Sachi's soul despite the dense grass. "What's she doing in there?" Drake hurried the others toward the clump of leaves off the road. As the big grass shimmied apart, Sachi stepped out, still buckling up her armor. She glanced irritably in their direction.

"Could this not wait? I am not a camel."

Drake realized his mistake too late. Also, they apparently had camels in this world in addition to horses. More to ask about later. "Anna's missing."

Sachi's ears went completely flat. She hissed, sprinted into the road, and raised her nose to the air. Drake could see her nostrils twitch as she searched the wind for any trace of her little blue cupcake. Not long after, her eyes widened.

"Behind us, lord."

Drake grinned with relief. "You smell her?"

"Yes." Sachi bared her teeth. "I smell her blood."

Emily gasped as Drake's own blood ran cold. It couldn't... not after all this, all he'd done to get her somewhere safe and warm, not after...

"She is alive," Sachi said. "But a good ways back."

"Go," Drake ordered.

"But, lord—"

"Go!" He bared his teeth right back. "I have two battle maids and a Thak to protect me, and no one's faster than you on open ground. Find her!"

His feral leapt past him and scampered off on all fours like the cats she shared many traits with. It was but a moment before she vanished into the dark. With nothing else to do, Drake led his people back to their camp, which was a way's off.

They were halfway back to the fires when a low hiss stopped Drake cold.

He spun around to find Thak collapsed in the middle of the road, eyes glazed and mouth filled with blood. Before he could ask Lydia what the hell had happened to the big zarovian, Emily dropped to one knee beside him, but not before gritting her teeth and pointing back up the road. "Ass...." she managed, before she collapsed as well.

Spectral purple butterflies lit the night as Lydia flutterstepped a good ways up the road, facing a clump of tall grass the way Emily had pointed. Lydia tossed a gleaming yellow dagger into the grass like a snake snapping. A man cried out in pain, but then Lydia also collapsed.

Drake finally noticed thin streamers of red blood flowing out of Lydia's eyes and mouth, disappearing into the tall grass like string winding its way out of a doll. He also finally understood why first Thak, then Emily, and then Lydia had all collapsed.

"We lost three rangers that night," Sky said. "Good ones, which means whoever got the drop on them in my own town was even better."

"You had rangers watching the house? After our negotiation went so well?"

"To protect you, both from anyone who caught wind of our arrangement or any of my own people who did the same. All were exsanguinated."

That was a big word, but he knew what it meant. "You mean drained of blood?"

It only took an instant for Drake to accept whoever was attacking them now was the same person who murdered Sky's rangers, and a moment longer for him to charge the tall grass toward whoever Lydia had been trying to kill. Where Emily had seen a person hiding.

Someone hiding in that grass had a bullshit superpower.

Drake wasn't simply furious about his people being attacked, nor was he foolish enough to let rage lead him to his death. He simply doubted he could escape this assassin even if he wanted to escape, and while the only weapon he had was the same trusty club he'd stolen from one of Captain Ro's men weeks ago in Redbow territory, it was still a club.

Any fool could use a club.

As the worst headache in the world slammed into him, he slowed. He stumbled forward as his vision blurred red. Ahead, streamers of his own blood flowed into the tall grass, and he could *feel* blood oozing from his mouth, his nose, his eyes.

This hurt. It felt like his blood was being vacuumed right out of his face, but even with the pain that caused, Drake pushed forward. He pushed into a jog, and then a run, teeth bared as his blood flowed into the grass. He followed the flow like a cat chasing a string.

He spotted a shadow just inside the grass. At his approach, the man turned and stumbled off. Even as he did so, however, blood continued to stream. It was streaming right into the man. While that would kill anyone else, all it did was show Drake where to go.

Tall grass slapped him in the face and arms as he stumbled after the shadow. So much blood had already left his body. No person could lose this much blood and still live.

As towering grass slapped past them both and Drake closed in on the shadow, he realized the figure wore a dark-brown cloak. The man was limping visibly, likely from the fact that he had Lydia's glowing dagger stuck in his thigh. Drake quickly caught up.

The man turned at the last moment, eyes wide and disbelieving. "How are you—"

Drake hit him as hard as he could with his stupid club.

2

SONGS WON'T BE THE SAME

The man dropped when Drake clubbed him as hard as he fucking could in the head. A moment after that, the thunderous headache faded. He was no longer being drained of blood. Finally, the glowing yellow knife in the man's leg just disappeared.

Drake hoped that didn't mean Lydia was dead now. He didn't know how to deal with her being dead. For now, he'd assume she'd just called her magical dagger back... or whatever.

He still felt a little dizzy, and the world was slowly spinning, but he didn't collapse. It seemed Samuel's burnished rarity could even generate new blood. Too bad for this asshole that he couldn't have known that, since Drake had just got his new rarity today.

He raised the club to finish off the unmoving man, but noticed then that his would-be assassin was more than a bit unconscious. In addition to the cut on his thigh, there was a massive welt on his head and a long stream of drool rolling down his lips.

The man was alive, but was he brain-damaged? It would be just Drake's luck to finally capture one of his many would-be assassins alive, only to club him so hard the man forgot how to talk. He wanted nothing more than to sprint back out of this tall grass and see if Lydia was alive, and Emily was alive, and Thak... fuck, he'd just *met* Thak... was alive.

But if this assassin woke up and escaped, he could attack them again. Drake wasn't a healer. He could only heal himself. If the others were alive, they'd still be alive when he got back with his captive, and if they were dead, well... they'd still be dead.

He couldn't let this man wake up, run off, and live to attack again. He'd been lucky that the assassin hadn't known Drake could lose a bathtub full of blood and still run after him. He doubted he'd get so lucky again, and besides... he owed this man some payback.

Drake hung his club back on his belt and then experimentally shoved one arm under the entirely unconscious man. He was heavy, but Drake hauled him to his feet. He shouldn't have been able to carry an unconscious man after losing that much blood, but he had Samuel's burnished rarity now. His survival was proof of just how useful regeneration would be.

With the drooling assassin hanging off his shoulder and weighing him down, Drake ground his teeth and walked. Given the weight and his trembling legs, it was more like a slow shuffle. He stayed ready to pull his club and brain the man again if he stirred.

Shouting was audible now, not far off, and Drake soon heard the grass rustling. People were coming to find him. Two zarovians burst from the grass first. Drake breathed out as he recognized a bright-orange lizardman and another pale-yellow one.

"Who you catch?" Korrag shouted.

"Assassin," Drake managed.

Xutag raised one hand and clenched his claws. The meaning was obvious.

"No. Don't kill him. We need to interrogate him."

Korrag reached out and plucked the heavy assassin off Drake with one hand, then dropped the man over his shoulder. "I carry. You come. You great warrior."

"Not a great warrior," Drake corrected as he fell in behind

Korrag and Xutag fell in behind him. "Just the only guy who could get close enough to hit that asshole with a club."

They emerged from the maze of tall grass not long after. Drake was relieved to see Valentia and Nicole already there, tending to Lydia and Emily with their magic healing gloves. Thak lay where he'd fallen. No one was tending to Thak.

Before Drake could ask, Korrag hissed like a snake. "Thak dead."

Shit. He must have lost too much blood to save. "I'm sorry, Korrag."

"Thak was best drummer," Korrag said mournfully. "Songs won't be the same."

Drake almost asked the big lizardman to crack the assassin in half right then, but he wasn't ready to kill a man in cold blood. At least... not until he'd interrogated him first.

"He'll pay for this," Drake assured the big zarovian. "But for now, I need him alive. So keep him that way."

"Torture fine," Korrag said. "But I kill after?"

"Not unless I tell you to. Sorry, big guy."

The big zarovian sagged with another heavy-sounding hiss. "Makes sense. Stop more dying by talking. Still, want to kill."

"Me too, buddy. Me too."

Xutag walked over to Thak and knelt beside his body. The pale-yellow lizardman placed both claws together and bowed his head. His tail thumped once, twice, thrice on the earth, and then collapsed limply to the ground. He made a stovetop-sounding hiss.

Valentia rose and strode over, gaze furious. "You should not have gone off alone!"

Drake met her angry gaze with a level gaze of his own. "I had Lydia, Emily, and Thak with me." He pointed at the man unconscious on Korrag's shoulder. "The man I just knocked out was hidden in the tall grass, could suck the blood right out of you, and dropped all three of them in a few seconds flat."

"Then you should have called for more of us!"

"And what would you have done differently in their place?"

Valentia opened her mouth, looked back at the two women covered in sweat and pale as the moon, and clenched her fists. She didn't answer.

"It's all right," Drake added calmly. "That wasn't a critique, just a reality check. No one could have dropped that guy alone, and the only reason I was able to drop him is because Emily spotted him, Lydia tagged him in the leg, and I had Samuel's rarity to keep me from going down. At least now we can finally find out who keeps sending these assholes."

"He will not talk," Valentia said. "If he is as good as you say he is, he will never talk."

"We'll see." Drake motioned to the man slumped over Korrag. "His rarity is stealing blood. Any idea how he did that through silverweave?"

Valentia considered. "Silverweave mitigates magical attacks but does not entirely prevent them, especially if they are truly powerful." Her normal calm quickly returned. "Can you describe how he did it?"

"He sucked blood out of my face and nose and... well, it was disgusting, and it hurt."

"A uniquely targeted rarity." Valentia shook her head in horrified wonder. "Those are exceedingly rare." She coolly evaluated Thak's body. "The difference in mass between the fallen zarovian, Emily, and Lydia is significant, yet Emily and Lydia survived. Given that, I can only imagine that their silverweave blunted the attack enough that it didn't kill them."

Drake was relieved to hear his battle maids would live, though he was still pissed off about Thak. "Do most rarities target the whole body?"

"That is why silverweave is so valued by those who face powerful opponents. The fact that he could still target you even in silverweave is remarkable."

"Any idea how to keep him from doing that again if he wakes up?"

"Blindfold," Valentia said. "Even if he can activate his rarity with only one's head exposed, if he can't see at all he won't be able to use it."

Nicole hurried over, reached into her apron, and pulled out a silky white blindfold. So she just carried one of those around? Of course she did.

Drake took the blindfold and looked to Korrag. "Lower that dickhead down here."

As the man's head lolled dangerously enough Drake worried they might accidentally snap his neck before they interrogated him, Drake strapped on the blindfold, or tried. With a small *tut-tut* of disappointment, Nicole stepped past and cinched it on the man's head with ease.

Drake glanced at her. "It's scary how good you are at that."

She kept her eyes on the assassin. "I'm good at a lot of things."

There was no humor in her words. Nicole's flat tone told him just how furious she was about what this man had done to Emily, Lydia, and Thak.

Poor Thak. He'd liked hitting things, he'd been a good drummer, and he'd been one more loyal soldier who'd died to keep his manor lord alive. Thak would be remembered. He would also be avenged.

With the immediate adrenaline rush of combat and the horror of watching his own blood sucked out of his eyes dealt with, fresh worry for the little blonde scamp who'd sent them all running out here returned. Yet he couldn't do anything for Anna here, and no one had a better chance of finding her than Sachi. He had to trust his catgirl.

This assassin must have been the one to abduct Anna. It was the only thing that made sense. He'd planned it all out... abduct Anna, use her to draw Sachi away so his approach wouldn't be detected, wait for Drake to leave the camp looking for her, and then strike.

Once more, Drake had walked face-first into a trap. He'd been reckless and foolish to leave his camp without a larger force. If not for his new rarity and the fact that it was also burnished, he would likely be as dead as Sky's rangers back in Skybreak Manor.

He *had* to be more careful in the future. As much as he worried about Anna, he couldn't keep her alive if he was dead. Moreover, if that assassin had managed to kill him *and* Lydia, he would have handed over his whole manor and every person in it to this bloodsucking piece of shit. Though... the assassin would have been surprised when Drake's people murdered his ass.

One more reason to be glad he'd defanged the blood pact. Like the old Lord Crow, Drake wasn't above a bit of petty vengeance. He took comfort in the fact that if the worst did happen, whoever managed to kill him and Lydia would be killed by the rest of his manor before they knew his people could fight back.

As the still-burning fire in their camp came back into sight and more zarovians rushed up to join them led by Cresh, Drake considered how the attack had gone down. The assassin must have focused his rarity on Thak first because he considered a large armed zarovian the biggest threat. His mistake.

He must not have known about Emily's ability to see souls with *rend soul*. Otherwise, he'd have targeted her first. When he saw Emily pointing at his hiding spot in the tall grass, he'd tried to eliminate her next, but Lydia had flutterstepped on top of him and tagged him with her dagger. That had forced him to switch targets before he could finish Emily off.

And then, of course, Drake had charged in like a maniac, which had given the assassin no choice but to run. Whoever this man was, he was one hell of an assassin. He was also Drake's prisoner, and he'd now need to decide what to do with the man.

Would this assassin tell him anything about who'd hired him? Even if he did, would Drake spare his life and take him prisoner? A man who could target people even through silverweave would be almost impossible to keep secure, and a single mistake would cost more lives... not to mention keeping watch over and handling a prisoner would slow down their travel.

If he made the wrong decision, more would die. His people would die. He wouldn't decide right now. First, he would wait for Sachi to return with Anna, who *would* be alive. Next, he'd interrogate this assassin. And finally... he'd handle the rest.

Whatever the rest turned out to be.

By the time they were back in the camp, Lydia and Emily had recovered enough to walk unassisted. Both still looked extremely pale, but they were likely used to being borderline anemic, especially Lydia, who spent blood to use *flutterstep*.

Come to think of it, everyone with active rarities spent blood to activate them, even Valentia, who could freeze blood. So the assassin they'd just captured was able to simultaneously weaken his opponents while draining their power source and, if Drake's hunch was correct, restore his own. What a wicked rarity. How many had this man killed?

A taunting possibility also then occurred to Drake. This man had a lethal rarity, and his rarity was to *emulate* rarities. He didn't even have to mix blood with this man in order to take and use his rarity, since he could just forcefully bleed him until he filled up one of the blood flasks Zuri had given him which he still carried in his hip pouch.

But would he? Could he? He had no interest in becoming a ravenous blood-sucking monster, and becoming a guy who cut people open and carried their blood around in his pouch was dark, even by manor lord standards. Still... it was an option.

He had no doubt that bleeding this guy and taking his blood would be immoral. He wasn't going to try to justify it to himself. But moral or not, the question now was if it would be necessary to protect himself and his manor. He already knew what Valentia would say.

Sachi soon came sprinting back into camp with Anna riding on her back. The little girl had tears streaming from her eyes, but she was obviously alive. Sachi sprinted to a stop and gawked at the procession, including the man on Korrag's back.

"That man smells like a wolf! Can he shift his shape?"

Drake leaned in and noticed a faint scent of musk and grass. "You can smell wolves?"

As Anna dropped off her back and ran for Drake, Sachi snarled. "I should have known a lone wolf wouldn't be hunting all the way out here."

Anna threw her arms around him with a tiny cry. Drake gently rubbed her back. "We all got fooled. Now, what'd he do to Anna?"

"I found her tied up and hidden in the bushes. He slit her calf enough to make her bleed. I could smell her, but I doubt anyone else would have found her back there."

"I was scared, lord." Anna clutched Drake tight. "But I knew you'd come for me."

Drake suspected the assassin had only left Anna alive because if she was dead, Sachi would have smelled that, too. His rage simmered as he once more considered asking Korrag to break the assassin in half. That was foolish. Anna was alive, and he needed answers.

"Sachi found you," Drake reminded her. "Sachi will always find you." He glanced at his huntress, who flicked her ears in acknowledgment. "Can you keep an eye on her? I need to have a talk with the man who pulled you out of our camp and tied you up in the grass."

Anna pushed back enough to stare up at him. "Don't let him hurt anyone else."

"I won't," Drake said grimly. "You can count on that."

Drake doubted Sachi would let Anna out of her sight when she was in camp and not scouting. That was fine. He wouldn't either. The little girl might have a habit of getting kidnapped at inconvenient times, but she could still teleport them all home if necessary.

And so long as he had Anna in his manor, so could he. If he was willing to give up the ability to regenerate and mixed blood with Anna, he could teleport himself and his people right back to Gloomwood Manor. There was no doubt he was now a powerful manor lord.

So, now the question would be just how ruthless he was willing to be.

3
WHAT KIND OF LORD ARE YOU?

Once they were inside his big command tent, Samuel flagged them down. His frown was something to behold. "This is the assassin? Korrag, may I see him?"

The big zarovian lowered the still-unconscious man again, holding him out like a baker might extend a long loaf of bread. "You know?"

Samuel pulled back the man's hood, and in the light of the tent, Drake got a better look at the asshole. The man who had murdered Thak and almost murdered the rest of them was a handsome man with tan skin and long blond hair, but there was a cruelty to his features that was impossible to deny. He had a small scar on his lip, but no other notable features.

"We have never hired him," Samuel said. "Lord Crow employed many assassins, but he rarely paid a premium. Can this man really target people through silverweave?"

Drake nodded. "He did it to half the people here."

"Then whoever hired him absolutely paid a premium. That means he is likely a member of the Gilded Blades. Your enemy is even more wealthy and powerful than we feared."

Drake sighed. "What else is new? Let's just tie him up and get some answers." He looked to Lydia and Emily, who were walking but pale. "You two? Go lay down."

Lydia frowned. "I don't think we should leave you alone now, lord."

"And I want to watch the interrogation!" Emily added eagerly.

"I've got Val and Nicole to watch over me, and you two need rest," Drake said calmly. "Get some rest, get some food and sugar, and get that blood back up. That's an order."

For a moment, he was worried they might argue. Drake was relieved when Emily sighed and nodded, and while Lydia didn't look happy about this order, both of them headed off to get some food and, hopefully, relax. Drake glanced at Valentia and Nicole. "You're up."

"Hooray," Nicole said darkly.

They headed into Drake's command tent. Valentia brought a chair over and slapped it down in the corner of the tent. Korrag lowered the unconscious and blindfolded blond man into it, then held him there as Valentia trussed him up and to the chair. Drake was unsurprised at how good she was at tying people up.

Drake looked to Sachi. "Take some zarovians and do a full sweep. We have to be sure this dickhead is the only assassin out here. If you smell a wolf, kill it. It's probably an assassin."

Sachi left with a grim expression on her face. That left Drake, Korrag, Valentia, Nicole, and Samuel in the tent with the assassin. Korrag spoke up next.

"Thak still back on road. Xutag mourns there."

Drake felt like an ass for forgetting they'd lost a man tonight. "Go get him. Do whatever you need to put him to rest."

Korrag slapped a clawed hand to his chest, then hurried out of the tent. That left only his two battle maids and his butler. It was time to get some answers.

"Nicole?" He glanced at her. "Wake him up."

As she advanced and drew a glowing spirit knife, Drake grimaced. "With your gloves."

She sighed. "Oh, fine."

As they waited, Nicole ran her glowing fingers over and around the giant bleeding welt on the man's head. Drake would swear he heard a small snap inside, which suggested some part of the man's skull had just uncracked. So if nothing else, Drake knew he could swing a club.

Nicole tended to the man a bit longer, then stepped back. The blindfolded assassin tensed, visibly tested his body to see how tightly it was bound, and then smiled.

"How did you live through that? I sucked three men worth of blood out of you."

"I had a big lunch," Drake said. "Who sent you?"

"I can't believe you're the lord of Gloomwood Manor. You're so young."

"I'm also the guy who's going to murder you if you don't give me a reason not to, so let's have less age discrimination and more answering my questions."

"We should not be rash," Samuel cautioned.

"Listen to your man," the assassin said with a smirk. "Killing me now gains you nothing, and you'll get a sizable bounty for turning me in to the authorities in Korhaurbauten. I'm sure you could make some good coin by handing me over to them."

"I'm not interested in your bounties. I want to know who hired you."

"Then I am afraid you'll find your night just full of disappointments, lord."

Drake wasn't ready to give up yet. "You know a lot about us. Did your research?"

The assassin said nothing.

"And this isn't the first time you've seen us, is it?" Drake thought back to a house full of poison gas. "You're the one who killed those three rangers in Skybreak Manor, then pumped that poison gas into Lord Skybreak's guest house."

Still, the assassin remained silent.

"You failed then. So you're what, zero for two on killing me? Seems like you're kind of a shitty assassin."

"I am curious," the assassin said. "I will admit I saw you in Skybreak Manor, but only because I must know how you escaped. Tell me that, and perhaps I can offer you information."

"Like who hired you?"

"Not that, lord. But other information. You will find I am a fountain of such."

"I've already told you what I want. Your employer. Will you tell me?"

"Of course not. Please ask something intelligent."

"Everyone?" Drake looked around at those gathered. "I need you to give us the room."

Valentia frowned. "It is unwise for you to interrogate this man alone. Even blindfolded and tied to a chair, he is exceedingly dangerous."

"I just proved out on that road he can't do a thing to me. And if he tries, I'll hit him in the head with my club." He looked around at his now tense people. "I need to speak to this man alone. Clear the tent. Even you, Samuel. Make sure no one's around to eavesdrop."

"And just what do you plan to offer him?" Samuel asked calmly. "You cannot be considering negotiating with him without first hearing the thoughts of your advisors."

"I am the lord of Gloomwood Manor." Drake put some steel into his voice. "You serve me, not the other way around, and I don't need you to make decisions. I *allow* you to *suggest*. Now, do I need to compel Valentia to escort you out, or should we do it the other way around?"

He didn't actually want to be an asshole here, but it was important the assassin *hear* him sounding like an asshole. He needed this man to know he was serious. He wasn't going to get anywhere in this interrogation if the assassin thought he was soft.

Samuel frowned, gaze moving to the blindfolded man tied to the chair and then returning to Drake. "I would simply ask that you not offer any deal to this assassin without first weighing all the possible ramifications."

"I won't. Now go." He motioned to everyone in the tent. "All of you, right now."

Casting curious or confused looks his way, they filed out one after the other, Samuel first and Valentia last of all. As she glanced back, he smiled and winked.

She stared a moment. Then, almost grudgingly, she nodded back. It was a relief to realize that, even without knowing what he planned, Valentia finally trusted him to handle his manor lord business. How far they'd come.

Once Drake was certain he was alone, he returned his attention to the man in the chair. "We're alone now. Nothing you say will be heard by others. So, ready to talk?"

"You seem quite new at this," the blindfolded, blood-sucking assassin said languidly. "Would you like some tips? I've served dozens of your kind over my long career, so if you'd like to know a few good ways to threaten your thralls, I'd be happy to help you out."

"By dozens of my kind, you mean other manor lords?"

"No one else pays as extravagantly as your kind, lord, and the challenge is always equal to the coin. When you are as skilled at your job as I, the challenge is all that matters."

"Doesn't seem like it's all that hard to suck the blood out of people."

"The murder, of course, is easy. Still, I must catch them unawares. Unsuspecting. Often in places filled with people who might not wish them dead. Targets like you, lord, are among the most challenging of all, yet even you would still be dead if not for your curious rarity."

"Or maybe I'm just better than you."

The man laughed. "Your attempts to prick me are delightful."

Drake rolled his eyes. "Look, I have to call you something if we're going to negotiate. Even if you won't give me your real name, don't you have an assassin name or something? Some edgy and pretentious title like Bloodrazor, or the Eager Edger, or Suckerfish?"

"None who hear my name live to tell it to others. So it shall stay."

"All right, I'm just going to call you Suck, then. Because you suck."

"If that is supposed to be an insult, I can offer advice about those as well."

"No thanks. Now, Suck, who hired you?"

"If you're simply going to repeat the same simple questions, please, kill me now."

"You say that. You act brave. But I still get the feeling you don't really want to die."

"Then you are a fool."

"I don't think so. You say the words and talk the talk, but deep down, I don't think you're ready to die just yet. Before I clubbed you, you flinched."

"It was a club, lord. These things happen."

"It wasn't just your reflexive reaction. I saw your eyes widen, and I saw your little moment of fear. You thought you were going to die, and you weren't okay with that."

"No one *wants* to die, lord. Even a man who sees death as often as me. Yet I am sworn to the Blades and to my profession. To answer your question would violate my oaths."

"If you're truly ready to die for your guild and your beliefs, and you're not just full of shit, I will end you. Make no mistake. I'm not going to let a man like you come at me twice."

"I would not. I have failed to kill you, so another Gilded Blade will come in my place. So long as our guild is tasked to end you, lord, you will be ended... today, or tomorrow."

"I understand that, but you've just described every day of my fucking life. It's not like you can threaten me with death. Now, answer my question. Are you ready to die?"

"Everyone who undertakes my prof—"

"That's not what I asked. Are you, personally, willing to die, right now? Not a hard question."

"It is always a possibility in my line of work."

"And there you go dodging it again. That's how I know you're full of shit. But fortunately for you, we don't have to do this dance all night. Instead, I'm ready to make my offer."

"I will listen, lord, though out of amusement more than any true interest."

"Tell me who hired you and I will release you unharmed. Moreover, I will hire you to kill someone else. Someone I very much want dead."

"Is this torture, lord? Asking questions to which you already know the answer?"

"Let me be very clear here, Suck. I want you to tell me who hired you. Only me. I will not ask you to testify, nor will I tell anyone else you told me. Not even my own blood thralls. Do you understand? I want to know who hired you to kill me, but once you tell me, no one other than the two of us will ever *know* you told me. Not even my own people."

"This is a strange offer."

"Yet you haven't said no. You see a way to live now, don't you? Just tell me who hired you. I won't even send you after them. I have multiple people I need dead, so if one of those is the person who sent you to kill me, I'll hire you to kill another one."

"You truly are a foolish lord if you think I'll take this deal."

"Yet there's my offer. Tell me, and just me, who hired you. Live and accept a new contract from me for a nice fat bounty and go on about your business. Do so knowing I'll never tell anyone you revealed your client to me. Not if you agree to my deal."

"No manor lord would make this offer." Yet Suck still didn't tell him no. "What kind of lord are you?"

"A kind you've never met before. I'm not from your realm, nor your land. I came from another world entirely. Now, I'm going to walk across the room and pick up my crossbow. You have until I get back to accept my offer. Otherwise, you're going to be target practice."

Making sure his footsteps could be heard, Drake walked across the tent and lifted Magnum off the table. He walked back. He stopped a few paces from Suck, then flipped the safety with a menacing click. The sound inspired the response he'd hoped for.

"Wait," Suck said.

4
THAT ISN'T A LIE

Drake hefted the weapon, rested the stock against his shoulder, and lightly rested his finger on the trigger. He focused on Suck's chest. "You have until the count of three. One—"

"State your offer again."

"Tell me who hired you. I will not tell anyone you told me, nor will I reveal who hired you to anyone else. Finally, I will hire you to kill one of several enemies and pay you well."

"Then... I accept your offer, Lord Gloomwood."

Drake lowered his crossbow. "I knew you were a reasonable man."

"Perhaps too reasonable. Even now I feel as though I have made my first mistake. Still, you are correct on one point. I am not ready to die. So. My client?"

Drake waited.

"I was sent to kill you by Lord Proudglade himself."

Drake had expected as much. Having it confirmed was wonderful—in that he knew now, not that a guy with the power of motherfucking Zeus wanted him dead—but still, he had successfully gotten the name of Suck's client out of the assassin. Now, for the rest.

"Very well, Suck. As I said, I wish to hire you to kill another target, but first, I need to know just how far you're willing to go."

"I'm not sure what you mean, lord."

"This won't be an easy task, even for you. There will likely be collateral damage. To be clear, others dying is acceptable to me so long as the person I name dies as well."

"Then name your target, lord. If I can reach them and defeat them, they will die."

Suck didn't simply say he'd kill Drake's target. He couldn't say that because he didn't believe it with absolute certainty.

"First question. Are you willing to kill unarmed peasants?"

"A fine jest, lord. But in the spirit of indulging your strange humor, yes."

"And women?"

"They must die just as often as men."

"And what about children, Suck? To be clear, I don't think you'll have to kill a child on this job, but it's possible. If it's the only way you can reach your target, can you kill a kid?"

"Of course, lord. I have done so before."

Anna was truly lucky he'd needed her alive. "Final question, and then we're in business. How many targets, specifically targets who you have been hired to eliminate, have you killed?"

"Seventeen, lord, but please don't let that lessen your opinion of my skills. Many others died on the way to those. In truth, at this point, I no longer keep count."

Drake had enough information to make his decision. "You've answered all the questions I had for you. Now, before I pay you for your trouble, I have one last thing to tell you."

"What is that, lord?"

"I can lie."

There was a moment when utter silence filled the tent. Then, Suck spoke.

"What does that mean, lord?"

"It means I'm going to kill you now."

The assassin tensed in the chair. "You cannot mean—"

As the man spoke Drake raised his crossbow, squeezed one eye shut to aim, and pressed the trigger. As Magnum thumped against his shoulder, the sound of the weapon unleashing a bolt echoed loud enough that he knew they would hear it outside. The bolt slammed dead center into Suck's chest, split his ribs, and cracked into the chair's back, pinning him to it.

It turned out it was pretty straightforward to aim this crossbow after all.

As this ruthless assassin who had murdered so many men, women, and children he'd lost count thrashed on the chair, choking on his own blood, Drake walked forward and fired again. The second bolt went through Suck's neck and almost out the other side. Only a trace of fletching remained, just visible inside the thrashing skin beneath his chin.

The assassin lost consciousness so quickly he couldn't even tip over his chair. He died soon after. The rancid smell made that clear. The sound of multiple booted footsteps arose behind him, and then Valentia, Nicole, Samuel, and even Emily and Lydia all rushed into his tent. He hoped they'd managed to eat *something* before hiding outside his tent.

Drake lowered Magnum. That had been a successful test of his new weapon. He turned to face their assorted faces and assorted emotions as they took in the scene. Him, armed, standing over the bound and blindfolded man he'd just straight up murdered.

Nicole looked visibly delighted by the carnage, while Lydia's calm gaze took everything in without visible judgment. Samuel frowned in obvious disappointment. Emily grinned wide and pumped her fist, and Valentia...

She simply nodded in what he assumed was approval.

"That man was our prisoner," Samuel said calmly.

"No." Drake popped open his hip pouch and pulled out a blood flask. "He was an assassin sent to kill every one of us, including Anna, and he's killed dozens more before us, including children." He uncapped the flask and placed it below the back of Suck's neck, which was now bleeding freely. "I have it from his own lips." Blood trickled eagerly into the flask. "Had we released him, he'd simply have murdered more people and come back at us."

Samuel crossed his arms. If he had any concerns about Drake collecting the blood of a bound man he'd just murdered, it didn't show on his face. "The noble court could hold him."

"And how long until a rich manor lord paid the proper tithe to get him out again? You think we're the first people to capture him? He's in a guild of assassins, and he could kill people through *silverweave*. Had we turned him over, he'd have been out in days."

The flask filled quickly. Suck bled profusely. Drake capped the flask.

There it was. He now had a flask full of blood that could turn him into a literal blood sucker. He didn't want to use it if he didn't have to use it. But if he *had* to use it... he was ready. He wasn't sure if everyone would approve of his decision, but this hadn't been their call.

"You may be right," Samuel said. "But now, we will never know who hired him."

"He never planned to tell us that. He made that clear. Or did any of you hear a different interrogation than I did? If I misinterpreted his intentions, tell me now."

No one contradicted him. No one could. They had heard everything he did... up until the point he'd sent them out of the tent. Drake tucked the filled blood flask into his hip pouch.

"We're done with this interrogation," he informed his people. "Nicole, fetch Korrag. He can have what's left of the assassin. I don't feel like burying this child-killing asshole, so tell Korrag he can do whatever he likes with the body."

Nicole saluted and hurried out, still wearing a grin. She actually looked proud of him.

As for Samuel, he still looked displeased, but Drake could understand his reasoning. In Samuel's eyes, Drake had acted rashly and, moreover, in a way that contradicted his recent vow not to be an *evil* manor lord. Were he Samuel, he too would be concerned.

Yet despite the fact that Lydia didn't look bothered by what he'd done, she was still the one he needed to talk to about it. She, he thought, would understand. Moreover, he had a question only she could answer which he needed to ask. He set Magnum back on the table.

"All of you may return to your duties. Lydia, walk with me."

As he moved to exit the tent, she fell into step beside him. "To where, lord?"

"The carriage. You and I need to have a chat about our next move."

"Samuel should—"

"In this case, Samuel doesn't need to be there." Drake glanced at her as they walked. "You trust me, don't you?"

"I do, lord."

"Then we'll speak more in the carriage."

They stepped outside into a cold night. In the distance, Drake spotted some zarovians stacking freshly cut logs. So that was how they honored their dead. They were going to build a pyre and send Thak off to Valhalla. That seemed like a zarovian-esque thing to do.

He opened the carriage for Lydia before she could open it for him—she was the one who'd almost died from blood loss recently—and glanced at her. She stepped inside, and while she was obviously trying to hide it, she was still visibly tired. He'd make sure she ate something after they spoke.

Drake glanced back at the tent and saw Samuel watching him. The man looked away the moment his gaze met Drake's, and then Drake closed the door and sat down. Drake had no doubt the old man was still upset with him, but he'd worry about that later.

Lydia now sat on the couch across from him. Speaking face to face would be best. Once certain they would not be disturbed or overheard, he leaned forward.

"It was Lord Proudglade."

Her eyes widened only briefly before she accepted how he'd learned that. "You lied."

"I did, but only to him."

He explained how he'd fooled the ruthless assassin into revealing his employer. He also revealed how the assassin had answered his questions. When he finished, Lydia nodded.

"You were right to execute him."

"And the blood? Was I right to steal his blood?"

"Given your rarity, it would be foolish to abandon such a weapon."

"Great. Good." Drake grimaced. "So why do I still feel like I've crossed a line?"

"A line, lord?"

"It's an expression from my world. It means when you've done so many bad things you can't ever be a good guy again."

"Good and evil are often a matter of perspective. All you have done, you have done to protect yourself, our manor, or our people... though I know it may not feel that way."

Drake nodded. "Like you said, I was right to execute him. I know that, and I want to *feel* that, but I'm not sure how I feel yet. Killing people who were trying to kill me is getting easier, but killing someone in cold blood, even a man like that..."

"I or any other maid would have done it for you."

"I know you would have. But it would have been selfish to ask, and this was my first execution. I needed to do it myself. I needed to know I could kill an enemy even if I had the option to spare his life and walk away, especially if he'd be a threat to us in the future."

"You still had doubts? You have killed before."

"Technically, but Lord Crow was self-defense, not a cold-blooded murder. And while I ate people as a dire rat, there was a level of disassociation I used as a crutch. It wasn't fully me who killed those mercenaries, those assassins, or so I could tell myself. It was the rat. Until tonight, I wasn't sure I could personally execute someone."

"And now that you have executed your first prisoner, how do you feel?"

There was no judgment in Lydia's question. There was concern, but the concern felt directed at him rather than at what he could do for the manor. He appreciated that she was looking out for him.

"I have no fucking idea," Drake admitted. "I just didn't see any other options. That man was too dangerous. A hero might be willing to show mercy to a defeated foe, but Val made it clear I can't do that. There was no way I could let that asshole come at us twice."

"And what of your blood pact? Did you consider forcibly adding him to it?"

Drake wasn't surprised Lydia had asked him about that possibility, nor was he angry she'd brought it up. If he hadn't thought about his ability to bind people with blood magic, he wouldn't be doing his duty as a manor lord. He also felt comfortable with his reasoning.

"It wasn't an option this time," Drake said. "And not just because I'm still not comfortable with slavery or torturing some dude until he's willing to say anything. We don't have that kind of time, and that guy was literally a *child* killer. I'd never let someone that shitty into Gloomwood Manor even if I was willing to enslave him. Dude had to die, and if we need a blood sucker for some reason, I can do it."

"I don't disagree," Lydia assured him. "With any of your reasoning."

"And it's fine that you asked. I'm glad you asked. I want you to ask questions like that."

"Then I shall continue to do so." She hesitated. "And though you know this, I have killed bound and defenseless prisoners before. It was never easy, and it is not supposed to be easy, no matter their crime." She held his gaze. "Not unless you're like him."

She still carried the weight from her time enslaved by blood magic to Lord Dickcheese. She likely always would. Perhaps, now, Drake would share a bit of that weight.

He had also spent enough time navel-gazing. It was time to get back to business. "So, setting aside whether I'm actually an evil manor lord now, what can we do with this? Now that I know Lord Proudglade hired this guy?"

"Very little. Unfortunately, you cannot reveal what you have learned without revealing how you learned it. In doing so, you would throw away your strongest tool to manipulate our enemies. Moreover, even if you did reveal this, Lord Proudglade could simply tithe."

"So sending an assassin to kill another manor lord on the way to a cabal isn't an unforgivable crime, just generally frowned upon?"

"An unfortunate fact. Attacking a manor is off limits, but lords on the road are not."

"So, all we've gained is that you and I know for certain it really is Lord Proudglade who wants to murder me. We can adjust our defenses and negotiate with this extra information during the cabal. My next question is going to be more difficult for you."

"There are few questions I won't answer."

"I need you to tell me if we can trust Samuel with the fact that I can lie."

"With..." She breathed out.

"To be clear, Samuel seems like a genuinely cool guy. I can tell everyone at the manor absolutely adores him, and so far, he seems all right to me as well. Savvy. Logical. But I've only known him a day. You've known him as long as you've served here. How would he react?"

"I..." Lydia looked down at the seat. "You were right."

"About what?"

"This is a difficult question."

"So you understand why I needed to talk with you alone."

"I do. Of course I do."

"You don't have to give me an answer now. In fact, I don't want you to. Think about my question as we travel and come tell me when you figure it out."

She looked up. "Until he knows what you can do, Samuel will have doubts about you."

"He still works for me. If you're willing, you can tell him you believe I made the right decision. That may appease him. Ultimately, however, you're still my rock."

"What is that?"

"The person I talk to when I have no idea what to do. You listen when I have doubts, you give great advice, and you always make sure I keep moving forward. There's no one in this entire camp I trust more than you. You've rewarded my trust time and again."

She pushed her hands together and blushed brightly. "Oh, lord."

"That isn't a lie."

"I know it isn't. And... I will tell you when I have an answer."

"Sounds good. Now, anything you think we should tell the others?"

"You saw Nicole and Val. They were thrilled with your decision. Sachi and Emily approved as well. We've already discussed Samuel, and you know my thoughts. So no, lord. That man murdered one of your blood thralls and intended to murder you. He needed to die. No one will question that."

"Great. The less I have to think about that asshole, the better. Now, you're going to eat something."

"Of course, lord."

"I mean it." Drake hadn't forgotten how quickly she'd gotten to his tent after he shot Suck. "I am personally escorting you and

Emily to the chow line. You need food and fluids and all that, and I also want to have Raylan look at you both. I'm not losing any more people."

Lydia eyed him. "Are those words you truly believe?"

Drake snorted. "Let's call them aspirational and leave it there for now."

5
GOOD CHOW

The next morning, the smell of fresh sausage roused Drake in his sleeping bag. He actually had slept—he'd slept just fine, in fact—and the fact that he had drifted off easily and had no nightmares after using a living man for target practice concerned him.

He should feel bad, shouldn't he? He should feel at least some small measure of guilt after executing Suck, but perhaps, in addition to acclimating to this fucked-up fantasy world in other ways, he was also growing numb to murder. At least the murder of his enemies.

He wasn't exactly thrilled about this fact, but it was convenient. The less time he spent feeling guilty about killing assholes, the more time he could spend protecting himself and his people. Some back on Earth might call him a monster, but... they weren't here.

He had a manor full of people to protect and ruthless enemies to kill. He'd worry about thorny questions of morality once he was safe and no one was threatening his people. Which, given the way things worked here, would likely be *never*.

Emily dropped to her knees beside his sleeping bag, already dressed in her battle maid best. She smiled down at him as she extended a silver fork with a sausage on it, then wiggled it under his nose. "Wakey wakey, Lord Gloomwood! It's time to eat."

He irritably pushed away the sausage. "I don't need you to feed me."

"I know." Emily grinned. "But I would like to."

"Just give me the fork and plate, please." He'd thank Meryl for this bounty after he got done scarfing it down. "And go get yourself some food if you haven't already."

With a small but playful pout, she rose. "I have already eaten. So have the zarovians."

"Oh? Good chow?"

"They devoured the assassin this morning. It was kind of you to give him to them. I think even Cresh was impressed with your generosity."

Drake was suddenly not quite as hungry for sausage. "They ate him?" He was suddenly glad he'd remembered to harvest the man's blood while he was still... solid.

Emily turned and walked away. "Cresh sent his apologies for not saving you a bite, but I assured him you wouldn't mind."

"Yeah... sure." Drake glanced down at the sausage on the fork, mentally debated as disgust warred with delicious smell, and then took a bite.

Meryl remained a miracle worker. He scarfed down two sausages and ate the fruit as well, then wiped the juice on his sleeve. Feeding his would-be assassin to his zarovians was, he supposed, a good way to get rid of a body. This was actually going to work out rather well.

Given how few people in Drake's camp had actually seen them lug that man into his tent, Suck's "Gilded Blades" might never know what happened to him. Drake could do without assassins taking a personal interest in him. He had enough assassins taking a financial interest.

Slipping out of bed in just the light tunic and pants he'd gone to sleep in immediately made him shiver. It was even colder in the morning, on the road, than it was in his manor. Fortunately, someone—likely Lydia—had stacked a fresh set of dark silverweave clothing on the chair beside him. A heavy fur cloak sat on the chair's back. His steward rocked.

Drake grabbed the clothing and stumbled into the private area in the big tent set aside for changing. Once he was suitably attired for manor lord business, he stepped out and stretched. Given he'd had his blood sucked out last night, he felt absolutely fine now.

Better than fine. He felt perfect. Despite sleeping on hard ground again last night, he felt none of the aches and pains he'd come to associate with roughing it in the wild. Every muscle in his body felt both alert and energized, and he suspected he knew why.

This was Samuel's rarity. The burnished regeneration now filling his body extended even to basic aches and pains. Given what he knew about aging and how human cells wore out over time, he wondered if this ability could even make him immortal. Would he want to be?

No. Not in this world. Sooner or later, everyone he liked would be dead and all he'd have left was constantly dodging murder attempts. And if he did eventually settle down with someone like Sky, or some *other* hot and sexily murderous woman, she'd die of old age as well.

He'd be alone. Being alone sucked. So no immortality, even if he survived all this. Eventually, he'd switch rarities and shuffle off into comfort or death.

Before he'd been trapped here he'd hardly ever thought about the future—it had been a struggle simply to keep an apartment and a construction job—and now, there seemed little point in planning for more than the next few weeks. Still... the fact that he still actually missed his mother and some of his friends back home assured him he wasn't actually evil.

He still felt things. He just didn't lose sleep over murdering child-killing assassins. As for the "I store vials of my defeated enemies' blood" bit? That was just planning ahead.

With his latest minor morality crisis resolved, Drake lifted the tent flap and stepped out into what was already a busy camp. Most of the other tents were already down, and servants were busy packing up the wagons. He also didn't miss the zarovians arrayed in a protective ring in all directions. After last night, Cresh and his people were taking no chances.

He and Emily had been the only people in the tent when he woke up, but a brief visual survey spotted Anna eagerly helping two women pack up a wagon. She was grinning and even laughing as they worked, so no ill effects from being abducted last night. At this point, the poor child must be more than used to it.

After a brief debate, Drake walked back into his tent and grabbed Magnum. As large and heavy as his crossbow/rifle was, he wasn't about to leave it in the wagon another day. It was going in his carriage as of today, and he remembered then that Magnum only held two bolts.

Reloading. It was time to learn how to reload while his people packed up. He hurried back out of the tent once more and searched until he found a man he recognized.

"Hugo! Morning."

The man he'd met yesterday night seemed surprised to see him, and even more surprised to see Drake actually remembered his name. "Lord Gloomwood? Is there trouble?"

"No trouble. Just need to grab my crossbow bolts. I test-fired my weapon for the first time yesterday night, so I need to reload."

Hugo nodded and hurried for the back of the wagon. The man grunted again as he attempted to lift out a large wooden box. It must be heavy.

Drake grabbed the handle on one side of the box. "Don't throw your back out. Grab the other end and we'll lift it together."

Hugo stared. "But, lord—"

Drake grinned at him. "You think I can't handle a box?"

The man blinked rapidly and then grabbed the other handle. "Of course not, lord."

"Three, two, one. Lift." With Drake's help, they easily lifted the box out of the wagon and then carried it to his carriage. The box was going in his carriage today too. He needed bolts.

"Just set it down here."

"But, my lord—"

This man really was protesting endlessly. "Lydia can help me load it. You've got more important things to do, don't you? Like packing up the rest of my wagons?"

"Yes, lord!" Hugo snapped to attention, pivoted on one heel, and hurried back to his business. Still, he didn't look frightened, just eager to please. Drake would take it.

He knelt beside the box and opened the latch. It wasn't locked. Once he looked inside, he whistled. There must be at least fifty bolts in this box, which explained the weight. Unlike arrows, which were wooden except for the tips, crossbow bolts were heavier.

Given how easily the single bolt he'd fired had gone through Suck, Drake wouldn't complain about the weight. His memory of the wet crunch vaguely nauseated him, which made him feel even better about not being evil. He picked out two bolts and closed the box.

He walked back into the tent and set the bolts on the table, then examined Magnum. Goktul hadn't sent any instructions, but this couldn't be that hard to figure out. The first thing he'd do was put the "safety" back in its original position. That made the most sense.

He next tried rotating the barrel mechanism manually, but it wouldn't budge. It seemed firing a bolt was the only way to rotate the mechanism, and he didn't want to impale some hapless servant through the wall of his tent. He was only just getting them to trust him.

Still, Magnum was easy to rest on its side—Goktul had likely designed it that way, since the "limbs" on each of the four sides were narrow—so he settled it with one empty rail facing up and pulled on the empty strings. It wouldn't budge. How was he going to reload this thing?

Given how hard it shot bolts, Drake should have known he couldn't string it manually without super strength. Did it have a hidden crank somewhere? He had asked Goktul to make it easy to reload, and the zarovian smith had done an absolutely bang-up job with all his other requests, so he must have prepared *something*. Drake looked closer.

He soon spotted a small depressed circle next to the front of the mechanism, one just big enough for a fingertip. It was the size of a button, but it didn't look like one. Still...

He pressed the little circle. To his delight, something whirred inside the mechanism, and then the bowstring, the "limbs" on either side of it, and the little moving rack on the rail cranked back of their own accord. Was this magic? Drake didn't care, so long as it worked.

Once it finished cranking all the way back, which only took about ten seconds, Drake grabbed a bolt and eased it into the notch on the rack, which sat just ahead of the now-taut bowstring. It fit perfectly, and a faint snap assured him it wouldn't fall out.

Easy to reload, indeed. Goktul had made this amazing crossbow absolutely idiot-proof, and as with Meryl, Drake suspected he could make a fortune if he somehow exported the talents of his blood thralls back to Earth. Was it possible Goktul had a rarity that let him make magic weapons? Or was he just *really* good at making weapons?

Regardless, any idiot could reload this thing, and Drake repeated the process with the remaining empty rail. He now had four bolts loaded once more, and could load one new bolt every ten seconds. He grinned. He was going to kill *so* many assassins with this thing.

He lifted Magnum with a grunt and carried it to the carriage. He doubted he could run with his weapon—the best he might manage was a lumbering jog—but still, he was more than satisfied with his magical revolving crossbow/hunting rifle.

Once he'd stowed his magnificent crossbow inside his carriage, he spotted Anna approaching with Robby in tow. He hadn't seen her creepy wooden doll for several days, and its faux green-emerald eyes gleamed in the light.

Drake chuckled when she arrived. "Taking Robby out for a morning stroll?"

"He does like his exercise," Anna said. "But, lord, I wanted to ask you something."

"What's up?"

"Could I ride with you and Lydia today?"

Perhaps she *was* just a little affected by being kidnapped last night. Now that Samuel wasn't taking up an entire couch, they had four seats. "You bet, squirt. Hop in."

"Oh, I will!" Anna grinned wide. "I just have to help the others finish packing up."

"Sure. Just find me when you're done."

As Anna hurried off with Robby bouncing in one hand, Samuel cleared his throat. Drake hadn't even noticed the man's approach. He glanced at Samuel to find the man not watching him at all. He was watching Anna.

"Got a problem with her sharing our carriage today, old man?"

Samuel simply shook his head. "Before we leave, we should talk."

He'd expected this. Samuel was still pissed about the murder last night. "Sure," Drake said. "Where do you want to talk?"

"Behind your tent would be fine. We should remain inside the zarovian perimeter."

Drake motioned. "Lead the way."

Samuel strode off with what Drake could only describe as military precision to his steps. He'd actually been growing to like the man, but it seemed their honeymoon period was over. Still, until he had a decision from Lydia, he'd let the man think whatever he liked.

6
I SAID I'D HANDLE IT, NOT IGNORE IT

Once they were hidden from everyone save the alert zarovians staring out over largely flat countryside, Samuel spoke again. "Where did Anna acquire her wooden doll?"

Drake took a second to mentally regroup from defending his actions last night to answering questions about playthings. "You mean Robby?"

"Is it hers, or was it given to her?"

"I mean, if you want one, I guess we can pick one up in the capital."

Samuel frowned. "I would appreciate it if you would limit your jests when we are discussing manor business. While you think yourself amusing, you are not."

"Brutal honesty. Just what I pay you for." Drake still wasn't sure why Samuel was mad about Anna having a friend. "What does our business have to do with Anna's doll?"

"I'd simply like to know where she acquired it. Did you purchase it for her?"

Drake realized that in recounting his tale of tearing apart Captain Ro and his men, and rescuing Anna and Jeremy, he hadn't actually mentioned Robby. He couldn't imagine why Samuel would want to know about Anna's creepy doll.

"The man who held her captive gave it to her," Drake said. "She also told me it was her only friend. Given they kept her in a cage while threatening to feed her dad to dogs if she didn't behave, I can see why. It's creepy, but it keeps her happy. What's the problem?"

"The eyes, lord."

"Do you really have a doll phobia?"

"It is possible it is simply tinted glass," Samuel said calmly. "Yet I have seen such gems before in other contexts. Not in a doll, but a very similar green gem was once added to a scepter Lord Crow secretly gifted to a rival he wished eliminated. I believe he used it to spy on his enemy."

All at once, Drake got a whole lot more concerned about Anna's creepy doll. His grin died. "Are you telling me you people have spy cams in this world?"

"While I can only guess at what 'cam' means, I assume you are asking if it is possible for people to view others remotely through magical items. It is. The green gems in the doll's eyes are the same color as the gem Gloomwood placed atop that scepter."

"And old Crow could see his rival through the gem?"

"I believe so. I once heard a voice I did not recognize in Lord Crow's study and entered to check on him. I recognized his rival in the bowl of water on which he was intensely focused. I also recognized the rival's voice. I believe Lord Crow could both see and hear his rival through the green gem atop the scepter."

Drake could only grind his teeth as he mentally traced his path back over the last few weeks. Robby had spent almost the entire trip from Captain Ro's camp to Skybreak Manor in a backpack, but hadn't they taken the creepy doll out when they got to Sky's guest house? He'd assumed the assassins had already been waiting for him there, but what if they hadn't?

What if Suck had just been in the area, then hurried to Skybreak Manor to take a shot at him while Drake waited for his own forces to come over from Gloomwood Manor? The assassin had even known what house he was in, despite Sky's caution. Robby had been out and about.

Moreover, Suck's ambush last night had gone off like he had satellite intel. Despite the short period of time that passed between Drake receiving the letter and this whole convoy trundling out of Gloomwood Manor—a matter of hours—Suck had known exactly where to meet them. He'd been an experienced assassin, but he'd also been perfectly prepared.

It was possible Suck had simply anticipated Drake's vanguard would take the Noble Road between Gloomwood and Korhaurbauten, and he'd simply waited on it. Yet his enemies had been doing an awfully good job of ambushing him repeatedly, and if Samuel was right...

"Fuck," Drake said. "We can't just take her best friend away. She'd be wrecked."

"Would you suggest we simply let whoever is viewing us through it continue to spy?"

"We don't even know if that's happening. But..." He looked up. "I can find out."

"How so, lord? Do you have a talent for identifying magical objects?"

Drake paused as he considered how to phrase this without mentioning the word 'lie.' "I have a way to find out if you're right. So why don't you let me handle this?"

"I don't feel comfortable ignoring this matter."

"I said I'd handle it, not ignore it. Now, can you answer some questions for me?"

After a long moment of placid staring, Samuel nodded.

"Are there any alternate paths to the capital? Or just this one road?"

"No paths that are as well-maintained as the Noble Road. There are several routes we could take if we wish to avoid it, but I would not recommend them. If we break an axle or lose a wagon on rough roads, we may not have time to make repairs and reach the capital on time."

"Which is why our enemy might not expect us to take those paths, which could save us time in ambushes. Which path is the second most direct? How quickly can we divert onto it?"

"If we travel steadily, we could leave the main road to Korhaurbauten and divert onto what is known as the Merchant's Roadway. It winds through Ashglaive and multiple towns before returning to the Noble Road at its end. We'd lose two full days if we took that route."

"But could we still make it on time if we pushed the horses?"

Samuel's brow furrowed in obvious concern. "Perhaps, lord. But as before, I do not think it is wise. Our force is sizable and strong, and Sachi will warn us of any larger force that seems to challenge us. We will be safer on the Noble Road, and more importantly, we will better be able to coordinate our defense."

"All right, Samuel. We'll stay on the main road today."

Given Drake seemed to be wasting his time, Samuel now appeared more than a bit exasperated. "And how will you handle the possibility that the doll is being used to spy on us?"

"My way." Drake held the man's gaze. "You told me yesterday a manor lord is expected to be perfect. I'm working on it. I've already survived a month in your world without your counsel, so while I still want it, I also need you to trust me to handle business. Will you?"

"It is difficult for me to trust you when you will not share your way of thinking. Are you so confident in your knowledge and foresight? Lord Crow felt much the same way."

Drake resisted the urge to mouth off in anger. Samuel had no reason to trust him yet, not without knowing all he could do. "I'm not Crow. But today, I'd like you to ride with the other battle maids. Lydia and I will speak to Anna about her doll. I don't want you there."

"And why not?"

"Because she doesn't *know* you, Samuel." Drake saw no way to divert his butler than to straight up lie to his face, which would be hard to explain if he slipped up. "She trusts me. She sort of trusts Lydia. But she trusts no one else, and if we're going to toss away the only thing that kept her sane while she lived through hell, I want her with people she trusts."

Samuel's jaw tightened. It looked like he might argue further, but after a momentary staring contest, Samuel relaxed. "You must do what is best for the child."

"That's right." Drake nodded. "And besides, the maids all love you. I bet they'll be thrilled to have you shacked up in the carriage with them. Just don't do anything I wouldn't."

Samuel narrowed his eyes. "All relationships I now maintain are professional."

"Glad to hear it."

"And as Lord Gloomwood, I will expect the same from you."

Drake chuckled. "No worries on that score, old man. If I was going to make a move on one of my stupidly attractive battle maids, I'd have done that weeks ago."

Samuel looked past Drake. "May I be dismissed?"

"You're the one who wanted to talk." Yet Drake paused before letting Samuel go. "I'm also glad you mentioned the doll. I get you may not fully trust me yet, but I'm not dismissing your concerns. I simply need to handle them my way. Finally... you decide when you're ready to go do something else. That's how I do things, remember?"

Samuel nodded curtly and walked past him to re-enter the camp.

At the moment, Drake was firmly hoping Lydia came down on the "tell Samuel you can lie" side of the argument. Because if not, working around the old man without letting him know what was going on was going to get frustrating. Now, to launch his fiendish plan.

Which would start by finding Sachi.

Soon after he spoke with his favorite feral and gave her his new orders, they were packed up and ready to roll out. Lydia arrived with Anna in tow, and Drake was both relieved and worried to find Robby with her. After Lydia helped him load his big crate of crossbow bolts into the carriage, Drake motioned for her and Anna to get inside. He followed.

As he reached to close the door, Lydia raised one hand. "Samuel is still coming, lord."

"No, he's not. We had a disagreement this morning, so he's going to ride elsewhere." He firmly kept his eyes away from Robby, who now sat in Anna's lap.

Lydia stared. "A disagreement?"

"Yeah. I don't want him with us today. I'm tired of arguing with him."

Lydia bowed her head. "Of course."

Anna hugged Robby tight. "I like Samuel. Is he really troubling you, lord?"

Drake closed the door to the carriage and thumped the front wall to let the carriage driver know they were ready to move. "He's fine. We just had an argument that got rather heated, and I wanted to let him cool off before we make camp tonight. That's all."

"And you're sure it's all right for me to ride with you today?"

Drake smiled at her. "Of course it is. You and Robby are both welcome."

Anna hugged her creepy doll tight. "Thank you!"

The carriage lurched into motion, which assured Drake they were on the road. Once they were moving, he executed the next part of his fiendish plot.

"Lydia? Close the curtains. I'd like you to teach me more about the various manors and their lands today, and I don't want any visual distractions. Anna can learn with us."

Anna grinned. "I would love that, lord! I know so little about other manors!"

"Then that's what we'll discuss today." Drake grinned right

back. "Lydia knows just about everything, and she's a very good teacher."

"I wouldn't go so far as all that," Lydia said. Yet her smile returned as she closed the curtains on the wagon windows, dropping them into darkness.

Drake activated the Zippo candle, then looked up. "Oh. I almost forgot to mention something to you."

"What, lord?"

"We'll be taking the Merchant's Roadway today."

Lydia's lips immediately tightened. "Are you sure that's wise?"

"Samuel didn't think so. That was the argument. Still, there may be more ambushes on the Noble Road. Diverting down the Merchant's Roadway is our best bet to avoid them." He eyed her meaningfully. "Also, I don't want any arguments about this. That's an order."

Lydia immediately nodded. "Of course, lord."

"Now. Let's start by learning about Lord Brightwater and the lands she controls."

As Anna turned to Lydia hopefully, she began to share what she knew.

7
DO YOU ACTUALLY HAVE TO PEE?

Talk of manor lords and their lands continued until the caravan stopped for lunch, which Drake insisted they take inside the carriage. When Anna mentioned she needed to pee, Drake decided she likely wouldn't know what road they were on just by looking and allowed it, but he asked Lydia to stay with him. He also offered to keep Robby in the carriage with him.

Anna, thrilled by the idea of giving her favorite doll some time for Lord Gloomwood, happily agreed. Thus the creepy doll didn't leave the carriage, and the curtains stayed closed. Anna, when she returned, said nothing about their route.

After taking their lunch inside the carriage—with the curtains still closed—travel resumed. Full of food and soothed by movement, Anna soon fell asleep with her head in Lydia's lap. That was the first stroke of luck. He might soon be able to clue Lydia into his plot.

When they hit a bump that sent Robby tumbling off the bench and flat onto his creepy doll face, hiding the gems, that was the second. Drake immediately leaned forward and beckoned for Lydia to move closer. He simultaneously put a finger to his lips.

Visibly surprised, Lydia nonetheless leaned forward as far as she could without disturbing Anna. Drake pointed to his lips and then mouthed *"I lied."*

Lydia tilted her head. As she did so, Drake pointed at the doll now face down on the floor of the carriage and mouthed, *"Spying on us."*

Lydia's eyes widened as she recognized his words, and then she settled back in her seat and offered a firm nod. She'd been visibly tense ever since Drake announced the route they'd be taking today, but she now appeared much more relaxed. As she glanced at the curtains he'd kept closed all day, she even smiled to herself. Perhaps she'd now guessed his ploy.

With little to talk about and even less desire to wake Anna, Drake decided to take his own midafternoon nap. It might make it more difficult to sleep tonight, but he doubted he'd be sleeping tonight anyway. He couldn't leave the task of waiting for Sachi to someone else.

He'd best get all the sleep he could now.

The soft couches in the carriage and the gentle, even movement made it all too easy to drift off. It seemed only a moment before a sharp lurch and the sound of routine shouting outside alerted him to the fact that they had once again stopped for the night. Anna came awake at almost the same time he did, and when she saw him, she giggled.

"Oh, lord, you dozed too. Did you have a good dream?"

He yawned and stretched. "Not really. But no bad ones either."

"I dreamed about my mother," Anna said. "She's with the Eidolons now, but sometimes, she comes to visit me in my dreams. Even though I've been bad, she still loves me."

So Anna's mother *was* dead. Drake had always suspected, but having it confirmed so casually was a kick to the gut. He forced a smile past his discomfort. "You're not bad, squirt."

She smiled bravely. "Not anymore."

Lydia cleared her throat. "With your permission, I will organize the setup for tonight."

"Sure, Lydia. Take Anna with you." He paused. "Oh, but leave Robby here."

Anna frowned in visible distress. "But why, lord?"

"I have an idea to dress him up for you. I just realized on the road today that when we got you nice clothes, we didn't get any for Robby. He doesn't have any."

Anna's eyes went wide as saucers. "You'd do that?"

He actually would, even if he ripped Robby's eyes out after. "You bet."

She hopped across the carriage and hugged him. "Thank you, lord!"

He hugged her back. "Now, go help Lydia, and no wandering off this time."

She nodded vigorously. "I promise!" She settled Robby on the couch facing Drake and fixed him with a firm gaze. "You be good. Lord Gloomwood is very nice to get you clothes."

"Come now," Lydia told Anna. "We've lots to do."

Anna eagerly exited the carriage with Lydia. As before, Drake stayed inside with the creepy doll. He wouldn't emerge until his tent was ready, and then he'd carry Robby with him. He'd also make sure to keep the doll's green eyes clutched to his chest the whole time.

Soon enough, the camp was ready. With Robby essentially blinded against his chest, Drake carried the creepy wooden doll out of the wagon and into his command tent. He then stuffed the doll into his backpack. His whole plan would fall apart if Anna found him and carried him outside. Then, he walked out to find a battle maid and good supper.

That night, as they were all settling in for bed, Anna wandered over. "Where's Robby, lord? It's about time for us to go to sleep."

"He's sleeping with the other maids tonight. They wanted to

spend some time with him so they could decide what outfit would be best."

Anna pouted. "But Robby's my *friend*. He keeps me safe."

"Well, you know what? Since Robby's having a sleepover, you can sleep beside me tonight. Move your sleeping bag over here. Nothing will hurt you with me around."

Anna gasped in delight. "Thank you, lord!"

"Now get settled."

Once Anna had her bedroll carted over, he caught Lydia watching him with a knowing gaze. She couldn't have failed to notice they were still on the Noble Road, but she hadn't said a word about it. Not long after, Anna was snoring softly nearby. Slipping out of his sleeping bag was easy, and grabbing his heavy fur cloak off the chair was easier than that.

Drake had only just reached the opening of the tent when the soft sound of slippers on fur hide assured him Lydia was right beside him. They slipped out together, and then Drake led Lydia to the nearby tent where the other battle maids slept. It was still well inside the camp perimeter, and the shadows of alert zarovians were barely visible around them.

He had learned today on his journey that zarovians could go days without sleep, though they'd need to hibernate afterward. That made them ideal for standing vigil on long trips. He doubted much of anything could get into this camp tonight.

He offered Lydia an amused glance. "Any questions about our weird day?"

"Just one, lord. Did you send Sachi down the Merchant's Roadway to scout for ambushes?"

He grinned. "What do you think?"

"If our enemy does attempt to ambush us on the Merchant's Roadway, the only reason they would do so is because of what you said in front of the doll. Sachi can slip away without being detected, and then we'll know your suspicions about the abilities of Anna's doll are correct."

"Samuel's suspicions, actually. If he's right, I'm going to kick myself so hard I might actually injure my own ass. If that creepy doll has been keeping tabs on us this whole time—"

"You could not have known."

"Which is the problem, and which is why I'm glad to have a man like Samuel."

As they sat beneath the stairs, Lydia glanced at him once more. "You know, lord, if we keep sneaking off like this in the middle of the night... it could present a problem."

He chuckled. "Rumors, you mean?"

The wind caught her dark hair and teased a few strands across her face. "They do arise."

"If you're worried about what Samuel might think about this, don't be. I made it perfectly clear I'm not ever going to be *that* kind of a manor lord."

She looked to the sky. "I have the answer to your question."

She meant about if he should tell Samuel he could lie. "Already? It's only been a day."

"You can trust Samuel with your secret. While his loyalty to Lord Crow was never strong, his loyalty to our manor is as strong as the silverwood trees around Gloomwood Manor. When he knows what you can do, he will be eager to help you exploit your unique gift."

"That's all I needed to hear. In fact... now that you've decided, why don't you go wake the old man up? Have him join us for the reveal. We'll quash his doubts and blow his mind."

She rose. "And if Anna awakes?"

"Tell her I had to pee and I'll be right back."

"I cannot do that, lord. Not unless... do you actually have to pee?"

Drake laughed as he remembered Lydia couldn't even tell a little white lie. "Tell her I'm waiting for Sachi, and as soon as she returns, I'll be back to keep her safe."

"That I can do." Lydia departed.

Not long after, a scowling Samuel returned with Lydia. He looked annoyingly dapper despite being in his fuzzy bedclothes. Drake motioned for them all to hunker down in the shadow of the other tents, where they could speak without being overheard or seen.

Samuel looked none too pleased about being roused in the middle of the night, but he was already alert and focused. "What is this about?"

"Nothing much. There's something we both need to get off our chests."

Samuel sighed. "If this is about our argument regarding our route—"

"It's not. It's time we told you what's been going on between us. All the stuff you've seen Lydia and I talking about in secret when you're not around."

Samuel waited.

"Lydia and I are having sex."

Lydia gasped. "Lord, how could you!" Yet as much as she blushed at the lewd implication, she also couldn't entirely hide her amusement at Samuel's expression.

Samuel's glower at Drake could have melted ice, yet when he directed it at Lydia, she had the decency to look a little abashed. "I expected better of you."

"Tell him, Lydia," Drake said. "Tell him the truth."

Lydia looked right at Samuel with every ounce of indignation a battle maid could muster. "Lord Gloomwood and I are not and have *never* had sex."

Samuel opened his mouth to berate her, then paused. His eyes narrowed, and Drake watched as the whirring gears inside the man's mind momentarily ground to a halt. He looked to Drake again, then to Lydia, and then frowned.

"Does sex mean something different in his realm? Is this a game of words?"

"Also," Drake added, "I burned the manor down before we left.

I tossed a torch through the front door and watched it collapse. Then I kicked you in the nuts. Remember that?"

Samuel gaped at him, then at Lydia. Soon after, he closed his mouth. He watched Drake with fresh caution and, perhaps, a hint of respect.

Drake leaned in. "Do you understand why I'm different from any other manor lord you've served? Or do I need to spell it out for you?"

Samuel nodded as if discovering a great truth. "This is what the passage meant."

"What passage?" Drake felt a rush of fresh excitement as a clue to why he'd been summoned here gleamed. "There's a passage about me in some old book?"

"It concerned your people, and Earth. There were only a few details in the account Lord Crow obtained regarding your realm, but some were deeply disturbing. In the words of an ancient explorer, people from your realm can defy the will of the Eidolons."

Did that only mean lying? Or could there be more to it? "So what does that passage mean to you, Samuel? Now that you've met me?"

"It means that you speak with the confidence of a madman."

"Oh, I like that." Drake glanced at Lydia. "Though I'm not quite sure how it applies?"

Lydia scooted closer. "We have discussed how we can only say that which we believe. Yet once a person loses the ability to process the world around them, they can say anything."

"They believe things that aren't real, so can say whatever they hallucinate." It made sense. "That's not quite what I can do... I'm still sane, relatively... but it's not a bad guess. I can lie. That means I can say whatever I want whether I believe it or not."

"And that is how you defeated Lord Crow's obedience fetish," Samuel agreed with visible relief. "I had great difficulty understanding how that was possible, but now it all makes sense. And when you recounted how you defeated him, you spoke a 'lie,' as you call it."

Drake nodded.

"Did you lie about anything else in your account?"

"Think hard about how manor lord debt works, and in particular, the rituals that went on that night. Is there anything in my account you wish had happened differently?"

Samuel's eyes narrowed as the possible truth dawned on him. Maybe. He didn't ask Drake to correct his account. He also didn't suggest Drake was lying about anything.

"Then it all happened exactly how I said it did," Drake said.

Samuel nodded with a calculated gleam in his eye. He no longer looked annoyed or suspicious. He looked intrigued. "How did you lie to the doll in the wagon?"

As a tall, svelte woman with cat ears and a silky tail slipped into view from behind Samuel, Drake rose and waved her over. "Let's see what Sachi has to say before I answer that."

8
I TAKE IT YOU'VE HAD A BUSY FEW DAYS

Sachi grinned with the satisfaction of a job well done as she joined their little huddle beside the tent. Her armor was covered in dust and her dark ears were also flecked with it, but she looked pleased, not exhausted. She'd spent most of the day moving at full speed.

"It's a good thing you did not take the Merchant's Roadway today, lord."

Drake both mentally celebrated his genius and mentally kicked his own ass for letting some asshole spy on him through a creepy doll for so long. "What did you run into?"

"I scented a large group of men crouched in the thick forest through which the road passes just outside Kara's Hamlet. I also smelled fresh oil and burning coals."

"Gods," Lydia whispered. "Would they really have set the whole forest on fire?"

"With us inside." Dak grimaced. "They must be pissed Suck failed last night, so they're escalating to full-on pyromania. What about wagons or horses?"

"I smelled both, lord, and their horses were quite lathered.

They must have run them forcefully before those men moved into position in the woods."

"Like they had to reposition quickly." Drake offered Samuel a meaningful glance. "As if someone gave them orders to move their ambush to the Merchant's Roadway."

Samuel nodded, then raised one eyebrow in curiosity. "Who is Suck?"

"The assassin who sucked blood out of people." Drake looked between them, receiving only blank stares for his trouble. "Because he sucked? C'mon, give me something."

Samuel turned back to Sachi. "Were you able to get any idea of their numbers?"

One of Sachi's cat ears flicked in annoyance. "Lord Gloomwood ordered me not to venture too close. He seems to retain some doubts about my abilities."

"That's not it at all," Drake told everyone. "Whoever is after me had pockets deep enough to hire a guy with a rarity so deadly it worked through silverweave, and he *did* kill Thak. There's obviously more bullshit where Suck came from, and I couldn't know what rarities their assassins might have." He looked at Sachi. "You're too important to lose."

Sachi's ears flicked back and forth. "I *am* very important."

Samuel stroked his chin beard. "On reflection, Lord Gloomwood's orders were correct. We need not know the enemy's composition, only that they waited in ambush."

Drake grinned and raised a hand for a high five. "Give it here."

Samuel ignored him. "There is a significant wealth gap between those who can afford to hire a Gilded Blade and those who cannot, but once one surpasses it, money becomes no object. The important thing is we have verified our suspicions."

Sachi's tail moved sinuously. "And what would those suspicions be, Sam?"

Drake raised an eyebrow in surprise. Sachi called Samuel *Sam*? He recalled Valentia telling him that Samuel was a mortal whom

Sachi prized above all others and the person who had convinced her to join Lord Gloomwood. They must go back a good ways.

As he once again evaluated the man's rugged good looks, he wondered just how well Samuel and Sachi knew each other. Was Samuel into catgirls as well? Had he actually *banged* a catgirl?

"I'm afraid only Lord Gloomwood can answer that question," Samuel said firmly.

The old man caught on fast. Drake grinned at Sachi. "I just needed to verify a spy report I received from one of my contacts. Oh, and me and the old man wanted to settle a bet."

Sachi snorted. "Samuel is experienced and wise, not old."

Drake realized he might inadvertently have gotten himself into a great deal of trouble. "It's a term of respect in my world."

Sachi's eyes fixed on him as her tail went still. "It had better be." After a suitably terrifying moment, she relaxed and rubbed her shoulder against Samuel. "I need a bath."

Samuel's face remained impassive. "I'm sure Tamara can have one drawn."

"I'm sure she can." As she leaned against him, Sachi's tail slapped against Samuel's thigh and then slithered up and along his midriff like a snake. "If you have any other questions about my scouting, please. Come join me. I have missed our nighttime chats." She slapped his belly and then sauntered off with her tail weaving sinuously back and forth... along with her ass.

Drake stared after her, then grinned and turned back to Samuel. "What was that you said earlier today? About all your relationships being professional?"

Samuel offered a flat stare. "Unlike you, Lord Gloomwood, I can only speak words I believe."

The old man had him there, and he didn't look in the mood to be teased about whatever was going on with Sachi. That made Drake all the more determined to tease him about this... once they all decided what to do about the creepy doll that was spying on them.

"So, what will we do with the doll?" Lydia asked. "Anna seems so fond of it. She will be devastated when we toss it away."

"We can't just toss in a bonfire," Drake said. "Besides, now that we know someone's watching, I say we use it to fuck with Lord Proudglade."

Samuel's brow rose. "How do you know Lord Proudglade is behind these attacks?"

"Suck told me. Last night. Before I shot him."

His butler finally seemed to grasp just how powerful lying could be. "Now I understand why you ordered us to leave the room." He paused, then nodded. "Well done, lord."

That was the first real praise he'd received from Samuel. It felt good, but Drake wouldn't let it go to his head. The important thing was they now trusted each other.

"I agree we should continue to feed our enemy false information through the doll," Samuel added. "If we haven't alerted them to our suspicions with today's ruse."

"I have a plan to handle that too," Drake said. "Tomorrow, after Anna wakes up, I'll give her back Robby and then you and I will have an argument in my tent in front of them both. I'll berate you for countermanding my orders yesterday about our route."

"I could not do that," Samuel said. "Whoever watches us would become suspicious."

"But what if yesterday, I gave you an order you could get around? Let's say... I told you I *thought* it would be a good idea to take the Merchant's Roadway. Then just assumed you'd do it. And because you're a smart man, you gave the order to keep us on the Noble Road."

"That makes me seem like a poor advisor, and you seem like a fool."

"Which is also what we want Lord Proudglade to think. The more he underestimates us, the more of an advantage we'll have when we turn the tables on that rancid chucklefuck."

Samuel stroked his chin beard in thought. "The words you

choose for your enemies are most colorful. Yet how will we argue when I did not countermand your orders?"

"You just keep your mouth shut and look sullen while I gripe at you, or toss in asides whenever you can slip a truth our watcher will misinterpret. The upshot will be that I, the master of lies, will berate you for keeping us on the Noble Road when I ordered you to take the Merchant's Roadway. At which point you can truthfully remind me we merely discussed it."

Samuel crossed his arms. "The possibilities your unique ability offer for spycraft are truly fascinating. I request a few days to consider all the ways we could adjust our current schemes to incorporate your talents. As ideas occur to me, shall I relay them?"

"In private, of course."

"Of course. Then, Lord Gloomwood, I would ask your permission to retire once more. I have much to think about, but I think better when rested."

"Probably a good idea for us all to get some sleep now that Sachi's back," Drake agreed. "Samuel, come find me so I can berate you in front of Anna and Robby, and then we'll play the rest of the day by ear. If Anna wants to join us again in the carriage, we'll at least know everything we say is being observed and can act accordingly."

Samuel inclined his head and headed back to the tent. Lydia took one more look around, then smiled his way. "Shall we retire as well, lord? It is very late."

"You go on ahead. I want to check something first."

She watched him calmly. "You know I do not wish you to wander around alone."

He sighed at her protectiveness. "All right. But after I grab my box, I'm going to hang out in my armored carriage for a bit. If it'll make you feel better, you can stand watch outside."

"It would make me feel better," she assured him.

Drake led her to his carriage and opened the small luggage compartment beneath, where he had personally packed his own stuff. He pulled out his backpack and then the sealed magic box gifted to him by Lord Skybreak. It was well past sundown, which meant she would likely not attempt to contact him again, but he hadn't had time to check.

After he stuffed his backpack in the carriage and rose, Lydia eyed him curiously. "You have been spending an awful lot of time with that mirror."

"I have to. You think looking this good happens naturally?"

Lydia *almost* avoided rolling her eyes. "I will be here when you're done grooming yourself, alone, in your carriage."

He considered her for a moment. "Actually, you know what? Why don't you join me?" He pointed. "In the carriage."

She pursed her lips. "And the rumors, lord?"

"Samuel's not worried." Drake looked around for any eyes and found only the distant backs of zarovians. "And if anyone else thinks we're doing anything inappropriate, fuck 'em."

"I was given to believe that 'fucking' was the very rumor we were trying to avoid."

Drake damn near choked on his next swallow, then thumped his chest. "Goddammit, Lydia, don't just clobber me like that. You're not supposed to hurt your manor lord."

"I apologize, lord." She did not look very apologetic.

Once they were both inside the darkened carriage, Drake fired up the Zippo candle and then spoke the name of his home. "Earth."

The box popped open, and as he had several nights ago, Drake removed the mirror. He peered into it at once and was thrilled to find no trace of his own face. Instead, there was simply an inky blackness. That suggested something he'd very much hoped for.

"Lord Skybreak?" he asked. "If you're there, pick up." Since Lydia didn't know Sky's real name, he didn't want to reveal it without Sky's permission.

The darkness didn't fade. No voice emerged from the mirror. Yet just before Drake turned to show the blackness to Lydia, a candle ignited in the pane.

"Lord Gloomwood." Sky peered blearily at him from inside the mirror, her blonde braids messy and in disarray. "I take it you've had a busy few days."

Lydia's mouth opened as she stared in surprise. Drake grinned at her, then focused on the mirror. "It's good to hear your voice. Just so you know, Lydia, my steward, is in my carriage with me, though we are otherwise alone. Obviously, she knows about the mirror now."

"So we're moving on to involving blood thralls in our pleasant nighttime chats."

"You involved Lucien first."

"You are, in this case, entirely correct. Hello, Lydia. We haven't met, but all of my spies speak very highly of your capabilities as steward and of your prowess in combat."

"Then please, Lord Skybreak," Lydia said, "thank your spies for me."

Drake was pleased. His steward didn't miss a beat.

"So, Clint." Sky paused and grimaced. "She does know your name, doesn't she? It is very late and I am operating on very little sleep."

"She knows," Drake assured her. "As my steward, I trust her with all my manor's affairs and most everything else, hence why she's the first person I've trusted to know about our little chats. With a cabal on the horizon, it feels like we both need to step up our game."

"I assumed you would already be traveling. Do you care to reveal your route?"

"Don't your spies know already?"

"They do." Sky smiled faintly. "But I was curious if you would trust me with it."

9
I'LL TRY NOT TO TAKE ALL NIGHT

"Then let's get right back to business," Drake said. "Has Lucien made any progress on our letters?"

Sky took a breath. "Since you have informed me you trust your steward with all your affairs, I will also trust that I can do so... at least in regards to what we have already discussed. Lucien feels confident he will soon grasp the cipher and has begun experimental translations. Unfortunately, there is no way to know which letter directed Captain Ro to abduct you, since they are in code."

"So what has he translated?"

"Only a few sentences so far, but he will gain speed as he gains confidence. According to Lucien, the code is, itself, more code. That is, even were it written without being coded in a cipher, even the plain language would be difficult to understand."

"Confusing," Drake agreed. "Just like your dates."

"We tentatively believe the first contract he deciphered was for the assassination of a minor nobleman in Blackmane territory. My spies were able to verify the man was assassinated, so if our translation is accurate, it seems this Captain Ro was at least marginally competent."

Just not competent enough to not get mauled by a wererat, Drake added silently. "So how's your travel going? How many assassination attempts are you up to now?"

"Three."

Drake whistled. "In two days? You've got me beat. Still, I bet I can impress you."

Sky leaned closer to the mirror. "How?"

"I took care of your assassin. The blood sucker guy. The one who killed your rangers and tried to gas us in your guest house. He tried to kill me yesterday night, but I killed him."

Sky went very still as she stared at him through the mirror. Even looking right into her light-blue eyes, he couldn't tell what she was thinking. Given what little she knew about the assassin and how much damage he'd done, her estimation of him might have increased.

"Who was he?" she asked finally.

"He didn't give his name before he died, but his rarity was literally sucking the blood out of people. He could also do it through silverweave. Val called it a targeted rarity?"

"Gods," Sky whispered. "Targeted how?"

"He sucked blood right out of my eyes and nose, which was gross. He was also a Gilded Blade. I assume you're familiar?"

"I am. That rules out both Mistvale and Frostlight. My spies are up to date on their finances and investments, and they couldn't afford a Gilded Blade."

"That's good to know, because I actually know who our enemy is now."

Across the carriage, Lydia frowned and eyed him. *"Are you sure?"* she mouthed.

Drake's enemies were getting more aggressive with every passing day. If he lost Sky, the only real manor lord ally he had on his side, on the way to the cabal, he might not have any allies left in Korhaurbauten. Plus, he actually liked her.

He nodded to Lydia, then raised the mirror to look Sky dead in the face. "The man who sent the assassin to kill me was Lord Proudglade himself."

"Do you have proof we can present in the noble court?" Sky asked.

He was a little disappointed she just accepted his magnificent revelation as if he'd told her the time of day and moved on. Still... she also hadn't asked how he had learned this truth, and moreover, she now appeared even *more* impressed. Maybe. He hoped.

"Unfortunately, no," Drake said. "Other than Lydia and Samuel, my spymaster, no one knows what I've told you. We also have no way to prove it."

"I'm glad to hear Samuel is on the mend. Yet you cannot testify to this yourself?"

"Not without causing more complications that would outweigh any benefit."

"I see." Sky considered him cautiously. "The assassin murdered three of mine and, no doubt, many others, so you have my gratitude. Also, while it is good to know the man who murdered my rangers is dead, we still cannot know if he was behind Rodney's assassination."

"Or my abduction." Drake sighed. "Because I have so many enemies that any number of them could have come at me from any number of angles."

"Yet it is nice to know you have allies as well, isn't it?"

He smiled at her through the mirror. "It is."

"I will forward what you've told me to my spies. Armed with this knowledge, they may be able to uncover more about Lord Proudglade's recent dealings with the Gilded Blades. If we find anything, I will of course let you know. Information for information."

"I'd appreciate that. Now if I can ask you a question, do you have any idea why we've been summoned for a cabal?"

"I'm as in the dark as I suspect you to be. I assume your

steward explained to you just how unusual it is to have a cabal called with so little notice?"

"Someone did," Drake agreed, remembering Valentia. "But you really have no idea?"

"All we know for certain is that it relates to something the noble court wants to immediately address and that event happened this month. That, unfortunately, does not narrow it down. Given how high tensions have been with Lord Brightwater on the verge of tilting the table, almost every manor's territory has been more tumultuous than usual."

"Any examples?"

"Lord Frostlight and several of her sworn banners barely stopped a splinter cult of apocalyptic cultists from opening a portal to the underside in a half-buried kromian temple. Lord Mistvale's forces put down an unexplained wave of extremely aggressive giant spiders some rumors suggest were actually bred and released by Lord Ashwind. And Lord Blackmane has been dealing with a manor in chaos after he was caught cheating on his blood thrall."

Drake remembered the spy report he read with Nicole just before they left for the cabal. "Hold on a sec. Lord Blackmane was cheating on his blood thrall... with *another* blood thrall?"

"It would be a salacious and amusing event, were he not one of the only manor lords we might count as an ally, and were his manor not now in an uproar as his thralls take sides with one spurned paramour or the other. If it comes to war, Lord Blackmane will be of little help."

Drake glanced at Lydia again. She looked empathetically pained by the news of Blackmane Manor in chaos. It was now all the more clear to him why he should *never* think about getting involved with someone who served him.

He turned his attention back to Sky. "So this cabal could be about any of those things and more."

"It could be." Sky didn't sound convinced.

"But ten to one odds says it's going to fuck me, specifically, in some new way."

"I have no interest in a wager. But given your luck since you arrived, I wouldn't bet against you."

"I appreciate your faith in me."

"Then let me show a bit more. My caravan is traveling light, primarily to counter any attempts to waylay us with speed, but as I said, we have endured three ambush attempts. I haven't had much sleep. My spies tell me you're traveling with a considerably larger host."

"Lord Skybreak, do you have someone watching me right now?"

"Not you," she assured him. "I'm the only one keeping an eye on you."

She was flirting with him. That was definitely flirting. And whether it was intended to soften him up for her upcoming offer or not, he already knew what she was going to suggest.

"Are you suggesting we join forces for the journey to the capital?"

"You did say we should formalize our alliance. Step out of the dark. The announcement of our official alliance could, on its own, be cause for a cabal, so we could save ourselves an extra trip if we announce our alliance shortly before we arrive at Korhaurbauten."

"I need to put the mirror down for a second," Drake said. "Do you mind waiting?"

"Not at all. But you do realize I can still hear you?"

Drake chuckled. "We're going to step outside a moment. I hope you're not offended I want to speak to my advisors before agreeing to your proposal."

"I would think less of you if you did not. I recognize this is a significant step forward in the relationship between our manors. With luck, I will still be awake when you return."

"I'll try not to take all night." He set down the mirror and motioned for Lydia to follow.

They exited the carriage, and Drake closed the door. Lydia was now watching him with an expression he wasn't sure he could quite read. Was she impressed? Or anxious?

"You and Lord Skybreak grew closer than even I hoped," Lydia said calmly.

Drake grinned. "Jealous?"

"Pleased." Lydia smiled back. "May I reveal something somewhat personal... Clint?"

She'd called him Clint. She'd only rarely called him Clint. What had gotten into her tonight? "If you're comfortable with that."

"I have followed Lord Skybreak's rise since before she took over for her mother, whom I also followed with equal interest. There is only one other manor lord at the table whom I would wish to serve. She has just asked to formalize an alliance with you."

"So you'd be in favor."

"Yet as much as I have long wished we could ally with her... we cannot."

He frowned in surprise. "Why not?"

"As much as I would love to ally with Lord Skybreak, her blood pact remains unchanged. I do not know how she would react were she to learn that you have altered our blood pact to remove all compulsions. She could see this as a sign of weakness, or worse—"

"Hold up," Drake interrupted.

"But, lord, I think—"

"You don't have to worry about that," Drake said. "She already knows."

Lydia stared. "You told her?"

"I did. Also, she did the same thing. Before me. She nullified her blood pact years ago, like right after she first took over as manor lord."

Lydia stared in wide-eyed shock.

"It came up in one of our earlier conversations," Drake said. "So... think about what this means. Sky has been running her manor without bullshit magic slavery for years, but the other manor lords could still say those are unique circumstances. But now, there's two of us."

"Two manor lords who have replicated this new method of organization," Lydia said quietly. "Two who have proven it does work. That is powerful evidence that changing our procedures would work for everyone. Your success is not a fluke."

"So as a bonus objective, Sky and I talked about, down the line, seeing if we can talk the other manor lords into doing things our way. We want to tilt the table against slavery."

"If that's the case, then I must empathically suggest we ally with Lord Skybreak, and not simply because I now admire her even more." When Lydia smiled, it almost looked like she was proud of him. "I had no idea you had already charmed her!"

Drake frowned at her implication. "Hey, I didn't just *charm* her. I pulled off some legitimately impressive feats using all my unique skills and tactical prowess. I impressed her with my stratagems!"

"That seems... certainly possible," Lydia agreed. "But if you wish my counsel in regards to formalizing our alliance with Lord Skybreak, knowing this, my answer is yes."

"All right. Should we go wake up Samuel for his opinion?"

"There's no need. He was the strongest voice in favor of allying with Lord Skybreak before Lord Crow forbade him from ever bringing up the topic again. The alliance Lord Proudglade started and has strengthened each year has been Samuel's most vexing concern. We could wake Samuel, but only if you want to see a grown man struggle to contain his glee."

"I really would," Drake said ruefully. "But our new ally has dealt with three assassination attempts in two days, so how about we give her an answer and let her get some sleep?"

Lydia opened the door to the carriage. "That would be very kind of us."

Drake stepped up after her. "Though we probably should have drawn this out a bit longer. When she sees how quickly we agreed to this, she's going to get a big head."

Once the carriage was closed again, Drake raised the mirror to find Sky peering into it, idly dabbing at her cheek with a handkerchief. She visibly startled at his return and banished the offending handkerchief from sight. "Did you need to ask me something else?"

"No. We've all made our decision, and it's a yes."

"That was faster than I expected. Did you already intend to ask me?"

"Please don't let it go to your head. We all think your idea is a good one. With your rangers and my zarovians, I don't think anything will be able to sneak up on or crush us. And now that I think about it, having us formalize right before the cabal could throw the others off."

"It will," Sky said firmly. "I was prepared to make that argument if you seemed hesitant, along with a number of others I carefully prepared between my second and third assassination attempts. Now, you have made a mockery of my preparations."

"I do that with other manor lords. How soon can you meet us?"

"If you continue at your current pace along the Noble Road, we should be able to meet up with you by mid-afternoon tomorrow. With your permission, I'll send a few rangers ahead of the main vanguard to inform you when we're close. Expect them shortly past midday."

"That's fine. I look forward to joining forces with you tomorrow afternoon. Oh, and just wait until you see my new crossbow."

She perked up. "You have a new crossbow?"

10
THIS IS A POLITICAL CALCULATION

Early the next morning, after Anna left the tent to help the others break down the camp, Samuel reported to Drake for his argument. With Robby the creepy spy doll looking on from a table, Drake loudly berated Samuel for failing to follow his orders about changing their route. Samuel then flatly responded by reminding Drake he'd given no such orders.

Which was the truth.

After Drake was satisfied with the show he'd put on for whoever was watching them on the other end of the doll, he unceremoniously stuffed Robby back into his pack and scanned his roster for the names of the people who'd traveled with his party. He spotted a familiar name from last night—Tamara—and tracked down Samuel again. The man had left his tent in a fake huff.

"Where can I find Tamara?"

Samuel pointed out a small group of servants all working efficiently to package up the camp's laundry and stored food stuffs. "She will be supervising the other scullery maids. She is the woman with the spectacles and blonde hair."

Drake nodded his thanks and approached the small group, which consisted of Tamara herself, two younger women in less ornate maid outfits, and a young man in a servant's uniform. All were packing up the camp with practiced efficiency until one of the younger women, a dark-haired girl, noticed his approach. She hissed urgently as if to warn them.

The whole group came to attention as Drake approached, which was just something he was going to need to get used to dealing with. And at least he knew how to get rid of Robby for today. He could use one day when he didn't have to worry about being spied on.

He produced the doll from his backpack. "Do we have any clothes appropriate for this?"

Tamara, a spectacle-wearing blonde who was likely only a few years older than Drake herself, eyed him curiously. "For your doll, lord?" At least she seemed at ease with him.

"It's for Anna," Drake explained a bit self-consciously, just to avoid any confusion about him owning a doll. "She's still a bit unsettled from her abduction, and I thought getting some nice new clothes for her doll help take her mind off what happened."

His servants stood straighter, and one, the young dark-haired woman who'd called them attention, touched her mouth and made the tiniest little "D'aww!" Drake pretended he hadn't heard her. Still, this was a far better reaction than having his people scatter at his approach.

Tamara smiled warmly and took the creepy wooden doll he offered. "I'm sure we can find or adjust something to fit her doll, lord. I'll have it to you by lunch."

Drake could actually use a full day without being spied on, but he couldn't just say that. "I appreciate that, but I'd like to keep her focused on learning for today's journey and surprise her before bed. Would you mind bringing the doll by the tent tonight after we set up camp?"

Tamara nodded. "We will ensure she doesn't see it while she works."

"Great. Thanks. And uh... good job with the camp." Drake

motioned vaguely at the efficiently folded, stacked, or rolled-up clothing and bedrolls. "You're all doing great."

His servants all nodded eagerly, and the young man even exclaimed "Thank you, lord!"

With what he hoped was a suitably dignified wave, Drake left so they could get back to work without their boss looming over them. Even if they were growing more comfortable with him, no one liked working with their manor lord scrutinizing their every move.

Soon they were ready to move once more, and after his footman opened his carriage for him—Drake had learned the man's name was Rodger, an old name for such a young dude—he stepped inside to find Lydia and Samuel already waiting inside, deep in a discussion.

As the door closed behind him—Drake assumed Rodger would open it again when Anna arrived—Drake settled on the seat beside Lydia and leaned back on the soft cushion. Both had ended their conversation the moment he entered. They now watched him expectantly.

He felt like he had to say something to justify interrupting them. "Robby's riding with the maids today. They're going to make him a cute little suit and bring him by the tent tonight. So we should have at least one day on the road without being watched."

Samuel nodded in approval. "How do you feel about our argument?"

"If it didn't convince Lord Proudglade or whoever's watching, I don't know what would. We had to know whether the doll was spying on us, and I didn't know a better way."

"We did as best as we could," Samuel agreed. "While the fact that you were lying about our reasons for not switching routes yesterday seems obvious to me, that is only because I know what you are capable of. Given most others could not even conceive of your ability to present alternate facts, there is a good chance they will find other explanations."

"You can just say lie. Make it easier on all of us."

"Best not to, even in private," Samuel said calmly. "Once one grows too comfortable speaking freely of manor secrets, it becomes easier to slip up when one doesn't intend to. Especially now that no one in the manor is compelled to *keep* your secrets."

That made sense. "So, what were you two talking about before I arrived?"

"The possibility of your marriage to Lord Skybreak, and the logistics involved in merging our territories and vassals."

Had Drake been drinking tea, he definitely would have spit it out. "The fuck, Samuel?"

Samuel looked truly surprised by his outburst. "Is something the matter?"

"Marriage?" Drake stared. "Didn't we just agree to ally with her yesterday night?"

"We did," Samuel said patiently. "I believe you made a fine decision, and I am pleased you were able to formalize an alliance with Lord Skybreak so quickly. I am even more pleased to learn that your opinions about blood pacts align. Perhaps it will be possible to change things."

"That's the dream."

"Yet while an alliance is strong, a marriage would provide a unique opportunity for us to burnish both manors. It would also further prove the veracity of your approach."

Drake frowned. "Where did this even come from? We don't even know if she really likes me yet, or if she's just angling for an alliance."

Lydia's brow furrowed. "If she... likes you, lord?"

"Like if she'd actually want to go on a date? Let alone marry me."

Samuel cleared his throat. "I'm afraid this may be a cultural misunderstanding. Your prospective marriage to Lord Skybreak has nothing to do with whether you are physically attracted to each other. It is instead a way to bind our manors together so firmly that even Lord Proudglade and his allies may hesitate to engage us in battle."

"Oh," Drake said, as both his shock at the idea and the fact that it was actually appealing crumbled beneath the weight of his manor lord responsibilities. "This is a political calculation."

Samuel now appeared genuinely confused. "When would it not be?"

"A political calculation that could benefit both you and Lord Skybreak," Lydia assured him. "Our silverwood is prized for its strength and durability, and lumber is one of the resources Skybreak Manor has the most difficulty acquiring thanks to their weak trees. By comparison, their quarries and underground vineries are among the richest in the land. Durable rock and fine wine are resources we must often trade for in Gloomwood Manor."

"I see," Drake said... reluctantly. "And how would a marriage be stronger than an alliance?"

Samuel looked all too eager to explain. "In an alliance, you and Lord Skybreak would formalize military obligations and negotiate favorable trade deals, but each of you would retain control over your manor's affairs. Were you to marry and merge houses, by comparison, you would also merge your resources. We would, essentially, become one manor."

Drake could see how that would be useful. He'd also never even considered getting married before now. He wasn't even twenty-four years old yet! Not to mention he could be dead any day if an assassin got lucky. Sky seemed nice and was absolutely attractive but... marriage?

Still, he had to consider how differently things worked here. He was in a world that operated far more like the countries of old than the modern world he'd left. People got married a lot younger here, and royals, in particular, almost always got married for political reasons.

His only reference for such arrangements was the gossip he'd occasionally skimmed over about the British monarchy, but he remembered it had been quite a scandal when one of their royals claimed he wished to marry for "love" rather than marry for their country. Arranged marriages had been a thing throughout history, and most of the time, the nobles made due.

He wasn't just a manor lord in charge of one manor and territory. He was nobility in this world, and nobles in history almost always married other nobles specifically to strengthen their fortunes or military power. That was why so many old stories were based around powerful people in arranged marriages stepping out with their forbidden side pieces.

"Any such marriage would be years in preparation." Samuel spoke as if hoping to assuage Drake's obvious discomfort with the idea. "If we are to consider such an arrangement, we should start making preparations now to be ready for such a merger, should it occur."

"Sure," Drake agreed. "I guess I can see why you'd want to plan for all possibilities."

Even if he wanted to date in this world, it wasn't like he could hook up with one of his own people. He also doubted he'd encounter a nice peasant woman he could date while running Gloomwood Manor. Some other manor lord would just abduct her and use her to get to him, or she'd turn out to be a femme fatale who'd ensnared him in a honey trap.

He didn't need romance. He wasn't necessarily even *ready* for romance. But if he did want to get serious with a woman at some point... his options were limited to a chosen few. And while he didn't know the other options, Sky was already an attractive option.

But what was he even thinking? Already he was looking at Sky like an objective, another goal to be obtained in his pursuit of not having to look over his shoulder all the time. He wasn't ready to be that type of manor lord yet. And as Samuel said, even if he somehow ended up eventually going in that direction, any decision would be years away.

Still, he was curious about one element of the logistics. "If Lord Skybreak and I got married, how would that change our blood pacts? What's left of them, anyway?"

Samuel nodded thoughtfully. "I had forgotten your world does not have those. Were you and Lord Skybreak to marry, you would also need to resolve any differences between your pacts. You would adjust them before any such marriage occurred to be identical."

"And if we disagreed, how would that work?"

"The two of you could negotiate whatever power-sharing arrangement you preferred. Ultimately, should you and Lord Skybreak agree to marry, the negotiations preceding your nuptials could take years. Such discussions can grow quite lengthy."

Drake chuckled. "So there is one hell of a pre-nup. And what about divorce?"

Again, Lydia and Samuel looked at each other in obvious confusion, then back at him. "Is that a term from your world, lord?" Lydia asked.

"On my world, people do get married, but since there's no blood pacts, there's less negotiation. Also, in most cultures, if the marriage doesn't work, people can get divorced. That means they dissolve the marriage and go their separate ways. Many even remarry later."

Lydia looked truly confused by the concept. "That is... very strange, lord. And your world's gods allow this?"

More cultural confusion. "Our world's gods don't give a shit. I don't even know if our world has gods, or what they believe. In fact, arguments about what our gods believe are responsible for a good number of the wars that happen in my world."

"I see," Samuel said. "It may then perhaps be best to clearly explain how marriage works between manor lords. Once you agree to marry, and the negotiations regarding who will maintain dominion over what have been concluded, you will then mix your blood in a ceremony blessed by the Eidolons who, if they approve, will unite your blood pacts."

"And you don't generally un-unite blood pacts," Drake agreed. "That's a forever thing."

"That is correct." Samuel nodded firmly. "Even if one of you subsequently died, the united blood pact would remain with the survivor. That is another way a marriage is stronger than an alliance. Any enemies must now defeat two people to seize it."

That did sound like an advantage he hadn't considered. So long as he remained a bachelor, anyone who killed him and his successor would immediately inherit Gloomwood Manor and all its people... though they'd get killed almost immediately. Still, he'd be dead.

By comparison, if he was married to Sky and one of them got murdered, the other could keep both their manors and their people safe. They could even keep their unique approach to manor management a secret until they were ready to push more manor lords to follow it.

It seemed "until death do you part" was quite literal in this world, with any marriage approved by and likely enforced by actual gods. That changed his mental calculations. Could he ever marry *anyone* knowing this world's gods would ensure it could never be undone?

That was a question he didn't need to consider for years, and only if he was still alive.

11
THEY WILL BE DELAYED

Anna joined them in the carriage soon after Drake learned Samuel and Lydia were already conspiring to marry him off to someone, which he still wasn't totally cool with. Still, at least they both took the hint to drop the subject. He knew neither would be foolish enough to bring up *marriage* in Sky's presence, and he *was* looking forward to seeing her today.

His people would probably continue making arrangements for an eventual marriage behind the scenes, but they couldn't just marry him off without his approval. He remained the lord of Gloomwood Manor. No one was going to make him marry anyone unless he wanted it.

Or, he supposed, if it would put him in a stronger position as a manor lord.

He really was considering the political benefits now. Samuel and Lydia had planted the seed. He'd liked what he'd seen of Skybreak Manor—the huge town Sky maintained with all its skilled workers, its strong stone walls, the obvious defensibility its narrow approach offered—and he also liked the people he'd met among Sky's folks, like Karth and even Head Ranger Cask.

Moreover, Sky herself appeared quite strong. Her blood thralls all followed her of their own free will, just like his, and from the casual way she spoke of dealing with assassins, she must be a competent warrior as well. And what about her rarity?

Drake needed to look that up on the road today. He didn't want to look ignorant when she and her rangers joined their caravan this afternoon. If Sky's rarity was powerful, and in this world, female rarities generally were, she'd also be an excellent addition to his army.

Or rather... their new joint army. If he ever married Lord Skybreak. Which could happen someday, maybe, years from now.

From the list of manor rarities Zuri had provided, he learned Lord Skybreak's rarity was simply called *void*. There was no additional information, and not even Lydia knew how it worked. Apparently lords only needed to report the names of their rarities, not describe them, and Sky had kept hers secret. That suggested it was even more powerful than he hoped.

Drake spent the morning having Lydia quiz him about things he'd learned yesterday regarding the other manors. He was pleased when he got more questions right than wrong. He still wasn't going to remember the date each new manor lord took power, but he did now know what resources each manor lord possessed and understood their leadership styles.

Lord Proudglade, as he'd suspected, was currently the richest and most well-respected manor lord thanks to the strength of the alliances he commanded, which he had pulled together by force of personality and will. The fact that his powerful rarity, *shock spear*, allowed him to toss bolts of lightning capable of blowing up walls obviously helped.

Proudglade Manor also sounded like a much nicer place to live than Gloomwood Manor, at least before Drake had taken it over. They were known realm-wide for their fairness and sense of honor, though Drake had some doubts about all that. Still, so far as Lydia knew, none of the former Lords Proudglade had ever tortured and killed their own servants.

Instead of battle maids, Proudglade Manor's elite soldiers were its golden knights, men and women with some sort of combat rarity. Proudglade Manor currently had eight golden knights, not five battle maids, but from the description of their rarities, Gloomwood Manor retained the edge in overall power. The rarities of his battle maids remained among the best.

The rest of Proudglade Manor's forces were a mix of silver knights (elite warriors with no rarity, or whose rarity wasn't useful in combat) and bronze knights, who were foot soldiers who didn't even wear real bronze, just leather armor. Lord Proudglade also had many servants in various roles just like he did, as well as skilled artisans and weapon smiths.

Proudglade Manor, like Skybreak Manor, was actually a keep built inside a town, and yesterday Drake had confirmed that Lord Proudglade (just like Lord Skybreak) did not actually have the entirety of his surrounding town as blood thralls. The upper limit of a blood pact remained around one hundred people. More than that, and the compulsion grew diluted.

Therefore, the majority of people who lived in the area around keeps like Skybreak and Proudglade Manor were just folks who swore fealty to the local manor lord, like the folks who lived in Shadowfort: the town back on Drake's lands. With other manor lords, only those who were part of the manor lord's blood pact were allowed inside the keep.

Drake had also learned that Gloomwood Manor was not the only manor that stood alone without a town around it. Gloomwood Manor remained remote due to the difficulty in clearing the massive silverwood trees, a process Drake was told was closer to sawing down miniature mountains than chopping down a normal tree. Given the resulting wood was much stronger than normal wood and also entirely fireproof, the effort remained worth it.

Gloomwood Manor was also remote due to the ability of Lord

Gloomwood to command vero, who in turn commanded the limbs of its massive silverwood trees. Drake now understood the other manors that stood alone, without towns, were similarly defended.

Ashwind Manor didn't have a town above ground at all. The manor and the small town built up around it existed entirely in a large underground chasm. Frostlight Manor was half-buried in a mountain atop a sheer cliff in a frigid territory, with small habitations scattered across those frigid lands. And Mistvale Manor was apparently built up in a giant tree.

When Drake included the size of the habitation surrounding it, Brightwater Manor was actually the largest of all the manors. In addition to a stone-and-wood fort on the coast, it included multiple buildings along the beach, as well as a whole armada of floating buildings moored just off the coast. Hurricanes weren't a big issue here.

Finally, he'd learned quite a bit about Korhaurbauten itself. The realm's capital city was also built near the ocean, though it had grown up around a large and peaceful bay that was so shallow most large ships couldn't even moor inside it. They had to drop anchor in the deeper waters beyond the bay and then take smaller boats to and from their big ships.

Korhaurbauten was the oldest and largest city in the realm, and the Eidolon temple was apparently the oldest known structure ever built. Given Lydia told him the Eidolons themselves had built it, that wasn't surprising. It still boggled his mind that actual gods not only existed in this world, but could also actually be *seen* by anyone who visited the temple.

Supposedly, the Eidolons slumbered in the center of the temple in an endless dream. If anyone ever somehow managed to wake them up, the world would vanish the moment they rose. Because this world, as its people believed, was actually a dream of the Eidolons.

He had enough troubles without debating theological theories about the end of the world. Still, when he got to Korhaurbauten, because he was a manor lord, he would be one of the privileged few who would be allowed to enter the ancient temple and get a look at the world's gods. He'd do his best not to sneeze loudly enough to accidentally end the world.

When they stopped for lunch, which Drake again took inside his armored carriage (Samuel insisted the surrounding hills would be perfect for archers), Drake half hoped Sky and her people would arrive and join them. Yet they concluded lunch and returned to their slow walk down the Noble Road without the arrival of his allied manor lord.

By the time the sun was most of the way to the horizon, Drake was more than a bit worried. Sky had said advance riders would meet them shortly after lunch and then the rest of her vanguard would arrive in mid-afternoon, but both had come and gone without any sign of them. Given she couldn't lie, she had obviously fully intended to have that happen.

So had she run into another ambush? This time, one she couldn't escape? His worries grew after he removed the magic mirror from its magic box and checked to see if Sky had contacted him on it. She hadn't. Where the hell was she?

Finally, with his caravan rolling on toward dusk and the sun little more than a red smear on the horizon, Sachi returned with news. A large group of riders was approaching... the vanguard of Lord Skybreak. Finally! Better late than never.

Drake ordered a halt so Sky's vanguard could catch up. He had no doubts they were actually Skybreak rangers, thanks to Sachi's intel, and he was very curious to know what they'd run into today. There were no wagons with them, so they must have left those behind.

Lydia and Valentia walked with him to meet Lord Skybreak and her rangers as the first six rangers approached his line of wary zarovians. From the way their horses were limping along, they had obviously run the animals hard. Not a good sign. Not remotely a good sign.

When Drake recognized Karth in the lead, he walked past a glowering Cresh and walked out to meet the man. The Noble Road and the area immediately around it were wide-open ground, so short of invisible archers, he had no worry about being attacked. With Lydia and Valentia at his side and Emily and Nicole in reserve, he went out to meet his weary allies.

Karth looked dead on his feet when he finally slid off his exhausted horse. The rest of his people looked the same. His dour expression told Drake the news was going to be bad. He looked like a man who'd seen his horse killed in front of him, yet his horse was right there.

"Lord Gloomwood," Karth said. "It is good to see you well."

"You too, Karth." Even so, Drake was already looking past the man into the crowd of distant faces, none of whom he recognized. "Where's Lord Skybreak?"

"She will be delayed."

So she wasn't here? Drake ground his teeth. "How long?"

"Perhaps a week. Perhaps longer. She sent me to give you her most sincere apologies and asks that you travel to the capital without her."

Sky's failure to show up for the cabal on time meant she would be censured by the noble court, which would be bad. It also meant Drake wouldn't have his newly allied manor lord to back him up, which meant he wouldn't have her vote around the table either. He needed to know what the hell happened today.

"Were you ambushed?"

"Lord Skybreak informed me that is none of your concern."

"Did she *order* you to keep your mouth shut, Karth? Or was it just a suggestion?"

The weary man, covered in dust from his ride and the road, eyed Drake as a man who had lost all hope. "And just what would you do if I told you about our day?"

"I don't know what I'd do. Because you haven't told me. If you tell me, I can tell you what I'd do, and if I can help your lord somehow, I'd like to do *something*."

Karth glanced back at the other five rangers with him, a group of three women and two men who all looked as weary as he did. He looked beyond to the host of other soldiers gathered further up the road, all as tired and dejected as he looked. Then, he looked back to Drake.

"It's Lord Skybreak's mother. Lady Skybreak. She's been taken hostage, and the leader of the group responsible demanded she deliver the ransom herself. If she refused, they informed us they would kill her mother slowly and painfully."

Lydia gasped at Drake's side, then glanced his way in worry. "Lady Skybreak is a powerful warrior, lord. Her rarity, *cleavage*, allows her to split stone. If a group of warriors managed to take her hostage, they must be truly powerful as well."

Drake had only just begun to process a rarity called "cleavage" when Karth spoke.

"Lady Skybreak was only captured because she surrendered to these mercenaries instead of allowing them to put Tallowhorn to the torch. She gave herself up to save the town. Over two hundred men, women, and children."

That was yet another problem with being a *good* manor lord. Drake glanced at Valentia. "I guess that's too benevolent?"

Valentia offered him a level gaze. "Lady Skybreak is no longer in charge of Skybreak Manor. Given she now has only her own life to consider, not a manor, her decision to offer herself in place of an entire town of her subjects is a heroic sacrifice I can respect."

This *totally* felt like a double standard, but Drake let it go since he actually agreed with her. He looked back to Karth. "So, Lord Skybreak knows this whole mess was absolutely orchestrated to keep her from reaching the cabal, doesn't she?"

"The possibility has been discussed. Many times, lord." Karth sighed. "Which is why I am now the lord of Skybreak Manor."

Drake blinked. "The *hell?*"

"This afternoon, Lord Skybreak passed the title and blood pact to me. I will lead our vanguard to Korhaurbauten in her place. She has instructed me to keep counsel with you and your advisors and to support you in representing our manor's interests."

"And do you feel confident you can do that, Karth?"

The ranger grimaced. "The former Lord Skybreak made it clear I don't have a choice."

12

SHE IS BELOVED

"Where is she?" Drake demanded. "Why send you in her place? Did the people who have her mother order her to deliver the ransom to some town in the opposite direction?"

Karth nodded. "The soldiers said she must personally deliver her mother's ransom to Fort Graystone, an old watch post at the edge of our territory. It is three days in the opposite direction of Korhaurbauten. That is why our lord could not join us in the capital."

All the more proof their enemies had put this all together specifically to ensure Sky didn't reach the capital as his ally. Drake was now all the more certain he needed to find some way to fix this, but he didn't know how. He also wouldn't figure it out standing out here.

The newest Lord Skybreak and his weary vanguard had traveled a long way under harsh conditions, and it was already getting dark. Drake had no idea what to do about this news, but for now, what he could do was offer his allied manor a place to water their horses, restore their strength, and rest after the grueling ride they must have endured today.

But first, there were the formalities to consider.

"Lord Skybreak." Drake eyed Karth. "I trust the alliance I formed with the former lord last night remains with you. However, I still need your word that you have come to join us in peace. Neither you or any of your blood thralls will harm my people or betray us. Agreed?"

"Agreed, Lord Gloomwood," Karth said. "Will you offer the same assurance?"

Drake repeated the same words on behalf of himself and his own people, which, had he not been able to lie, would have ensured Karth—or Lord Skybreak—could safely enter Drake's camp and mingle with his blood thralls. If he ever decided to break bad in this world, his ability to lie was going to make him exceedingly dangerous to literally everyone.

At least until his enemies figured out he could do it.

Yet because he was already a manor lord, Drake could not seize another blood pact even if he wanted to. He'd learned that from Lydia when he asked. While one of his blood thralls could become the lord of Skybreak Manor if they managed to kill Karth, assuming the man had not named a successor, they'd have to go through the army of determined soldiers guarding Karth first. Given their skill, that would be a bloodbath.

Since he and Karth had just agreed to compel their blood thralls not to harm each other, that wouldn't be possible. Thus, an alliance could be maintained. So far, so good.

Drake looked back at his army of glowering zarovians and the camp his people were already setting up, then back at Karth. "Come get something to eat. You've had a very long trip, and we welcome you to our vanguard. We'll also handle your horses."

"Our horses stay with us," Karth said. He took the lead of his exhausted animal and slowly led it to the camp. "But if you've feed to spare and water to provide, we'd welcome it."

Skybreak rangers must be pretty tight with their horses, which was odd given their whole territory wasn't all that great for riding on horseback. Perhaps they just rode their noble steeds around fields and practiced drills when they didn't have a trek to the capital to complete. Since he wasn't going to obtain a loyalty oath from horses, Drake allowed it.

As he walked back to his caravan with Lydia beside him, he found himself increasingly unwilling to accept just leaving Sky behind. Now that she had surrendered her leadership of Skybreak Manor to Karth, she would be as free to be *benevolent* as her mother.

From what little he knew about her, he suspected Sky intended to be rather *non*-benevolent instead. Given she'd once promised to crucify the assassin who murdered her rangers beneath a cold sky, he doubted she'd be much kinder to the people who threatened to torture her mother to death. Sky would be out for blood.

In other words, far too reckless for her own good.

Drake wanted to go help her. Were he some basic hero in a basic fantasy story, it wouldn't even have been a question. Unfortunately, he had the welfare of his entire manor to consider, his alliance with the *new* Lord Skybreak to maintain, and the fact that the noble court would censure him if he didn't show up for the cabal on time.

He didn't have the luxury to simply *be* benevolent. Moreover, even if the odds were stacked against her, Sky would put up a good fight on her own. She didn't require a rescue.

So the question that was most important to him now was if Karth could fill Sky's shoes. Because if not, Drake would walk into the cabal crippled to the point where the other manor lords could roll right over him. He knew Sky could handle the cabal. But could her replacement?

Lord Blackmane, one of his only other possible allies, was dealing with an entire manor in an uproar over him sticking his dick in multiple blood thralls, while Lord Ashwind, from everything Drake had learned in his studies with Lydia, was a massive pushover who would only fight back if someone threatened to take his precious ferrocite mines away.

Meanwhile, the lords of Mistvale, Frostlight, and Redbow were all ruthless fighters solidly behind Lord Proudglade and out for blood. It was now looking quite likely he would walk into the cabal at Korhaurbauten as one against four, and that was assuming Lord Brightwater maintained her so-called neutrality. Even if he somehow found a way to use his ability to lie to his advantage in negotiations, he doubted that would save him from being rolled over.

He left Lord Skybreak—the newest Lord Skybreak—to get some food and some rest with his exhausted blood thralls. Karth looked to be walking purely through willpower and stubbornness, and while he was now the lord of Skybreak Manor, he didn't seem inclined to issue any orders. Another sign he might not be the strong ally Drake needed in the capital.

It might not even be that Karth wasn't strong. He'd certainly shown swagger and resourcefulness in their previous meetings. Now, however, the woman Karth respected more than anything had ordered him to leave her behind, possibly to die, and dropped a manor of responsibility on his head. So far as he knew, Skybreak Manor still didn't have a steward.

Once he was certain Lord Skybreak and his people were getting settled in, Drake motioned for Samuel to join him and Lydia for another impromptu strategy session in his armored carriage. Once he had them gathered, he quickly filled Samuel in on the current situation. The old man looked none too pleased.

"So?" Drake asked. "What do you know about Karth? Can he pull his weight if he's the only manor lord we can rely on at the cabal?"

"I know very little about his skill in politics," Samuel said. "The only thing I can say for certain is that he is a childhood friend of Sky's. My spies suggest they were inseparable as children, and that while Karth eagerly took the blood pact at sixteen to serve the former Lord Skybreak... Sky's mother... he always intended to serve her instead."

"So the reason Sky chose to pass him her blood pact was his very real loyalty to her, rather than his talent for politics or ruthlessness as a manor lord." Drake grimaced. "If she's smart, and she is, I bet she'd be hesitant to trust any blood thralls who she thinks would make a strong manor lord with her blood pact. They might be less likely to give the title back."

"She obviously intends to reclaim her title should she survive," Samuel agreed. "Whether she will survive her attempt to rescue her mother is another issue."

"You really think whoever's behind this could take her down? I didn't see any of her lady bodyguards in the vanguard, and from what I remember, they stood out. Those women are close in skill to our battle maids, aren't they? She's not going after her mother alone."

"I would not wish to face Mary in open combat," Lydia agreed. "Her rarity affects blood just like Valentia's. However, she causes it to course from the pores of her target. She does not suck blood away like the assassin you killed, but anyone who faces her in combat will bleed out quickly if they do not find a way to defeat her."

"And the other bodyguards?" Drake scanned his memory for the other names she'd mentioned. "When we met inside her manor, she mentioned two other women by name."

"Kari and Ali," Lydia offered helpfully. "Kari's rarity, *impact*, allows her to increase the weight of any blade she uses in combat, but only for her opponents. So while she cannot simply slice through ferrocite like Emily, a blow from her rapier hits like one from a greatsword."

"And Ali?"

"I believe she is a shapeshifter, lord, though there are few accounts of her actually shapeshifting." She looked to Samuel. "We don't actually know what she shifts into, correct?"

Samuel nodded. "In the capital, Ali's rarity is listed as *dire wraith*. If anyone outside of Sky's inner circle has seen what form she takes when shifted, they did not live to report."

Drake didn't fail to note that Samuel was calling Sky "Sky" now. Samuel had already stopped treating her as the Lord of Skybreak Manor, even though, so far as most everyone who served her believed, she still was. His butler was a stickler for accuracy.

He focused on what they needed to know. "So if we can't dig further into what Karth can offer us as the leader of Skybreak Manor, what about Sky? Lydia told me how strongly you wanted to ally with her. Do you think she would be a better ally in the cabal than Karth?"

"Without question," Samuel said. "Sky has been attending cabals in Korhaurbauten with her mother since she was old enough to walk, and she has trained every moment of her childhood to take over for her mother as Lord Skybreak. Moreover, all reports from Skybreak Manor suggest her people's respect for Sky is genuine and strong. She is beloved."

"And her mother?"

"Equally so."

"But her mother's still alive, isn't she? Why'd she hand over the manor to Sky?"

"I do not know for certain. My spies suspect that the reason Sky took the title so young was because her mother contracted a wasting illness, but I have been unable to confirm this beyond the rumor. Others simply believe Sky took the title because her mother judged her rarity strong enough that she should do so immediately when she came of age."

"And no one knows what her rarity can do? Other than it being called *void*?"

"Correct," Samuel said. "However, based on the spy reports I have received from those few cases where those outside Sky's blood pact witnessed her fight others, she is truly skilled in martial combat. Whether her skill is natural or due to a rarity is unknown."

"Or it could be both," Drake said. "Like Lydia."

Lydia offered a small smile. "There is no need to flatter me."

"I'm not," he assured her. "I could say the same of all my battle maids."

"Regardless, this leaves us in a difficult situation," Samuel said. "I wish I could say I am surprised that Sky chose to pass her title to a thrall and pursue her mother's abductors when it was obvious they intended her to do so, but unfortunately, I suspect the spy masters for the manors arrayed against us have the same intelligence as I."

"Which is?" Drake prompted.

"Sky is ruthless and talented in negotiation and well-versed in battle, but fiercely protective of her people and family. Her mother is the only family she has left. Thus, she can be manipulated into rash action when those she cares for are threatened."

Drake sighed. "So basically, she's still too benevolent to be a ruthless manor lord."

13
CONGRATULATIONS, OLD MAN

"It would not be accurate to call Sky simply benevolent," Samuel said. "Her enemies would certainly not agree, and she has not hesitated to execute many of them in the past."

Drake frowned. "So how many enemies has she taken down? That we know of?"

"According to my latest reports, Sky has personally defeated a number of warriors and assassins in direct battle. She has also ordered the execution of twenty-eight captives."

Given Drake had personally executed an assassin two nights ago after capturing him, he couldn't judge Sky based on just that. She'd survived as a manor lord a lot longer than he had. Moreover, she had released a man who personally tried to shoot her… granted, without his ear.

"And what did the prisoners she executed do?"

"All committed various crimes against her people, her thralls, or her manor. After a trial, they were judged guilty. By the laws of our realm, their executions were just."

"So she's not into torture." That was a relief.

"All she ordered executed were humanely beheaded, save one. After his capture and confession, she ordered his testicles ripped off. She had her healers stop the bleeding and left him to die of dehydration on a cross high atop a mountain. He took days to die."

Drake winced both physically and mentally. He'd heard Sky talk about how she intended to crucify the assassin who killed her rangers, but knowing she'd actually done it was a little beyond what he'd been prepared for. "What the hell did that guy do?"

"According to the trial records, he abducted, abused, and murdered several children."

As he reflected on the man's horrific crimes, Drake couldn't help but understand Sky a little better—or hope he did. While such a brutal execution felt at odds with Sky's own hesitance to ally with him when she thought he was the same as Lord Crow, this felt different.

It didn't feel like sadism. It felt more like Sky intended to make it clear there were crimes she absolutely would not tolerate in her lands, and making a gruesome public example of this child-killing asshole had been her way to do that. Once more, he had to consider her actions as they existed in this murderous world with its murderous rules, not his own.

This made it all the more clear to him that Sky was a fierce warrior and a strong manor lord. He needed someone like her as his ally, and if Samuel was concerned Karth couldn't cut it in her place, Drake was even more concerned. But what could he do to help her?

He supposed, if he had to, he'd simply go get her and teleport her back with him. "Where's Fort Graystone?"

"Is that where Sky went?" Samuel asked.

Drake nodded. "Karth said it's a three day's ride away from the capital."

Samuel considered for a moment. "If they were a day's ride away when you spoke last night, and they did set out from Skybreak Manor on the same day we did... then, yes. That would force Sky and whoever went with her to ride three days away from the capital."

"Which means there's no way she can possibly get back by the time the cabal starts, and if we were to turn around to go get her, we'd all miss it by a week or more."

"Correct." Samuel grimaced. "As such, I believe we have no choice to—"

"We're going after her," Drake said.

Lydia tilted her head in obvious concern. "We can't."

"We can if we teleport her," Drake said. "If Anna's rarity works how I think it does."

Samuel's grimace turned into a possibly thoughtful frown. "You would reveal one of our most powerful rarities to Sky and her people?"

"We're allied now. Also, won't we have to report Anna's rarity in Korhaurbauten?"

"Only once she comes of age," Samuel said. "All citizens are required to register their rarity at age sixteen, if present, but you told me Anna is only ten. That means we could legally use her rarity in secret for six years without revealing it to the other manor lords."

"I think the big four already know," Drake said. "Remember Robby and his creepy green eyes? I know Anna and I have discussed her rarity in front of him, so Lord Proudglade, at least, already knows what she can do. Keeping it secret from the other manors probably isn't possible anymore."

"Perhaps," Samuel agreed. "Still, that is all the more reason not to go after Sky. If Lord Proudglade has taken Anna's ability to teleport others into consideration, he may expect her to come and have a trap prepared for her."

"I understand that," Drake said patiently. "Here's what else I understand. The same assholes who have been hammering us this whole time just abducted Sky's mom. The fact that they took the *one* person they knew Sky wouldn't let die and then requested she come to personally deliver the ransom, when she was expected at a cabal, proves they want her gone."

"That is simply what we suspect," Samuel corrected.

"But if I'm right, it means Lord Proudglade and the others are already freaking out about what'll happen if Sky shows up in Korhaurbauten allied with us. If they've gone to all this effort to ensure she can't make it, she may be critical to our success in the upcoming negotiations."

Lydia offered Samuel a firm glance. "He might be right. We could fail without her."

Samuel lightly stroked his chin beard. "So you suggest we send a fast-moving force and Anna to meet Sky and her people at Fort Graystone, and, if they are still alive, teleport them to a recall spot... where?"

"On the floor of this carriage," Drake said. "Or the floor of a wagon."

Samuel's brow rose in obvious surprise. "The recall spot can move?"

"When Anna teleported me into Captain Ro's wagon, it was on wheels. So while it's possible they kept the wagon parked the whole time they set up their abduction, it seems like all we need to teleport is a big round circle of blood. We might even be able to cart the spot around on a plate if we wanted."

Samuel nodded thoughtfully. "So while a small force protecting Anna proceeds to Fort Graystone, our main vanguard and the recall spot would proceed toward the capital. If we can verify your understanding of Anna's rarity, that could work." He hesitated.

"I'm sensing a but in there, Samuel."

"This would only work if Anna and her escort could find Sky's force in time, and if Sky's force had not already been captured or defeated by the people who captured her mother, and if Lord Proudglade has not anticipated that we might send Anna and laid a trap for her. If anything goes wrong, our force and Anna could be captured or killed."

"Would you take that sort of risk for me?" Drake asked.

Samuel said nothing. He appeared to be thinking about it.

"Yes," Lydia said. "We would absolutely take such a risk for our own manor lord. Sky is now allied with us in all but an official proclamation in the capital. Lord Gloomwood is also correct about Lord Proudglade's motives. If we don't help Sky, we may face him alone."

Samuel looked to her, then back to Drake. "In this case, I cannot offer you a definitive recommendation. If we attempt to reach Sky and teleport her back to the capital, we risk losing Anna as well. If we proceed as Sky intended, we risk arriving without a critical ally we need to navigate this cabal. Our allied manor also loses its powerful leader."

"So what you're saying is, it's my call?"

"Yes, Lord Gloomwood. I will accept your decision."

"Then we're picking up Sky," Drake said. "Without risking Anna."

Samuel's eyes widened, and then he scowled. "Absolutely not."

Drake grinned. "You just said you'd back my decision. No take backs."

Lydia looked between them in confusion, but then she too gasped. "You cannot be thinking of going yourself!"

"Why not? Lord Proudglade might be expecting Anna to show up, but he sure as hell won't be expecting me. I'll copy Anna's rarity and use it to teleport myself, Sky, and her people right back here to my armored carriage. That'll throw the old fucker for a loop."

"Risking valuable blood thralls to save a crucial ally is an acceptable risk," Samuel said grimly. "Risking our manor lord is not. You cannot place yourself in harm's way."

"Oh yes I can. Because even if I die, your next manor lord can't do shit to you."

"That doesn't mean they might not report what you have done to the noble court, or execute us after we act against our new manor lord."

"So push him down a flight of stairs."

"We need you as our manor lord," Samuel said firmly. "We need your unique ability to maintain our secrecy. Once the noble court learns how you have changed the Gloomwood Manor blood pact, our manor could be censured, or worse."

Drake mentally shook his head. "You really think the noble court will go apeshit because I made it impossible for manor lords to murder their own people?"

"You have made it possible for blood thralls to murder their *manor lords*," Samuel corrected firmly. "They could see that as an attack on all manor lords, and in particular, the authority of the noble court. That is not a risk we can take in the current political environment."

Drake looked to Lydia. "How would you feel about me naming Samuel my successor instead of you?"

She nodded immediately. "I believe that would be wise."

His butler's next words died as his mouth opened, but no words emerged. Drake had finally said something to rattle him. He looked to Samuel again.

"Congratulations, old man. You're next in line to the throne."

Lydia squeezed Samuel's shoulder. "You are the best choice."

Samuel recovered enough to frown at her, then at Drake. "I cannot be your successor."

"Why not? Everyone here loves you. Sachi, the battle maids, the staff. Hell, I bet even old Cresh has a soft spot for you. Moreover, you may not be able to regenerate as fast as me when I copy your rarity, but you're still one tough SOB. You're hard to kill."

"I am your spy master and advisor. I am not an acceptable choice for manor lord."

"Because you care about your people?" Drake asked. "Because you'd hesitate to sacrifice Olivia or Lydia or any of the others if that was the only way to keep Gloomwood Manor safe? Well tough titties, old man, because that's just what I'm asking you to do if I die."

Samuel watched him with increasing unease.

"You've told me how hard I must be many times. Valentia just came out and said it. I have to be ruthless enough to order executions and even order people I care about to go to their deaths if it'll keep the manor safe. Are you telling me you can't do what you advise?"

"Lord, I..." Samuel appeared to be a true loss. "This is not what I want."

"Which is why I feel completely comfortable naming you as my successor. I named Lydia when I got here because there was no one else I felt could protect our people as well as she can. However, you'll need her as steward. So it's time for you to step up."

"We do not even know if this plan of yours will work," Samuel said insistently. "While you have been able to successfully absorb a few rarities, Anna is not part of your blood pact."

"Neither was Lord Crow, and I still snagged his dire rat. Showed him how to use it, too."

"This is unwise," Samuel insisted. "It is exceedingly reckless. Even were you to succeed in obtaining Anna's rarity, you could lose your ability to regenerate. Every rarity you have thus far absorbed only came after the one before it disappeared."

"I'm pretty sure I will lose *regrowth*," Drake agreed. "That's why I can't do this alone. I'll need a few battle maids to keep me safe, and Sachi to track Sky and make sure we don't stumble into anything we can't handle. The rest I'll leave with you, along with Anna."

"Your ability to absorb rarities and deceive others is far beyond my talents," Samuel cautioned.

"And your ability to navigate murder politics and run our manor's affairs is far beyond mine, not to mention your ability to deceive isn't so shabby either. Overall, it's a wash."

His butler frowned in consternation.

"But I'm still more handsome," Drake added. "Right, Lydia?"

She ignored his question and touched Samuel's arm. "We should consider this."

He stared at her in exasperation. "Now even you are considering his reckless plan?"

"I have seen Lord Gloomwood in battle," Lydia said firmly. "I have also seen him navigate traps and situations that would have tripped up or ruined even a veteran manor lord. He has not only navigated these challenges, but survived and grown stronger. He can do this."

Drake felt a warm rush at her praise.

She smiled at him. "However, Samuel is more handsome. I am sorry, lord."

He stared, betrayed. "Oh, come *on*."

14
I WON'T TELL A SOUL!

"I will not endorse your mad plan without first speaking to Anna," Samuel said firmly. "We do not even know if this plan of yours will work. This discussion is moot if it will not."

"That's fair," Drake said. "I'll need to get the lowdown from her on how to use her rarity anyway, and we'll need to test it before I leave to pick up Sky. But now that we know what we're going to do, talking with Anna is our next order of business."

"Shall I fetch her, lord?" Lydia asked.

Drake loved that she hadn't fought him on this. Once again, Lydia had his back.

"The maids should have delivered Robby to her by now," Drake said. "I actually did have them make her doll a new outfit, so be careful not to reveal why we want to talk to her."

"Understood." Lydia exited the carriage and closed the door behind her.

Samuel turned his frown on Drake again. "Why are you so eager to save Sky?"

"Because we need her for the cabal, and because she's a bad ass mother..." He paused and considered how Samuel, who took everything literally, might interpret that particular colloquialism. "She's a strong warrior and a powerful manor lord."

"So your desire to ride to her rescue herself is not simply because you fancy her?"

It took Drake a moment to remember that was old people talk for "you think she's hot," and then he could only chuckle. "No, Samuel. God. You and Zuri."

"What does Zuri have to do with this?

"You both seem to think I'm constantly being led around by my dick." Though Zuri, Drake supposed, had been compelled into thinking that.

Samuel's expression hardened. "As your advisor, I would be remiss if I did not ensure you examined your motives in detail. Is what you say what you believe?"

"I've examined my motives plenty. We're going to have to move fast and ride hard if we go after Sky, which will be difficult for Anna. If we get into a scrap with whoever took Sky's mother, an assassin could pick off Anna the moment she shows up, which leaves us no way home. Yet no one in the enemy force will expect *me* to have a teleport rarity."

"No. They will simply target you to eliminate the lord of Gloomwood Manor."

"They'd do that anyway, which is why I have battle maids to protect me. And finally, I'm simply not ready to order a child on what could possibly be a suicide mission. That kid's been through hell already. Whether we succeed or not, she deserves a good life in the manor."

"So while you are not allowing yourself to be unduly influenced by your attraction to Sky Skybreak, you are allowing yourself to be influenced by your worry for Anna."

Drake frowned. "Of course I'm factoring Anna's age into my decision. I've told you repeatedly I'm not going to lead like an asshole. That doesn't invalidate my arguments about them not expecting me to have a teleport rarity or Anna's trouble keeping the pace."

Samuel's frown didn't fade. Still, he also didn't offer any more arguments. Drake was getting exhausted from dealing with the old man, but he had asked for counsel. If nothing else, Samuel continued to ask the hard questions others would not.

A knock from Lydia announced her return. After Samuel opened the door, she and Anna then entered the carriage together. Anna immediately leapt across it to throw her arms around Drake, and he only barely managed to catch her in time. What had gotten into her?

"I love it, lord!" Anna all but squealed. "His clothes! They're perfect! You've made him so happy!" There were little tears squeezing out of her eyes.

Oh. Right. Robby. Drake gave her a moment before he cautiously disengaged her and sat her on the bench. "I'm glad Robby likes his clothes, but if you really like them, you need to thank Tamara and her maids. They're the ones who made them for him."

"I will, lord!"

"But that's not why I called you to see me."

She dabbed at her cheeks and settled on the seat beside him. "Of course. I may not be your blood thrall yet, but I'm going to be!" She sat up straight. "How may I serve you?"

"I have questions about your rarity."

"Would you like to copy it, lord?" She didn't seem alarmed about that.

"I'm thinking about it. First, I need to know how it works. Tell me how you use it."

Anna now looked truly excited. "You know about the recall point. I have to cut my arm and drain the blood in a circular pattern. But I can show you, lord! It's not that hard, I promise."

That was a reminder that this little girl had to *literally bleed* every time someone forced her to make a new recall point. Another reason to avoid asking her to teleport people as much as he could manage. "And then?"

"Once the recall point is ready, I can feel it. I can always feel it, even when I'm days away, though the feeling goes away the further I get. I only stopped feeling it once."

"When?"

"A big storm washed away the recall point. I couldn't get back to Daddy, and I was so worried they'd kill him. Finally, Captain Ro came to pick me up."

Drake suspected Ro had known just how valuable his adorable teleporter was for abductions, and he had been bluffing about killing her father. Not that any of that helped Anna now. She'd still endured... all that.

"And how do you actually teleport? You just pick a door and walk through it?"

She nodded eagerly. "I convince myself the door goes to the recall point."

"I have to believe it, lord." She leaned forward. "When I took you to see Captain Ro, I believed the door out of your manor would take us back to him. It did."

"But you have to step through that door first."

"Yes, though I don't teleport right away. Everyone else who agrees to teleport with me has to step through the same door after I have... believed it, I suppose. And when the last person who's agreed to teleport with me steps through the door I believe will take us all to the recall spot, that's when I go too. I go at the same time as the last one."

It sounded complicated, but everything Anna had just described matched what he'd experienced. As Drake considered the two times he had been teleported by Anna's rarity—first from his manor, and second from Sky's guest house—it all made sense. Easy enough. Now to ensure the other part of his brilliant plan was actually brilliant and not... suicidal.

"And the recall spot can move, correct?"

Anna nodded.

"And how many people can teleport at once?"

"The most I've ever teleported is four."

That was a lot less than Drake had hoped. "Is there any cost?"

"It tires me," Anna admitted. "I only teleported four people one time, and I blacked out after. Captain Ro wouldn't tell me for sure, but I think... I almost died, lord."

So teleporting people consumed blood, just like other rarities, and the more people Anna teleported, the more blood she lost. Drake offered Samuel a meaningful glance. The man must understand what this meant.

If Anna tried to teleport Sky, her warriors, Drake, and his battle maids, she could literally die of blood loss. By comparison, if Drake burnished Anna's teleport as he had all the others, he might not have a problem at all. If they wanted to use Anna's teleport rarity to deliver Sky to the cabal on time, they really did have only one option.

"Are you going to save Lord Skybreak?" Anna asked hopefully.

This child was too clever by half. He could just lie to her, but that seemed unnecessary. "I can't talk about our plans. I'd appreciate if you didn't either."

She nodded vigorously. "I won't tell a soul!"

"Not even Robby. Can you keep a secret from Robby?"

She frowned. "Why would I need to keep secrets from my friend?"

"He might worry about me if I leave to go after Lord Skybreak. You'll worry, won't you?"

The little tremble of her lips assured him she would. She was so damn adorable.

"So let's not tell Robby," Drake insisted. "He might be your friend, but you keep him safe too. If he doesn't know I'm leaving, he won't worry about me. So promise you won't tell him?"

This time, Anna nodded vigorously. "I won't!"

"Then I think we're all agreed." He glanced at Samuel and Lydia. "Aren't we?"

Lydia nodded immediately. Samuel nodded, but grudgingly. Perhaps learning that Anna teleporting more than four people might kill her had finally convinced him to agree to Drake's plan... or at least not fight it any longer.

Anna pulled a small hat pin from her dress pocket and then stabbed her own palm. She did it before Drake could speak, and so casually it made him blink. She must be used to stabbing herself and bleeding for others. Another reason to keep this poor kid safe.

She raised her bloody palm and smiled. "Ready, lord!"

He ruefully withdrew his letter opener and stabbed his palm, then grimaced as the wound immediately sealed up. That would be a problem. His ability to physically regenerate so quickly was going to make swapping out his rarity a lot more painful than he'd realized.

He looked at Anna. "Because I can heal so quickly, I'm going to have to cut myself a lot more than you. Don't worry. I'll be fine."

While she looked a bit uncertain, she nodded. "All right, lord."

Drake set his teeth and then jammed the point of the letter opener into the top of his forearm. It stung, but he knew it wouldn't be nearly enough. He growled and dragged the sharpened edge down, blinking as the pain speared his arm.

He couldn't stop. Not if he wanted to salvage their chances at the coming cabal. He gasped when he finished slitting open his arm. Anna immediately slapped her bleeding palm over the large gash.

Dammit. His skin was already starting to heal up despite the length, so Drake cut his arm again and again. Anna moved her hand to the new wound, and after several very painful minutes of constantly savaging his arm, he'd had enough.

Gasping, Drake eased Anna's hand away. She looked to be on the verge of tears, but he smiled to assure her it had all been necessary. That had fucking *hurt*.

"I'm fine. I'll be fine." The last of his self-inflicted wounds were already sealing over, and he moved his arm to show her. "See? Not a scratch left."

Next time, it might be easier to place Anna's blood in one of the vials Zuri had given him instead of trying to swap it with her in real time. Hopefully, they wouldn't have to do this often. Drake also decided he'd gather a sample of Samuel's blood to take with him if worst came to worst and he had to switch back to regeneration. Best to be prepared for every outcome.

Lydia moved to Anna's side and wrapped her hand in a handkerchief before Drake could ask, then pulled out one of her white healing gloves. As she put it on, Drake smiled in relief and approval. Unlike him, Anna wouldn't heal so quickly, but Lydia could fix that.

"Okay." Drake looked up. "So last time, how long did Hugo say it took for Samuel's rarity to replace *flutterstep*?" That was the blood thrall whose rarity allowed him to keep precise time.

"Just a little under an hour, lord," Lydia said as she mended Anna's cut.

Drake looked to Anna again, and then, against his better judgment, opened his arms. She hopped forward once more. He gave her a firm hug to calm her down after all that blood.

He soon eased Anna back. "I'll see you as soon as we all get back," he promised. "But now, I need you to do one more thing for me."

"What's that, lord?"

"I'd like you and Robby to sleep with Tamara and the maids tonight."

She nodded immediately. "So Robby won't know you've left."

"That's right. We don't want him to be sad."

"I like Tamara," Anna said. "And I can thank her for Robby's clothes."

"Make sure you do that."

She offered the cutest little curtsey. "Is there anything else, lord?"

Drake kept a straight face with great effort. "That's all, Anna. You're dismissed."

With her features as serious as a heart attack, Anna bowed, rose, and then hurried out the door of the carriage the moment Lydia opened it.

Drake glanced at Samuel. "Seriously, Samuel. Tell me you'd send that adorable little girl out on a dangerous mission. I want you to mean it."

He sighed. "I would prefer not to send either of you."

"It's good to know you care. But trust me, old man. I'll be back before you know it."

15
STILL BEING NICE

Lydia settled on the carriage bench beside him. "Who else will join you, lord?"

He glanced at her. "Who would you recommend? We'll need enough firepower to reach Sky and possibly mix it up with those mercs, but we also can't leave Samuel undefended. If worst comes to worst, he'll need protectors in the capital."

"Nicole and Valentia should join us," Lydia said. "Emily will stay with Samuel."

Drake chuckled. "She's not going to like that, so you can tell her. But tell me why."

"Nicole's ability to scout invisibly will serve us if we have to locate Sky or her mother in hostile territory. My rarity will allow me to deal with any watchers in elevated positions or open any locked gates from inside. And Valentia is simply very good at killing people."

"So's Emily," Drake pointed out.

"Yet Emily is a very visible, very intimidating threat." Lydia glanced to Samuel. "That is why she will be the ideal protector for Samuel in the capital if he arrives without us. Emily can also see the souls of anyone who attempts to sneak up on Samuel or others."

"Sounds like a plan to me," Drake agreed. "Any objections, old man?"

"I am not old," Samuel said irritably. "Why do you insist on calling me that?"

Drake grinned at him. "Mainly because I know it pisses you off."

Samuel sighed. "While I still do not fully endorse this course of action, if we must proceed with it, I agree with Lydia's tactical assessment. If you take a larger force, you may have difficulty teleporting them all back. And without the ability to scout, bypass locked doors, and assassinate enemies silent from a distance, you may not succeed at all."

Drake glanced at the carriage door. "Then I guess we should all get some grub, like normal, before we head out. In fact, let's all eat in the tent." He looked back at his two closest advisors. "So Robby sees us all doing it."

Just past midnight, Drake and his chosen battle maids rode out of their camp under cover of darkness, wearing feathersteel. While he'd contemplated asking one of Sky's rangers to join them, Drake had decided to let the poor bastards rest. Sachi knew the territory over which they'd be traveling as well as any Skybreak ranger, and he trusted her implicitly.

Before he left, with Anna's guidance, he'd created a "recall spot" in his armored carriage. Even now, he could feel that spot as a faint tingle at the back of his mind. He'd also verified he could teleport himself, Lydia, Valentia, and Nicole back to it without issue.

Using Anna's teleport rarity was a little like *flutterstep*, except the disorienting change of scenery was much longer and happened only after everyone passed through the door he "believed" would take them home. He also didn't feel remotely tired after using it, while Anna said teleporting three people would have exhausted her. So he was in good shape.

He also carried Sky's magic mirror. Karth hadn't brought one, which suggested Sky still had hers. He couldn't call her on it, but perhaps she would call him to check in.

Their fresh horses had been drawn from those in his vanguard, and while that would leave Samuel and the others without scouts for a little while, Lord Skybreak's rangers could easily take up those duties and many more once they rested up. By the time they realized Lord Gloomwood had gone to rescue their former lord, Drake would be long gone.

As they rode at a steady trot, Sachi ranged out ahead and vanished more often than not. She was slowing herself down so they could keep up, since they couldn't all move at catgirl speed unless they exhausted their horses. There was no need to do that yet.

Sky was likely not running her horses ragged either. She and her bodyguards had more than a day's head start on them, but they'd want to be rested once she arrived at Fort Graystone. Lydia had suggested a gallop later tonight, while they still had largely level land that would suit the horses well, and then walking the horses until just before morning.

This was going to be a grueling trip. They wouldn't have time to sleep late or lounge around camp enjoying Sachi's yummy meat. When they weren't riding, they would be walking, and when they weren't walking, they would be grabbing a few hours of sleep.

Still, Drake felt ready for this. He felt more prepared for this journey than he'd been even a few weeks ago, and thanks to his recent time with Samuel's regenerative rarity, his body was in peak physical condition. He also knew his battle maids and their gloves could help him recover each morning if he woke up sore from riding.

Sadly, he also knew Magnum was going to get heavy fast. He'd debated a good long while about the plusses and minuses of bringing his heavy revolver/crossbow on the road, but ultimately, he couldn't just rely on his battle maids if he needed people dead. The weapon was much heavier than a paintball gun, but he'd still rather have it than not.

Goktul had put his heart and soul into this weapon, and it had already served Drake well by killing one assassin. Leaving Magnum behind would have been foolish. So he'd carry the weight and use it to kill people.

As they rode, it wasn't long before Valentia spoke up. Drake had been expecting her to berate him about risking himself since she left. He braced himself for a tongue lashing.

"You were wise to choose Samuel as your successor," Valentia said.

Drake had anticipated a lot of arguments, but he hadn't expected that. "Yeah?"

"While Samuel currently doubts himself and fears the responsibility, he will make an excellent manor lord. He has the wisdom of years serving and surviving under lords of Gloomwood Manor and the temperament to make the hard calls."

"I take it you're also saying I lack all those qualities?"

"Not at all." Valentia offered a surprisingly warm smile. "Your leadership style is simply different from a traditional manor lord. While I am more partial to Samuel's approach, given it is that to which I am accustomed, you have had too many successes for me to dismiss them as luck. You have cunning and guile equal to the challenges you undertake."

Nicole chuckled quietly. "Gods, Val, you're never this nice."

"I am simply offering feedback," Valentia said primly. "Moreover, you did not me finish."

Drake grinned knowingly at Lydia. "Uh oh."

Valentia continued. "No matter how often I caution you against it, you continue to risk your own life. As your blood thrall, I cannot in good conscience endorse your decision to do that.

However, that does not mean I do not respect your bravery or skill in battle."

"Still being nice," Nicole reminded her.

"In short, lord, I still do not think you should have led this mission. But since you have chosen to do so, and you have named Samuel as your successor so Gloomwood Manor will remain safe if you fall, there is little point in berating you. I will support you as best as I can."

"Thanks, Val," Drake said. "Oh, and Nicole?"

"I'm not going to like this, am I?"

"I'm glad you're here as well. Even if you still don't trust me."

Nicole glanced his way. "Yet despite my best efforts, you have yet to prove my suspicions correct. So please, continue to disappoint me."

After that, there wasn't much to say, and Drake was happy to settle into a comfortable silence with his three overprotective battle maids and the open countryside through which they rode. Sachi came back close enough to speak only once to warn them she'd detected a group of riders. After a short debate, Drake decided to go around them. No point in taking chances.

It was well into the night when Drake finally found a chance to speak to Lydia in relative privacy. Nicole and Valentia were riding ahead now, speaking quietly, and they seemed involved in whatever they were up to. With Sachi's recent assurance there was no one around for a good ways, everyone felt a little safer simply focusing on the ride.

Drake was pleased when he managed to successfully convince his horse to move closer to Lydia's animal. He was getting better at riding. He still wasn't a skilled rider by any means, but he could give his mount basic commands and not fall off it when it galloped.

Lydia looked up from some recollection and blinked at him. "Is something the matter, lord?"

He hoped he hadn't shocked her out of anything pleasant. "You doing all right?"

She smiled at him. "Why would I be anything less than fine?"

"I don't know, but I do want you to know I have total faith in you. I know you could excel as Lord Gloomwood if I die. But I needed you with me, so changing Samuel to my successor made the most sense. We can't have both the lord and his successor on a mission."

Lydia frowned and looked to the countryside, then met his eyes again. "Lord... I hesitate to admit this, but now that I am no longer your successor, I am relieved."

That was a surprise. "You... really?"

"In those few rare times Samuel and I could speak in privacy, we dared speak of who might inherit the manor if Lord Crow fell. It was always a risk to speak of such things, as the old lord could compel us to reveal such discussions at any time. He could punish us simply for speaking of it."

"So why are you relieved not to be my successor any longer?"

"Because I am a coward."

Drake narrowed his eyes. "Now hold on. That's not true at all."

"I can only say what I believe."

"Right, but you can also believe stuff that's not true. How are you a coward?"

"The day you asked me why you wished me to be our manor lord, I omitted something."

"That's fine, but that doesn't make you a—"

"Please let me finish," she interrupted calmly. "I have wanted to say this for some time, but have never found the right opportunity."

He felt like a heel for interrupting her. "All right. I'm listening."

"I do, of course, believe everything I said to you that day. I did believe you would be the best choice to lead the manor under your new blood pact, given your experience with leading others without it in your world. I also trusted you to lead us because you gave us the ability to protect ourselves from future manor lords. You risked yourself to keep us safe."

Drake listened in silence. That seemed like what she needed.

"Yet I kept another belief from you as well, the first time I was able to keep anything from my lord." Lydia took a breath. "The other reason I wished you to become our manor lord, instead of taking the title myself, was because I did not wish to become a target."

Drake nodded as it all fell into place. "That doesn't make you a coward. Nobody would want a job that puts them in the sights of every assassin on the planet."

"So that is what I wished to tell you, lord. I was not entirely... truthful... with you that day about my reasons for turning down the title of Lord Gloomwood. In retrospect, I preferred to let you seize the title and bear the risk in my place. Even today, your bravery inspires me."

"I had no idea," Drake said softly. "But you know it wasn't bravery, right?"

"How do you mean? Your decision was incredibly brave."

"No, my decision was ambitious and reckless, and you absolutely made the right call by staying as steward to protect the manor. We're both very lucky I didn't fall flat on my face."

Her eyes widened. "What do you mean by that?"

"Lydia, I'd been in your world a few *hours* when I took this title. I've had time to think back to our first day as well. Knowing what I know now about what goes into this job, I should have run screaming from the room. I wasn't qualified to lead anyone."

"Yet you did step up to lead us," she said firmly.

"Only because I had no idea what I was signing up for. Maybe I was brave, sure. Or maybe I was simply excited by the chance to have my own manor and people to serve me, to live like a king instead of a peasant. Looking back now, I wonder. If I'd known back then, like truly known the dangers I'd face... I might have turned this title down."

Lydia frowned. "I don't believe that."

"I'm just saying, a lot of what you're crediting to bravery could also be credited to having no fucking clue what I was signing up for. You knew what this job and world were like. You'd seen multiple manor lords die and knew every way your world could destroy you. Also, you had the manor to think about in case I fucked it all up."

"That was a concern," Lydia agreed hesitantly.

"So can I offer an alternative suggestion? Would you mind if I did that?"

"I will listen."

"You're no coward. You just decided to protect Gloomwood Manor another way."

As she tilted her head, her dark hair coursed down one shoulder. "I truly don't know what you mean, lord."

"You serve as our steward. That's how you protect the manor."

"My role as steward is to support you and ensure the manor runs smoothly. Anyone could do that. I am nothing special."

"I disagree, and so do you if you think about it. You've already admitted there's no one at the manor you think will make a better steward than you."

She said nothing.

"You may try to hide it, but don't think I've noticed how completely carefree my time as a manor lord has been so far."

She looked away. "I really would appreciate it if you wouldn't jest about such things."

"I'm not jesting. I've been through a hell of a lot, barely escaped death half a dozen times, but those are problems I would always have encountered. Yet because I have you, I have never once worried the manor would fall apart while I was busy not dying."

Her gaze returned to him, confused. "How would the manor... fall apart?"

He thought of how frazzled Sky had seemed after she lost her steward. "I sometimes think the only reason I was able to accomplish half of what we've managed since I became Lord Gloomwood is because of the dozens of equally vexing problems you've intercepted before I heard about them. You can be modest all you like, but I can't even imagine how much you handle for me. Problems I don't even *hear* about."

"That is kind of you to say, lord, but it is not courage. At a minimum, it is competence."

"That is one part. But that's not the only courage I'm talking about."

"Then..." Lydia hesitated. "What do you see as courage, lord?"

"The way you've held everyone in the manor together while you dealt with the worst and most homicidal bosses anyone could have. No matter how much of a complete tool Lord Gloomwood has been, you've been there as a barrier between the vulnerable staff of our manor and whatever asshole was running the place. You've had to manage dickish lords while keeping everyone else alive and keeping the manor from going under."

"That is simply what Esme charged me to do, and it is not a task I take lightly. Even so, I will never be half the steward she was."

"Esme was the steward before you." Drake nodded. "The one who died."

"It is hard to talk about her, lord, but if I have worth as a steward, it is thanks to her."

"That's... well, a little unreasonable," Drake said. "The way you see your worth, I mean."

Lydia shrugged. "I can only speak what I believe. Moreover, you have made *my* role so much easier. After you arrived and I began to understand what kind of a man you were, I was pleased to finally have a lord I could serve *eagerly*. Yet I do not want your title."

"Because you might have to protect the others again someday,"

Drake said. "I think the real reason you want to remain steward is so if Samuel and I both die somehow, and an asshole takes over the blood pact, anyone who kills us might still decide to keep *you*. Right?"

Her lips pressed together.

"They'd keep you alive because you've got a great rarity and you know how to run the place. As a lord you'd be a target, but as a steward, you're indispensable. And if you're indispensable, you can keep protecting everyone, even if you're stuck serving another asshole."

She simply offered a deep sigh.

"So here's where you're wrong about being a coward. Your choice to remain steward to protect the others isn't cowardice. It's one of the bravest reasons I've ever heard."

She looked away again. "You are very kind."

"It's not kindness, it's fact. You're right that dodging assassins is terrifying, but at least I could fight back and kill my enemies. Thanks to the blood pact, you never had that option."

Still Lydia said nothing.

"You spent years living under the same roof with homicidal dickheads who could fillet you if you said the wrong word, yet you never gave up and never stepped down. Instead, you acted as a barrier between your evil lords and everyone else, and even after I showed up, you intended to do the same. I believe that is incredibly brave."

Finally, her gaze met his again. "As I said, you are very kind."

Now that she was looking at him again, Drake grinned to put her at ease. "Also, you should cheer up. Since I'm such a great manor lord, and I'm so skilled at defeating assassins, you can be my steward as long as you want. I'm too clever and talented to die."

She frowned. "Your overconfidence is often vexing."

"It can be."

"Yet there is no lord I would rather serve."

"Not even Lord Skybreak?"

She looked to the road ahead. "Only if I could no longer serve you."

16

I AM SO VERY POKEY

Grueling days passed as they rode hard, walked hard, and rested however long they could. Fortunately, Sachi picked up a trail she identified as belonging to a group of Skybreak rangers on their second day of travel, at about the spot they suspected Sky had split with Karth and the rest of her manor's vanguard. Sachi had Sky's scent now, which was *great*.

Knowing they'd managed to pick up Sky's trail motivated everyone. They pushed harder and longer each day. Every time they set out again one of his battle maids used their healing gloves on Drake, and he was surprised when they also used them on each other. At least that proved he was getting better at long hauls. Together, they kept each other going.

Sachi even managed to catch some game as they moved. While they had to cook it rapidly and couldn't season it, any fresh meat was welcome when their only option was dry cheese and stale bread. Fortunately, water was plentiful in the countryside leading to Skybreak territory, and Sachi knew where to find more once they hit the rocky mountain terrain.

Drake also took what time he could to practice with Magnum. He still couldn't drill fast-moving bunnies, but he could hit man-sized rocks with precision close to what he'd managed back on Earth with a paintball gun. Magnum was meant for man killing.

He also checked Sky's mirror every night. She never called him. If he had to guess, she didn't want him to berate her about her decision to chase down her mother.

As hard as the journey was, after three full days of travel, they finally approached the rocky, mountainous terrain that made up much of Skybreak territory. That would mean leaving their loyal horses behind. Walking them into danger would simply slow everyone down.

Riding the animals at anything other than a walk over Skybreak's mountainous terrain would risk the horses snapping a leg or worse, and Sachi assured them there was plenty of good grazing and fresh water in this area to keep them alive. Drake knew she wasn't just saying that to reassure him. She couldn't lie, and she seemed to like the horses well enough.

It felt wrong to just let the horses wander off after they'd brought him all this way, but Drake accepted Sachi's assurance they'd be all right on their own and might even be found by locals at some point. All horses belonging to Gloomwood Manor were branded as such, and the manor offered rewards for their return... or reports of them being stolen.

After freeing the horses of their saddles and packs, they took what they could carry and left the rest. Now on foot and carrying only their light packs and weapons, Sachi led Drake and his battle maids after Sky and her loyal warriors.

While Sachi couldn't identify who was who, she had reported four distinct scents in the trail that *weren't* horses. That matched Drake's understanding that Sky was traveling with Mary, Ali, and Kari. While four warriors might seem a little light for dealing with a whole group of mercenaries, it was possible not all of the mercenaries waiting at Fort Graystone had rarities. Given what he knew about the ratio of those with divine blood to those who didn't have it, the composition of the mercenaries could be similar to Captain Ro's.

When he'd faced men without rarities after escaping Captain Ro's hospitality, Drake had ripped apart twenty trained mercenaries simply by shifting into a dire rat and having lunch. He suspected Kari's rarity, *dire wraith*, could be as powerful, and who knew what Mary and Ali could do? The guys who came after Sky's mother might already be fucked.

Finally, there was Sky herself. He was looking forward to finally learning just what *void* was capable of. He'd imagined all sorts of ways it might work: summoning a black hole to suck away enemies, creating a black hole inside enemies, or even erasing parts of the walls or floor with a touch. It could be anything, but he hoped it would be cool.

Regardless, he knew she wouldn't go down without a brutal fight. And after the mercenaries who'd abducted Lady Skybreak (Sky's mother) had threatened to slowly murder her if Sky didn't come, he doubted they expected much in the way of mercy. Or if they did, they didn't know Sky Skybreak.

After another hard day of alternating between fast walks and slow jogs, all of which irritated Sachi, they finally made camp after darkness fell in a narrow split in some high rocks. Even if they didn't have Sachi's feral senses to alert them of anyone's approach, it would be impossible for anyone to come at them without entering through the narrow opening.

The high rocks also meant they could have a fire without worrying about the light giving them away to anyone in the distance, which meant meat. Cooked meat. After the long haul he'd had today and the three days prior, Drake eagerly chewed through a whole bunny.

They were also able to remove their armor, or at least most of it. That gave Drake's sore muscles room to breathe. Feathersteel was absurdly comfortable as armor went, but even it began to chafe after days on the road. His body needed to decompress.

Once the meal was done and the fire was fading, Sachi spoke up. "We should leave before first light. A few hours after midnight is best. If we do so, we'll reach Fort Graystone shortly before dawn. Any lookouts will be at the end of their shifts and eager for the morning."

"Which means they'll be sloppy." Drake idly rubbed his own shoulder in hopes of easing the tension of carrying Magnum all day. "Still, doesn't the fact that everyone's sloppy in the morning mean they'll expect someone to show up at that time?"

"Expectation become less important as monotony weighs it down. Given Sky and her warriors likely arrived yesterday, whatever took place in that fortress may already be over. If it isn't, I doubt any survivors will be expecting anyone else."

Possibly. "Yet Robby has to know we've left the camp by now. Lord Proudglade knows Sky might be getting some reinforcements soon. He might warn them."

"You still haven't told me how you got that assassin to talk," Nicole complained. "It's so cruel. It's like handing me a puzzle without all the pieces."

"You know I can't tell you yet," Drake reminded her. "It's for your own good and our security." As much as he trusted his battle maids, no one but Lydia and Samuel now knew he could lie, because the more people who knew, the more chances they could be forced to reveal it. "The important thing is, these guys may still be expecting us."

Nicole leaned forward. "Then once we sight the fort, Sachi and I will go poke around a little. That's why I'm here. To poke things." She wiggled her fingers. "I am so very pokey."

Valentia shoved another chunk of meat at her. "Eat. You always get like this after a long hike ahead of a battle. You need your energy."

"Aww, Val. Will you feed me? Little bites, please."

"I will cut your food into smaller chunks if that will make it easier for you to swallow."

Nicole pouted. "I see someone doesn't want their post-hike massage."

Drake could actually use a good massage after four days of riding and hiking, even with the healing from his battle maid's gloves to help him, but he wasn't about to ask. Especially since he suspected any of his battle maids would jump at the opportunity to impress him.

As much as he respected these women as warriors and professionals, asking any of them to massage him after a long ride would just feel icky. Which was why he almost jumped up when Lydia's firm fingers began kneading the tension out of his shoulders.

"Hey!" he protested. "I'm fine!" Yet as a tingle filled his body and tension melted from his sore muscles, he lost the will to ask her to stop. That felt goddamn *amazing*.

"We face battle tomorrow with an unknown number of opponents," Lydia said firmly as she continued to knead his muscles. "Our healing gloves can only do so much, and we cannot risk you slowing down or missing a step because you are sore. You no longer have Samuel's regenerative rarity, and I'd prefer not to intercept more crossbow bolts on your behalf."

As Drake groaned despite his best efforts to keep quiet—damn, Lydia was good at working the tension out of his shoulders—Sachi growled in amusement.

"That's not fair. I've done more walking than anyone. Who will massage me?"

Nicole grinned her way. "I'll do you, kitty."

The huntress purred. "Do not offer what you do not intend to provide."

"Though I know you'd be much happier if *Sam* was here to do you."

Sachi's ears flicked back and forth. "He does have powerful hands."

Drake groaned, and not from what a terrific job Lydia was now doing with the sore muscles on his upper back. "I'll give you a lot of leeway with the old man, but can you not all talk about how much you want him while I'm right here? I have an ego too, you know."

Nicole snickered. "It looks like Lydia is doing just fine with your ego, lord. You should return the favor. She has this super sensitive spot just above her lower back—"

"Nicole," Lydia interrupted calmly. "You need to eat."

Nicole rolled her eyes and tore off a chunk of meat, then chewed. "See?" she said with her mouth half full. "I'm eating."

Valentia leaned forward. "We should discuss our tactics for tomorrow's battle, should it come to one. Our lord had fought several battles against multiple opponents, but only in his former dire rat form. He needs to know how we prioritize opponents."

"That's good," Drake agreed, then groaned as Lydia's firm fingers dug into his lower back. "Holy shit, how are you so good at that?"

"Practice," she said simply. "Listen to Val."

"Should we be engaged, Nicole will vanish," Valentia said. "If there are ranged opponents beyond forty paces, we will take cover while she moves invisibly to deal with them. Otherwise, she will remain in reserve to kill anyone who sneaks up on Lord Gloomwood."

"I won't quite be breathing down your neck," Nicole told Drake. "But you can imagine I'm doing that if it makes you feel safer."

"Once visible hostiles approach, I will freeze any who move within forty paces," Valentia continued. "In such a case, I will not be taking prisoners. People will die."

Drake believed her. "Just how many bad guys can you freeze in a fight?"

"Perhaps ten," Valentia said. "More than that and I will begin to flag. However, I cannot freeze blood through silverweave. So if we do encounter enemies wearing armor resistant to magic, I will leave those to Nicole and Lydia."

"And me," Drake reminded her. "I bet a crossbow bolt will fuck up silverweave."

Valentia gave no indication as to her thoughts on that. "Regardless, once I have frozen the initial wave of attackers, if more enemies remain, Lydia will leave her position as your bodyguard and enter the fray. At that point, lord, you must focus on protecting yourself."

"So I'll hunker down and snipe fools while Lydia *fluttersteps* the shit out of them." Drake gasped as Lydia's hands wrapped around his calves. "Hey! My legs are fine."

Lydia settled herself at his feet and began kneading his calves with her heavenly hands. "Your leg muscles feel as tight as silverwood. Stop acting childish."

"Right, but... that part's a little sensitive!"

Nicole grinned wide. "Oh, so he's ticklish!"

"Shut up," Drake ordered, then grimaced. "I mean, not literally. You can still talk." The muscles in his calves were sore, certainly, but still... this was Lydia!

Valentia continued as if Lydia was *not* currently kneeling at Drake's feet while massaging the back of his legs. "If we were to face more than fifteen mercenaries at the same time, even without rarities, I would not feel comfortable about our chances. But we would not face such a force because Sachi would inform us before they arrived. We would evade them."

"Also, I'd be killing them too, lord," Sachi added. "Which Val keeps leaving out."

Valentia glanced at her. "Having you in reserve is the only way I feel comfortable engaging in a battle with an unknown force when Lord Gloomwood must also be protected. That is why I have not included your efforts in my estimate. Even with Nicole watching over our lord in lack of other threats, we need wiggle room."

"I think our lord's going to wiggle out of his pants if Lydia goes any higher," Nicole said.

"Oh, shush," Valentia said crossly. "Unless you want to massage him."

"Ooh, can I?"

"No!" Lydia, Drake, and Valentia all said at once.

Nicole tore another bite off her meaty bone. "Rude."

Drake sighed as Lydia finally began working the tension out of his lower thighs. If she went any higher he *was* going to stop her, accusations of childish behavior be damned. Yet he now felt as relaxed as if he'd settled into a warm bath. He knew Lydia was also using the power of her healing gloves in concert with her massage, which felt divine.

Fortunately, Lydia concluded her work before it got to the point where Drake felt obligated to order her to stop. He really shouldn't be so sensitive about this. Lydia was his steward, his chief operational officer, and a loyal ally he trusted implicitly.

The fact that she was also a damn good massage therapist was just a bonus.

17
WHAT ARE YOUR ORDERS?

Drake got very little sleep in the little time they set aside for it. Still, he felt alert enough after Sachi roused them. They armored up, bundled up, and set out a few hours past midnight to make their final trek to Fort Graystone. Today, he would finally learn if Sky had successfully saved her mother and was standing triumphant over her foes, waiting for a ride home.

Or if this whole trip was all going to conclude with a very depressing end.

As they picked their way over mountain country littered with loose stones, hidden holes, and slick mud, Drake was glad they had freed the horses, even though he still worried about them. Leading horses across terrain like this in the dark would have been exceedingly dangerous. It was dangerous enough for him, and all he had to do was follow Sachi closely.

As the hours passed, Drake focused on little more than ensuring he didn't slip on the mud or twist his ankle in a hole. This world was not like his own in many ways, but the most striking at the moment was how quiet it was at night. There was no noise save the gentle wind over the hills and the barely audible sound of their boots on grass or scree.

No matter how many times he glanced up at the night sky here, he was always struck by how many stars burned there. Unlike home, where the sky was filled with stars, in this world, without ambient light, it was more like a god had vomited glitter across the sky. There were so many stars up there that many overlapped, and he suddenly wondered if one was his.

Had Lord Crow teleported him through time and space? It was certainly possible this world, wherever it was, could exist somewhere in the same galaxy or universe as the world he'd once called home. That wouldn't explain the magic, of course—so much here defied his grade-school understanding of the laws of physics—but still, was it possible?

Probably not. Too much was different here. Real gods, real magic, and this crazy blood pact shit. None of it was possible in a universe with laws anything like the one he had come from, so even the laws of physics had to be different here. Tonight, the night before he might face his first battle without a powerful rarity to keep him safe, was an odd night to miss home.

Yet he did miss it. He wondered if his mother had held a funeral for him yet. It had been almost a month since he vanished, so someone must have found his empty truck by now. Without a body, he'd likely be listed as "missing"... so was his mother still holding out hope?

It was odd that he'd thought of her so little since arriving here. The fact that he'd been so busy trying not to die was part of it, but if was being honest with himself, he'd also admit that they'd grown apart in the past few years. He'd basically relied on himself since fifteen.

So why was that?

The kind and attentive woman who'd nurtured and raised him had grown less attentive each year, all but leaving him to his own devices by the time he started high school. He'd been a latch key kid from ninth grade on, with his own hobbies and friends to hang out with. With his mother working most nights, they sometimes only saw each other on weekends.

He'd been making his own breakfast, lunches, and dinners since eighth grade, other than when his mom left him pizza or he grabbed whatever she'd left in the fridge. He'd even done his own shopping once she'd started leaving him money for it. He'd only splurged once, after which he'd learned that getting a new video game wasn't fun when he didn't have anything to eat.

His mother's inattention had made him fiercely independent, forced him to do things for himself, and taught him to budget and manage resources... but was that *good?*

In the past few years, since he'd decided college wasn't going to work after two years of building up debt he couldn't pay off, he and his mother had barely spoken at all. Maybe a short phone call every few months. So it was possible, given his mother still lived in Iowa, that whoever had found his empty truck in New Mexico and reported it to the police hadn't even told her yet.

As Drake walked what felt like endlessly with only his thoughts for company, the way his life had changed in the last month seemed almost impossible to believe. The rarities and the battle maids were one part, but so was the way he, himself, was changing. The harrowing challenges of life as a manor lord still felt more like a challenge than a curse. And killing people as easily as he could now made him feel like a different person entirely.

Still, what was the alternative? Back on Earth, he'd been killing himself digging holes, hammering nails, and moving wheelbarrows full of concrete for a basic wage he blew on beer, games, and the occasional strip club with his construction buddies. He hadn't had any savings, and he'd had no way to pay off college debt. What would he have been back on Earth?

Not much. Back on Earth, he wouldn't be much at all. But here... he was someone.

He might not deserve the head start he'd gotten in this world. Even so, unlike all those assholes back in his world who started with money and connections, at least he could use his head start to protect his manor and his people. It wasn't just that the people of his manor were loyal to him now. He felt responsible for them as well. He *wanted* to keep them safe.

Not to say that being rich wasn't also nice. Being rich remained absolutely fucking awesome. Yet without perks like wealth, why would anyone ever sign up for this insane job?

"Lord?" Lydia's soft voice snapped him back to the world. "We are close."

Drake set aside the introspection summoned by his silent and meditative multi-hour journey across fantasy mountain land. It was time to focus on the business of not being dead... and pulling his weight in whatever conflict came next. He might have powerful allies now, but he was still responsible for protecting himself. Magnum would let him do that.

Sachi diverted from her path and led them to higher ground, which required some scrambling up uneven hills and even some straight up rock climbing. Fortunately, even with the weight of his pack and Magnum, Drake managed. He was already more fit than he had been.

Once they finally came to a stop on a narrow, rocky ledge overlooking a steep descent, Drake saw Fort Graystone for the first time. It wasn't much. Just a big rocky rectangle built halfway into the rock, with a couple of sad-looking watchtowers.

It didn't have a moat, though there was the faint blue sliver of a shallow river winding its way up to the fort. None of that mattered right now, however, because there were at least eight burning flames gathered all around it.

"That is a large force," Lydia said quietly as they gathered on the ledge. "That cannot be Sky and her people."

"No," Valentia said. "And those are not camp fires, Lord Gloomwood. Those are watch fires. Those are likely maintained by a sizable force of soldiers all intent on preventing whoever is inside that fort from sneaking out without being filled with arrows."

"So... Sky brought some friends and surrounded them?" Drake asked hopefully.

"More likely she was lured to the fort and trapped inside," Valentia said. "The fact that a force that large has not invaded suggests a stalemate has resulted. With their powerful rarities, Sky and her bodyguards can defeat a much larger force in close quarters. But should they attempt to cross an open field, they would be cut apart by arrows."

Drake groaned. "And the mercs don't need to invade. They just need to keep Sky bottled up in there until they're sure she can no longer make it to the cabal. They've done that already, since there's only two days left. So why are they still there?"

"It could be whoever hired them simply wants to ensure nothing unexpected happens," Lydia said. "Or there are warriors with powerful rarities on their way to eliminate Sky and her bodyguards. The mercenaries now gathered may simply be holding the line until their reinforcements arrive."

"Or Lord Proudglade figured out I snuck out of my camp with my badass battle maids and unstoppable huntress," Drake said. "And he doesn't want us getting in to help."

Lydia's face gave no window into her thoughts. "Regardless, reaching Sky will be very difficult." She glanced at him. "What are your orders?"

Drake frowned as he considered options. He'd decided this mission was necessary, so he wasn't about to give up this easily. He needed more information.

"We need to know exactly what we're dealing with." Drake glanced at Sachi, then Nicole. "You two want to rock-paper-scissors for it?"

"I will scout along the ridges," Sachi said. "Nicole, you have the camp."

"Hooray," Nicole said in a manner that was definitely *not* enthused. "Hey, Val? If I die while scouting a camp full of mercenaries, I just want you to know I enjoyed the sex."

"Just don't do anything foolish," Valentia said firmly.

"Why would I do that?" Nicole crouched low and moved off.

She didn't activate her rarity, *penumbra*, which let her go invisible. There was no need to do so this far from the watch fire and soldiers. While Drake didn't know how long she could maintain her invisibility, he knew it wasn't forever. She'd save it for when she got close.

As for Sachi, she'd vanished entirely in the short time he watched Nicole leave. His feral huntress still came and went like the wind. Given her body count, that left him glad she was his ally and actually seemed to like him. He was now alone with Valentia and Lydia.

"So... they going to be awhile?" Drake asked.

Lydia nodded. "Caution is best when dealing with an enemy force this large. I would not expect them back before dawn."

"Cool. So if we've got some time, I guess I'll try the mirror again." Drake dug into his backpack for the big magic box he'd hauled across four days of travel. "Earth."

It popped open, and then he removed the mirror inside. A brief inspection offered the same disappointment as all the prior times he'd looked. His reflection. Nothing else.

Valentia glanced his way. "It's possible she may never contact you on that again."

"Possible," Drake agreed. "But if she did and I didn't check, she might like me less."

He'd just finished stowing the mirror in his pack when Lydia's hand slammed down on his shoulder and pushed him against the ledge. Before he could complain, he saw Valentia flatten herself as well. A glance at Lydia showed a finger to her lips.

So they were being quiet now. There must be a good reason for that.

The low sound of voices became audible in the distance, far enough away he couldn't make out the words. He could, however, hear what sounded like multiple people approaching. If they weren't worried about being ambushed by the people running all those watch fires, the soldiers were probably with the bad guys.

Moving cautiously and quietly, Drake all but slithered to the edge of the ledge to join Valentia in peering over. In the distance, the tiny flames of torches bounced. Drake saw only two visible flames, suggesting a small force. They looked to be in no hurry.

He had a worrying suspicion these were the reinforcements the mercenaries who currently had Fort Graystone surrounded were waiting for. So now... he needed to decide whether to let them by or ambush them.

18
YOU DON'T JUST CALL A TRUCE WITH THE ENEMY!

As Lydia joined him and Valentia in their survey of the enemy group, Drake glanced at her and kept his voice to a low whisper. "What are the chances those are good guys?"

Lydia whispered back. "There is a remote possibility they could be Skybreak soldiers or traveling merchants hoping to take shelter in Fort Graystone, but I doubt that."

"Should have kept a scout in reserve," Drake said. "Guess it's up to us then."

"You wish me to ascertain their identities?"

"Sneakily," Drake agreed. "We can't even get a good look at them from here. Let's see if we can get close enough to at least hear whatever they're chatting about so amiably."

"Lydia should go alone," Valentia said. "You and I will stay here until she returns."

"That's a good plan," Drake agreed. "But it won't be nearly as fun for me, and I like Lydia alive. So let's go, battle maids."

Valentia sighed. "At least, if we all die, I will no longer have to worry about stopping you from taking foolish risks."

Drake grinned at her. "See? There's an upside to every plan."

He looked toward the sound of their oncoming enemies. "Now, let's mosey."

Drake let Lydia lead the way, and he wasn't surprised when she led them back the same way Sachi had led them up here. Going back down was a bit more harrowing than climbing up, mainly because he was looking at the distant ground instead of the sky. If he missed a step and fell to his death, Samuel would get the manor a whole lot faster than they planned.

Once they were back on mostly-level ground without broken necks, Lydia set off in the direction they had seen the distant torches. Drake followed closely in her footsteps. He didn't even hear Valentia behind him. He had to look back to verify she hadn't simply vanished.

Soon, the voices were audible once more. Lydia slowed. Fortunately, a stroke of luck or, more likely, Lydia's competence with reading and choosing routes across mountain terrain brought them along a narrow ledge ahead of and above where the folks below were ambling. As Drake flattened himself and wriggled along it, unconcerned voices carried on the wind.

"...no way she's still there," one voice said, a young woman. "This is the Asp we're talking about. She's probably already burned their flesh off and sauntered away!"

"Not if she couldn't get close enough to burn them," another voice said, a young man. "She can't burn men alive if they're constantly lobbing arrows at her."

"I'm telling you, we're walking to a fort full of gooey dead men," the first woman said. "This whole trip was a waste from the moment we set out, and it'll smell."

"We get experience either way," the man said. "So if everyone is dead and they've already left, consider this a training mission."

"And if it isn't, we face the Asp!" the first woman said. "Which is terrifying!"

"You should both turn back if she truly frightens you," a second woman said vengefully. "That woman took everything from me. She will pay in blood."

The man groaned. "Please don't mention your blood vendetta to the mercenaries. We're trying to present ourselves as professional and experienced bounty hunters."

"You weren't there," the second woman said. "You didn't see all she did."

"No, I wasn't, but that's no reason to just tell anyone you see you're out for revenge," the man said. "Now, we're getting close, so we should probably..."

The man trailed off. Drake didn't like that the man trailed off. The steady sound of approaching footsteps had stopped as well. While he saw torchlight below, the torch that was casting it hadn't yet rounded the narrow bend in the rocks that would bring it in sight.

Lydia nudged him and mouthed four words. *"Have we been spotted?"*

The answer came when a literal flaming rock came hurtling out of the sky.

Instincts honed by dodging men carrying long steel beams across a busy construction site allowed Drake to roll to one side as Lydia rolled to the other. The rock crashed down between them and shattered into searing, rocky shrapnel. That peppered his raised hand and arm and left some shallow cuts, but did nothing worse.

None of them had said a word and been quiet as the wind, so one of those mercenaries must have a rarity that allowed him to detect nearby danger or nearby enemies. That sucked.

"Did you get them?" the first woman called frantically. "Are they dead?"

An angry grunt followed. "Shut up, Gaby!"

At least the enemy force seemed to be comprised of idiots. Drake urgently motioned for his people to fall back. As they all stayed low and attempted to retreat, another flaming rock hurtled from the sky. That was definitely a rarity, but this time, a small but glittering ball of ice hurtled up to meet it. Valentia really could freeze just about anything.

The two projectiles collided in midair. Rocks and flaming debris scattered like a firecracker above their heads, showering them with pebbles. While that was annoying, it was surprisingly non-fatal. A shadow rushed around the distant cliff edge below.

More than forty paces away. Not that much further though. Drake brought Magnum to his shoulder and aimed down its barrel. He pressed the trigger. His assault crossbow bucked against his shoulder as the bolt whistled away.

The bolt slammed into the rock only a hand's length from the distant shadow's head. So close! They cursed and leapt out of sight.

"Crossbow!" the first woman yelled. "It just fired!"

"Which is why you don't just charge out blindly!" the second woman yelled. "Gods!"

Another flaming rock rocketed into sight, and this time, Drake saw where it was coming from. Someone in the distance was lobbing the damn things up into the air like they were carrying around a trebuchet. If this was like other rarities, he imagined it was tiring them out. They had also just revealed their position. Drake and his maids held the high ground.

This time, the rock was far enough off target Valentia didn't bother to intercept it, or perhaps had no ice available to do so. That allowed Drake to close in without being attacked, though the commotion might be loud enough to alert the soldiers at the watch fires.

Before he could finish advancing, a slim female shadow rocketed into view from the ledge that had been out of sight below. She seemed to be, for all intents and purposes, flying, and also already had a bowstring drawn taut. He caught a glimpse of dark flowing hair and a grim smile, and then an icy wall popped up in front of his face.

The arrow hit the wall and sliced straight though, with the tip coming to a stop right before Drake's nose. A smarter man would have taken that as a cue to not be so reckless, but Drake stepped around it and aimed Magnum instead. As the woman landed gracefully on the ledge and reached to her quiver for another arrow, he fired.

This time his bolt hit home, though it only caught her in the shoulder. Her anguished cry as she tumbled off the ledge tugged at what part of him hadn't gone full murder machine. He hoped he wasn't going to go soft whenever he had to kill women. Lydia wouldn't.

From below, the first woman gasped. "Oh Gods, are you okay?"

They now had the advantage in momentum. Drake was determined to take it. He rose and crouch-walked forward with Magnum, aware he only had two bolts loaded now. He was pleased when both Lydia and Valentia fell into step beside him. They advanced together.

The urge to stop and reload was strong, but that meant he'd have to take his eyes off the ledge. If that long-haired archer leapt up to take a shot again, he wanted to be ready. He was all too aware he was only alive right now because of Valentia's icy intervention.

"You said he'd just fired!" the second female voice called angrily.

"He did!" the man called.

"But he just *shot* me!"

"Crossbow reload rarity?"

The first woman called up to them with just the slightest tremor in her voice. "Hey, fellow bounty hunters?" She sounded hopeful. "Team up? We can split the bounty!"

Drake slowed. He didn't like it when the people he had to kill sounded so young and terrified. Still, these people had attacked them first, and they might have dangerous rarities. He couldn't risk losing a battle maid to a fatal strike… or die himself.

As they approached the ledge and a possible path downward, Lydia pointed toward a narrow path down. She brushed her hands across her waist and pulled two glowing yellow daggers from her hips. She pointed to a second path and narrowed her eyes.

Pincer attack. Seemed like a good plan. The enemy was probably huddled up in fear.

"You don't just call a truce with the enemy!" the second woman said. "Now get ready!"

Ahead of him, Valentia hissed. "Silverweave, lord," she whispered.

Drake ground his teeth. "Can't freeze 'em?"

"No. They came prepared to face rarities."

"Then you're my shield."

As Lydia moved down the path she'd indicated, Drake looked for another way down. He could probably get an angle on them once he reached the ledge... assuming he didn't get a burning rock in the face for his trouble. He'd just have to trust Valentia to handle that.

He'd just reached the ledge when someone gurgled in pain, and then a woman shouted out in triumph. "Got her! I got her!" She shrieked. "Carl!"

Had they hurt Lydia? Drake rushed to the edge and swept Magnum around and down, from the high ground, to find a sight that was less horrifying and more... mildly horrifying.

The dark-haired woman who had turbo jumped earlier had collapsed with her back against the cliff, clutching the bolt buried in her shoulder. Blood pumped past her fingers. A young man who might even be younger than Olivia—Carl—stumbled away from Lydia, clutching his bloody stomach in an attempt to keep his gleaming intestines from sliding out.

And a third woman, Gaby—a tall, slim, blonde-haired girl in what looked like patchwork silverweave clothing—stood with both hands out and golden light flaring from her palms. She stood like she was holding back a falling wall, one foot braced with her ankle up.

Lydia stood frozen paces away from the blonde-haired girl, face flat and eyes cold. One dagger was raised while the other looked as if it had just finished a slash. She wasn't moving. She looked to be, so far as Drake could tell, frozen in place.

The blonde woman physically slid back despite the only sign of resistance being the air ahead of her glowing hands. "Carl? Carl! Did she get you?"

"Oh yes." Carl dropped his knees. "Not good."

He glanced up at Drake. As he did so, Drake got a clear look at a young olive-skinned face, short curly hair, and wide dark eyes. His target looked like he was still in high school, and the terrified despair in the young man's eyes kept Drake from taking the kill shot.

From up here, from this close, he could put a bolt through a kneeling man-sized target just as easily as he'd killed Suck. Yet it was obvious that, other than whatever Gaby was doing to freeze Lydia, these three assassins were out of the fight.

He still needed to find out what they were doing out here.

Ice crackled into being beneath the young blonde-haired woman's boots. When some invisible force drove her back, she lost her footing. Lydia stumbled, face still hard as stone. She caught herself and dashed forward with knives raised to make the kill.

"Lydia, stop!" Drake shouted.

Lydia froze a hair's breadth from slicing the throat of the terrified blonde girl who, having now fallen on her ass, had managed nothing but to raise her hands to ward off the knives. Beside him, Valentia cursed softly. "Don't do this."

"Surrender now!" Drake called as loud as he dared. "Or you're all dead!"

Gaby looked up at where Lydia stood paces away, glowing knives raised. Eyes wide as saucers, she stared pleadingly at Drake. "We surrender!"

"Gods." Carl collapsed onto his side in his own blood. "Ow."

"I will never surrender," the dark-haired archer said, still clutching her bleeding shoulder. "You'll have to kill me first."

"Don't be an idiot!" Gaby pleaded with her. "We can still live through this!"

Valentia was now seething at his side. "This is not the time to be *benevolent*."

"I know." Drake kept Magnum trained on the dark-haired woman, the only one of them who still looked capable of putting up a fight. "But we still need answers about what's going on out here, and these folks might have some."

And as much as this world was changing him, he wasn't yet ready to slaughter a bunch of high school kids.

19
NOW, YOU FEEL LIKE LIVING?

Carl, still clutching his sliced-open stomach, was coughing hard by the time Drake and Valentia safely descended to the ledge where the three defeated assassins clustered together at the mercy of Lydia's glowing knives. They looked to have completely given up on fighting.

Judging from the blood still pumping out of the dark-haired archer's shoulder, it wouldn't be long before she bled out. As for the dark-skinned man, Drake had no idea how long you could survive with your intestines attempting to leave your body. Not long, probably.

He lowered Magnum. He didn't need to shoot any of these people unless he did it to spare them a painful death. He glanced at Lydia. "Can you save them?"

She frowned. "I would not recommend that, lord."

"Please just answer the question. Can you save their lives?"

Lydia grimaced and looked back to their new captives. "With great effort, Valentia and I together could mend their wounds and save their lives. I will not be able to *flutterstep* afterward, and her ability to freeze enemies will be greatly reduced."

"Please!" Gaby begged softly. "We've surrendered, so just help them! I'll pay you!"

"Shut up," the dark-haired archer hissed. "Pleading is useless."

"But I don't *want* to die, Robin," the blonde-haired girl hissed. "This was all your idea!"

"Hey." Carl coughed. "Decide quick? Getting dizzy."

"Agree you won't use your rarities on us and won't try to escape," Drake said. "You also have to answer any question I ask or I'll let you bleed to death right here."

"I agree!" Gaby said. Then, she glared at Robin. "Agree, right now!"

"I won't."

"If you don't agree then Carl dies! Of intestines!"

Robin bared her teeth and glanced at the man coughing up blood beside her. Finally, she met Drake's gaze with a glare. "I surrender. I agree."

"Get them stable," Drake ordered. "We're just going to assume Carl's agreed too."

Though she looked visibly angry about it, Valentia dropped to Carl's side and forcefully pressed his own hand against his intestines. "Hold here," she ordered coldly.

She obviously didn't agree with Drake's order. The fact that she still followed it was a sign of how far they'd come in trusting each other. Her trust was flattering.

As Carl did his best not to die, Valentia's gloves flared white. Drake continued to stand a few paces away with Magnum in case they tried anything. Meanwhile, Lydia was grimly working out the bolt buried in Robin's shoulder.

The woman quickly passed out, either from pain or blood loss. The bolt came out with another spew of blood. Lydia then went to work as well.

Drake looked between the three slumped would-be assassins, the narrow mountain path leading to the distance watch fires, and his battle maids. Every *non*-benevolent voice inside him screamed he was making a mistake. He was wasting time, he was standing in the open, and he was expending the valuable blood of his battle maids to save assassins.

Yet they were just kids, and they looked to have some interesting rarities. Rarities he might find useful in the future. Rarities that might make a good addition to his manor... if he could convince them not to mention his changes to the blood pact to the noble court.

The whole time Gaby hadn't moved. She remained locked somewhere between fear, hope, and desperation. She almost touched Carl to check on him before a low hiss from Valentia sent her arm slapping protectively against her own chest.

Finally, Lydia rose. "This one will live."

"The boy too," Valentia said grudgingly. "Though he won't enjoy relieving himself. That is going to be painful for some time."

Lydia was now visibly paler than she had been, and Valentia was practically moon white. Both had spent a great deal of their blood—blood they needed to use their rarities—to heal two people who had just been trying to kill them. Had he made a mistake?

It didn't matter now. He'd made his call. Time to see where it went.

"We should get them off the road," Drake said. "Gaby? You're our prisoner now."

"Of course," she said meekly. "We did surrender."

"And my battle maids just saved your lives," Drake said. "So unless you want to make me undo all their fine work, you're going to do everything I say."

Gaby blinked rapidly before her eyes once again shot open wide. "Gods!" She stared fearfully between Lydia and Valentia, her jaw dropped. "You... you are..."

"We should move," Valentia reminded Drake grimly.

"You're Gloomwood Manor's battle maids!" Gaby whispered

fearfully. "What are you doing out here?" As her eyes fixed one more on Drake, she squeaked. "So that means you're..."

"Lord Gloomwood," Drake agreed impatiently. "Now, you feel like living?"

Gaby nodded in wide-eyed, fist-clenching terror.

"Then you're responsible for your dark-haired friend there. Get her up. We're moving."

Gaby urgently shook and even slapped Robin several times until the woman groaned and opened bleary eyes. "We need to move now, right now. Right now! Or we die."

Drake looked at Valentia and Lydia, both still pale from blood loss, and sighed as he settled Magnum over his shoulder with his leather strap. "I'll get the other kid."

"He could stab you," Lydia warned.

"Not through feathersteel." Drake walked forward and offered an arm. "Time to move, Carl. Unless you want to stay here and wait for my feral to eat you."

With a numb, half-awake nod, Carl allowed Drake to help him to his feet. As he tossed the young man's arm over his shoulder and walked off with Carl stumbling beside him, he wondered how many times he was going to stupidly risk his life tonight. He had a few more in him.

Carl wore silverweave, but it looked *old*. It also hung on his spare frame, so if he was hiding a blade, it was small enough feathersteel would stop it. Drake wasn't worried. The kid could barely keep his eyes open.

Behind him, he heard a shuffle of unsteady feet that suggested Gaby was helping Robin walk as well. From Valentia he heard nothing, but he knew she was back there, silent and seething. He hoped she'd come around eventually.

Lydia once more took the lead and chose a path up and off the narrow mountain road that would be easier for three wounded high-school-age assassins to navigate. From there they doubled back toward the ledge where they'd observed the distant watch fires and then stopped.

Lydia glanced back. "This should be safe enough, lord."

"I'm so sorry we attacked you," Gaby said fearfully. "We had no idea you were Lord Gloomwood. Please, forgive us!"

"Shut *up*," Robin managed.

"It was my idea," Gaby said. "To attack you. So if you have to punish someone—"

"Shut up, Gaby!" Robin hissed. "You can't reason with a manor lord!"

"But you can't—"

Drake turned on them. "Both of you shut up." He pointed at a nearby slope leading up. "Sit down, stay quiet, and wait until I'm ready to interrogate you."

Gaby meekly hurried over to the spot he'd designated. Once Drake gave Carl a gentle shove, the man stumbled over as well. Robin looked hesitant, but one glance back at a visibly murderous Valentia sent her skittering forward. Once more, the three were contained.

"May I ensure we were not followed?" Valentia asked. Her tone remained hard as stone.

He glanced at her in concern. "You can't freeze people right now."

"I need only keep watch." She stared. "Resolve your interrogation of these three quickly. If I do spot anyone approaching, I'll return and bring warning."

She spun and stalked back the way they came. Drake let her be. He still wasn't sure he'd done the right thing, sparing his enemies, but at least he didn't feel like an asshole. He'd thought he was ready to kill anyone he faced, but it seemed he wasn't.

So good news? He didn't just kill everyone. Bad news? He didn't just kill everyone.

Drake looked to Gaby first. She seemed the most pliable. "Ready to talk?"

She nodded fearfully.

"All right. Tell me exactly what you're doing out here."

"We came for the bounty, lord," Gaby said. "On the Asp."

Drake frowned. Who the fuck was the Asp?

"And for revenge," Robin added. "This was my idea. I forced the others into it."

"We both agreed to come along!" Gaby protested.

"Only because I twisted your arms, and shut up!" Robin turned her hard gaze back to Drake. "I lead this group. I know you must take vengeance for our attack, but I beg you, consider taking Gabriel and Carl as your blood thralls instead."

Robin reminded him of Lydia. When faced with her own death, she immediately focused on protecting her friends. That made him resent her attempt to murder him less.

He tapped his chin as he considered taking his first new blood thralls since Jeremy. He'd already made peace with the fact that his pact would protect them from other manor lords and that he would free them of compulsion after they joined. Still, Samuel's caution about how the noble court might react stayed with him. Would these three keep his secret?

If he invited these people to join him, and they accepted, he wouldn't have any way to compel them not to share that his blood pact no longer compelled anyone to do anything. On the other hand, like his own people, the desire to protect their new manor could convince them to keep his secret. Even if he believed that, bringing in new people remained a risk.

Yet he'd lost five servants and a zarovian patroller in the assassin raid. He'd lost Thak a few nights ago. He was down seven people and could lose more. Adding these three young people to his manor would bring him back up to... seventy-two? He'd have to check the roster.

Moreover, if he did intend to stay here and lead Gloomwood Manor, his manor would eventually fall if he refused to recruit new warriors. Building a manor's roster and keeping it strong enough to protect everyone was his responsibility. He needed powerful people and powerful rarities, especially since those rarities were ones he could copy and burnish.

So... he would consider recruiting these three. But only if they volunteered to join him, knowing they had freedom to refuse while understanding what they were agreeing to.

"Why would I recruit you?" Drake asked.

"Carl can draw forth, ignite, and propel solid rocks," Robin said. "You saw the results of his aerial bombardment. Such a rarity would strengthen your manor. And Gabriel can immobilize even the strongest warriors with shields of force."

"Temporarily," Gaby added quickly. "And I'm so sorry I did that, miss battle maid!"

"I fully intended to kill both of you," Lydia reminded them calmly.

"Well... thank you for not killing us!"

"Thank Lord Gloomwood. He is the only reason you still breathe."

Drake was perfectly fine allowing Lydia to play bad cop while he considered his options. The rarities these kids had weren't as terrifying as his battle maids, but they still beat the hell out of the domestic rarities most servants in his manor had. He was curious to know more.

Drake fixed Robin with a hard gaze. "What's your rarity?"

"I can jump rather high," she said calmly. "As you no doubt noticed."

So she could. Robin's rarity was like a much weaker version of *flutterstep*, and she also set herself up to get drilled by a crossbow bolt as she came down. Still... she'd had him dead to rights with that arrow, and she'd made the shot while flying through the air. If Valentia hadn't crystalized that icy shield from water vapor, Samuel might be in charge of the manor now.

All of that, however, could come later. He turned his gaze to

Gaby. He needed to know more about this bounty, and in particular, the Asp. Whoever that was.

"Who is the Asp?"

Gaby blinked. "Is this a test?"

"No, I really don't know who that is. Who are you hunting?"

"A monstrous woman who brutally murders whoever displeases her," Robin said fiercely. "Her rarity allows her to produce and toss acid as easily as you or I would toss water. She answers to no manor, only coin and her own avarice."

"She sounds fun," Drake agreed. "So what the hell is she doing out here?"

"Mercenaries have cornered her in Fort Graystone and called for brave warriors with rarities to slay her," Robin said. "We came here intending to put an end to her for good."

These three weren't anywhere near powerful enough to take on a woman as powerful as this Asp sounded, but he'd give them points for ballsiness. Seeking out a woman who could toss acid was pretty brave.

Also, what the hell was this all about? Was the Asp the woman who had kidnapped Lady Skybreak? Had Sky put out a bounty on the woman? When would she even have time to do that?

"Who posted the bounty?" Drake asked.

Robin glanced at Gaby, then back at Drake. "Lord Redbow."

As Drake finally put two and two together, he slapped his forehead. "Oh, that's slick."

"What is, lord?" Lydia asked.

"If we've stumbled over what I think we have, it's low down dirty as fuck." Drake focused on the trio of would-be bounty hunters. "Where was this bounty posted?"

"In Corinian, lord," Robin said.

"No, that's wrong," Gaby said in visible confusion. "It was posted in Ashglaive, remember?"

"You might have seen it there," Robin said. "But it was also posted in Corinian."

Drake now suspected this particular bounty was posted in a number of places. "How long ago did you see it posted?"

"Six days, lord," Robin said. "But I believe it had been up longer."

In retrospect, this plot was so simple Drake could have devised it. Lord Redbow had started by hiring the Asp for a job: go to Fort Graystone, enter the fort, and wait there. Then, he'd had his army of mercenaries surround her. All of that had actually occurred.

Redbow had then posted the bounty offering to pay anyone who traveled to Fort Graystone and slew the Asp while she was trapped inside the fort. This wasn't a lie, as he did intend to pay them. *If* they killed the Asp *while* she was inside the fort.

Lord Redbow had then let the Asp leave Fort Graystone about the same time he had more of his mercenaries abduct Lady Skybreak (Sky's mom) and deliver the ransom ultimatum. Thus, Sky had come to Fort Graystone, killed those inside, rescued her mother... and been trapped inside after the rest of Redbow's men once more closed the noose around them.

Now, thanks to Redbow's doublespeak, Sky and her people would spend the next few days being attacked by every bounty hunter with a hard-on for the Asp. Either they would succeed and kill Sky (thinking she was the Asp) or they would die in the attempt (leaving Sky thinking Redbow had sent them). Either way, Lord Redbow lost nothing and had a great deal to gain once Sky fell.

If he wasn't such an evil douchebag, Drake could almost have respected the man.

20
CAN I PLAY WITH THEM?

"All right," Drake said. "So, I have good news and bad news."

"Good news?" Gaby asked hopefully.

"We'll do that first. I'm not going to murder you all just yet."

Gaby breathed a huge sigh of relief. Carl slumped against her and breathed, looking close to passing out despite Valentia's healing. Drake doubted she had done anything but her best with him. He simply suspected getting your guts sliced open fucking hurt.

As for Robin, she simply watched him with cautious eyes. She no longer looked angry, but she didn't look at ease either. He couldn't blame her.

"The bad news is, if I'm right, the Asp isn't here any longer. Or she never was."

"No, you're mistaken," Robin said firmly. "Do you seek to defend her?"

"I really couldn't care less what the evil acid lady gets up to," Drake assured them. "What I'm telling you, boy and girls, is you've been played."

Gaby was getting that vacant look again. "Like... music?"

"I happen to know who's holed up in that fort, and it's not the Asp."

"Then who is it?" Robin demanded.

"Lady Skybreak, Lord Skybreak, and her three most terrifying bodyguards."

Robin turned pale. "How could you know that?"

"I'm Lord Gloomwood." He smiled his creepiest smile. "Remember?"

"But... that..." Robin now seemed to recognize how much trouble she was in. "They would murder us. Lady Skybreak alone could swallow us in stone!"

"Good to know," Drake agreed. "Now, in Ashglaive and Corinian, when you were there, were there other people interested in the bounty on the Asp?"

"That's why we rushed here so fast, lord!" Gaby said. "We were worried someone would get here first and defeat her before we got the chance!"

Drake glanced knowingly at Lydia. "So if you had to guess, how much more cannon fodder has Lord Redbow just aimed at everyone inside that fort?"

Lydia looked grim. "If it is as you suspect, both seasoned mercenaries and anyone with a rarity capable of combat may be headed here right now. Or they've already arrived."

"It's Redbow's go-to strategy," Drake agreed, remembering his earlier conversation with Sky about how they casually tossed assassins at people. "They don't care if the assassins they send die because they're a dime a dozen, and if they actually kill the target, bonus."

"We are not a... dime a dozen," Robin said with a glare. "Do you treat everyone so callously?"

"Mind your tongue," Lydia snapped. "Lord Gloomwood's benevolence is the only reason any of you are still alive right now."

Drake was again surprised by how quickly and fiercely Lydia defended his honor, and he didn't know whether to be amused or proud. He now knew what they were up against, and that it was all the more important to get Sky out of here soon. He was glad he'd come.

Robin, for her part, seemed sufficiently cowed by Lydia's rebuke. She didn't even look like she wanted to fight anymore. With her chance for revenge snatched away, she looked lost.

Drake needed to get to Sky and get her out of here before dozens more bounty hunters showed up. But first, he'd needed to hear from his scouts. As Nicole melted into being directly beside him, he found her watching the three captives with visible amusement.

"Did you find puppies?" Nicole asked coyly. "Can I play with them?"

That was *definitely* one of the creepiest things she'd ever said in his presence. He hoped she was trying to intimidate the new kids on his behalf. Otherwise, he might worry about her.

"They're bounty hunters." Drake frowned at her. "And wait, how long have you actually been here?"

She shrugged.

"Were you going to make me repeat that whole conversation despite the fact that you already heard it?"

Nicole smiled at him. "What an interesting question!"

He wasn't about to take that bait. "Where's Sachi?"

"Here, lord."

Drake didn't jump and congratulated himself on his fortitude. The way Sachi always seemed to pop up out of nowhere made him half-wonder if she could turn invisible, but Zuri had said nothing about that. Either way, he had the answers he sought.

Ahead, his three captives were all speaking in low tones.

"Were we really tricked?" Gaby asked. "Did we come all this way for nothing?"

"Apparently." Carl coughed. "Team effort."

"Hush now," Robin said quietly. "I need to think."

Drake looked at the trio of now-dispirited bounty hunters. "I need all three of you to tell me you're not going to try to escape. If you try to run, I'll let my maid play with you."

All of them nodded quickly and fervently. "We won't run, lord!"

"Now, I'm going to have a chat with my associates," Drake said. "Sit tight."

He assumed Valentia was still keeping watch for enemy soldiers and scouts. He moved far enough away from the trio of would-be bounty hunters that he could speak with Nicole, Sachi, and Lydia without being overheard, then motioned for them to crouch down.

"What's it look like by the fort?" he asked.

"Depressing," Nicole said. "At least sixty soldiers ring the fort. While most are armed and armored like mercenaries who lack rarities, they could be hiding them. Either way, even though I can sneak through their lines, they'd attack as soon as I knocked on the door."

"And the front door of the fort? I assume that's locked tight?"

"Barred from the inside. There isn't even a window for Lydia to *flutterstep* through."

"Sixty soldiers." Drake whistled softly. "Kind of wish I could still rat out and chow down."

"There's more on the ridges, lord," Sachi said. "I didn't explore the entire ridgeline, but there are archers and assassins camouflaged above the visible soldiers. All have a clear line of sight to the fort and could easily rain arrows down on anyone who emerged."

"That's all very encouraging," Drake agreed. "It sounds like just charging up to the place and knocking on the door is going to get us slaughtered."

"It would get you slaughtered," Sachi corrected. "Then, no one goes home."

She was right. Even if the rest of his people could somehow fight through all that and get inside the fort, without his current ability to teleport people back to his carriage they'd just fight their way into a trap.

"We have to do something," Lydia said. "After we've come all this way, it seems like a waste to simply give up. If they truly do plan to pit would-be bounty hunters against Sky and her people, it will be a massacre on both sides. Sooner or later, she will fall."

Drake glanced back at the three bounty hunters he, Lydia, and Valentia had nearly murdered tonight. He already had an idea to get inside Fort Skybreak. It was almost a good one… but it was all going to depend on if Sky would pick up the damn phone.

He looked to Sachi. "Will any of those soldiers come looking for us?"

"I don't believe so, lord," Sachi said. "They seem focused on penning in anyone who emerges from Fort Graystone. Up here, we're clear of their lines."

"Then we have time." He looked to Lydia. "Here's my thought. We still know Sky has her mirror, so we're just going to have to hope she contacts us soon."

"She must be warned," Lydia agreed. "But what else do you intend, lord? You have that look you always get when you're hatching some new plot."

Drake frowned. "I have a look?"

"You have a look, lord," Sachi said. "A plotting look."

"I was not aware I had a plotting look. That sounds like it could get me in trouble, since it reveals that I am plotting."

"Gods," Nicole said softly. "You want to pose as bounty hunters and march inside!"

Drake grinned and poked her arm. "Gold star for you."

"That's an exceedingly bad idea," Nicole added.

Drake's grin faded as he considered her tone. "Why?"

"You know the Asp doesn't reside within that fort," Nicole said. "Moreover, whoever commands those mercenaries will certainly demand to know if we plan to claim the bounty. You cannot refuse to answer. They might attempt to take us hostage if you refuse."

"Ah... right." Drake recognized the one speed bump in his latest clever plot. If he went this route, he'd have to reveal that he could lie to Nicole, Valentia, and Sachi.

Still... how long would it be before they figured it out on their own? And what was he gaining by keeping it secret? Valentia and Sachi had proven their loyalty to him time and again, and Nicole seemed on the way there. What did he lose by telling them?

He lost the ability to have them testify in Korhaurbauten. He couldn't risk letting any battle maid testify before the noble court, because there was a chance someone might ask them about something they couldn't lie about and then it would all come out. So was there some way he could pull off his latest scheme without revealing the truth about his lies?

Plenty of time to consider that. First, he had to see if he could even get in touch with Sky. If he couldn't reach her through the mirror his clever plan wouldn't work regardless, because even if they managed to open the barred door and get into Fort Graystone, Sky's cadre of murderous bodyguards were waiting inside to kill them.

Drake doubted they'd be in the mood to fire warning shots at people they believed were coming to take down their current lord... and their former one.

"Let's hold off on our 'invade the fort' plan for now," Drake said. "I hate just sitting on our hands, but it's clear we can't fight our way in. Bluffing our way in is going to be difficult as well. We still have two days until the cabal, so we still have to figure something out."

"And if your fair-haired manor lord still doesn't answer you?" Nicole asked.

"Then I'll make a decision," Drake reminded her. "That's what I do. Decision making. Now, I have another question for you three."

Sachi cocked an eyebrow. "Even me, lord?"

"Is there some reason you don't want to be included?"

"I am not a battle maid."

"Right, but you are a Sachi. You know how much I like my Sachi."

She purred loudly. "Ask what you wish."

"How do you feel about the kids over there? Are they Gloomwood Manor material?"

Sachi's ears twitched. "I thought your suggestion to recruit them was a jest."

"That exploding rock thing was pretty cool," Drake said. "And, Lydia, just what happened when Gaby stopped you dead? Did she really paralyze you?"

"She did, lord." Lydia looked thoughtful. "She even caught me mid-*flutterstep*. I was not aware, until that encounter, that anyone could catch me mid-*flutterstep*."

"A puppy caught you?" Nicole asked with a grin. "You're slipping, Lids."

"She obviously cannot hold a person forever," Lydia said. "I was able to force my way forward. I would have freed myself and killed her in another moment."

"And you did free yourself the moment Gaby lost concentration after Val iced her boots," Drake agreed. "Still, that's not a half-bad rarity. I bet it'd be pretty badass if I burnished it. I wonder if I could stop a whole damn carriage?"

"Robin, the archer, has a strong will and is skilled with a bow," Lydia said. "Her disposition seems compatible with ours. However, I worry about her blood vendetta."

"Against the Asp," Drake agreed. "I imagine that could be inconvenient, since I can't compel her not to go kill that lady."

"That is correct, lord," Lydia said. "She also believes that joining a blood pact will compel her to follow your orders. If she believes you won't let her pursue her vengeance, she may refuse to join us."

"Right," Drake agreed. "It's still her decision, and I don't want to tell her the truth unless she joins us. So it's a chicken and egg situation."

"You could just threaten to kill her little friends," Nicole said. "If you were to threaten to murder the boy and blonde girl unless she submits to your blood pact, she'd join us."

Drake frowned at her. "You already know I don't work that way, and we've already verified these three didn't come here to assassinate me. They're just kids who got played by a dickhead manor lord, so I'm inclined to let them walk."

Nicole sighed. "Val's gonna' be so mad at you."

Drake grinned. "She already is. Still, I'm inclined to offer them a chance to join us, if they *want* to join us. And *if* they join us, we'll tell them how my pact works... but not before." He didn't need any rumors getting out. "Now, any objections?"

Lydia shook her head. Nicole shrugged. Sachi bared her sharpened teeth.

"Right, then Val's the last." Drake stood. "Sachi, could you go relieve Valentia?"

21

I HAVE A REQUEST

Drake waited as Sachi disappeared into the darkness. Not long after, Valentia returned. She took one look at the three people still huddled together against the ledge, and they all flinched at her murderous gaze. She marched over to join Drake and the others.

As Valentia crouched in Drake's impromptu council circle, she frowned. "I see your would-be assassins are still breathing. We still have a use for them?"

"They actually aren't assassins," Drake said.

As Valentia watched in stoic silence, Drake filled her in on everything he'd learned from his interrogation. As he spoke, Valentia's hard features eased. Once she finished, she glanced at their three captive young people with what might be actual sympathy.

And when she turned back to Drake, she looked visibly annoyed with him.

"Oh, no." Nicole giggled. "He did it again, didn't he? His knack for making a dumb decision that somehow turned out right."

Valentia said nothing.

Nicole rubbed Valentia's shoulder in obvious sympathy. "I

know that's frustrating. I'll help you kill the next group of assassins before he can spare them."

"So you *do* wish to spare them," Valentia said flatly. She no longer looked opposed to the idea. Given Robin had almost put an arrow in her, that said a lot for her turnaround.

"Actually, Val... I was thinking of recruiting them."

"And their rarities?"

"Robin, the dark-haired girl, can jump really high," Drake said. "The blonde can do some cool force magic that managed to catch and hold Lydia mid-*flutterstep*, as you saw. And we all saw what the dark-haired kid can do. Meteor kaboom."

Nicole frowned. "Is that truly the name of his rarity?"

"Hell if I know. But it was a meteor, and it went kaboom. Don't you people just make up the names for your rarities anyway?"

"The Eidolons give us their names," Nicole said. "After we activate them for the first time, they speak the name in our head. That is the only name we can give to others."

"Oh," Drake said. "Well... all right." He felt a bit annoyed the Eidolons had never given his rarity an official name, but he obviously played by different rules. "Even so, we're going to call it meteor kaboom until I decide otherwise. Now, would they make good recruits?"

"Their rarities are weak to middling," Valentia said. "None would survive as battle maids."

"Sure, but it's hard to find people as powerful as you five. I also know Lord Proudglade has various grades of knights. If we started, like, a junior varsity team, would they qualify?"

Valentia sighed. "Can we please just use terms from our world?"

"A backup squad," Drake said. "Or useful folks who could help us out in battle, like Lord Proudglade's silver knights."

Valentia shrugged. "We have less powerful rarities in our manor, and we have plenty of space. Do you intend to reveal our unusual blood pact to them before they join us?"

"No. I'm not that reckless."

Valentia visibly pondered. "With training, the boy and the blonde girl could make passable warriors. The dark-haired girl's rarity will simply get her killed when she jumps in front of an arrow. However, she could still make a good archer."

"All right. Thanks, Val."

Valentia frowned. "I am the last person you consulted?"

"I wouldn't make the offer without hearing from you."

"That is..." Valentia paused.

"Benevolent? Silly? Weak?"

"Wise," Valentia finished. "Once again, I find it difficult to judge your unusual decisions as harshly as I would wish. You have a knack for making unwise actions seem wise."

"I'll take it," Drake said. "Let's go ask them."

"And if they do not agree to join your blood pact?" Valentia asked. "What then?"

"They walk," Drake said. "They already know the person they came to kill isn't here. If we let them go, they might even warn off some others. That'll save Sky some grief."

Valentia offered an incremental nod of her head.

With that, Drake rose and walked back to the three people he'd taken captive tonight. They all watched him with varying levels of unease and outright fear. Time to change that.

"I'm going to make you an offer, but first, I need to make sure you're all of age for all this. How old are you?" He pointed at Robin. "You first."

"Eighteen, lord." She spoke softly and without hesitation.

He pointed at Gaby next.

"Sixteen." She gasped. "Lord!"

Drake pointed at Carl last.

"Seventeen, lord."

So Gaby was the baby of the group. She was just old enough to be able to sign up for a blood pact, which might explain why she was still available. Her ability to stop people in their tracks was arguably the most powerful rarity these three possessed, at least in regards to keeping her manor lord alive. Drake might be getting a good deal if he signed her now.

This really was like recruiting players for a football team. He also had the space. Now, he just had to make sure they knew what they were getting into, and that they *wanted* to get into it.

"I've consulted with my battle maids. They have agreed to allow you to join us at Gloomwood Manor, *if* that is what you truly wish to do," Drake said calmly. "But first, I need to make sure you all understand what joining my blood pact truly means."

Robin frowned. "We understand."

"You think you do. I assume you've heard what manors offer. A place to live, a wage for life, food, drink, maybe even adventure. It probably sounds great. But there's a downside."

"We know," Robin said crossly.

Drake ignored her, because the others might not. "You'd be sworn to serve me. That's not always fun. Do you know how a blood pact works?" He couldn't risk telling them they'd need to serve him, since that would be an obvious lie... and he supposedly couldn't do that.

"We know what we'd be swearing to do, lord," Gaby assured him. "Serving in a manor is a great honor. I've dreamed of an opportunity like this since I learned I had a rarity."

Drake frowned at her. "I don't need you to flatter me. Think this through. Joining me could get you *killed*, and if you join my manor, you're joining our fight. Are you willing to kill for me if I order it? Have you ever even killed someone before?"

That was an even more pointed question, since it would be her choice to obey his orders... and she didn't know that. She might assume that being compelled would make it easier to kill people and balk when she realized she'd have to make that decision herself.

"I am willing to fight and kill to defend my friends," Gaby said.

"I'd never have come on this hunt otherwise. I would do whatever I must to defend you, lord."

Before Drake could probe further, Robin stepped forward. "And what if we refuse to join Gloomwood Manor?"

"Then you walk," Drake said. "No consequences. No punishment. You leave this place and forget you ever met me. However, I *would* ask that you inform any other bounty hunters you run into on the way back home that the Asp is no longer here."

Robin looked truly surprised by his answer. "You would spare us? After we attacked you? Even if we don't agree to join your manor?"

Drake nodded. He didn't mind her asking him to repeat something he'd literally just said because he knew how badly most manor lords treated their blood thralls. He and Sky remained unusual in that regard.

"I would be honored to join your manor, lord," Gaby said. "I mean that. I understand all you've said, and I know it could be dangerous, but even so. I'll be set for life!"

Drake looked to Carl. "And what about you?"

He bowed his head. "I, too, would be honored to serve you. I've thought about this before, and I always promised myself if I got the opportunity... I would accept."

He looked to Robin last, knowing she would likely be the holdout. "Robin?"

"I have a request," Robin said.

Gaby hissed and frantically slapped Robin on the arm as if she'd suddenly caught on fire, but Drake raised a hand to stop that nonsense. "What is it?"

"I will join your blood pact, but I would first ask your leave to hunt down the woman who murdered my family and burned down my home. The Asp took my father, my mother, my younger brother, and many others in my village. She burned them alive with acid."

No wonder she wanted revenge. "How did you survive?"

"I wasn't there, lord." Robin's fists clenched. "I found them after."

This young woman must blame herself for the murder of her whole family and a whole bunch of other people. It was another reminder of how cruel this world could be and how easily people with powerful rarities could tear through those without. Even the way Drake had torn through twenty mercenaries as a dire rat proved how unfairly the odds were stacked against normal, non-rarity wielding folks in this world.

It sounded like this Asp was a real monster. Drake suspected Lord Redbow had picked her to bait bounty hunters because as many people would come to Fort Graystone for revenge as would come for gold. The ruthless manor lord was too clever by half.

"I won't just let you run off after her," Drake said. "I may have other duties for you, and as far-fetched as it might seem now, I might need to work with the Asp at some point."

"Then I cannot join your blood pact."

Gaby gripped her arm. "Don't be an idiot! This is perfect for us!"

"I can't join if I won't be free to avenge my family," Robin said. "Do I still walk?"

Drake nodded. "I guess so." He looked to Gaby and Carl. "You two still in?"

Gaby shook the other woman. "We promised we'd stay together!"

"And I almost got you both killed, tonight, for my revenge," Robin said. "I have no right to drag you off on a task for me. Joining a manor has always been your dream, Gaby. Take it."

"But then you'll die!" Gaby all but wailed.

Carl grimaced. "She's right. There's no way you beat the Asp on your own."

Robin pulled away from Gaby and straightened. "Lord Gloomwood, am I free to leave?"

Gaby rose as well. "Then I'm going with you!"

Robin stared at her in shock. "You can't."

Carl grimaced and looked to Drake. "I am truly sorry, lord. I would love to join you. But..." He hesitated. "If you will truly let us walk, I can't let Robin go alone."

"You're both taking his deal," Robin insisted. "You can live in a manor! Don't be idiots."

"You're the idiot!" Gaby said stubbornly. "I'm not going to go live in a manor if it means you go off and get melted!"

Drake mentally facepalmed. Was he really going to let these kids get enslaved by another manor lord just because one girl couldn't give up on her quest for revenge? He understood Robin's quest, but he was starting to see why some more brutal manor lords enforced blood pacts. And if he let these kids walk... they *could* be enslaved.

If a more ruthless manor lord recruited them by force, next time he might be forced to kill all three of them. But what were his alternatives? He still refused to force people to join him, and revealing that his blood pact didn't enslave people would endanger his whole manor. He had to weigh the freedom of three people against the lives of everyone he protected.

He also couldn't make Robin *not* want revenge on the lady who melted her family, and he was never going to force anyone to join his blood pact... but perhaps he could give Robin a chance to actually achieve her revenge. That might accomplish all their goals.

"I have an alternative offer," Drake said.

All three of their worried gazes snapped to his. They looked more than a bit afraid. He suspected they'd all just concluded their hesitance had left them fucked.

"Robin, if you join my blood pact, you will serve me. You'll need to follow my orders."

"I cannot do that, lord, if you refuse to let me kill the Asp. She must die."

"Let me finish. I demand you serve me until you turn twenty-five."

Robin's brow furrowed. "One cannot leave a blood pact."

"I didn't say you'd leave. I said you'd wait seven years. I'm giving you the chance to take your revenge, because while you serve me, we'll train you, equip you, and actually give you the skills that *might* allow you to have a chance against the Asp."

"I don't understand."

"If you go up against the Asp right now, you're dead," Drake said evenly. "We all know it. But if you join me and train with my huntress, and my battle maids, and my warriors, you'll have seven years of real battle experience by the time you turn twenty-five."

Her eyes widened.

"And when you turn twenty-five, I will no longer forbid you to kill the Asp. You can hunt her down if you choose to do so, though you will do so of your own volition. I won't order her dead unless she harms me, but I also won't stop you from going after her."

None of that was a lie. He couldn't actually forbid her from killing anyone, but she still thought he could. It was also true he wouldn't forbid her after she turned twenty-five.

"After seven years," Robin said quietly. "I serve you for seven years, then kill her."

"Gods, Robin, just take the deal!" Gaby said. "He's being impossibly generous!"

"He is," Carl said. "This gets you all you wanted. It even gives you a chance to win!"

Robin looked at her friends. "When the time comes, I won't ask you to come with me."

"You won't have to," Gaby said. "And if we can't go with you because we have other duties, you'll still be ready for her. You'll have a real chance to get your revenge."

Robin looked once more at Drake. Her features were calmer now, her gaze firm. This time, he had no doubt how she would answer.

22

WE'RE HERE TO RESCUE YOU

Once the sun showed itself on the horizon, Drake decided to engage in some light sabotage while he waited to get in touch with Sky. While he couldn't yet tackle the mercenaries surrounding Fort Graystone directly, and he couldn't bluff his way through without risking a fight with Sky's bodyguards, he could cut down on the number of bounty hunters and mercenaries who made it to the fort simply by telling them the truth.

The Asp was long gone.

As for his new *employees*, that was handled. He'd inducted them into his blood pact for the first time last night and then revealed his pact actually didn't compel them to do jack shit. All three had been shocked, and he still wasn't entirely certain Robin was going to hold off her revenge for as long as they'd agreed... but at least now he knew they could never be enslaved by another manor lord. They were safe... relatively.

Still, their reaction overall had been positive, and all had sworn not to tell others the truth about how his blood pact was different from that of other manor lords. Since all his blood pact now did was prevent people from being enslaved by another lord, it did serve a positive purpose. Not being compelled also continued to win him brownie points.

He was also here for the long haul. He would have to recruit new blood for his manor or everyone he wanted to protect could die. Robin, Gaby, and Carl had just proven people would agree to join him of their own free will and then agree to serve him after, even if they'd expected this arrangement to work in an entirely different way.

More proof to present to the other manor lords that blood pacts needed to go.

Intercepting unwitting assassins was the first task he gave his new recruits. Working in pairs, he ordered them to form a loose perimeter around the soldiers and cautiously approach any small groups who seemed to be on the way to Fort Graystone. He paired his newbies with experienced people to make it more likely they wouldn't get into too much trouble.

He paired Robin and Sachi—their shared enjoyment of archery was obvious—and paired Gaby with Nicole, mainly because Gaby's ability to immobilize people would be a good complement to Nicole's talent for sneaking up on them. Finally, he paired Carl with Valentia, which would give them the ability to use meteor kaboom at range and *flashfreeze* up close.

Carl's rarity, it turned out, was called *firestone*. But Drake was going to keep calling it meteor kaboom. He didn't care how many odd or exasperated looks he got.

Drake ordered his people to avoid any Redbow soldiers or large parties of mercenaries who might be coming to reinforce the soldiers already at the fort. He gave them permission to approach smaller groups or those dressed more like bounty hunters or independent warriors.

Sachi assured him there was a good chance most halfway decent people wouldn't just attack without warning. If they did, Drake gave his experienced warriors freedom to retreat or attack at their discretion. If someone was stupid enough to attack his people unprovoked, they'd get what was coming to them. It was a big rough world out there.

Ultimately, he hoped his people could head off anyone coming to claim the fake bounty on the Asp long enough for him to get in touch with Sky and "claim" it for himself, but he couldn't be certain his strategy would work or the soldiers wouldn't catch on. So he and Lydia set up a camp on a ledge beyond the visual range of the ring of soldiers to keep watch.

There, they would wait to go to the aid of anyone who got in over their head or warn the others if anything unusual happened among the soldiers laying siege to Fort Graystone. He'd pondered sending Sachi up to eliminate some of the archers camped away from the main group, but decided there was too much risk that it could alert the others.

As the day wore on, Drake alternated between staring into a perfectly normal mirror and looking in the direction of Fort Graystone for any sign something had changed. He could barely see the tall wooden towers that had burned the entire night before, but he couldn't see the soldiers stationed around them. Which meant they couldn't see him. Which was good.

Finally, just when he was about to choke down a lunch of stale bread and the last of their cheese, the mirror changed from showing him to showing darkness. Moments later, he saw a pale, exhausted face staring at him from within. Her light-blue eyes went wide.

"Sky!" Drake jumped up and grinned. "Are you okay? Did you find your mom?"

"She's safe," Sky agreed. "But, and I'm sorry, I won't be able to join you any time soon." She paused. "Were you waiting for me to call you all this time?" She looked somewhere between pleased by his persistence and a little disappointed in him.

"Just the morning."

"Then you're at the capital, or close? Is Karth with you? Is he all right?"

"He is, but... okay, this is a funny story."

Sky's exhaustion faded as disbelief replaced it. "You didn't."

"Didn't what?"

"Is that *my* territory behind you?"

Drake glanced behind him at the scrub and grass that must be barely visible behind him in the mirror, then back at her. "I mean, technically, it's Karth's now."

"*Clint.*"

"We're here to rescue you." He smiled his most charming smile. "You ready to go?"

Sky visibly seethed as she glared at him through the mirror. "You idiot."

"Sure, but—"

"What in the realm gave you the idea *I* needed to be rescued?"

"That's a fair reaction," he agreed with a raised hand. "But before you tell Karth to cancel our alliance, just listen. I have a good reason to be here."

He explained the reason the mercenaries had her bottled up in Fort Redbow and Lord Redbow's plan to toss unwitting groups of bounty hunters at her until she died or surrendered. Sky's ire faded as she listened. When he was done, she visibly ground her teeth. At least she didn't seem angry at *him* any longer.

"I suppose that explains last night," she said quietly.

"Rough one?"

"We were attacked twice, once by a man who attempted to melt the front door with some sort of burning rarity, and later by a woman who somehow slipped inside the fort despite there being no secret passages or open windows. She was decent with a spear."

"Both of those folks sound powerful. Did you capture them?"

"No."

Drake grimaced as he chalked two more unwitting victims to Lord Redbow's treachery... and Sky's bodyguards. "There was no way you could have known who they were."

"There was not," Sky agreed. "It seemed so odd to me that each would attack alone, without coordination and without support from the mercenaries. Now it makes sense."

"Is it going to bother you?"

Sky looked away. "If I can find out who they were, and I can verify they came to slay the Asp, I will compensate their families. I have regrets far greater than these."

She most likely did.

Her gaze met his again. "And while I'm grateful for this information about my enemy's plans, it changes very little in regard to our larger problems. Why are you here? Who will represent our interests in Korhaurbauten? "

"You and me, together."

"And how will you and I get to the capital in just under two days, which is now a six-day journey away? After we somehow defeat a mercenary force of sixty or more in elevated positions with poisoned arrows? Do you have a plan for that?"

"I do, actually," Drake assured her. "And I bet you're going to love it."

Right about mid-afternoon, Drake set off to claim Lord Redbow's bounty.

From talking with his people after they rounded everyone up, his people had saved six lives today. Six would-be bounty hunters had turned around upon being informed the Asp was long gone. Six wasn't a lot in the grand scheme of things, but it had kept more people from falling into Lord Redbow's trap and kept the danger to Sky and her warriors to a minimum.

Though, he suspected, the danger was more to anyone coming after them.

Sadly, none of the warriors he'd "saved" had seemed interested in joining his manor. They'd all been older folks who had likely already decided to do the independent bounty hunter thing. More evidence he'd need to make a good offer quickly when someone with a badass rarity came of age. Hopefully, Samuel's spies could keep him informed in that regard.

Despite Anna drawing the line at four people, he remained confident he could teleport more than that. Every rarity he'd thus far absorbed had been considerably burnished. While twenty might be a stretch when Anna could do four, twelve seemed easily within reach.

Since his manor was only two days away, he'd considered sending his new recruits back to Gloomwood Manor instead of taking them to the capital. However, he needed Carl to pull off the scam he planned, and he doubted Gaby and Robin would want to leave him. Plus, the more people he had to protect him in the capital, the better off he'd be.

After Drake and the others swapped out their feathersteel for silverweave, Drake set off down the same road where he had intercepted Robin, Gaby, and Carl. Feathersteel, while durable, wouldn't stand up against the number of soldiers guarding the fort. It was important for Drake to look as if he actually had come to fight the Asp.

Silverweave wasn't just good at stopping magic. It was also highly resistant to acid. By comparison, Robin had confirmed acid as powerful as that tossed by the Asp could melt through feathersteel and into the flesh beneath in short order. So they'd look like idiots dressed in feathersteel, and they needed to look at least *marginally* competent.

Drake led in his dark silverweave clothing and ominous ankle-length fur cloak, with Valentia and Lydia at his sides. Each now wore one of his extra silverweave outfits in lieu of their maid uniforms. While Lydia's borrowing clothing hung on her slim torso and Valentia's was almost absurdly tight in the chest area, their cloaks made the mismatch less obvious.

Nicole, unfortunately, had to make due with normal clothing.

Since she could turn invisible if things went bad, she'd volunteered to go in light. They had no other option.

Fortunately, the worn and mismatched silverweave worn by his new junior varsity team helped sell the illusion of a group of newbie bounty hunters who had completed just enough jobs to afford silverweave, but not *nice* silverweave. He'd learned Robin, Gaby, and Carl had pooled all the wealth they had to purchase their silverweave outfits. They looked it.

Even though he had no intention of fighting anyone today, he had a decent battle party. If the Asp was inside that fort, Drake suspected the seven of them could take her even if her own silverweave stopped Valentia from freezing her blood. Hopefully, the mercenaries surrounding the fort would agree with his assessment.

Sachi wasn't with them. She had already slipped past the sentries and crouched somewhere in the cliffs above, hidden. She couldn't get inside thanks to the fort's sturdy structure and its sealed door, but she could easily join them once he'd knocked on the door.

Which Drake now planned to accomplish through judicious use of meteor kaboom.

He was encouraged when four soldiers in gray-and-brown leather armor moved from the mountainous cover ahead with bows drawn. They didn't attack, which was the encouraging part. Another soldier in the same armor walked forward with one hand on the hilt of his sword and the other raised palm out.

"Halt! Identify yourselves!"

Drake casually spread two hands to slow the party. They wouldn't advance until they'd been cleared to do so by the soldiers. Since these men weren't wearing silverweave, Valentia could freeze all four of them dead in a matter of moments... but that wouldn't get them inside.

"We're here because of the bounty!" Drake shouted.

Not a lie. He *was* here because of the bounty, even if he knew it was fake. After much mental debate, Drake had decided he might not even have to lie to get past the mercenaries. He just had to say little enough that they would draw their own conclusions.

It was time to practice his doublespeak.

The soldier nodded. "You're just in time. There's seven of you?" He looked pleased.

This soldier seemingly had no intention of warning these "bounty hunters" they were about to walk into a butcher's den. That made Drake feel absolutely fine about killing him if it came to that. He still didn't want to kill innocents or those who surrendered, but manipulative mercenaries who sent people to their deaths were something else entirely.

"We're more than enough to defeat the Asp," Drake said confidently, which was, again, not a lie. "Is she still bottled up in the fort?"

"No one's seen her leave," the soldier confirmed. "So you lead this party?"

Drake nodded.

"What's your name?"

Drake looked him dead in the eyes. "Some call me Maverick."

Also not a lie. Lydia and Valentia had both called him that just this afternoon... after he asked them to do so. He didn't care if they both thought it sounded strange and silly. If it was good enough for Clint Eastwood, it was good enough for him.

The soldier's brow furrowed. "And that's the name you want on the bounty? If you claim it?"

Drake nodded.

"You may approach," the soldier said. "But don't forget we're all on edge after days sieging this fort. If you make any overtly hostile moves, we'll fill you with arrows."

"We're here because of the bounty," Drake said. "Not to fight you guys." *Unless we have to,* he added silently. *In which case, at least you four boys are fucked.*

23
ARROWS ARE DUMB

Drake was all too aware of more armored soldiers watching his small party of "bounty hunters" as they approached Fort Graystone. Almost all of them were men, and he understood why a lot better now than when he'd first come here. If you didn't have a rarity in this world, or a rarity powerful enough to get picked up by a manor, you made your way however you could.

Since the Eidolons gave men the shaft in regards to rarities in general, many often took work as sellswords taking contracts from the manor lords. Pretty much any manor lord had the coin to hire disposable mercenaries for tasks they chose not to leave to their blood thralls, and to most manor lords, these men were just that. Disposable.

He suspected most of the soldiers in this company didn't even know who they had cornered in this fort, or if they did, they justified it by telling themselves they'd send the money they earned home to their families. Despite his and Valentia's attempts to file down what he still considered a conscience, outright slaughter wasn't his only option.

Fortunately, none of the gathered soldiers looked to be in the mood to challenge them. A number actually seemed encouraged by the fact that seven bounty hunters with rarities had shown up to deal with "the Asp." They were probably hoping their long vigil here would soon be over. With Sky dead, they could all head home with their ill-earned coin. If Drake's plan worked today, everyone might even get what they wanted.

Soon they were in sight of the front of Fort Graystone. It stood across a stretch of open ground, a blocky gray structure that hunkered like a stone giant against the cliffs. There was no cover for at least fifty paces between the closed doors of the fort, which meant even the fastest warriors who emerged would be riddled with arrows before they crossed half of it. It was obvious why Sky and her warriors hadn't tried to escape.

The soldier who'd met them on the road had left long ago, probably to return to his post leading to the fort. It was another soldier who greeted them. He was an older, muscular man who had multiple visible scars on his face and neck. He also had an extra big shoulderpad that was red as opposed to brown and a nifty-looking eyepatch.

This must be the captain. Life was rough out here. This dude had obviously seen some shit. "Name?" the captain asked.

Drake once more looked him dead in the eyes. "There are some who call me Maverick."

"Real name," the man said grimly.

Drake wasn't going to give that up yet. "You have all the information you need."

The captain scowled. "I can't let just anyone face the woman holed up in there. How do I know you can handle her?"

Drake jerked a thumb behind him. "I have them."

The captain looked Drake's party over with his keenly evaluating eye. Lydia and Valentia, no doubt, cut intimidating profiles, and he hoped he did as well. As for the kids and Nicole, they'd do all right. He hoped Gaby wasn't offering her nervous grin. He didn't look back to check.

The captain finished his evaluation and frowned at Drake. "What's your plan?"

"Get inside, take care of business, leave. Does it need to be more complicated?"

The captain chuckled darkly. "I'm not sure it'll be that easy, *Maverick*."

Drake shrugged. "If you can't afford us—"

"No," the captain interrupted. "We will pay you what that bounty offers *if* you manage to kill the Asp. Though you understand, in that case, you'll all have to split it."

More doublespeak. Even if they were really bounty hunters and they actually did survive a fight with Sky and her bodyguards, they still wouldn't get paid since the bounty was for the Asp, not Sky. This captain was obviously an asshole.

Drake considered letting the veiled truth slide past, but the real "Maverick" wouldn't do that. He had to push. Every conversation he had outside his manor taught him more about this world's speech. Just because people couldn't lie didn't mean deception wasn't common.

"Is the Asp still in the fort?" Drake asked.

The captain scowled. "You think we'd still be stuck out here if she wasn't?"

The captain hadn't said "yes." Instead, he had answered with a question. People in this world could ask any questions they liked because asking a question wasn't a lie, but it was still a tell. If they wouldn't give a straight answer, they were almost certainly hiding something.

"You didn't answer my question," Drake said. "Did you actually see her go in there?"

The captain scowled. "*I* didn't see her do anything. My scouts saw her enter the fort, which is when they sent others to post the bounty. Do you have any idea how this works?"

Drake scowled back. "I'm not taking my people in there

without knowing what we're up against. I need to know the Asp is still inside." That's what a bounty hunter leader would say.

The man's scowl grew to a glare. "If you're too soft to take the job, then you can walk right back the way you came. There's plenty more waiting to fill your shoes."

Another redirect, and more pressure to take the job. This captain had been doing this awhile. Still, Drake would push. He would push until it made sense not to.

"So what can you tell me? What have you been doing the past six days?"

"Standing watch *here*," the captain growled. "No one here has seen the Asp leave the fort, and we've been here for six days. Since she entered. That's all I can tell you."

So no one here had seen the Asp leave? Easy. All these soldiers had simply closed their eyes while she left the fort. Still, Drake would let this one slide as well. He'd let the captain feel he'd outsmarted him and then outsmart him in return.

He made a show of considering his options. Finally, he nodded. "I assume we can trust you to have our backs?"

"No," the captain said. "If we could go inside that fort and kill her ourselves, we wouldn't need you folk, would we? We wouldn't be *paying* you to kill her. So you go in, kill everyone in there, come out, and you get paid. That's the deal. Take it or walk."

Drake had made enough of a show of arguing with this man about this bounty. And better yet, he hadn't had to lie once. This man thought he was deceiving "Maverick," which made it all the easier for Drake to deceive him. This was almost fun.

"You'll want to give us some room," Drake said.

The captain smiled grimly. "May the Eidolons guide you." He didn't look like he meant it.

Drake smiled back. "Trust me. You're going to be shocked at what we can do."

That was pushing it, but Drake couldn't resist some more

doublespeak of his own. Fortunately, the captain looked amused instead of suspicious. Boy would he be surprised.

"Now pull back your men," Drake said. "I don't want to harm any of you by accident."

Watching them with obvious curiosity, the captain of the mercenaries made subtle motions with his hands. Any nearby soldiers backed up a respectable distance, clearing a path and some space about Drake and his party. Fort Graystone sat ahead, tightly closed.

Drake glanced at Carl, snapped his fingers for attention, and pointed. "Kaboom time."

Carl grimaced as he walked up beside Drake. "It really is called *firestone*... sir."

Drake had asked his people not to call him "lord" in front of the mercenaries, and Carl, at least, had remembered. He hoped the others wouldn't slip up before they got inside.

"I know," Drake said. "Now, give me some meteor kabooms."

Carl set his booted feet slightly apart like he was about to do a lift and curl, lowered both hands and curled them into Cs, and took one deep breath. As he breathed in, actual chunks of earth tore themselves free of the earth and roiled together in a ball of fiery rock.

Drake watched with keen interest. That did look to be a fairly useful rarity. If he copied it, he'd bet he could easily make a rocky fireball three times that size.

Carl raised his curled hands and the molten ball now spinning between them, brought one back like a shot-putter, and tossed the ball of flaming rock with one heave of his hand. The rock blasted away with far more momentum than just that motion could offer, suggesting Carl's rarity was in play as well. It even made a faint shriek as it arced down toward the fort.

Carl's meteor exploded against the door of the fort in a shower of smoke and flames. The nearest mercenary gasped audibly at the show. While Carl's meteor kaboom charred the wood and left a noticeable chunk of wood missing, it would take a lot more fireballs to take down that door... which was exactly what Drake had hoped for.

"Again!" Drake shouted loud enough he was sure the mercenaries would hear.

Carl breathed, summoned, and tossed. Each ball of molten rock slammed into the door in almost the same spot—the young man's aim was incredible—and then shattered in all directions. Bits ignited the dry grass. Soon the entire area ahead of the door was cloaked in reams of roiling smoke caused by a dry grass fire.

That smoke obscured the front of the fort and much of the area above it. It would be Sachi's cue to slip out of her hiding spot, wherever that was. She had actual cover now.

"Advance!" Drake roared. "Bring that door down!" He charged in like an idiot.

As over sixty mercenaries watched in what he hoped was slack-jawed disbelief, Drake charged across the open ground between the ring of mercenaries and the distant fort... and into the smoke. His people charged right behind him, with Lydia on his left and Val on his right. The sound of huffing and boots pounding behind him assured him the rest of his crew was following close behind, though one of them did start coughing.

Yet no one shot them in the back. The archers waiting to kill anyone who emerged were likely too busy gawking at his recklessly stupid charge to bother ending it prematurely. Drake hoped everyone watching was waiting with bated breath to see them fall.

"Now!" Drake shouted from inside the smoke. "Bring those doors down!"

That was the vocal cue he'd agreed upon with Sky. He hoped he'd shouted it loud enough for them to hear it inside the fort. He couldn't shout much louder.

Ahead, a loud rumble announced the doors opening. That sound was clear enough the captain would recognize it. They would have only moments before the man realized Drake had pulled the wool over his... eye. Hopefully, by then, everyone would be inside.

Drake pushed into a huffing sprint. "Go, go, go!"

Magnum was heavy. His backpack with its share of feathersteel armor was heavy. His whole body was heavy, and from behind him, he heard the captain roar three words.

"Loose! Loose! Loose!"

So the old one-eyed asshole had already figured out they were here to help Sky.

Drake was already inside the fort, huffing hard, with Valentia and Lydia right beside him. The moment he spotted a woman in dark-colored leather armor crouched in an alcove just off the open doors, he dived in beside her. He had no idea who she was—Mary, Ali, or Kari—but he did know she was with Sky.

He ignored the dark-haired woman's shocked glare. He couldn't flee until he knew all his people were safe. Three people sprinted past—Robin, Carl, Gaby—and then he waited.

Sachi must already be inside. He had to assume she was already inside. When dozens of whistling arrows followed by a tortured cry came from the smoke instead of Nicole, Drake dashed back out again. He had only heartbeats before the next volley.

Valentia howled from behind him.

Drake found Nicole stumbling along with at least three arrows in her back. He went low, slammed into her stomach, dumped her over his shoulder, and then spun around. He sprinted back toward the door as the terrifying whistles of more arrows sounded above. Was he fast enough? He better damn well hope so.

Above Drake, ice crackled as the moisture in the air expanded and froze. An icy sheet crackled out above them like an umbrella. Arrows shattered the ice as Drake charged inside.

Ice, metal, and wood clattered against his back and stung, but even that thin sheet of airborne ice had been enough to stop the arrows in midflight. Even the brief collision with the ice had reduced them to dropping, not falling. Without the momentum they'd gained on the way down, they wouldn't kill him.

Drake heard angry shouting from outside and the sound of gears grinding as the doors groaned closed. Sky's people were cranking those doors shut. He slowed inside the safety of the stone walls as he realized they'd made it, then pumped his fist. "Fuck yes!"

"Ow..." Nicole reminded him from his shoulder.

She had been the only one not wearing any armor, and she'd volunteered to guard the rear since she could go invisible using *penumbra*. However, even when you were invisible, a forest of falling arrows could still puncture you just fine.

A thunderous boom announced the thick doors of Fort Graystone slamming shut once more. That locked the angry shouts of the mercenaries outside where they belonged. Valentia rushed him along with Lydia, and then Drake handed Nicole off to both of them for treatment.

"Robin! Gaby! Carl! Sound off!"

The shouted greetings of his JV team were a relief.

"Sachi!" Drake called. "Where are you?"

No one answered that.

"Sachi!" He spun back around toward the closed doors. If she was trapped outside...

A long, thin, fuzzy object curled affectionately around the back of his thigh. "That was impressive, lord."

Drake glared at the huntress who'd once more seemingly appeared from thin air beside him, then slapped at the long tail she'd wrapped dangerously high around his thigh. She winked and sauntered deeper into the fort. He should have known better than to doubt.

"I do not like arrows," Nicole proclaimed loudly from down the hall. "Arrows are dumb."

The sound of booted feet in a cadence he almost recognized turned him back around. Sky approached at a determined pace and stopped a few paces away, glaring a challenge with her light-blue eyes. Her pale face was streaked with dirt and blood caked her feathersteel. He pondered offering a hug and immediately decided against it.

"You could have died," she said angrily.

Drake shrugged. "Comes with the job. How long you plan to stay mad?"

She forcefully gripped his left forearm in one strong hand. Surprised, he belatedly gripped her other forearm with his free hand. As he clasped arms with her and stared into his eyes, a genuine smile lit up her face. That smile felt good.

"You are going to make a powerful ally, Lord Gloomwood."

Drake grinned back. "Same goes for you, Lord Skybreak."

"Yet I cannot help but feel your antics are going to keep me awake at night."

As Drake suddenly imagined a soft four-post bed, a lot less clothing, and nighttime antics aplenty, he cleared his throat and released Sky's muscular arms. "How long do we have?"

The sound of a huge object slamming into the front doors of the fort made them both take a step sideways.

"About as long as it takes their ram team to batter down a fort's door," Sky said.

24
IT'S NOT YOU, IT'S ME

"On me!" Drake made a "circle up" motion with his hand and looked at Sky. "Show me the door you picked for our escape."

Sky took off to lead him deeper into the fort, and the sound of boots assured him others were following. He stopped to check on Valentia and Lydia, who now had Nicole on her feet. Nicole's whole back was soaked in blood, but the arrows were out of her.

She looked pale, but she was walking with their help. Healing gloves could only do so much, and they'd only had moments to work on her. There was also the possibility those arrows had been poisoned, which would require Raylan's skills back home.

Still, it looked like Nicole was going to make it. They'd taken no casualties, which was the second good news of the day. The first had been the call from Sky on her magic mirror.

As for Gaby, she looked to be having the time of her life. Her face was flushed and her grin was huge. Carl was still pale from tossing so many meteor kabooms. He leaned heavily on Robin as her keen eyes scanned the fort for threats. No one other than Carl had been forced to use their rarities during Drake's clever plan, though they would have if needed.

"I still can't believe your rarity is to teleport people," Sky said softly. "No wonder you were able to escape the assassin in my guest house. I can't wait to see that trick."

He grinned at her as they walked. "You won't have to wait long."

As they moved into the fort, it didn't take long for them to start walking past bodies. All looked to be mercenaries similar to those outside, though these wore different armor. Several were drenched in blood, and one looked like he'd had a hole punched straight through him. These must have been the men charged with holding Lady Skybreak hostage.

Drake ignored the carnage. Some part of him suspected these soldiers had been duped into defending this fort against Sky and her people—no sane man would hold a fort against this woman and her overpowered bodyguards—but he hadn't done this to them, and they'd been part of a group that abducted Lady Skybreak and threatened to torture her to death.

Distant and menacing booms continued to echo through the fort. Drake suspected Lord Proudglade had ordered the mercenary captain to move in and take Sky out if the lord of Gloomwood and his battle maids showed up to extract her. The mercenary captain must suspect that was exactly who he'd let get past him and charge the fort.

That was another reason he'd been glad to add Gaby, Carl, and Robin to his party, and to have Sachi sneak in on her own. If Lord Proudglade was working off the intelligence he'd received from watching them through Robby, he'd warned them of four humans and a feral... not seven humans. Every little bit of deception helped.

As Sky led them around a corner, a menacing demonic shadow detached itself from a distant wall. Before Drake could raise Magnum, Sky touched his arm. "She's with us."

The shadow shimmered closer, red eyes glowing, before it resolved into a tall, slim, dark-skinned woman who was entirely too naked. Drake averted his eyes out of courtesy as soon as he recognized her—Ali—and mentally processed what the rarity *dire wraith* could do.

Ali came out of her shift naked, sure, just like he almost had with dire rat. But she was basically a demon once her rarity kicked in, and apparently she could control her change. He definitely wouldn't want to meet demon-shifted Ali in a dark room. Or any room.

But wow, would it be nice to get just one vial of her blood.

Out of the corner of his vision, Drake watched Sky pull off her cloak and toss it to Ali. The other woman wrapped it around herself and fell into step beside them.

"None slipped inside," Ali said. "Your mother awaits us."

Right! Lady Skybreak, Sky's mother, was in this fort as well, because Sky had come all this way to "pay her ransom." Which Sky paid in blood rather than coin, as Lady Skybreak's abductors should have known. As they passed a set of closed wooden doors, the distant smell of corpses that wafted through suggested a lot more bodies might be piled behind those.

As Ali pushed open another set of double wooden doors, Sky raised an arm to halt him. Drake paused outside as the doors revealed a large dining hall beyond. Inside stood a tall, blonde woman wearing an ornate silverweave tunic that rose to her neck and sturdy-looking pants. She was dressed for battle, not supper, and had a sword hanging from her belt.

This noble, Drake knew immediately, was Lady Skybreak.

This was what Sky would look like when she was twenty years older, and she looked good. She was a bit taller than Sky and visibly athletic, with taut muscles. Her blonde hair hung in braids similar to her daughters, though it was a bit messy given her recent captivity.

Her face was similar to Sky's with a slightly longer nose and faint wrinkles at the edges of her eyes. She was an attractive woman, but Drake had yet to meet anyone here, male or female, who wasn't at least marginally attractive. It seemed the Eidolons passed down good genes.

Another boom echoed throughout the fort. Those mercenaries were persistent.

Sky glanced at him. "It's time to go, Lord Gloomwood. If you're ready."

Drake nodded. "Lady Skybreak, could you step out here with the rest of us?"

He didn't think his teleport rarity would work if she was already inside the door she needed to pass through to be teleported. Best to do everything exactly as they'd practiced back at his camp. Lady Skybreak strode to the doors and moved past him.

She didn't look at her daughter. Sky didn't look at her. There was obviously some awkward tension there, which had him curious despite the perilous situation.

Was Sky mad at her mother because she gave herself up to save a whole town? Was Sky's mother mad at Sky because she gave up her whole blood pact to save her mother? That seemed like the type of thing these two might get mad at each other about.

Drake focused on the doorway and convinced himself it would lead to his carriage. Before, it had been easy. He'd felt the connection form almost immediately.

This time, nothing happened. He didn't feel it. He focused harder, even as the next boom from the battering ram was followed by what sounded like a splintering crack.

"Is there a problem?" Lydia asked warningly.

"No problem," Drake said with a grimace. "I just need to focus."

Sky huffed. "Gods, I was afraid this would happen." She pointed at him. "Stay there."

He frowned at her in confusion. "What?"

"It's not you, it's me."

"What does that mean?"

"Stay there and use your rarity. Do not move." Sky then backed away from him, and she continued backing up. Away from the door. Further down the hall. What was she doing?

"Lord?" Lydia reminded him. "They'll be here soon."

Drake turned back to the door frame, and this time the connection with the door frame was immediate. Finally! What had been the problem before? "I've got it!"

With his connection to the portal inside his carriage back at his vanguard now confirmed, Drake turned to face everyone gathered in the hall. "Will you come with me?" Drake shouted. "Everyone, say yes!"

A chorus of yesses greeted him from the others. Good enough. He stepped through the door that led to his carriage and felt the pulse of his recall spot, though he remained in the fort.

Perfect. He wouldn't teleport until everyone who'd said yes did so. So far, everything was working just as it had when he'd tested this with his maids and feral before he left his vanguard to come here. Distance didn't seem to matter.

Drake turned to face those clustered behind him. "Form a line! Lydia goes first. No one walks through this door until I say so, then I need each of you to wait a few heartbeats after the last person goes. You got that?"

Most of them nodded. Another loud crack echoed down the hall from the ram in the process of obliterating the front doors of the fort.

"Lydia? Go through and get everything ready on the other side."

"Yes, lord." She walked through the open doorway and vanished.

Gasps from those assembled greeted Drake as he resisted the urge to pump his fist. "Hold!" he called to the others. A stampede through the doorway could be bad.

He mentally gave Lydia ten full seconds to prepare their exit even as more splintering sounds came from the door. His steward needed time to catch her balance after the teleport, stop the carriage if it was moving, open the door, and get out. She'd had enough time.

"Val, Nicole, Sachi, go!"

Sachi sauntered through the doorway and vanished just like Lydia. Nicole and Valentia stumbled through next, together, which Drake allowed because he knew his carriage could hold two people easily. More than that and they could end up teleporting on top of each other. Given what generally happened in videogames when they did that, that would be bad.

With his people now teleported successfully, Drake looked to everyone who hadn't walked through an invisible teleporting door before. "Through the door you will find a carriage! Step immediately out of the open door on the other side! Don't dawdle!"

"Go!" Sky shouted. "Ali, now! Through the door and out the carriage!"

Ali walked through the open doorway and vanished, followed a few heartbeats later by a short, blonde-haired woman, then a woman with spiky black hair. He'd get those two straightened out later. As Gaby rushed through and vanished, Drake started feeling dizzy.

That was... seven people? Already three more than Anna could manage.

Carl went through next, followed by Robin. Spots were dancing before Drake's eyes now, and the room was slowly starting to spin. That was nine. Three left, including himself.

"Mother!" Sky shouted. "Go now!"

Lady Skybreak stepped through the door and vanished. That made ten. Everyone he'd come here to rescue was now safely back with his vanguard on the Noble Road less than a day from Korhaurbauten. The only people he wanted to save in this fort were Sky and himself.

Drake's heart hammered as his knees trembled. He'd just teleported six more people than Anna could manage, and he wasn't dead yet. He really had burnished this rarity!

"You may have to leave me here!" Sky shouted.

Despite the spinning room, he found the strength to stare at her in shock. "What?"

"It's my rarity!" she shouted. "*Void* cancels other rarities if I get too close!"

Doors loudly shattered deeper in the fort. Men roared as footsteps thundered inside.

Drake mentally cursed. Of course Sky hadn't told him her rarity could cancel other rarities. Once she knew his rarity could teleport everyone she cared about to safety, including her mother, she'd kept it from him, even if it meant she might not escape herself.

Such. Heroic. Nonsense. Drake stumbled deeper into the room to put more space between them. "How far?"

"I don't know!" she said. "You have to go without me!"

"I can't!" he shouted back. "You already said yes! I literally can't leave unless you do!"

"What?" she shrieked. "You didn't tell me that!"

"Well I didn't know you were going to be a hero about it!"

Men roared as boots pounded. Drake thumped back against the far wall of the dining hall, as far as he could get from the door. "Run through the door now! Try!"

As shouts sounded almost on top of them, Sky darted for the open doorway into the dining hall. Drake's vision flickered dangerously as the shadows of armed men grew large on the wall beyond. Was this it? This might be it for both of them.

A warm body slammed into him hard enough to drop him into his back on hard wood. He gasped and blinked back spots as the world spun above him, but it was a world that existed inside his armored carriage. Not the inside of Fort Graystone.

He'd done it. He'd teleported home twelve people, three times what Anna could have managed, but she was ten and a third of his body weight. He'd hoped his burnishing of her teleport rarity would be a bit more powerful than this, but twelve wasn't bad at all.

"Can you see me?" Sky cried above him. "Speak to me!"

Drake smiled up at her. He tried to speak and didn't quite manage it. Still, he knew his battle maids would be here in moments. Their healing gloves would likely provide enough healing to stabilize him so he didn't die of blood loss. He was fairly certain. If not, well...

He'd done everything he planned to do.

Though he would have appreciated a *little* more time to enjoy the feeling of Sky lying on top of him before he blacked out.

25
NOT ENOUGH SNACKS

Drake smacked his lips, rolled onto his side, and cuddled up in the warm soft sleeping bag for more shuteye. But... wait. This was a rather fuzzy sleeping bag. Fuzzier than a sleeping bag should be. Also, the world smelled like leather and smoke. Was something burning?

"How are you feeling?" a soft female voice asked. "Can you speak?"

Wait a moment. That was Lydia, his flutterstepping battle maid, and he was still stuck in a fucked-up fantasy world where everyone was trying to kill him. Which was *still* better than living in a drafty one-bedroom apartment back in New Mexico.

Drake forced his eyes open and experimentally stretched. He didn't feel bad at all. Actually, he felt amazing, like he'd just come awake after a long and restful nap. The last thing he had done was... drain himself of blood teleporting twelve people out of an old fort... so it was surprising to feel this good afterward. In fact, he felt so good that...

"You gave me Samuel's rarity again, didn't you?" Drake asked. He reflexively reached for the pouch of blood vials and found it missing, then spotted it nearby.

Lydia grimaced. "Had we not done so, Samuel would now be the lord of Gloomwood Manor."

So he really had almost killed himself by teleporting twelve people using Anna's rarity. Good to know for next time. Anna's rarity had sucked him dry.

"Ten," Drake said. "We'll settle for ten. No reason to get overly ambitious."

Lydia's warm hand rested on his forearm. The gesture felt far more caring than he expected. She looked genuinely concerned about him.

He patted her hand. "Hey, I'm fine."

"That is good to hear." She released his arm. "Everyone who you teleported from Fort Graystone arrived safely. You have been unconscious for approximately four hours, and we have made camp for the night. Our vanguard will easily reach Korhaurbauten before lunch tomorrow. That gives you a night before you will officially be required to attend the cabal."

"Can't wait for my first cabal."

"Robby remains with Tamara and her maids in their tent, so we have leeway to speak freely. You may also be unsurprised to learn that Sky is, once again, Lord Skybreak."

"Figured Karth would hand the blood pact back," Drake agreed. "Not everyone enjoys constantly dodging assassins and making the hard calls."

"Now that you're awake, would you feel comfortable attending a formal supper with our new allies? Meryl and her cooks are almost done with their preparations."

Drake sat up. "I could eat." He idly rolled one shoulder in its socket, then flexed and tested his forearm. Nothing felt off. "And by allies, we're talking Lord and Lady Skybreak?" Both were women, but he had to keep to the odd conventions here.

"I took the liberty of suggesting the idea of a supper and strategy session in preparation for tomorrow's cabal, assuming you came awake in time. I hope I haven't overstepped."

"You never do." He frowned. "And wait. Have you been watching over me for four hours? Without a break?"

"It is my duty to keep you safe, lord."

He pulled up the top of his sleeping back and looked inside. "So... where are my pants?"

Lydia blushed brighter than he expected. "Samuel and Raylan weren't sure of the extent of your injuries, so they looked you over after Samuel mixed his blood with yours. While you were unconscious. No one else was allowed in this part of the tent."

"Not even Emily?"

"*Definitely* not Emily. Though, fair warning, she may be prickly for a few days. She was not happy about being left out of the rescue party."

"At least she got to hang out with everyone's favorite Samuel."

"I have laid out an outfit that's suitable for supper," Lydia said. "I've left it on the table. With your permission, I'll leave to inform the others you're awake and allow you to dress."

"You don't need to be so formal when we're alone." Drake shrugged and paused halfway out of the bedroll. "Though... you do need to leave."

She rose and offered a faint smile. "It's good to see you awake, Lord Gloomwood."

Once Lydia left the screened-in part of his big command tent, Drake slipped out of his furry bedroll—he *was* wearing a pair of those silky faux boxer things, which was better than waking up naked—and checked out the clothes Lydia had left out from him.

The shirt was dark-colored, just a shade off black, and laced with gold trim that formed a complex and almost flowery pattern across the chest. The weight of the garment despite its thin appearance suggested it was silverweave, but he doubted a manor lord would attend a fancy dinner in anything less. The pants were dark as well with flared cuffs, fancier than he normally wore, but fortunately not so floofy he would feel self-conscious.

Drake dressed easily without enduring any aches or pains from draining himself of blood four hours ago—having Samuel's physical regeneration rarity back was amazing—and was pleased to see Magnum in the room with him. He loved that crossbow. He pulled out Sky's magic mirror, which was, at the moment, just a mirror, and gave himself a once over.

The dark shirt looked good on him, as did the pants. Both flattered a frame he would swear was more muscular and toned than it had been a month ago. He had, in fact, been working out. He finished the outfit by pulling on his ankle-length fur cloak.

His long black hair was still a mess, however, haphazardly sticking out in all directions. He would definitely need a haircut before he presented himself at the capital. For now, he'd simply find some water and slick down the worst parts. It would have to do. Unfortunately, in this world, baseball caps were not acceptable dinner attire.

He stuck his head out of his screened-in private area to check who was currently in his tent. He spotted Korrag on watch immediately—the big orange zarovian had to bow his head to fit inside the tent—and Valentia sitting at a table nearby, legs propped up casually on another chair as she read yet another book. The tent was otherwise empty. No Anna?

As Valentia glanced up, her ice-blue eyes were warmer than he expected. "Did you have a good nap?"

He stepped into the tent at large and nodded. "How's Nicole?"

"Resting comfortably." A faint smile joined the warmth in her eyes. "I haven't thanked you for saving her life."

"It was a group effort, but you're both welcome." He glanced at Korrag, who was obviously doing his best to stand at attention like a manor guard. "How's life, buddy?"

"Lots of watching," Korrag said. "Not enough snacks."

"Sounds about right." Drake took note of the long wooden table in the main portion of his command tent, one that had not been there previously, and then looked to Valentia and her book. "So this supper's going to be inside?"

"In attendance will be you, Lydia, Samuel, Lord Skybreak, Lady Skybreak, and Head Ranger Cask standing in as acting steward for Skybreak Manor. As this will be a small but formal supper, the rest of us will be on duty outside or eating with the rest of the camp."

That was useful information. "How are we doing on food and such?" They had added a large number of people to their vanguard four days ago, which must have presented a problem. He doubted his cooks had packed enough food to feed two vanguards.

"Tonight's supper will be a bit light," Valentia agreed. "I'm certain your new allies will understand given the circumstances. Fortunately, in the days you were away, Lord Skybreak's rangers spent most of their time assisting with extra hunting. We do not lack for food."

It sounded like everything back at his camp had run just fine in both his and Lydia's absence, so Samuel had done a fine job keeping the lights on while everyone else was gone. That didn't surprise him. The old man had been playing this game for decades.

"Great," Drake said. "So, I'd like to walk around the camp now to see how everyone has held up." And to make sure his people knew he was back in fighting shape. If they'd heard he'd blacked out from blood loss, they might be concerned.

Valentia set down her book and stood. "I will accompany you."

"Thanks, Val." He glanced at Korrag again. "How about you, buddy?"

"Cresh told me to guard tent."

"The tent? Not me?"

"Tent," Korrag agreed.

Drake chuckled. "We wouldn't want you disobeying orders. See you in a bit."

Korrag nodded gravely.

With Valentia at his side, Drake stepped out into a camp that already felt familiar despite him only spending a few days here. Several nearby servants glanced his way and one even smiled at him. They didn't look nearly as afraid as they had days ago.

Perhaps it had been his time in the soup line. Or his work with Hugo and Tamara. Or maybe just weeks going by without him murdering any of them. Either way, it felt good to see people who were happy to see him alive rather than people who winced like whipped dogs.

The camp was as he'd expected it to be, given Samuel was in charge. Every tent was arranged close enough to the others to create an efficient camp but far enough away there would be enough room for zarovians or horses to rush through if needed. It wasn't quite sunset yet, so the soup line hadn't started yet, but there were a lot more people here.

The addition of Sky's vanguard hadn't quite doubled their numbers, since her vanguard was smaller than his, but there were far more people around. Also, Sky's people were dressed in various types of light armor and most carried bows. They made a strong contrast to his people, who were primarily dressed as servants and laborers.

Drake wondered then if Sky even had any domestic servants, or if that was a luxury the prior Lords Gloomwood had allowed themselves. He could see how having more people capable of combat would be beneficial, but he wasn't about to fire loyal people who'd decided to serve him by choice. Everyone here was his responsibility now.

Drake looked to Valentia. "How's the JV crew settling in? Any problems?"

Valentia glanced at him. "You really should come up with a different name for our warriors-in-training. No one understands what that means."

"You're probably right." They walked past where the cooks were setting up, including two he didn't recognize. Sky's people. "So, is there any precedent for bringing in folks who we're going to use as warriors, but who aren't battle maids?"

"The last two Lords Gloomwood had no interest in training warriors unless their rarities were of unequaled strength. So, as you have seen, even Olivia was inducted as a battle maid when she joined the manor."

"And historically, have there always been five of you? Or have there been more?"

"Official records only go back around three hundred years. However, if I recall, the most battle maids Lord Gloomwood ever had at a time was eight."

"So we have three more silverweave maid uniforms back at the manor, gathering dust?"

"They are sealed away in magical boxes that can only be opened by the blood of the current Lord Gloomwood. However, you are correct that they sit unused. If we are ever fortunate enough to come across a person with a rarity powerful enough to join our ranks, I hope you will take the opportunity to recruit them."

Now that he'd finally recruited his first new folks, Drake was curious to learn more about how he might strengthen his manor. With willing warriors. "So if I wanted to recruit more people, where would I find them? Are all my folks drawn from towns that swear fealty?"

"That is most often where you draw new thralls and why Samuel maintains a list of births and rarities that manifest in all territories. It is considered disrespectful to poach thralls from the territories of other manor lords unless they specifically approach you first. While it is not a crime, it can certainly lead to difficulties in manor relations."

"But if people seek me out voluntarily, there's no issue recruiting them?"

"There is not, though when a young person manifests a powerful rarity, many lords often take an interest. One of Samuel's duties as your spymaster is to track the appearance of powerful rarities and provide you with information about them when they arise."

"So I can recruit them if I have the interest and space." Drake nodded as Valentia confirmed his earlier speculations. "You and the others are absolute badasses, but I do think we need more capable warriors. Will I have any chance for recruiting in Korhaurbauten?"

"That pronunciation was almost passable."

"Thank you. I'm going to kick all sorts of ass at the cabal."

26

I WON'T GIVE AWAY THE MANOR, VAL

Valentia visibly considered Drake's questions about recruiting as they passed the line of horses and then turned around to avoid stepping outside the line of highly alert zarovians. Drake's lizardmen soldiers were now reinforced every so often by one of Sky's rangers. As they headed back into the camp, Valentia spoke again.

"I do not think there will be much chance for recruiting in the capital, especially once the cabal begins. Kohaurbauten is the one place in this land where the authority of the manor lords is not absolute. Typically, those who travel there wish to be left alone."

"What do you mean, not absolute?" Drake had discussed this a bit with Lydia, but he wanted to make sure he'd understood her properly.

"A manor lord has complete authority in their own territory," Valentia said calmly. "This includes the right to reward, recruit, or punish whomever they see fit. In Korhaurbauten, however, the noble court holds power. Manor lords cannot simply do as they wish there."

"So if I was a person with a powerful rarity who didn't want to get pressed into joining a manor by a dickish lord, I'd go chill in Korhaurbauten."

"If by 'chill' you mean 'live,' then yes."

Drake nodded. "So even if we run into someone as powerful as the Asp or one of the Gilded Blades in the capital, I couldn't force them to join me. They'd have to volunteer. Which they likely wouldn't, since they're in the capital in the first place."

"Correct. As such warriors have chosen to remain independent of any manor, it is unlikely any would choose to become your blood thrall. Also, manor lords can offer extravagant deals when they are interested in a powerful blood thrall, so there is also fierce competition when one makes it clear they will entertain joining a manor. So even if a thrall was interested in joining a manor, they would likely seek offers from all interested lords."

"And I guess people with powerful rarities could also become a manor lord if they manage to take one down," Drake said. "So if you have a powerful rarity, you have a choice. Serve a manor lord, or carve your way through the world until you kill one."

Valentia nodded grimly. "That was the route taken by the current Lord Frostlight. She survived eight years as a Gilded Blade until she killed the former lord of Frostlight Manor and took it by force. She purged all blood thralls she considered insufficiently loyal afterward. When a manor changes hands by force, such a housecleaning is not uncommon."

Valentia said that so calmly. It must have been exactly what she had expected would happen once he took over from Lord Crow. Lydia had likely expected the same, which explained why she was so relieved when it turned out he wasn't an asshole.

"So Lord Frostlight's rarity is one of the deadly ones?"

"*Windshear*, lord. She can harden and use air to such a degree it can actually cut flesh."

Drake whistled. "So she does what you do, but with air. Which is everywhere."

Valentia nodded. "My ice projectiles remain stronger, but any duel in which we engaged would be a difficult one. Other than Lord Frostlight, you are the only manor lord now sitting at the table who killed his predecessor and took his manor."

If it was true the Eidolons—the gods of this world—were the ones who decided who got what rarity, they obviously had a real sadistic streak. Why else would they create a world full of normal people and a bunch of superpowered folks who could rule over them with fear?

Either way, it *was* good that someone on Team Proudglade had killed their former manor lord and seized the manor. That way if Lord Proudglade brought it up during the cabal, Drake could simply point out Proudglade was allied with a former assassin who'd done the same. It also brought up another interesting aspect of how he might be perceived at the cabal.

"Does the fact that I killed Lord Gloomwood to seize his title mean the other lords will respect me more or less?"

"I cannot say. Lord Proudglade no doubt sees your assassination of the prior Lord Gloomwood as a despicable act, despite the fact that he wished Lord Gloomwood dead. He would have preferred to kill our former lord in open battle."

"And he says that while allied with Lord Frostlight. Suitably hypocritical."

"Lord Redbow would likely see your success as proof of your prowess as a warrior, were he not currently opposed to us due to his alliance obligations. And I do not know enough about the other manor lords to say with confidence. This is a question you should ask Samuel."

"But the rest of the current crop got their titles handed down?"

"Handed down voluntarily, like Lord Skybreak, or inherited after the former lord died and named them their successor. Such is the case with Lord Brightwater. She gained her post as manor lord nine years ago when the former lord was killed by an assassin."

"Did anyone ever find out who the assassin was working for?"

"No official responsibility has ever been assigned, but as you would expect, common wisdom suggests Lord Redbow or one of his sons was behind the attack. That may be the only reason Lord Brightwater has not yet joined the other four in the alliance."

"But she has no interest in joining us?"

"Correct. A blood thrall working for the Lord Gloomwood two before you managed to kill the former Lord Brightwater before the one most recently killed. So bad blood remains."

Drake sighed. "Once again, I'm stuck paying for the crimes of assholes who pissed people off before I was even born. That's my least favorite part of being a manor lord."

"You like that even less than the constant assassination attempts?"

Drake glanced at Valentia. "Okay. Second least favorite."

Valentia's features turned curious. "May I ask you something personal?"

Drake was so surprised by the question he stopped walking. "Sure, Val." Since when did Valentia ask personal questions? She must really be warming up to him.

"Did you have a family back on your world?"

Drake realized then he'd never discussed anything about his home with her. He'd mentioned his mother to Lydia, but she'd never share personal details without his permission. "I do. I mean, I'm not sure if I'll ever see her again, but I have a mother, and I miss her."

"But no one else?"

Drake shook his head. "My dad isn't dead, but I think the last time I saw him I was… four, maybe? He was never a part of my life. And my mother's parents were killed in an accident before I met them, so no grandparents either."

"So your family was just you and your mother, whom you may never see again." Valentia motioned for them to resume their journey to his command tent. "We have that in common."

"We do?"

"That is also how I was raised. My parents were originally from

Brightwater territory, but my father died at sea shortly after I was born. Not long after, unsavory individuals used the circumstances of his death to demand an unseemly amount of coin from my mother to pay his debts. Or, they advised her, she could offer me and consider her debt expunged."

Drake grimaced as Valentia recounted her story with absolutely no emotion in her voice, like she was telling him the history of some dusty old building. Not even Lydia had shared details about her past or family with him before now. What had prompted this from Valentia?

"My mother had no rarity. She was not powerful enough to kill those who sought to claim us, nor could she keep me safe from those who wished to abduct me had we remained in Brightwater. So she fled to the territory of Lord Gloomwood, which remained hostile to those from Brightwater territory due to recent events. She hoped our enemies would not follow."

Drake looked toward the command tent and said nothing, though he already suspected what Valentia would say next. She really must have had it rough growing up.

"Those men killed my mother not long after we arrived, but not before she presented me to Lord Gloomwood and I demonstrated my *flashfreeze* rarity on a rabbit. I was eight."

"I'm sorry, Val." Drake grimaced. "I didn't know any of that."

"I would not expect you to. Fortunately for me, Lord Gloomwood saw my potential as an assassin and agreed to protect me until I came of age."

"So those evil debtors lost out in the end."

"They did. I asked that Lord Gloomwood see to the deaths of all who harmed my mother in exchange for my pledge to become his thrall. He found the trade worthwhile."

So Valentia had ordered the deaths of the men who murdered her mother at age eight. She had started killing early. Drake couldn't blame her, given the circumstances and the world in which she lived. Still... that would leave some emotional scars.

"Lord Gloomwood sheltered me in his manor until I turned sixteen, at which point, as we had agreed, I accepted his blood pact and became his assassin."

Drake hesitated before asking his next question, but he doubted Valentia would tell him all this if she wasn't open to discussing it. "Do you wish you'd ended up somewhere else?"

"I have no family left in any territory," Valentia said softly. "Gloomwood Manor was all I knew after my mother passed. With her dead, I had no reason to travel, and the only thing I was ever good at was killing people." She shrugged. "To this day, that remains the case."

"That's not true, though," Drake said.

She paused at the entrance to his tent and glanced at him. "How do you mean?"

"You've saved my life twice now with your *flashfreeze* rarity. First when you blocked Robin's arrow, and again when you saved Nicole and me with that ice barrier you used to blunt the arrow volley at Fort Graystone. I'd be dead if not for you."

"Those were isolated events, and we were fortunate my desperate action blunted those attacks. Using my rarity defensively is not my strength."

"Well... would you want it to be?"

"I do not understand what you are asking."

"The prior lords have all used you as their personal assassin, haven't they? They've ordered you to assassinate those they needed dead or employed you exclusively to kill other warriors in battle. It seems like your protective potential is going to waste."

Valentia now looked unsure of herself. "My potential?"

"All I'm saying is... if you want a break from being asked to freeze people to death all the time, I could give you a different role in combat. You're amazing when it comes to blunting attacks and slowing the enemy. You could protect us with your freeze powers."

She actually smiled. "That is kind of you, Lord Gloomwood."

"It's not just me being benevolent. It makes sense!"

"Perhaps." Valentia looked back to the camp. "Yet there is so much blood on my hands that I feel there would be no point in walking a different path. I protect those I care about by killing those who would harm them. It would be irresponsible and inefficient to act otherwise."

"But if you wanted—"

"I know." Valentia impulsively gripped his arm with one chill hand. "And I truly appreciate your consideration. But I will best serve our manor and those I care about by acting as I have until now. So when you wish your enemies dead, please call upon me first."

She seemed to mean this. Drake wasn't about to question her choice when she seemed so resolved to follow it. He simply patted her hand and nodded. "Then I'll just say thanks."

"No other Lord Gloomwood has." Valentia released his arm. "Be careful at dinner. Lord Skybreak I trust, but I do not know what to expect of Lady Skybreak. Before she passed down her title, she was among the most shrewd manor lords to sit at the table."

"I won't give away the manor, Val."

"See that you don't." She walked off to take up position outside the command tent.

It felt strange to see Valentia smiling, let alone sharing details of her past, but maybe it wasn't. Perhaps the fact that he'd saved Nicole's life at Fort Graystone had eased the last worries she had about him not being ruthless enough to succeed as a manor lord. She hadn't berated him even once for risking his life to save a blood thrall, though... it had been Nicole.

Hypocritical of her? Maybe a little. Still, given what he now knew about the horrors she'd suffered growing up, he was all the more willing to cut her some slack. Now, it seemed she felt the same way about him. That made for a good working relationship.

Drake entered his tent to find two servants inside, Tamara and another woman whose name he didn't know. It looked like they had finished setting six places at the long table with fine dishes, spoons, forks, and folded white napkins with gold trim.

Tamara straightened. "Supper will be served in a few minutes, lord."

"Thanks." He glanced at the private area in the back of his tent. "Say, do you have any water you can spare?" He still needed to do something about his bedhead.

27
THE SUPPER WAS DELICIOUS

Drake knew very little about formal dinners. He'd meant to learn and even practice this manor lord stuff on his six-day journey to Korhaurbauten, but that had all gone out the window when he had to spend two-thirds of it traveling to Fort Graystone. So for tonight, the best he could do is watch Lydia and Samuel for cues and try not to spill soup on himself.

Lydia entered not long after Tamara left, then motioned to the seat at one of the two short ends of the table. "You will be sitting there, lord. Once we are assembled and you are ready to receive your guests, you need simply call 'Send them in' to those outside."

Drake appreciated her explanation of the seating chart. He walked over to his high-backed chair and ran his hands over it. The wood was dark, but not as dark-colored as his wagon. This wasn't silverwood. Given how expensive it was, it likely wasn't used for chairs.

Lydia walked over to join him at the table. "As steward, I will sit at your right hand, while Samuel will sit at your left."

Drake grinned at her. "Because you're my right hand?"

"I am not certain, lord. That is simply how it is done."

"And Lord Skybreak sits at the other head of the table?"

"Correct. As her acting steward, Head Ranger Cask will sit beside Samuel, while Lady Skybreak will sit beside me."

"So either Sky doesn't have a spymaster, or he's not joining us for dinner."

"Or it could be that Lady Skybreak requested to take the place of whomever Lord Skybreak intended to invite. While this supper was thrown together quickly, given the circumstances, arranging formal suppers between lords is often a convoluted affair."

Drake nodded and sat down in his chair. It wasn't as soft as the chairs back in the manor, but at least his butt wouldn't be sore immediately. He'd remember not to slouch.

Lydia continued her explanation of manor lord suppers. "Multiple factors must be agreed to by both lords in advance, including the number of thralls who will attend, who will sit at the table and where, the number of courses, and whether alcohol will be served."

"So it's not great when a manor lord gets drunk off his ass and starts ranting about how the noble court is all lizardmen?"

Lydia frowned. "You mean zarovians?"

He was going to have to learn how to make cracks that involved this world's conspiracy theories instead of Earth's. "Never mind. I'm attempting to be funny and failing at it."

"Perhaps a more measured approach would be best for supper?"

Drake chuckled. "We'll see what happens." He was relieved to see only a single fork and spoon, rather than an assortment. "How about eating? And do I start seated or standing?"

He doubted Sky expected her to pull a chair out for her. This was a formal dinner between manor lords, not a fancy date. Plus, Sky's mother would be chaperoning.

"You will be seated before your guests arrive, with Samuel at your side," Lydia said. "I will rise when your guests enter and invite them to join us, then seat myself once all of your guests are seated. That will be Tamara's cue to deliver the first course, which tonight will be small slices of fresh bread and slathered meat cubes."

Drake's mouth watered at the mention of Meryl's delicious meat. "Got it."

"Keep conversation limited to surface pleasantries to start. Your guests may consider it rude if you move to matters of politics or warfare before the first course is consumed."

Drake nodded to show he understood.

"Since you are inexperienced in formal dining, for the first part of the supper, I would suggest you simply let Lord Skybreak suggest topics and offer the same type of conversation she does. She wishes this supper to go smoothly, so you can trust her to guide its direction."

"As opposed to having dinner with Lord Proudglade, where he'd be trying to trip me up on every point." This was also a practice session for Korhaurbauten politics with a friendly audience, which was a good idea. "Makes sense."

"When speaking to us during supper, refer to me as 'steward' rather than Lydia, and refer to Samuel by name. Lord Skybreak must always be addressed by her full title or, as the night wears on, simply 'lord.' And you should address Cask as 'Head Ranger.'"

So no "Clint" or "Sky" at supper. Given the preference of most manor lords to not give their names unless forced, that custom made sense.

"With Lady Skybreak, you should always address her using her full title unless she invites you to speak informally, in which case it is permissible to use the name she offers. That is up to your discretion, but I would recommend you use her name if she gives it. Offering her name to one who does not know it is a gesture of respect and trust. Moreover, even should she ask you to speak informally, she will still refer to you as Lord Gloomwood. This is normal."

This was a lot to remember, but at least Drake didn't have to figure out when and how to use three different spoons. So far, he felt confident he would nail all of this, and again, he had a friendly audience who would want him to succeed.

Now to focus on what he'd actually be doing at this dinner. "So other than small talk, what should I expect to discuss tonight? And when should we start discussing it?"

"Once the second course is on the table, which will be tonight's main course, it is permissible to begin delving into manor politics and any matters related to your plans for tomorrow's cabal or the specifics of your new alliance. I do not know what Lord Skybreak and Lady Skybreak will wish to discuss, but I would assume it will be planning for tomorrow's cabal."

Drake nodded.

"The second course is where the meat of such discussions resides. You should expect to speak with them both until all your business is concluded, even if you finish your meal. Only once you and Lord Skybreak agree all business is concluded will dessert be served."

Drake wondered what dessert would be. He just knew it would be delicious.

"During and after dessert, small talk is again acceptable, and it is considered rude to return to matters of politics or alliances with such business concluded. At some point either your guests will excuse themselves, or you may do so. Stand when the other lord leaves."

Meals really were a lot more formal between manor lords. Still, at least there was a clear order to how these things flowed. He could covertly take notes ahead of time.

"There is one last matter. Once the official supper is ended by one manor lord excusing themselves, the hosting lord may offer to walk the visiting lord out, or the visiting lord may request a word with the host. Either can refuse with no offense given, but if they agree, this last meeting will take place between the lords and no others. It should be kept brief."

"And that's when the real secret deals are made," Drake said.

"Stuff the manor lords may not even want their stewards to know about."

Lydia nodded. "Once again, whether you ask for a private conversation or are asked for one, either party is within their rights to politely decline. In some cases it may be in your interest to decline, especially if you feel the manor lord will ask for an accommodation you do not wish to give them. To refuse, simply apologize and suggest speaking at the next supper."

Drake felt like he had all that. "One more question."

"What's that, lord?"

"If I'm about to say something dumb or move onto a topic I should ignore, can you like... bump my knee under the table? Or maybe clear your throat?"

Lydia smiled. "The former may be more subtle, lord. You can trust me to advise you."

Not long after Lydia finished his briefing, Samuel entered the tent. He sat in the chair to Drake's left side, then glanced at Lydia. "Our guests have arrived. All is prepared?"

She nodded. Samuel might as well have asked *"Is he prepared?"* but had decided to be subtle about it. Drake was more amused than annoyed.

He glanced at Samuel. "How many of these dinners have you done in your time?"

"A good number."

"Anything I should know about before we begin? Spy stuff?"

Samuel offered him a calm glance. "Nothing comes to mind."

"Guess we're good to go." Drake looked to the tent flaps. "Send them in!"

Head Ranger Cask lifted the flap to admit Sky, who was dressed in ornate silverweave similar to Drake's. Hers was blue. After she entered, Lady Skybreak entered as well, wearing another fancy tunic, silky-looking pants, and tall boots. She didn't carry her sword.

Fortunately, his first formal supper as a manor lord went as smoothly as he could have hoped. Lady Skybreak barely said a word and let Sky do the talking, and she led the way through a number of pleasant and innocuous conversational topics like she'd been practicing formal dinners all her life. Which, given it was Sky, she had.

The second course arrived soon enough, and then matters turned more political. This was the point where Lady Skybreak began to speak more often, but only to answer direct questions from her daughter about what she'd learned about other manors or her thoughts on recent events. It was obvious to Drake that her relationship with Sky remained strained.

He was truly curious about all that, but decided not to ask, even in private. If Sky wanted to talk about what was going on with her mother, she'd tell him, otherwise, he was going to leave well enough alone. He trusted Sky not to let whatever personal issues she had with her mother currently interfere with tomorrow, and would trust Lady Skybreak the same way.

Drake had halfway hoped that Sky's spies would be more informed than his own, but apparently, she had left her manor in a rush as well. There was no doubt in Drake's mind that someone had conspired to ensure they both received late notice of the cabal, but he couldn't prove it. So neither of them had any idea what the cabal was about.

Sooner than Drake expected, the main course was concluded, as well as all the political talk. Dessert arrived—sweetened orange fruit slices that were both juicy and delicious—and not long after, Sky excused herself to do one more last check on her soldiers.

Drake stood. "Then I'll bid you good night, Lord Skybreak."

"My lord." Lady Skybreak spoke up the moment Sky began to rise from her seat. "Before you retire, might I speak to you about another matter?"

Drake mentally froze. Everything Lydia had told him had prepared him for a private chat with Sky, which would be fine—he felt comfortable with Sky—but she hadn't told him Sky's *mother* could ask to speak with him in private. Which she apparently could.

He barely resisted the urge to glance at Lydia, but she couldn't bump his knee while he was standing. He wanted badly to glance at Samuel, but he suspected that would give away he had no idea what he was doing. From Sky herself, he detected nothing but passive disinterest.

Time to make the call. "Of course, Lady Skybreak." He hoped he hadn't screwed up.

Sky rose for real this time and offered Drake a curt nod. "Thank you again for hosting us tonight, Lord Gloomwood. The supper was delicious. Head Ranger, with me."

As Cask rose, looking as visibly uncomfortable as Drake was trying not to look, Sky turned and walked for the exit to the tent. She didn't glance at her mother. Cask did, received a kind smile for his trouble, and followed after his manor lord.

Had he pissed Sky off by agreeing to chat with her mother alone? Too late now.

Lydia rose as well. "I should make one last check on the security arrangements for tonight. Samuel, would you accompany me?"

Samuel rose as well. "Of course. Lord Gloomwood, we leave you to your guest."

Neither glanced back as they left the tent, so Drake still had no idea if he should have refused Lady Skybreak's request. As for Lady Skybreak herself, she was looking increasingly amused, which suggested his discomfort was showing. What now?

At least he hadn't spilled soup on himself.

28

I WANT THIS ALLIANCE

Moments later, Drake stood alone in his command tent with the former lord of Skybreak Manor, a still-formidable woman who managed to remain intimidating despite carrying no weapons of any kind. That he could see. He assumed his people would have searched her.

Though her rarity, *cleavage*, would apparently allow her to split open the earth and swallow him. As humorous as the name was, the way it could murder him was not. Yet Lady Skybreak's blue eyes remained visibly amused, and her soft smile was as nice as her daughter's.

"Thank you for agreeing to speak with me, Lord Gloomwood."

"Of course." Drake needed to sound as formal as he could, especially if he wanted to impress her. "What matter did you wish to discuss?"

"You need not trouble yourself on account of my current disagreement with Lord Skybreak. While we have reached an impasse in personal matters, rest assured that we remain aligned in all other matters... including the security of our manor and yours."

"Thank you for that reassurance." Drake was this close to

asking her why they were still so upset with each other, but he'd literally promised himself he wouldn't do that.

"With that said, that isn't the matter I wished to speak with you about."

"Of course," Drake said. "What is it?"

"Would you mind telling me a bit about your parents?"

Drake couldn't help but hide his surprise, and from the way Lady Skybreak visibly hesitated, he immediately suspected she'd taken his surprise the wrong way.

"I realize the question is unusual," Lady Skybreak continued. "But if you will indulge me, I'd like to know a bit about the people who raised you."

"Like... what exactly?"

"In your world, do they sit in a position of power?"

Drake couldn't help but frown as he considered her. "So you and Lord Skybreak have discussed my origins?" It made sense she'd share with her mother, but... still.

"My daughter has said very little to me about you, lord, other than that she considers you worthy of an alliance. Your recent actions have proven that beyond any doubt. I hope you will not be angry with me if I reveal I've had my spies check up on you."

Drake pondered a moment. "You still speak to Lord Skybreak's spies?"

"These spies are my own."

So Lady Skybreak maintained her own private spy network independent of Skybreak Manor. Even if she wasn't the manor lord any more, it made sense she wouldn't leave herself out of the loop. He wondered how many of Sky's people still reported to her.

"And what have your spies told you, Lady Skybreak?"

"You may call me Viktoria if you wish."

She was offering her name to one who didn't know it to show both trust and respect. She was likely attempting to blunt any concerns Drake might have about her strange questions about his parents. He was in uncharted territory here, and the one thing he knew was that overthinking this conversation would just make him look indecisive.

So he'd let it flow where it would flow and hope he didn't step on a rake.

"Of course... Viktoria," Drake agreed. "And I'm curious what you know about me." He forced an easy smile. "If your spies have slandered me, I'd like to correct the record."

"I know you were brought here against your will from another realm, yet immediately accepted your post as Lord Gloomwood without hesitation. I know your approach to handling your blood thralls is the same as my daughter's. Finally, I know teleporting people isn't the only rarity you've demonstrated since you became Lord Gloomwood."

All Drake could do was struggle to keep his poker face. Her spies were well-informed, but had they figured out he could absorb rarities? And how bad would it be if they had?

"Be assured, I don't wish to antagonize you," Lady Skybreak—no, it was Viktoria now—continued. "An alliance with your manor will benefit my daughter and our manor, so if I've overstepped in asking any question tonight, you may dismiss me without worry I will reveal any part of this conversation to my daughter. I want this alliance."

Since Viktoria couldn't lie, she meant every word. He mentally parsed her words for doublespeak and found nothing he could question. Her words seemed clear, and given Viktoria was clearly still plugged into realm politics and had her own independent spy network, he could benefit from forging a stronger alliance with her. She wasn't asking much.

"Your question didn't offend me," Drake said. "But I am curious why you want to know about my parents."

"I do not know how it is in your realm, lord, but in this one, a person can intuit a great deal about another based on who raised them and how they were raised. In the interest of improving relations between our manors and between us, I'd simply like to know a bit more about your upbringing. I will, of course, share similar information with you."

That sounded like doublespeak. Samuel, Valentia, Lydia, and basically everyone had warned him Lady Skybreak had been one of the most shrewd manor lords when she sat at the table. She wouldn't inquire about something like this out of idle curiosity.

There was more to Viktoria's question than simply wanting to learn about his parents, so should he press her to clarify further? A more egotistical man might have assumed she was asking about his parents to see if he'd make a good match for her daughter, but Drake wasn't about to make that mistake. She likely had a different agenda here.

So what was it? The best way to find out might be to answer a few of her questions. He couldn't think how any of his answers could come back to bite him in the ass.

"My mother's in clerical work back where I came from," Drake said. "In terms of my realm, that means she handles matters similar to what I imagine a mediator handles in your world. She reads documents, types documents, and sometimes makes the coffee."

"And your father?"

"Not in the picture."

Viktoria paused to consider, and he realized then she might be trying to parse another of his strange Earth phrases. "So your father has passed on?"

"No, he's still alive somewhere, but he's not a part of my life and never has been." He wondered what she'd make of that fact. "My mother raised me. It was just her."

Viktoria nodded thoughtfully. "I also raised Sky on my own. Her father was killed shortly after she was born. So you and my daughter were both raised by a mother alone."

It was sad to hear about Sky's dad, but also, Viktoria had just referred to Lord Skybreak as Sky in his presence. Should he do the same?

Probably not. Samuel had made it clear he should never refer to Sky as anything but Lord Skybreak. Best to err on the side of trusting Samuel instead of offending Viktoria.

"I'm sorry to hear about your husband," Drake said.

"Your sympathies are appreciated," Viktoria said. "I loved him very much."

Drake nodded. She was now offering personal information about herself. The question was, why? A woman who'd been a manor lord this long didn't do anything without a goal.

"One last question, lord. Would you say you have your mother's eyes?"

Drake considered her in silence as the strangeness of that question bounced around in his brain. People back on Earth only asked questions like that if they were comparing children to parents for similar features. But Viktoria couldn't be asking that, could she?

Was this a weird cultural thing? Did eye color mean something here that Samuel hadn't told him about? He'd seen other people with blue eyes, including Anna and Valentia, so his eyes weren't unusual by the standards of this world. His mother's eyes were also blue.

Again he considered the question and again could find no reason not to answer. Was Lady Skybreak—Viktoria—simply asking innocuous questions to soften him up for something bigger? It was tempting to simply dismiss her, and he suspected she'd leave if he did, but he'd also be admitting he was worried about her. He didn't want to admit that.

"Yes, we do have the same color eyes," Drake said. "I'd say people have even commented upon them looking similar before." He watched her cautiously. "I could say the same about you and Lord Skybreak. Your eyes look almost identical."

"Thank you, lord." Viktoria smiled warmly. "I appreciate you indulging me, and of course, thank you for the meal. As one final gesture of good faith, I will share something with you I did not share with the former Lord of Gloomwood. One of your blood thralls, Celia Thornton, has standing orders from Lord Gloomwood to deliver letters to a woman at Hearth's Shadow tavern in your sworn town of Shadowfort. Those letters eventually come to me."

Drake kept his poker face as he remembered his interrogation of his blood thralls for standing orders before he left the manor. Celia's standing order had stood out because of how odd and intriguing it was. She'd taken unknown letters to the tavern Viktoria had mentioned.

"Is that a tavern?"

"Yes, lord." Celia nodded vigorously, looking as frightened as he'd expect her to look. *"I do not know the contents of the letters. I am not allowed to read the letters. The woman who receives the letter is always different, but always greets me by saying 'These moons will turn to ash one day.'"*

"So Celia is one of your spies," Drake said. "In my manor?"

"Celia is not my spy," Viktoria said. "But she does deliver letters that often speak of events inside your manor. The order was first given by the same Lord Gloomwood with whom I formed our covert alliance. I don't know if you've completed a vetting of your blood thralls for standing orders from prior lords, but if you have not, I would suggest you do so."

"And why are you telling me this now?"

"Before your arrival, Celia and her letters were one of the only ways I could slip information about Lord Gloomwood and his activities out of your manor. Now that you're Lord Gloomwood, I felt it best to reveal this to avoid any perception I was working against you in secret. Celia was only following her lord's orders, and I'm trusting you not to punish her."

Drake had already decided to let the letters continue, but he hadn't thought about where they might be going since the cabal had come up shortly after he discovered Celia's nocturnal activities. It was a relief to have an explanation for Celia's odd standing orders, and he understood why Viktoria had wanted the intelligence.

The prior few Lord Gloomwoods had been assholes—Drake knew that from his blood thralls and Sky—so it made sense that Lady Skybreak had kept tabs on their activities to protect herself and her manor if they made any idiotic plays... like trying to summon a leviathan. That was the type of thing Viktoria would have wanted to know about to cover her own ass.

Still, it was interesting Viktoria hadn't passed such a useful resource on to her daughter. Unless she had, and Sky hadn't told him about it. Which made a lot more sense.

"Since we're sharing information, you don't need to worry about Celia," Drake said. "I discovered what she was doing recently and decided to let her continue. I'd set the matter aside given everything else going on, but learning the reason does ease my mind."

Viktoria smiled warmly. "Then I'm glad we spoke before any misunderstandings resulted. Thank you for your time, lord. My daughter is waiting, so I'll bid you good night."

Drake could only nod as Viktoria inclined her head, turned away, and walked confidently toward the flaps leading out of his tent. She really wasn't going to explain why she'd asked about his mother. He decided he wasn't willing to let her leave just yet. He could ask questions in this private meeting, too.

"Lady Skybreak, one moment."

She stopped, then turned. "Yes?"

"Why did you want to know about my mother?"

Viktoria smiled pleasantly. "Your mother is from your realm, lord?"

She hadn't directly answered his simple question. She'd deflected by asking her own. So she was hiding something from him... so how far did he want to push her?

"She is," Drake said. "And as I know of no way I can ever return to my realm, I also don't know any way she could come here. So why the sudden interest?"

"As I said, lord, I merely wished to know a bit about the people who raised you."

"And that's all?" That obviously wasn't all.

"Could I ask you to clarify your question further, lord?"

What *was* he asking? He couldn't compel Viktoria to answer any of his questions. They could do this dance all night without a resolution.

"Do you know of any way to travel between realms?" Drake asked finally.

"I am sorry, lord. I do not know how to travel between realms."

Drake nodded. It had been foolish to hope she might.

"But if you will share it, may I ask your mother's name?"

That set off warning bells in his head. Names had power here. Knowing the name of someone let you cast spells on them or whatever.

But also, you'd need a full name to do that... at least in his world. Just giving Viktoria his mother's first name likely wouldn't give her any power, since "Marissa" was a name shared by hundreds of women back on Earth. Viktoria had also given him her first name.

He could just make something up, but what if, by some weird twist of fate, his mother's real name somehow came up? Viktoria would then know he'd lied about it, which would be bad. He also couldn't stand here considering her question for too long without looking like an idiot. In the end, he decided to go with the simplest solution.

"My mom's name is Marissa. I'd prefer not to share anything else about her."

Viktoria smiled warmly. "Thank you for sharing her with me. Knowing what I do about how difficult it is to raise a child alone, I have no doubt your mother is a strong, capable, intelligent woman. While I know it to be unlikely, I hope you get to see her again someday."

She wasn't going to him what she was really after. He should just accept it and move on with his life. Perhaps Samuel would have some ideas when they discussed this later. Drake was certainly going to run this conversation by him and get his insight.

"Then good night... Viktoria. It was a pleasure speaking with you."

"Good night, Lord Gloomwood." She slipped out of his tent without a look back.

29
SO YOU'RE SAYING THERE'S A CHANCE

With Drake riding in his private armored carriage and Sky in hers, the joint vanguard of Lords Gloomwood and Skybreak finally reached Korhaurbauten early the next morning. With the capital city finally in sight, Drake couldn't resist the urge to pull back the curtains of his carriage to take a look. The Noble Road had gained a lot of additional traffic this morning, and they were far from the only people heading into the capital.

Drake spotted everything from peasants walking on foot to slightly better-dressed peasants riding on wagons to exceedingly well-dressed coachmen driving fancy carriages that looked as ornate and expensive as his own. No one else they passed had a vanguard of armed lizardmen, however. He didn't fail to note that even the most well-dressed coachmen gave his army of zarovians a wide berth, which was probably wise.

Korhaurbauten was, as Lydia had told him, a massive city built along the shore of a huge open bay. The Noble Road was now sloping down to allow his vanguard to travel into the (relatively) shallow bowl that sheltered the city. From up here, he could see the city below laid out in perfect detail. It was absolutely the most impressive city he'd seen in this world.

The huge Alicean Bay was a perfect blue and exceedingly calm, stretching off to a distant horizon where Drake could just make out the top of its C-shape. The shoreline itself was alternately beach and rocky cliffs, with the white foam of breakers just visible at this distance.

What must be hundreds of boats and sailboats dotted the yawning bay, but there was no sign of larger sailing ships or galleons. Lydia had told him the bay was shallow enough that huge sailing vessels couldn't enter without bottoming out. They had to anchor further out. So all of the boats he saw must be local fishermen or boats ferrying people to or from shore.

Most of the buildings directly along the shore of the bay looked to be wooden structures on stilts, while buildings that looked vaguely Mediterranean cropped up as his eyes moved inland. They presented a unified patchwork of red-tiled roofs. Drake had learned there were also waterways crisscrossing the city through which small boats could move and ferry passengers, but the buildings were dense enough he couldn't see those from this angle.

The vast majority of the buildings looked to range between one to three stories, with the castle tower-like outcroppings of some larger stone edifices rising higher than that. Yet despite the wide carpet of buildings below, Drake had no problem spotting the Temple of the Eidolons. It was set in the center of Korhaurbauten and towered over the city.

The temple had to easily be ten stories or higher, and it looked equivalent in size to one of the huge commercial football stadiums back on Earth. It was formed of successive tiered domes, each slightly less wide than the last, featuring rows of dramatic arches that reminded him of some of the famous mosques he'd seen in history books back in grade school.

The biggest difference between the Temple of the Eidolons and the famous mosques he'd seen in pictures was there were no minarets—the skinny towers that typically sprouted up around big mosques—surrounding it. Yet had he seen this city and temple from a distance, he would have assumed it was just another historical Mediterranean town on Earth.

Beside him, Samuel was pouring over more spy reports. However, Drake spotted Lydia also peering out the window. She looked to be enjoying the view almost as much as he was.

"It's an impressive city," Drake said.

"It is, lord." She smiled at him. "Like you, I have never before seen the capital."

"Really?" He hadn't expected to hear that. "You never came here with Lord Crow?"

"The former lords of Gloomwood typically left me to handle matters at the manor when they traveled to Korhaurbauten. However, I know Valentia has traveled here before with Lord Crow, as did..." Her smile faded slightly. "Esme."

Drake remembered that name. Lydia had mentioned Esme only once, revealing that she was Gloomwood's steward before her and that Lord Crow had Esme executed for some slight. It was shortly after Crow executed Esme that Olivia joined Gloomwood Manor.

He didn't want to push Lydia into any painful memories, so he decided to change the subject. "Well, assuming the cabal doesn't completely fuck us over the moment we arrive, we could be here for a few days. Anything you want to do while we're in town?"

She tilted her head in obvious confusion. "What do you mean, lord?"

"Do you want to do any tourist stuff? When we're not dealing with political bullshit?"

Samuel looked up from his spy scroll. "I'm afraid we'll have very little time to explore the city or enjoy its many amenities. The cabal and our negotiations will occupy the majority of our time here. We should return to the manor once those conclude."

Drake frowned at him. "Oh c'mon. You can't tell me we're

going to travel all the way out to your magnificent capital city and not do a little sightseeing."

"I would advise against that. This city is crowded, security outside the temple will be light, and assassins could strike from anywhere."

Samuel was probably right. It was disappointing to accept he couldn't just take a day to tour the capital, but that didn't mean his people had to suffer as well. He doubted anyone would pay a Gilded Blade to kill some random person with a rarity for heating soup.

"So even if I can't go out and tour the city, what harm would there be in allowing Tamara and the maids a day off? Or Hugo and his boys? Or anyone who's not me? I get everyone wants to kill *me*, but there's nothing to be gained by killing any of you."

Samuel tapped his lips. "If you wish to provide the staff with a day of leisure, that would be less risky from a security standpoint. Some could still be taken as hostages by your enemies, so you would need to be prepared to lose them if negotiations went poorly."

Samuel really did prepare for the worst. Drake ruefully shook his head. "Doesn't the city have security? They must have some sort of police force."

"The capital guard handles security within Korhaurbauten itself," Samuel said. "However, given the cabal, the guard will be stationed in and around the Temple of the Eidolons to ensure the security of the manor lords and their thralls. Travel beyond the immediate environs of the temple comes with many risks."

"So what if we paired people up?" Drake asked. "Zarovians and humans? Have people travel in small groups instead of alone, and make sure no one goes off alone. I get there's risk, but there's always risk. There's more risk in having my people die of boredom."

"I'm still not certain—"

"Lydia's never been here before, and I'm sure everyone on the staff would benefit from a little R and R. How long has it been since they got to relax?" Drake was now all the more certain he wanted to let his folks have some time off to enjoy themselves. "Even if I have to be stuck in the temple all day, we should give the others time to explore, shop, and chill in what is the closest thing I've seen on your world to a beachside paradise."

Samuel looked back at his spy scroll. "I still advise against it. However, if you cannot be dissuaded, I will organize such an outing. I do acknowledge the benefit to morale, and pairing zarovians with our people will make them harder to abduct."

"That's the spirit, old man. All work and no play makes Jack..." He paused, then sighed. "Every reference I make to my world goes over your heads. Do you have any idea how depressing that is?"

"The guarded crab dies alone in sand," Lydia said.

Drake glanced at her with fresh interest. "What does that mean?"

"It's a saying where I grew up, lord. I come from a small seaside village, and there, small crabs burrow into the sand where they are safe from predators. Yet they do not remain buried forever. They emerge to forage and even play with one another despite the risk this presents. Some are snatched by birds or other predators while out and about, but they still come out."

Drake smiled. "Because staying buried in the sand for their whole lives is the same as being dead. I like that lesson." He looked to Samuel. "What about you, old man? Got any lessons from your elders or words of wisdom from where you grew up?"

Samuel looked up from his spy scroll. "Trust not the roots of a treacherous tree."

"And what's that mean?"

"A sparse marshland near where I was raised is rife with shallow quicksand. The terrain is difficult to navigate safely, and the unwary often find themselves sinking. However, there are wiry trees with sturdy brown roots throughout the area. Rope trees."

"And I take it these rope trees are... treacherous?

"To an outsider who stumbles into a pocket of quicksand, the strong, sturdy-looking roots of the rope tree offer a way to pull themselves free. Upon grasping them, a toxin secreted by the roots is absorbed through the skin. It causes both euphoria and lethargy."

"Bad trees," Drake agreed.

"Thus, a person who stumbles into quicksand seeks to save themselves by accepting an offer of help from one they do not know. They soon pass out and then drown in shallow quicksand. Had they simply relied upon themselves, they could have escaped."

Drake nodded thoughtfully. "I just got a better understanding of why you think the way you think."

Samuel shrugged. "It is foolish to accept an offer of help when one cannot verify the other party has one's best interest in mind."

"Cynical and paranoid. Just what I need in my spymaster." Drake grinned. "Anyway, we're giving the thralls a free day. Or two. Since you're my paranoia chief, Samuel, I'll let you figure out the best way to organize small parties to minimize the chance of abductions."

Samuel eyed him in placid resignation. "If that is your order."

"And Lydia, how would you feel about taking the maids and Anna out for some fun?"

She frowned. "That would leave you unprotected, lord."

"But we're allied now. Remember? So I could hang out with Sky's bodyguards while you all took Anna someplace to unwind. And then, if Sky's bodyguards wanted to go out, you all could guard Sky in their place so they could do the same. Call it... team building."

Samuel finally appeared interested in the conversation. "While I am not at all in favor of leaving either you or Lord Skybreak so sparsely protected, allowing our thralls to intermix could increase support for a closer alliance. We could test this idea with less important positions."

Drake was feeling ever better about this. "So you're saying there's a chance."

"I would not be comfortable leaving you in the care of Lady Skybreak's thralls, nor, if she is wise, would she trust herself to ours. Yet we could suggest a manor summit at which you and Lord Skybreak could speak about the affairs of your manors over the course of a day. If we are lucky, you might even grow closer as allies."

"And how would that work?"

"For security reasons, it would be wise for the summit to take place in the secure rooms of the temple. If you were together, we could then task one thrall from each of your manors to stand guard over both of you. This would allow the others to explore the city."

"And give me some more time to charm Lord Skybreak with my clever stratagems and keen wit. Now I understand why you're so popular with the ladies."

Samuel watched him placidly. "I would be surprised if Lord Skybreak agrees to a summit, given her extensive responsibilities. But if you wish, I will suggest it to Head Ranger Cask."

"Don't bother," Drake said. "I'll run it by Sky the next time we talk."

"It is likely you may not see Lord Skybreak outside of times set aside for all manor lords to meet at the cabal. She still lacks an experienced steward, and while I am certain her head ranger is helping as best he can, Cask is also doing double duty leading her vanguard."

"All the more reason to find a time when she can relax and get a break from all that," Drake said. "Don't worry about pitching this to Sky. I'll pitch it myself when we have a spare moment. If she shoots me down, no harm done."

Samuel shrugged. "If that is your approach, I leave arranging the summit in your hands."

"Thanks, Samuel. Now, if you had to choose, what place has the best seafood here?"

"We will not be able to visit local restaurants."

"Sure, I get that. But that doesn't mean we can't order out."

30
I HAVEN'T HAD A DROP ALL NIGHT

Once they were actually inside the city, progress slowed significantly. Even though almost no one on the capital's narrow streets had any desire to stand between a vanguard surrounded by armed zarovians, let alone two impatient manor lords, there was only so fast the vanguard could move without rolling over people. Which was *apparently* not allowed.

As they rolled onward, Samuel tapped his chin and leaned forward. "Lord, I have one other suggestion you should consider before we enter the temple."

Drake did his best to be interested. "What's up?"

"You should compel both Lydia and me not to reveal that you can lie."

He hadn't expected to hear *that*. "I can't compel you to do anything."

"That is not correct," Samuel said patiently. "Over the past few days I have considered the ramifications of your decree, and I believe we can still use the blood pact to our advantage. All of your thralls may still *choose* to follow blood pact compulsion of their own volition."

Drake silently considered Samuel's statement and came up with nothing useful. "Yeah, and? Why would anyone do that?"

"If you compel us not to reveal that you can lie to others, we could *choose* to be compelled. That should protect us from revealing the fact that you can speak that which you do not believe... even if one or both of us were to be compelled by an obedience fetish."

Drake's eyes widened. "That's something they can do?"

"Only in cases where they expect a manor lord is not sharing important information," Lydia added quickly. "They do not routinely interrogate thralls or lords."

"Yet it is a risk," Samuel said. "While I have no precedent for how the court would react to the revelation that you can say things you do not believe, we should take all precautions. If you compel us not to speak of such things, we can choose to obey that compulsion. That will improve our security situation."

"I don't like it," Drake said. "I took this job with the understanding I wasn't going to use the blood pact to make you do anything."

Samuel frowned. "You would not be—"

"You'd be choosing to obey, I know." Drake sighed. "It makes sense, and I can see how it might work how you say it will. Do you really think we need to be that paranoid?"

Samuel simply stared at him. The answer was obvious.

"All right," Drake said. "Lydia, Samuel, I compel you not to tell anyone that I can speak words I do not believe." He paused. "Did that do it?"

Samuel nodded in satisfaction. "Based on my understanding of the blood pact, I believe so. We should perhaps confirm by having one of us don an obedience fetish—"

"We aren't doing that," Drake interrupted firmly.

His butler looked almost disappointed. "Then... we shall take other precautions as well."

Drake peered at Lydia. "How do you feel about this?"

"Samuel is right," Lydia said. "We must protect you, and by choosing to accept the compulsion you've given me, I no longer have to worry about being forced to betray your secrets if compelled by other magic. This is a great relief."

"I'm glad you feel that way," Drake said. "I still feel like kind of a jackass."

As they continued toward the Temple of the Eidolons, they still moved at a crawl. They were moving slowly enough that Tamara was able to walk up beside the carriage and deliver lunch when it came time for that, which Drake appreciated. He had read his dossiers on the other manors multiple times by the time his wagon finally slowed.

"We're here?" he asked hopefully.

Samuel pulled back to the curtain to glance outside. "Yes." He'd spent the day reviewing spy scrolls, so it made sense for him to check. "It should be safe to step into the courtyard. We are now in a walled and heavily guarded area reserved for arriving lords."

"Glad that's over. God." Drake rubbed his face. "I'm amazed the manor lords put up with a crawl through the whole damn city without running people over."

"They do not," Samuel said. "A set of streets leading to the temple is always closed off for several days preceding a cabal. This allows manor lords and their vanguards to reach the temple with a minimum of trouble several days ahead of time. The route was closed yesterday since closing the roads causes difficulty. Most manor lords arrived days ahead of time."

Drake groaned. "Yet more fuckery from Lord Proudglade and his three muskadicks. I'm still convinced he got our letters delayed. I can almost appreciate that level of pettiness."

"Remember, that sort of talk must stay inside our carriage or our private chambers," Samuel said firmly. "And I would not speak one ill word about the noble court within these walls. I cannot be sure someone will not overhear, and that would cause us difficulty."

"I know, Samuel," Drake said. "My mouth will be on its best behavior." He glanced at the carriage door as Lydia opened it. "So long as it gets to eat delicious steamed crabs."

Drake expected someone to attack him in the highly secured courtyard. He also expected someone to attack him in the halls of the Temple of the Eidolons, or for assassins to be waiting in the private chambers reserved for him and his thralls. He even expected some sort of magical bullshit to turn his big guest bed into a ravenous flesh-eating monster, but it turned out to be just a bed. A soft, fluffy, comfy bed.

He hadn't slept on one of those in almost a week.

How could he continue to exist in this world if he had to be this damn paranoid? How could he *not* be this paranoid and continue to exist? These were the paradoxes he imagined a manor lord encountered between their twentieth and thirtieth assassination attempts. He had little to do but pace as his servants settled in, and then night came.

Along with the delicious steamed crabs Samuel claimed were the best in the city.

Once Drake was stuffed with crab meat and more than a little buzzed on some delicious intoxicant that was a mix between mead and wine, he was in a considerably better mood than he had been earlier that day. He'd made it to the capital despite the obstacles Lord Proudglade and his cavalcade of assholes had tossed in his way, and he'd gotten Sky here as well.

He hoped Lord Proudglade was still seething about that. Drake would like nothing more than to march up to the man and break his nose, but he'd settle for giving him an ulcer. Once Emily verified no souls were close enough to shoot him and Samuel verified there was no more manor business to conclude, Drake even got to sit outside on the balcony and have a drink.

From up here, at least, the city smelled like salt and stone, with a warm breeze and warmer temperatures to back it up. He only realized how constantly he had been cold when he once again felt truly warm air. While Emily and Lydia both vetoed him removing his silverweave on the balcony—magic could strike him from anywhere—he at least got to kick off his boots and enjoy the feeling of warm air on his feet and toes.

This. This was why he'd decided to become a manor lord. The assassination attempts weren't fun, but he also got his own chambers in the noble temple and a view off a balcony that was only available to privileged SOBs like himself.

From ten stories up, the sprawling city below was laid out before him like a red patchwork blanket leading to the beautiful blue bay. If he could get away with it, he'd toss on a swimsuit tomorrow and go for a swim in that gorgeous blue water. Maybe he could find a way to slip out in disguise and check out the beach before he returned to his cold silver trees.

Drake was sitting barefoot on the balcony, pleasantly buzzed, with Emily leaning contentedly on the balcony railing, when the sound of slippered feet against stone told him he wasn't going to get to relax any longer. It was time for more manor lord bullshit.

He glanced up to find Lydia waiting. "What just exploded?"

"Did you request another meeting with Lord Skybreak?"

"I did not. I'm not quite that stealthy yet."

"She has just arrived and is asking to speak with you. Along with her mother."

Drake straightened in the chair and nearly tipped over his drink. "All right, so, not the worst surprise. And it makes sense to meet ahead of the cabal tomorrow, right?"

"Perhaps. However, I do not know why Lord Skybreak would wish to meet with you in the temple this late. If she had business to discuss with you beyond that which we covered at supper yesterday, she would have stopped us before we entered the city."

"Unless she's just learned something important she had to bring to me at once, despite whatever consternation it might cause among the other manor lords." Drake pulled on his boots. "You'd better show her in."

Lydia still looked somewhat annoyed. "Once the other manor lords learn of your late-night meeting, they will suspect all sorts of conspiracies are afoot."

"That's great! Keeps 'em guessing." Drake looked in disappointment at the city sprawled out below. "Though I guess I'll have to enjoy this view another night."

"Or," Emily loudly suggested, "you could invite Lord Skybreak out here to share some of this lovely mead with you!" She smiled coyly. "And you could enjoy the view together. Grow... closer."

"Stop," he warned her. "This isn't that."

"Isn't what, lord?" Emily's grin only widened. "An unannounced, late-night visit from the beautiful and unattached manor lord you so recently snatched from the jaws of certain doom? Perhaps she has come up to show her gratitude for your bold rescue?"

"Her mother's with her."

"Then perhaps her mother has decided to show you gratitude as well?"

Drake groaned. "No more mead for you tonight, young lady."

Emily chortled as she turned again to look over the city. "Enjoy your date, lord!"

As Drake followed Lydia off the balcony, she led him to a smaller room off his main chambers with a round table and four wooden seats. There were no servants in here and no luggage, so this room was likely reserved specifically for private meetings.

Drake didn't fail to note there was only one way in and out of this room and absolutely no windows. Even this far inside the private rooms set aside for him and his vanguard, security remained as tight as ever. Good. After the last few weeks, he could use some decent security.

"If you'll wait here, lord, I'll admit your guests," Lydia said.

Drake smiled as she turned away. "Finally comfortable enough to leave me alone?"

"Of course not," Lydia said as she strode away. "Nicole is sitting right behind you."

Drake jumped in his chair as Nicole then melted into view and thumped the table with a closed fist. "You absolute traitor!" she called after Lydia. "I was hoping he'd pick his nose!"

He scowled at her. "Well, good evening to you too."

Nicole offered her most impish grin and brushed her brown hair back from her gray eyes. "Thank you for the lovely supper. It really was delicious."

Drake nodded as several things became clear. "Now I know why we were five crabs light on our order. You didn't want to eat with the rest of us?"

"Val needed feeding," Nicole said. "And indulgences."

And now Drake knew why Valentia had missed supper too. He'd assumed she was outside patrolling the halls or watching the doors. Good for them.

He turned back to watch the only door leading into this room. "Well, whatever you've been doing, keep doing that. She needs to relax more than she does."

"Oh, trust me, lord, I know how to melt Val. I get her all gooey."

Drake simply nodded, hoping that would be the end of this discussion.

"Also, do you have any suggestions for prying one's tongue off an ice cube?"

Drake rubbed his face with both hands. "No more mead for you either."

"That's cruel, lord. I haven't had a drop all night."

Drake's savior from awkward conversations, Lord Skybreak, chose that moment to make her approach known by the clicking of her heeled boots. Lydia walked into view and then spun to face the direction from which Drake heard Sky approach.

"He's right in here," Lydia announced.

Nicole pushed back her chair with a loud creak, rose, stretched, yawned, and sauntered around the table. "That's my cue to go be inconspicuous elsewhere. Have fun!"

He waved sarcastically. "You too!"

Drake remembered he should stand a moment before Lord Skybreak rounded the corner, then stared when she arrived. She wore the same silverweave she'd worn at their dinner last night, but it looked like she'd dressed hastily. Only one braid was in any sort of shape to be called a braid, and the rest of her blonde hair was pinned up messily.

Also, he smelled alcohol on her breath. Strong alcohol. She'd been having a good time.

"You've been drinking?" Drake asked before he could stop himself.

She stepped into the small room. "I didn't expect this meeting to occur tonight."

"Oh, it's fine. Me too. I drink. All the time." He nodded to Viktoria as she entered as well. "Lady Skybreak."

"No need for formality," Viktoria told him. "Can we speak freely?"

"Hey, Lydia?" Drake called. "Can we speak freely?"

"Yes, lord!"

"We're good," Drake told them. "What's up?"

Viktoria walked past him, pulled out a seat, and settled herself with all the dignity he would expect of a former manor lord. "You should sit down, lord."

"That bad, huh?" Drake sighed, backed into his seat, and sat. "Lay it on me."

Sky continued to stand, even visibly fidgeting as her gaze alternated between the door, the wall, and her mother. He had never seen her look this out of sorts. Even after he surprised her with Valentia's testimony, she'd only been shocked for a few seconds.

"Lord Skybreak," Viktoria said calmly. "You should sit as well."

Sky scowled, then walked around the table to snatch a seat

facing the door. She pulled it out, plopped down, and crossed her hands in her lap. Drake didn't fail to notice she hadn't looked at him since she first walked into the room.

He focused his attention on Viktoria. "Do I need to call my spymaster for this?"

"If he has not spoken to you yet, then I would expect him to speak to you about this matter shortly after we leave. While I would otherwise take pleasure in knowing my spies outpaced those of the Rope Tree, I take no pleasure in tonight's news."

"You folks call Samuel the Rope Tree?" Drake remembered the story Samuel had told him in the carriage, about a tree that knocked people out with its roots and drowned them in quicksand. "Now I wonder if I should be worried."

"Never about Samuel," Viktoria said confidently. "Not so long as you are Lord Gloomwood. And since my daughter has allied us with Gloomwood Manor, we are obligated to stand beside you in all matters save if you commit an unforgivable crime."

Drake's whole body chilled as Viktoria brushed far too close to the matter he'd thought he'd concluded weeks ago. When he'd lied to Westin and assured the man Lord Crow had passed his title onto Drake before he attempted to summon a demon in the manor's torture dungeon.

This couldn't be about that. He'd solved *that* problem, hadn't he? He'd even planned to deliver his official cover story to the noble court tomorrow before the cabal, so...

"Despite their best efforts, my spies in the capital have been unable to uncover the purpose of this abrupt and unusual cabal," Viktoria said calmly. "However, my spies were able to uncover the *subject* on which the cabal is to be focused."

"Focused?" Drake looked between Viktoria and Sky, then groaned. "It's Gloomwood Manor, isn't it? It's always us. I fucking knew this was going to happen."

Viktoria watched him calmly. "Is there something you wish to share with your allies?"

"I knew this would happen because it's just my luck. Since the moment I arrived, I've had one grenade after another tossed my way. And if I understand what you're telling me, this cabal was called because of something the other manors think we did."

"No, Lord Gloomwood," Viktoria said. "Something you did."

"Something..." Drake paused. "You mean me personally?"

"Yes. This cabal was specifically called to discuss *you*."

31
MAYBE HE JUST NEEDS TO GET LAID

Drake considered this new bombshell in detail for a moment. A long moment. He was really glad he'd sat down. That had been a good suggestion from Lady Skybreak.

Finally, he looked to Sky. "This can't be about what went down at Fort Graystone. The cabal notice went out before that. Maybe it involves our tithe deal over Rodney?"

Sky's eyes met his at last. She shrugged. She still looked more than a bit uncomfortable.

"Is there something else?" Drake asked.

"No," Sky said calmly. "Whatever ambush they have planned for tomorrow, we will weather it as a team. New alliances are first on the agenda at a cabal, so we'll get that out of the way before any other obstacles present themselves."

"So why do you look like you're about to break that chair in half?"

"I'd prefer not to discuss it." Sky straightened. "Now, do you have any idea why five manor lords would all agree to call a cabal to discuss you?"

"I'd prefer not to discuss it" must be this world's version of *"It's*

nothing." Made sense, since people couldn't lie here. Another weird fact to worry about later.

As to why the other manor lords would call a cabal about *him*, Drake had several terrible ideas, including that Westin had somehow not believed he was Lord Gloomwood when he arrived in this world. It was also possible word had somehow gotten back to Lord Redbow that Drake had lied about staying in Captain Ro's camp and then left, or even that there was some new bullshit rule forbidding manor lords from eating their enemies.

Despite being allied with Sky, Drake didn't feel comfortable revealing that he could lie, and he didn't see how it would help either of them. It would simply mean more people who couldn't lie would know his secret power, and worse, it might make Sky trust him less. He had to consider how her opinion of him might change if she knew the truth.

Sky had grown to trust him so quickly because they were the only two manor lords to ever end the compulsion in their blood pacts, and she accepted he was different from Lord Crow because she believed he couldn't lie. He hadn't lied... not to her... but like Lydia, Sky might begin to wonder if he *had* lied once she knew he could do it. This was not the time.

Drake resolved to keep to the truth as best he could. "I can't say why the other lords would call a cabal about me. However, there is one thing that differentiates me from all of you."

Lady Skybreak nodded. "Your origin."

"That's right. I was summoned here from another realm, and as far as I know, I'm the only manor lord who wasn't born here. Could this be some attempt to change the rules so only native-born people can be manor lords? An excuse to take my title?"

"That is one possibility," Viktoria agreed. "Rules can change, and when they must, a cabal is always called. Yet there are no laws stating that a manor lord must be born in this realm, only that they must have divine blood."

"Because it's never come up until now," Drake said. "If it did, in my world, you better bet our politicians would get some law passed against it real fast. Immigration is a tricky enough subject where I come from without factoring in people coming in from whole other universes."

"Changing the bylaws of the noble court is an involved process," Sky said. "It requires agreement from two-thirds of all current manor lords to even begin such a process, and even then, ratification takes years. I can't imagine they'd call a cabal to attempt to disqualify you from being a manor lord unless they already had six votes."

"So do they?" Drake asked. "Four votes are a given. You said Brightwater is leaning their way as well. Who would be the last vote? Ashwind, or Blackmane?"

"Neither benefits from a weak Gloomwood Manor," Viktoria said. "Unless Lord Proudglade or another manor lord has made them guarantees that they will be compensated."

Drake groaned. "*That* sounds plausible. If Lord Proudglade considers the two of us a big enough threat, he might have tossed Blackmane or Ashwind a bribe to sell me out."

"House Blackmane is in a particularly weak position given the division among their thralls," Viktoria agreed. "If any house has bowed to pressure or bribery from Lord Proudglade, it may be them. This is one case where an assassination would be useful."

Sky straightened in her chair. "We agreed we wouldn't do that."

"I'm not saying we should assassinate Lord Blackmane," Viktoria assured her daughter smoothly. "Simply that it could be convenient for us if someone did."

Drake snorted. "It would be convenient if someone assassinated all of them."

The way Sky and her mother frowned at his suggestion made it obvious he needed to clarify his statement. "Which I am also not endorsing!" He raised his hands. "Just saying. Lord Proudglade has no problem sending assassins at me. Seems rude not to return the favor."

"The fact that you have *not* attempted to assassinate Lord Proudglade is one strong point in our favor," Viktoria said. "Ever since the death of the former Lord Brightwater, the current lord has despised all who employ assassins. I suspect the fact that Lord Redbow deals in assassination so freely is why Lord Brightwater has not already joined the big four."

Drake sighed. "If only we could prove Lord Proudglade sent an assassin after me, not once, but twice. But we can't, can we? And while I do have proof of who was behind another assassination attempt on me, I doubt pointing out it was the old Lord Gloomwood will help."

Viktoria's eyes widened noticeably. "The former lord attempted to assassinate you?"

"Yes." He almost added *"Didn't Sky tell you?"* but caught himself. He didn't even know if Sky had revealed their private chats to her mother, though Viktoria obviously knew about the magic mirror. "So if I'm asked to speak tomorrow, should I mention the attempts on my life?"

"Only if they seem pertinent to the discussion," Viktoria said. "Otherwise, I would not bring up mundane conflicts. The other manor lords could simply deny any involvement, and the noble court would not get involved. Some would also see your complaints as weakness."

"In other words, don't cry to teacher when the other kids bully you." Drake ruefully shook his head. "Your world is a lot more like mine than I sometimes remember."

Viktoria glanced at Sky to find Sky looking at a wall. Drake really wanted to know why she seemed so uncomfortable around him at the moment, but now wasn't the time to ask. Viktoria's mask slipped but a moment before she returned her gaze to Drake.

"Now, unless there is anything else you feel we should know

before tomorrow, we should return to our chambers and prepare for tomorrow."

Drake's mind was already whirring with plots and possibilities about tomorrow's cabal, and one worry in particular stood out. From what he'd read about cabals, he knew that in addition to allowing a manor lord who took the floor to demand direct testimony from another manor lord, manor lords could also demand to interview each other's thralls.

That could be bad if anyone asked Samuel or Lydia if he could lie.

But he couldn't go into the cabal tomorrow without an experienced advisor to keep him from falling on his face. He'd get eaten alive by the other manor lords. He'd already compelled Lydia and Samuel not to share his secret, but that might not be enough. He looked up.

"Lady Skybreak, I have a proposal before you leave."

She smiled. "As I said last night, Viktoria is fine when we're in private."

"I know, but I figure I should address you formally for this request." He glanced at Sky. "Lord Skybreak, who do you plan to have with you at the cabal tomorrow?"

The rift between Sky and her mother remained. He didn't know if it extended to Sky refusing to invite her mother tomorrow, but it couldn't hurt to ask. If he pitched this idea to them properly, he might be able to secure an advisor without risking awkward testimony.

Sky raised one eyebrow in obvious curiosity. "Why do you ask?"

"If it's acceptable to you, and to Lady Skybreak... I would like Lady Skybreak to join me in the cabal as my advisor tomorrow. Assuming she won't be advising you."

Sky's curiosity was immediately replaced with visible suspicion. "That's an odd request. Don't you trust your own advisors?"

"I do, but given what we've just learned about the focus of

tomorrow's cabal... there's something else I'm going to need them to handle." *Like not being available to testify.*

"Such an arrangement would not be entirely unprecedented," Viktoria said thoughtfully. "Allied manors have and do share resources as a part of their operations. My appearance as your advisor could also demonstrate the strength of our alliance to the other manor lords." Viktoria looked to Sky. "Unless you wish me to join you tomorrow."

Sky looked between them. "I see no problem with this. I have no need of an advisor for the cabal. If you'd like to have my mother advise you, Lord Gloomwood, I'll allow it."

So either Sky agreed it was a good idea to show a strong alliance in front of the other manor lords, or she hadn't planned to have her mother along to advise her anyway. Either one worked out well for Drake. He looked to Viktoria.

"Then, Lady Skybreak, I would request you join me as my advisor at tomorrow's cabal."

"I accept your proposal." Viktoria rose. "Now, we really should be going."

Drake stood as well. "Thanks for the head's up about all this. I don't know what we'll run into tomorrow, but it's reassuring to know we'll face it as allies. My steward will show you out."

Lydia arrived on cue, suggesting she'd been listening to the whole conversation from outside the room. He assumed both Viktoria and Sky would be fine with that. They had to assume he'd share all the pertinent details with his advisors anyway after they left.

He half hoped Sky would stop and explain whatever was bothering her after her mother left, but she walked past him with scarcely a glance. Something was *definitely* bothering her, something that hadn't been bothering her when they clasped arms in Fort Graystone. Given how pleasant she'd been at dinner yesterday night, it must have happened recently.

Was it simply knowing she'd allied with a manor lord who was now the focus of a whole goddamned cabal? Did she regret her haste in allying with him so quickly? Or had her own spies caught wind of some of the same rumors as Lady Skybreak's spies and now she had doubts?

Maybe one of the Rope Tree's spies would have some clue as to what was going on in Skybreak Manor, and why Sky would have gone from warm to chilly toward him overnight. He hoped he hadn't inadvertently said something that would offend her, but since they hadn't *talked*, that remained unlikely. It was more likely she'd learned something she didn't like.

Once Lydia returned, Drake looked around for Samuel and saw no sign of him. "Hey, you seen the old man recently?"

"He stepped out shortly after supper," Lydia said. "I'm not sure when he'll return."

"Did he say why?"

"No, lord." Lydia frowned. "I will advise him to inform you before he leaves again, and to ensure he tells you what he plans to do."

"I don't need to hover over Samuel. It's a beach town. Maybe he just needs to get laid."

Lydia cocked an eyebrow. "Is that more slang, lord?"

He chuckled. "Yes, but it's probably not suitable for you."

32
THIS IS NOT A SEX THING

Lydia considered him for a moment. "Is that a euphemism for sex?"

Drake grinned. "Nothing gets past you."

"I see." Lydia pondered. "Though you may not be aware of this, Korhaurbauten is known for the quality of its courtesans. It is late, but I could arrange one for you tonight if you wish."

Drake damn near choked on his next swallow, then stared at her. "Are you serious?"

Lydia seemed confused by his surprise. "The matter will stay between us, of course."

"Uh, no." Drake cleared his throat. "I don't need you to hire me a courtesan." If he remembered his history correctly, a courtesan was a high-class sex worker. Did Lydia really think he was that eager to get laid?

She tilted her head. "Have I offended you, lord? If so, I apologize for overstepping. Are liaisons with courtesans frowned upon in your world?"

"In parts of it, though it's stupid," Drake said. "To be clear, I've never had a problem with consenting adults being consensual, but… isn't that a huge security risk?"

"Those who are approved to become courtesans in Korhaurbauten are registered in the city roster, cannot possess rarities, and are selected for their talent and discretion," Lydia said. "Moreover, they must state they will not harm you before entering your presence. Finally, I or another maid will be close by in case you encounter trouble, typically in the next room."

He genuinely couldn't tell if Lydia was dead serious about this or if this was the most elaborate joke she'd managed to come up with since they'd met. Either way, the idea of banging a professional while all his battle maids listened through the wall was not appealing, and it wasn't even due to performance concerns. It would just be *weird*.

"Thanks for, uh… thinking about my needs." Drake managed a grin that was almost convincing. "You haven't offended me. I just don't need any distractions right now."

"Of course, lord." Lydia inclined her head. "Now, what will I be doing tomorrow?"

"Right." He was all too glad to get back to the problem at hand… she couldn't lie. "Given we now know the cabal is going to be focused on me, I'm concerned about having you and Samuel anywhere near the temple tomorrow. You understand why, don't you?"

"I do. We should not be available to testify."

"So how about the two of you take Anna out for a trip around the town? Maybe bring Tamara and another maid along? In plain clothes?"

Lydia raised an eyebrow. "And do what, lord?"

"See the sights," Drake said. "Get Anna some cookies, or whatever treats they have here that a little girl would like. I don't have a particular preference for what you get up to, but do it anonymously and avoid the capital guards. It's important you can't be found."

Lydia smiled thoughtfully. "I think Anna will very much enjoy this trip."

"To be clear, I expect you to enjoy it too."

She raised one eyebrow. "Is that an order, lord?"

"Absolutely. Go see the sights you've always wanted to see, get all the delicious food you can eat without falling over, and maybe see if you can make Samuel crack a smile."

"I will do my best." Lydia looked genuinely pleased by this idea. "Now, if you wish, you can return to the balcony or retire. I will inform Samuel of our plans when he returns."

Drake was actually more tired than he expected. A good night's sleep in a big soft bed would do wonders. He was just about to agree when a fresh and very devious thought hit him.

"Hey, hold up."

She paused halfway to the door and turned back around. "Yes, lord?"

"I'm going to ask you a couple of awkward questions now, and I don't want you to take them the wrong way. When you say this city has the best courtesans, how many are there?"

She eyed him curiously but without obvious judgment. "I would estimate there are easily a hundred within the capital, lord. There are multiple pleasure houses specializing in all sorts of preferences. But you said you did not need a distraction tonight."

"Stay with me here. Are there also male courtesans?"

Her eyes widened with understanding. "Of course, lord! Now I understand your earlier hesitance. I will—"

"Stop right there," Drake cautioned. "To be clear, I like girls, and that also has *nothing* to do with why I'm asking this. If I sent you out tonight, would it be possible to recruit a female courtesan and male courtesan for an all-day engagement tomorrow? Do they do those?"

Lydia nodded thoughtfully. "I could arrange for such, lord, though it would be considerably more expensive. But won't you be rather busy tomorrow?"

Drake rolled his eyes. "Judging from that smirk, you already know what I'm thinking."

"That you wish me to find a courtesan with long dark hair who is approximately my height, weight, and proportions?"

Drake grinned as she finally caught on... he hoped. "And *purely* for a platonic engagement. Just in case that wasn't clear. This is not a sex thing." He paused at her placid expression, then raised his hands. "This is not a sex thing!"

"Of course not, lord." Lydia could scarcely hide her amusement at his consternation. "And the male courtesan should also resemble Samuel?"

"At least in the body. We'll get him a hood. And get veils for our battle maids."

"While I believe I can fulfill your request, I am curious as to why you wish to engage in such complicated subterfuge. Do you wish to present our manor at full strength?"

"That's one benefit, but I actually have another reason." When he told her, she nodded with understanding. She even looked pleased.

"Now, the second question is more sensitive, and it's all right if you say no. Are you comfortable with whatever courtesan we professionally engage borrowing your uniform?"

"If that is what you wish, I will offer it," Lydia said. "However, we do have regular uniforms that look identical to those worn by me and your other battle maids. So if it is simply a matter of making the courtesan appear as one of us, those will do."

"Good enough," Drake agreed. "No need for you to let her borrow your uniform then. Though... you'll probably still want to wear a different outfit out and around town. Do you have any silverweave outfits that will protect you but don't scream Gloomwood battle maid?"

"We all do," Lydia assured him. "While I do not have a tremendous amount of covert field experience, since I am primarily needed to run the manor, I am more than capable of blending into the population of the capital. I will not be found."

"Then that's your covert mission for tomorrow. You have four objectives. One, don't be found. Two, fill Anna with sweets. Three, make Samuel crack a smile. And four—"

"See whatever I wish to see," Lydia finished with a soft smile. "Thank you, lord."

Even if he hadn't been worrying about one of the other manor lords asking her awkward questions tomorrow, he loved this idea. "If anyone has earned a day off, it's you. As for getting in touch after..." Drake pondered, then nodded. "Follow me to my room."

Lydia followed without question, and Drake entered his private room which was, unfortunately, without a balcony. A balcony and a portal to that warm sea air would be nice, but the upside of not having a balcony was less nighttime visits from assassins. He walked to the reading desk where he'd stowed his magical box when he arrived.

"Earth."

The box popped open, and Drake pulled out the magical mirror he'd used to communicate with Sky. "Take this with you tomorrow. Sky has the other half. Once night falls, find somewhere you can lay low and check for us to contact you every hour or so. That way I can contact you without knowing where you are, and no one can follow me to you."

"You seem remarkably well-versed in spycraft, lord," Lydia said appreciatively. "Do you have prior experience in your world?"

"I just watched lots of spy shows over the past few years. More of those stories we tell to entertain. And I had way too much time to read Samuel's spy books during that agonizing trip through the city. Now, do you have any suggestions or things I've overlooked?"

She tapped her lips and thought for a moment. "I do not. Your plan is sound."

"Nice. Thanks."

"With your permission, I will leave at once to engage the courtesans you requested. We will need to pay an extra fee for discretion, but there are routes throughout the city and within this temple that are ideal for covertly allowing exit and entry."

"So not everyone knows who the visiting manor lord has warming his bed."

"That is one use for such passages, lord. They are staffed by capital guards, however, who are also sworn not to reveal what they see to anyone, save the noble court. So our doubles can arrive undetected without issue."

"That's perfect. The cabal is going to start a few moments after second bell tomorrow?" He was still getting used to the fact that they didn't have precise times here. He did know the city rang huge bells to announce daily events, but the book hadn't offered a list of them.

"Correct, lord. I will request our courtesans arrive at our rooms at first light. That should provide more than enough time to outfit them however you see fit."

"That's perfect. You're cleared for launch."

She paused. "That does mean you wish me to go, doesn't it?"

"Yes. Thanks. And be careful."

"I always am." She strode out of the room, once again all business and determination.

Once Lydia left, Drake was finally alone in his big warm room with his big, warm bed. All alone. He knew Valentia, Nicole, and Emily were all right outside the door, and one would be on watch the whole night, so he knew he could finally relax... but he found he couldn't.

It still bothered him that Sky had seemed so standoffish tonight. It wasn't like he'd had his heart set on dating her, but it *had* been nice to have someone close to his own age who understood what he was dealing with. He only now realized how much he'd liked having those nighttime chats with her about their duties as manor lords. It was a way to feel sane.

He hadn't even asked if she wanted to do a summit so their thralls could go have a day on the town. He'd been too focused on racking his brain for why five manor lords, the minimum number who must agree to call a cabal, had called a cabal to discuss *him*.

Lydia's offer to hire him a courtesan had also thrown him for a loop. He hadn't expected to suddenly feel this lonely. He'd been too busy trying not to die to *feel* lonely.

He had mentally vowed from the moment he decided he was going to command this manor that all relationships with the people who served him would remain professional. He was not Lord Blackmane. Yet Lydia's offer to hire him a courtesan, just like when Samuel had blatantly tried to marry him off to Sky, was another reminder of how alone he was here.

As much as he trusted and cared for his people, he was their lord. A line in the sand had to remain between a leader and his followers. It would also be difficult to maintain friendships with anyone who wasn't working for him, at least if he wanted to avoid undercover assassins, and it would *definitely* be impossible to date without some absolutely mood-killing limitations.

It wasn't like he didn't want some sexy times once he wasn't in danger of being killed. He wasn't a monk. He was a dude. A dude who, apparently, had only one real prospect who might *already* be reconsidering her alliance with him.

Still... as problems went, a lack of dating options was the least of his. Another cup or two of that delicious wine/mead would solve the loneliness issue for tonight. He'd need to do one last skim of Zuri's dossiers as well, which would definitely put him to sleep.

Tomorrow would be his first cabal as the lord of Gloomwood Manor, and given all the trouble his enemies had gone through to stop him and Sky from being here, he was more determined than ever to fuck over every last one of them.

33
DO NOT OVERSHARE

Despite not falling asleep until early in the morning, Drake woke before dawn and couldn't get back to sleep. He was simultaneously excited and nervous about his first cabal. Excited because he finally had a chance to directly confront the manor lords who had attacked him, and nervous because he worried they had traps he wasn't prepared for.

Simply passing his hand over a lightly glowing metal tile on the wall caused four metal lamps to ignite on four sides of the room, giving him light in the otherwise entirely dark room. Korhaurbauten had useful magic items. The door to his private sleeping chamber was closed, so Drake dressed for the day and pondered taking one last look at his dossiers.

The thought of shoving his face in those books again made him feel physically unwell. He'd done enough reading for this trip. There was nothing he could do to prepare himself for today that he hadn't done already, so he simply had to keep his mind clear and focused until second bell. That would ring a few hours after sunrise.

As they'd discussed last night, Drake knocked on the door to his private chambers before unlocking the door. A moment later, he got a response.

"It's just horrible out here!" Nicole called from the other side of the door. "It's so dark and cold. Just think about how nice and fluffy your warm bed—"

Drake opened the door and stepped out, which caused Nicole to sigh and turn to him in disappointment. "Why did you not listen to my warning?"

"Because I'm hungry. You?"

"Vexed. Any chance you could sleep until it's Emily's turn to guard you? We have wine. I'll get you wine."

"Nope, I'm up." As he closed the door, Drake was pleased to annoy *her* for a change. "How was the night shift?"

"Uneventful."

"Well, good job standing guard."

"Standing in one spot is one of my many skills." Nicole fell in beside him as he wandered for the kitchen. "Meryl will not be preparing breakfast until first light."

"That's fine. I'll just grab a pastry."

"There is a problem with that, lord."

"What?" Drake frowned at her. "You can't tell me the pastries are poisoned."

"If they were, we would all be very dead."

Drake groaned. "You ate them? All of them? There were like twenty of those things!"

Nicole now looked genuinely abashed. "Emily assisted! She ate more than me!"

"Wow," Drake said. "Way to throw your fellow battle maid under the bus."

"Emily pressured Val and me to join her in eating pastries so she wouldn't feel guilty. We were only supporting her as we all support each other!"

"And your sweet tooth," Drake reminded her. "So I guess I'll just have... bread." And maybe some jam if he could find it.

Drake wandered into the small private kitchen included with the rooms set aside for his manor and found it all but spotless. His people were efficient as always. He rummaged through the cupboards as quietly as he could manage, hoping not to wake anyone up.

Valentia wandered into the kitchen with a yawn. "Are we preparing breakfast already?" She then stopped, eyes narrowed at Drake. She wore a thin shift and little else.

Drake stared in involuntary and acute shock before immediately turning to face the cupboards. "Morning! Val." He busied himself searching the labels on small jars.

"You are awake." Valentia sounded equally surprised and annoyed by this revelation.

"Woke up early. Couldn't get back to sleep. Was going to eat a pastry for an early morning snack, but apparently my battle maids got very hungry overnight." Why was he explaining himself?

"It's *really* hot in the capital!" Nicole explained unnecessarily, which had absolutely nothing to do with Drake's current dilemma. "Val has trouble staying cool even back in Gloomwood, so you're just lucky she wasn't walking around na—"

"Do not overshare," Valentia interrupted firmly. Though Drake wasn't looking, he was pretty sure she was glaring ice shards at Nicole. "I will leave you to your breakfast, lord." He assumed, by the silence that followed, that Valentia had left the kitchen to get dressed.

Drake took a deep, calming breath. This was like living in a college sorority house as the only dude, which, a few years ago, would have been his absolute dream. The problem was, he was also the head of the college in this absurdly inappropriate metaphor, which made what would have been otherwise thrilling accidental interactions awkward as fuck.

When he turned the next jar around, he saw that it was clearly labeled as peach preserves. Sweet! That would make the bread a little more palatable. He pulled it out of the cupboard and was relieved to find himself once more alone with a fully dressed Nicole.

With focus, he popped the lid on the jar of peach preserves. The true power of a manor lord. "Did Lydia and Samuel ever make it back last night?"

"Samuel returned shortly after you went to bed," Nicole said. "Lydia a few hours later. Both still sleep, which is what *normal* people do before the sun has risen."

Drake knew Lydia must have been successful in hiring his courtesans. She would never have come back otherwise. That improved his mood. He couldn't wait to see the expression on Lord Proudglade's face when that fucker finally figured it out.

He found a fresh loaf of bread easily, but he had nothing to cut it with and didn't want to just rip it apart. That would get crumbs everywhere. "Where can I find a knife?"

"Drawer to the left," Nicole said.

Drake opened it to find a wide variety of napkins.

"Your other left," she added.

He only now caught how she'd phrased her response. *The* left, not *your* left. She'd been fucking with him, again. "For future reference, that is your left, not mine."

She smiled innocently. "Isn't that what I said?"

A short time later, Drake had two slick slices of bread lumped with peach preserves which, as he bit into one, was definitely *not* one of the delicious pastries he'd sampled last night after he was full of steamed crab. This wasn't bad, though. He chewed thoughtfully.

Nicole thumped down beside him and rested her elbows directly on the counter. "How did your midnight meeting with Lord Skybreak go? Lydia wouldn't tell me anything."

A reminder of Sky's standoffishness last night dampened the rush of satisfaction he'd had after learning Lydia had acquired his courtesans. "They just had some information for me. We could be in for some real fuckery today at the cabal." Drake shrugged. "But what else is new?" He took a big bite of his peach-preserve-covered bread.

"I hope it's an exciting day," Nicole agreed. "The gossip has certainly been interesting."

Drake glanced at her. "You have gossip?"

She pouted in disappointment. "Do *I* have *gossip*. You truly are grumpy this morning."

"You ate all my pastries. Now tell me what you've heard."

"Well, to start, the town is abuzz with news that the new Lord Gloomwood and Lord Skybreak will announce an alliance between your manors. There's even talk of a marriage."

Drake grimaced. Nicole had to be fucking with him again, except... this wasn't doublespeak, and she couldn't lie. And telling him the truth fucked with him more.

"Rumors a manor merger is in the works have already taken hold across the capital," Nicole continued. "In fact, some gossip claims that Lord Skybreak has fallen hopelessly in love with the dashing young lord of Gloomwood Manor. A man who rescued her and ensnared her with his devilish charms."

Drake sighed heavily and set back what was left of his toast. "That explains that."

"Explains what?" Nicole asked eagerly. "I wish things explained."

"I can't imagine Sky's thrilled with having the entire capital claiming she's some lovestruck little girl wrapped around the finger of another manor lord." Sky's visible discomfort with him last night finally made sense. "That sort of gossip would piss me off."

Nicole tilted her head. "So she has soured on the idea of our alliance?"

"No, she's still on board, she just seemed awkward last night. Probably because she assumed I'd already heard the gossip about her being head over heels in love with me." Drake popped the last of his peach bread in his mouth. "At least the city says I'm dashing."

"If it helps," Nicole said, "most of this city doesn't know what it's talking about."

Drake side-eyed her.

"Though Lord Skybreak *is* quite dashing," she added with a coy smile.

"I'm telling Val you said that."

"Oh, she agrees with me! If you two get married, we have already agreed who to ogle."

Emily chose that moment to wander into the kitchen wearing even less clothing than Valentia, eyed the two of them while barely awake, and then walked out without another word.

"I did suggest you stay in bed," Nicole said smugly.

Drake honestly didn't even care any longer. "Just tell me when the courtesans get here."

He expected Nicole to make another joke about that and was almost disappointed when she didn't. Given he had no idea where his battle maids and servants were and who was actually dressed, he decided to hang out in the kitchen until the sun rose. Fortunately, Emily re-entered in full battle maid attire not long after she left.

"Morning, lord!" Emily said cheerily. "Did you sleep well?"

"I slept alright," he agreed. "Did you enjoy your pastries last night?"

"Oh yes. I was going to save you one, but then I remembered I was hungry."

He motioned with his head. "Want to clear the balcony for me?"

"At once, lord!" She strode out with new purpose.

Once Emily had once again verified no souls were anywhere in evidence that could shoot him on a tenth-floor balcony, Drake walked out and sat down just as the first faint blush of red began to color the dark sky and tint the blue water. The sunrise was already gorgeous.

Emily took up her protective position at the railing, where she could keep an eye out for any souls that shouldn't be nearby. Not long after Drake settled himself, soft footfalls announced Lydia's return. She, thank the Eidolons, was fully dressed.

Lydia grabbed a seat and settled herself beside him. "All is prepared."

Having a steward this competent was a benefit he was never going to take for granted. "Nice. Did you hear how dashing the capital thinks I am?"

"I can certainly understand why Lord Skybreak would be annoyed by the rumors regarding her romantic relationships. However, I doubt she blames you for loose talk in the capital. I wouldn't worry about her commitment to our alliance."

"I'm not worried. I just hope she doesn't think we started those rumors. Did you tell Anna the good news about today?"

Lydia smiled. "I did not feel it right to wake her. But I will let her know once she rises."

"And when Samuel got back last night, did he have anything to tell you?"

"Only that he continues to gather information with his spies. He, too, has learned of the purpose of the cabal. He seemed rather cross Lady Skybreak's spies beat him to it."

Drake grinned. "Good reminder for the old man to step up his game."

"He also agrees with your caution for today, though he is not thrilled with the idea of us all freely wandering the city."

Before Drake could say anything, Lydia spoke again.

"I eased his doubts. Your plan is sound, and he eventually accepted it."

Of course she had. "Thanks, Lydia."

She offered a warm smile in response and then looked to the rising sun.

As the sun rose, it tinted the once-blue bay the color of blood. The sight of a bay-sized expanse of human blood was not the best omen for today's cabal, unless, of course, Drake visualized it as the blood of his enemies. In which case, it was fucking metal.

Valentia joined them on the balcony as the sun continued to rise, but Nicole did not. She must be watching the door. Despite how much she vexed him sometimes... or most times... Drake appreciated her taking one for the team.

No one spoke as the sun crept upward and a line of light marched inevitably across Korhaurbauten. Light turned the dark roofs below to a bright crimson. They all watched as the first tiny dots of boats set out for the day. From up here, they were rice grain-sized specks of white that spread across the bay as the water faded from red to orange to a brilliant blue.

Next the great bells of the capital tolled, the audible signal that would announce the start of a new full day for many in the city. Drake knew from his reading that not everyone in the city had the luxury of eternally burning magic lights. Therefore, those who didn't take advantage of every moment of daylight would quickly fall behind.

A faint knock sounded just before Lydia rose. "Those would be our courtesans, lord."

Drake stood as well. "Great. Let's go see how you made out yesterday night."

Emily grinned wide. "You sent Lydia off to round up some courtesans?" She gave Lydia a hearty slap on the back. "You should get one for you too. It's time to end that dry spell."

Lydia cleared her throat *very* loudly. "Would you kindly go don your veil?"

"Is that an order, mistress?"

Lydia offered her a narrowed gaze. "What do you think?"

34
DO I MEET YOUR APPROVAL, LORD?

Emily hurried off to the nearby servant rooms, still grinning to herself. Once they entered the main room where guests were greeted, Lydia stood at Drake's side as Valentia opened the door. Two people stood outside, both dressed in heavy robes that obscured their sex. One was slim, however, and the other obviously much bigger.

"I am a courtesan from Lark House here at the request of Lord Gloomwood," the slim woman said quietly. Her soft, breathy voice was absolutely lovely. "I have no intent to harm him, and I have come to offer the services requested by his steward. May I come in?"

Valentia gave her a once over and nodded.

The man repeated the same words, though he was from "Fox House." Their words removed any chance they were assassins sent to get massacred by Drake's battle maids. As the woman entered she pulled back her heavy hood, and Drake was struck by just how much she looked like Lydia. The resemblance was remarkable.

Her nose was a bit more narrow, and her bust might be a bit bigger, but otherwise she was practically Lydia's twin. She was also rather gorgeous. Not to say that Lydia wasn't also gorgeous, but she was Lydia. This woman was *available*. Drake reminded himself he had no time for distractions today.

Once the man entered, he walked up to stand by the woman and pulled back his hood. His similarity to Samuel wasn't nearly as close—he lacked a beard, as it would be impossible to grow one overnight—but his build was similar enough he could pass wearing a hooded cloak. They could use some charcoal to darken his chin to give the *appearance* of a beard.

Once they were both inside and the door was closed, both courtesans bowed low and waited for him to acknowledge them. He allowed that. He didn't want to freak them out.

"Rise," Drake said. "We'll speak again once you're properly attired for today's business." He glanced at Valentia. "Take these two to the servant's quarters so they can get changed for today."

"At once, lord," Valentia said.

After Valentia had led off two people who were dead ringers for his blood thralls, Drake glanced at Lydia. "How long did you have to look to find these two?"

"Not very long. As I said, all courtesans in the city are registered, and this information includes their height, weight, and proportions, as well as the services they offer."

"Right." Drake worked very hard not to *think* about those services. "Well, again, great job."

They stood for as long as it took Emily to return wearing a veil, just as Lydia had ordered. While Emily currently had her veil lifted up over her head, he could see that it would easily obscure her facial features once lowered. It would be perfect for their courtesans.

"May I leave you with Emily?" Lydia asked. "I need to prepare for today's outing."

He nodded. "Just don't forget sunblock."

"What is that, lord?"

He hoped she didn't get too terribly sunburned. "Never mind."

As Lydia moved off, Emily sidled up beside him. "So who will you have guarding you at today's cabal, lord?"

He glanced her way. "You, of course."

The amount of pleasure on Emily's face was slightly terrifying.

"As I mentioned, Lady Skybreak will be with us as well," Drake continued. "As will Val. Nicole volunteered to guard our chambers, which I think just means she doesn't want to go."

Nicole would also spend today whipping Robin, Gaby, and Carl into shape as warriors, which he suspected she would enjoy immensely. He just hoped she wouldn't literally "play with the puppies." He at least trusted she wouldn't actually harm them.

Emily's smile dampened a little. "So you're inviting everyone but Lydia and Nicole."

"Yes, but you're going to be my guardian."

Her face lit up again. "No one will get past me, lord!"

From what he'd read about cabals, a manor lord could bring up to six thralls with them during the meeting, but could only designate one as his guardian. That person was the only thrall allowed to have a weapon in the council chamber (other than the manor lords themselves) and would be entrusted with the defense of the entire party.

Valentia didn't need a weapon to destroy people, and Emily could slice through souls with her spectral battle axe. Between them, he'd have significant threats at both range and up close. And since a manor lord was allowed to bring his own weapon, he was bringing Magnum.

He knew from his reading that most manor lords went with smaller personal weapons at cabals, such as enchanted knives or magical swords, but Drake didn't have any of those. Besides, he'd always been more of a "go big or go home" guy, and he'd simply feel better with his four-shot repeating crossbow in his personal manor lord box. Fuck fighting anyone up close.

Not long after, Valentia emerged from the back room, also wearing a veil, followed by "Lydia" and "Samuel." As Drake looked the female courtesan over, he was impressed. Dressed in a replica battle maid outfit with her veil obscuring her features, her height, figure, and dark hair almost made him wonder if Lydia was pulling a fast one on him.

"Samuel" was slightly less convincing—from up close, anyone could tell his beard wasn't real—but Drake knew the boxes that separated the manor lords to be distant enough from each other that no one could tell unless they entered his box. He didn't wear a veil, but he did wear a fine cloak with a hood that would shadow his features. It would have to work.

Once the thralls arrived, "Lydia" bowed, then rose. "Do we please you, lord?"

That was a question Drake was going to answer as platonically as possible. "You look just as I hoped. However, no bowing from this point on. My thralls don't do that."

"Of course, lord," Lydia said calmly.

She even *sounded* like Lydia. Could she do voices?

"Samuel" cleared his throat. "Do I meet your approval, lord?"

The man's voice was a silky baritone that Drake suspected would be supremely popular with just about anyone who liked men, however, he spoke more crisply than Samuel. Drake couldn't completely pin down the difference, but if he had to guess, he'd say Samuel sounded a bit more folksy. This guy sounded more like a nobleman.

"You look fine," Drake said. "However, I won't need you to speak today, so I'd like you both to remain silent unless you're unclear about your duties or I ask you a question."

Both courtesans nodded. Neither answered his question with speech. They were quick on the uptake, but he imagined people who made their living catering to rich folks had to be.

"Now, how should I address you today?" He didn't ask *what are your names* because that question, coming from a manor lord, would demand information they might not be comfortable giving him. Names had power in this world.

"I would be pleased if you would refer to me as Lark, lord," the woman said.

"And you may call me Fox, lord," the man added.

So, they were named for their courtesan houses. That must be how they commonly addressed each other unless ordered to do so in some other manner. It would work just fine.

"Has my steward explained your responsibilities for today?"

"Only that we are yours for the day and are to obey your every command, lord," Lark said. Fox nodded to agree with her.

"Good." Lydia hadn't mentioned the specifics of what they'd talked about so news couldn't spread. "For now, my commands are simple. We're going to all relax here until the second bell rings, at which point we'll leave this room and head to the cabal."

Neither courtesan spoke, but Fox visibly stiffened in a way that suggested he was freaked out. Drake wondered if either of these people had ever been to a manor lord cabal. He doubted it, but he also suspected they handled more harrowing situations every day.

Drake pointed to his Emily, who waved. "Lark, when we leave, you will walk ahead of me and directly beside Emily here. Don't worry if you don't know where we're going. Just keep an eye on her and follow her lead. Also, if anyone asks you any questions, don't answer. You can tell them I ordered you not to speak if they insist, but nothing other than that."

Lark inclined her head to show she understood.

"Fox, you'll walk just a bit behind me," Drake said. "Keep your hood up and your face down, but not in a subservient manner. More like you're watching the floor for traps."

Fox again nodded his understanding.

"Same orders for you. No talking other than to tell people I said you can't talk. When we get to the cabal, Lark, you'll sit to my left, and Fox, you'll sit behind me and to the left. Finally, during the cabal, I may lean over and speak to either of you quietly. Simply nod or respond as you see fit. It doesn't really matter what we say to each other, only that we do it quietly."

Both courtesans nodded to show they understood.

"Now, you're both free to relax until second bell tolls. There should be a cool pitcher of wine in the kitchen. You're welcome to have a cup if it'll take the nerves off, but don't step out on the balcony or anywhere anyone can see you."

Fox inclined his head and immediately headed for the kitchen. News that he was heading to a cabal full of ruthless manor lords must have unnerved him a little, which was an understandable reaction. Lark, however, remained where she was.

"You can relax," Drake assured her. "It's not a trick. I'm fine if you have a glass of wine."

"I understand, lord," she said quietly. "But if you will forgive my presumption, I have a matter I hoped to discuss with you before we leave."

Emily leaned in with a visible frown. "What's all this about?"

Drake raised a hand to stop his murdermaid from doing something violent. Lark had been unfailingly polite and made it clear she wouldn't harm him. He also suspected asking to speak to a manor lord required a significant amount of bravery, given how dickish most were.

"We have a few minutes before second bell," Drake said. "What did you want to talk about?"

Lark gratefully inclined her head. "It concerns my brother Darion, lord. His rarity allows him to mend flesh. If you seek a healer for your manor, I would beg you consider him."

A rarity to mend flesh sounded extremely useful. It also sounded like a rarity one of the other manor lords would have snapped up already if they could. There had to be a reason this guy wasn't already with another manor, but Drake was curious enough to want to learn more.

"Why ask me?"

He expected the question to throw her, so was surprised when Lark answered immediately and as confidently as if she'd expected him to ask.

"Courtesans of Lark House speak often with those who work in the temple. Those who work in the temple speak with those who work with manor lords, including your own thralls. To a one, your thralls have spoken of how different you are from prior lords they've served."

That immediately worried him. "Different how?"

"They say you are fair to your thralls," Lark said. "That you reward loyalty and do not torture or execute those who displease you. It is also said you have held memorials for fallen thralls. That is unheard of among most manor lords."

So his people weren't telling others he'd removed the compulsion of the blood pact, only talking up him and his manor in generic terms. Drake was pleased his efforts to change how his people perceived him were already bearing fruit. He might not even need to recruit new people to join his manor because his people would recruit for him.

Just like with companies back in his world, employees talked about the boss and culture with one another... and whether the boss was an asshole. If he'd behaved like Lord Crow since he arrived, he likely never would have gotten the chance to recruit this "Darion."

Lark continued. "My brother is now nineteen and has, thus far, managed to avoid being conscripted into a manor by remaining here in the capital. However, Lord Redbow is now aggressively pursuing him. The lord has given him a week to agree to join Redbow Manor before he escalates to firmer measures."

Drake knew exactly what that meant. "So Darion would like to work for me instead."

"Yes, lord." Lark bowed her head. "If you would simply agree to interview him, I'm certain you would find his rarity has value."

This was a no-brainer. Drake could get a second healer for his manor, help out Lark, and fuck over Lord Redbow by stealing his talent. It was a win/win/win. "Have him report to my chambers tomorrow morning. I'll interview him. If I like him, he's in."

Lark's gasp of delight actually made him tingle. This woman was *definitely* a talented courtesan. "Thank you, lord!" She looked as if she'd expected to drown and ended up getting a warm bath instead. "Now, if you'll permit me, I think I'll have some of that wine."

Drake motioned with one hand. "You're dismissed."

Soon after Lark left, the second bell tolled. It was time to head out to the cabal. If all went well tomorrow, Drake might have another healer for his manor.

But he still had to get through today without losing his title as manor lord.

35
IT IS CERTAINLY AN IMPRESSIVE WEAPON

Once Drake emerged from his chambers with his entourage, an older man with dark hair and fine clothing arrived. He offered a low bow. He wasn't Drake's blood thrall, so Drake didn't complain about the gesture of respect.

"Rise," Drake ordered.

The man rose. "If you would please follow me, Lord Gloomwood."

This man was here to lead him to the chamber where the cabal would take place. Drake knew where the central chamber where all the manor lords met was from his study of the capital, but he knew it was procedure to have a guide take him there to ensure no manor lord got "lost" on their way to a cabal. Having guides (who were also spies reporting all they observed to the noble court) cut down on any shenanigans preceding the day's meeting.

The trek to the cabal, with his entourage, took place along internal corridors within the Temple of the Eidolons. All of those corridors were guarded by warriors in glistening black armor. Drake knew from his reading about the capital and its capital guards that those inside the temple all wore full ferrocite, a material that was almost impossible to melt, as resistant to magic as silverweave, and very difficult for traditional weapons to crack.

The armor looked almost like plate mail, if plate mail were formed of volcanic rock instead of steel and iron. It had grooves and ridges that looked hand-carved, obviously ornate instead of functional, but nothing that would catch a blade. The helmet covered the entire head and left only a thin T-slit through which the guard inside could see out.

Ferrocite armor also weighed a lot, which meant the men and women of the capital guard were universally strong and athletic. Also, like the capital's courtesans, none of the capital guards had rarities. Since they were charged with the protection of manor lords, Drake knew prior manor lords had insisted no capital guard could have divine blood.

Otherwise, one could kill an unsuspecting manor lord and steal their blood pact.

Lark walked ahead of him and beside Emily, following Emily's lead without being obvious about it. She was terrific at following his instructions, which Drake had to keep reminding himself had *nothing* to do with their time together today. As tempting as some alone time with a willing Lark might be, he didn't have time for *that* sort of distraction.

He didn't glance back at Fox—doing so would suggest he didn't trust his steward—but he did trust Fox was holding up his fake Samuel act as well. So with Emily and Lark ahead of him and Fox and Valentia behind, he followed the dark-haired tour guide through corridor after corridor until they finally emerged in a hall much larger than the rest.

This hall was easily two stories tall and wide enough that several carriages would travel down it abreast. More capital guards in gleaming black ferrocite stood at attention along the walls by open arches leading to other hallways that led elsewhere into the temple. Ahead, two large wooden doors reinforced with ornate metal bars stood closed.

In addition to the two capital guards standing at either side of those doors, Lady Skybreak waited there as well. She stood dressed in a blue silverweave tunic, dark silverweave pants, and black knee-high boots. Her braids were done atop her head in a complicated tower of hair, and a golden tiara glistened there as well. She dressed to impress.

No one spoke as they approached the doors. Once they were close, one of the armored guards standing beside them left his post and pounded, loudly, on the doors. A moment later, they creaked open. Emily strode forward confidently and then stopped before entering.

"I am Lord Gloomwood's guardian," she declared calmly.

The capital guard on the left nodded. "You may keep your weapons. The rest of you, save for Lord Gloomwood, must surrender any weapons. Do you carry any weapons?"

Drake looked to his people. "Answer the man."

"I carry no weapons," Lark said confidently in Lydia's voice.

Hopefully, since people here couldn't lie, the guards wouldn't need to search Lark. That would ruin the disguise. The rest of his entourage repeated those words, but Lady Skybreak did not. She had probably already assured the guards she had no weapons once she arrived.

"You're cleared to enter," the capital guard said, but he eyed Drake as he did so. "Is that a... crossbow, lord?"

Drake raised Magnum for display and grinned. "You like?"

"It is certainly an impressive weapon," the guard said cautiously.

Drake wasn't sure if the guard was really impressed by Magnum or simply annoyed Drake was bringing such a massive weapon into the cabal. Still, the man didn't try to stop him. He assumed the other manor lords would have protection against crossbow bolts.

Once through the doors, he got his first look at the chamber manor lords for their cabals: the Chamber of Council. It was round inside, as he'd expected, and about as big as a large high school auditorium. The seats, however, wrapped around in a circular pattern like those in an ancient Greek theatre, high at the edges of the circle and descending in tiers.

The only thing that made it different from a standard theater was that the seats were set in a C rather than an O. Tiers descended inside the C to meet at what looked to be a stage on the side of the open side of the C-shape. Odd.

The domed stone ceiling was several stories above his head, braced by arched wood and stone that looked both complicated and expensive. There were also huge stained-glass windows up there that admitted brilliant light and showed creatures that looked like some sort of cross between a unicorn and a Pegasus. These had six legs instead of four and had small wings on the hooves of all six legs, in addition to the two big ones on their backs.

So the Eidolons were winged six-legged horses... or were represented as such in these stained-glass windows. It seemed entirely plausible that this whole world and all of its dangerous rarities had been created by a bunch of My Little Ponies with a god complex. Though, given they *were* gods, Drake supposed he couldn't fault them for that.

The theater was divided in a straightforward manner. There were aisles between each row of descending benches and armored wooden boxes built around the perimeter of the C like pizza slices. There were twelve slices, which reminded Drake there had once been twelve manors in this world. Now, after two manors had married and one was destroyed, there were nine.

There were also four different doors into this theatre, one that Drake immediately judged must be located at the cardinal points on a compass: north, east, west, and south. He judged he had entered from the eastern door, and his box was on the upper side of the C... or north. Sky and her entourage were already seated in the box to the right of his, or west.

He saw it then. The pizza slices were set up in the directions that each manor stood in relation to the capital. Drake knew Gloomwood and Skybreak Manors to both be on the northern top of this realm, with Skybreak's mountains to the northwest and Gloomwood's silverwood forest to the northeast. That explained why his and Sky's boxes were on the top of the C. They stood north of the capital.

The capital city, Korhaurbauten, was naturally represented by the platform on the open part of the C, just as it sat on the bay on the eastern side of the total land mass. Also, the stage wasn't empty. A single figure in fine red robes sat in the center of the stage in a raised seat/dais. That would be the noble court's judge, who would administer today's proceedings.

The woman—Samuel had informed Drake to always refer to her simply as Judge—would be as old as his grandmother if he had one, and mid-sixties was old for a world where there were so many ways people could die. The Judge had brown, weathered skin and pleasant features that would have been kind if she didn't look as intense as someone about to hand down a life sentence. He also understood her rarity, *ultimatum*, to be quite powerful.

There was no question in Drake's mind. He did not want to piss that woman off.

As he walked to his box, he glanced at Sky to see if she would turn around to greet him. She did not. Emily reached the box first and opened the door, and Lark walked in before him as if she'd been attending cabals for years. Drake stopped to allow Lady Skybreak—Viktoria—to precede him into the manor lord's box.

A faint smile was his reward for reading and re-reading the order of operations for cabals—if a manor lord brought an advisor from outside their manor, that advisor was always to enter after the steward and before the lord—and then Drake followed Viktoria into the box, followed by Fox and then Valentia, who closed the gate behind them.

There were only six designated seats inside the armored box, whose wall would rise to chest height once he sat. Drake also understood the box itself to be built with powerful magic that would flare to being if anyone or anything unauthorized tried to enter it. Even if he shot across the theater at Lord Proudglade, the man's box would stop the bolt. Still, if it wouldn't get him censured and possibly kicked out, it would be amusing to try.

Drake sat with Lark to his left and then waited for Viktoria to seat herself to his right. Fox then followed, sitting behind and to his left as instructed, and Valentia sat behind and to his right. That left the seat directly behind him empty. Emily chose to stand by the entry to his box, a choice that made sense, given she was his guardian today.

The rest of the manor lords and their entourages, save three, had already arrived. Lord Blackmane wasn't here yet—Drake imagined the negotiations about which of his spurned blood thralls would and would not be in his box was still ongoing—and also, judging from how the positions of the boxes matched up with the location of the manors, Lord Frostlight and Lord Brightwater were also not in attendance. The rest of his enemies were already assembled.

For the first time, Drake found himself directly across from the man who had repeatedly tried to assassinate him over the past few weeks: Lord Proudglade. Even without the name emblazoned on the front of his box, the glare of challenge the blond asshole offered was exactly what he'd expect from this pompous, entitled prick. Drake offered his own wry smirk in response, which seemed to only make Lord Proudglade's glower grow.

Good.

Though he hadn't seen Westin in weeks, there was no doubt this man was his father. Especially since Westin was sitting beside him. Westin even smiled when their gazes met, and Drake offered a shallow nod. That seemed to piss Lord Proudglade off.

Lord Proudglade had Westin's stoic, annoyingly heroic features, including his fine nose and piercing blue eyes. His styled blond hair was immaculate and probably shampooed vigorously every night. The man also wore a thick fur cloak with a golden clasp at his chest.

As to why Lord Proudglade had Westin with him, it wasn't hard to guess. The only reason Lord Proudglade would bring Westin today would be to call him as a witness at today's cabal. Drake already knew what Westin would say... or hoped he knew.

Drake also recognized Orson, the absurdly mustachioed golden knight who had stolen Cresh's magical axe. He stood as Lord Proudglade's guardian and stood holding Blood Woe, the magical axe he'd stolen from Cresh. Of course he did. The rest of the people in Lord Proudglade's box were unknown to Drake, though they all looked to be golden knights.

Lord Proudglade seemed content to keep up their glaring contest until the cabal was called to order, but Drake had better things to do. Given the position of his box to the right of Lord Proudglade, on the man's western border, Lord Mistvale was next on his list of enemies.

Given the name of the man's manor and the fact that he lived up in a giant tree, Drake had expected a guy who looked like an easygoing hippie. Instead, Lord Mistvale looked like a fucking vampire, except one of the evil and sexy ones who taunted the hero between rounds of sucking blood out of maidens. This man had a gaze he'd describe as "intense."

Lord Mistvale's hair was longer than Lydia's and platinum blond, which made Drake think the man must be growing some strong dyes up in his tree. Moreover, the suit/armor Mistvale had worn to the cabal looked almost like it was made of wood, except wooden armor would be stupid since an axe would destroy it. The armor was absurdly detailed.

Finally, Mistvale had just a hint of a blond goatee on his chin, completing his image as a brooding asshole vampire. Drake was glad they were enemies. He wouldn't want to be friends with this guy even if he wasn't with Lord Proudglade. He looked like Eurotrash.

Drake didn't recognize any of Lord Mistvale's entourage—three women dressed in brown-and-green leather armor and one man in the same—but assumed they were all Mistvale's bodyguards. Probably archers or assassins. At least they weren't elves.

As strange and overwhelming as this world might be, Drake wasn't ready for elves.

36
HE'S AN OVERCONFIDENT PRICK

The box to the left of Lord Proudglade likely belonged to Lord Frostlight, judging from the name carved on the wood in front of it. Which said "Lord Frostlight." The box beyond that was empty, suggesting it belonged to one of the two manors that had married into one of the others or the manor that had been wiped out. He'd find out later.

Drake swept his gaze back to the right along the south of the C, past Frostlight, Proudglade, and Mistvale. He passed another empty box and then found the box for Lord Brightwater. Her box was set due west of the Judge, so her territory must be clear on the other side of the land from where they were now. She also wasn't present yet.

Next to Brightwater was another empty box, followed by the box for Lord Redbow, which sat on the northwest of the C. It was beside Sky on her western border, which made sense with how Drake understood the geography of the world. Also, he'd had to walk through Redbow's whole damn territory after Anna teleported him there. Not fun.

Unlike Lord Proudglade, Lord Redbow seemed genuinely pleased to see him... the same way a lion would be pleased to see a fox. Given how many times this man had tried to assassinate both of them, his obvious hunger wasn't surprising. Drake took great pleasure in the fact that he'd survived every last assassination attempt. He even offered Redbow a mocking smile. Oddly, that only seemed to increase Lord Redbow's pleasure all the more.

Lord Proudglade was pompous, and Lord Mistvale was intense, but Lord Redbow was just *creepy*, like the single adult male who drove around in a white van offering candy to kids. Redbow was dressed in a leather robe despite the heat with a fluffy white collar surrounding his neck. He wore an odd little red hat Drake would have described as a fez if it had a tassel.

Redbow's black beard and thick eyebrows completed his sinister appearance. His face was ruddy and about as dark as Drake would expect from someone born in South America, but his teeth were immaculate, which made his smile all the more unnerving. If it came down to killing one of these manor lords, Drake would absolutely kill Lord Redbow first... or, if he wanted to be all poetic about it, send a dozen hired assassins to kill him.

Redbow's box had five other people in it, but all wore hoods and masks. Only their eyes were visible, and Drake would take ten-to-one odds every last one of them was an experienced assassin. That was Redbow Manor's stock in trade—assassination for hire—and while the scrubs he and Sky had both killed over the past few weeks weren't Lord Redbow's best, these five likely were. All five were also watching Drake with keen interest, which wasn't great.

Back to his left again. Two boxes sat between him and the Judge on the northeast circle of the C. Blackmane was directly to his left, and Ashwind was directly beyond that. While Lord Blackmane wasn't present yet, Lord Ashwind was... and he looked like was either badly constipated or simply displeased to be in the room.

Of all the manor lords gathered, Lord Ashwind looked to be the oldest in attendance, or maybe he'd just had the hardest life.

Ashwind had his head shaved bald and wore a loose black robe that looked more appropriate for skulking about in shadows than a cabal.

Odder yet, Ashwind only had two people in his entourage, which meant he was the least protected manor lord in the room. Though, given his guardian easily stood as tall as Lord Crow—a full head above Drake—and the man's muscles had muscles, he probably didn't need another one. He also carried a giant axe Drake knew would make Emily envious.

If Cresh, the giant zarovian leading Drake's vanguard, had been born a human, Drake suspected Lord Ashwind's guardian would be that guy. The fact that the giant had a long beard and half-lidded eyes that practically screamed *Berserker!* made Drake all the more glad he'd brought a crossbow. Though it might take more than four bolts to bring this giant down.

Lord Ashwind's only other companion was a man who was as calm as Lord Ashwind wasn't. He looked like this world's equivalent of a pencil pusher, a short, thin, balding man with spectacles and a look like he'd swallowed something sour prior to the cabal. He probably didn't want to be here either.

He and Lord Ashwind were still allies... supposedly. The same went for Lord Blackmane. Yet if Lord Proudglade intended to challenge his right to be a manor lord based on where he'd come from, he needed six manor lord votes to change the bylaws—which meant he was confident either Lord Blackmane or Lord Ashwind would vote with him.

Proudglade, Mistvale, Frostlight, Redbow, and Brightwater could call this cabal on their own—it took five manor lords to call one—but they couldn't actually change anything without an additional vote. So who'd taken Lord Proudglade's bribe to betray him? Lord Blackmane or Lord Redbow? Or did they have something else in mind entirely?

Drake looked away and reminded himself speculation was pointless. He'd know soon enough, and then he could take action...

whatever that action was. It was too late to make an offer to Lord Ashwind or Lord Blackmane that might keep them on his side.

According to Samuel, there was only one vote Drake could be sure remained undecided: Lord Brightwater's. She was the wildcard. Every lord today would be attempting to either form an alliance with her or at least get her to agree not to oppose him. He'd read her dossier multiple times to make sure he knew all he could about her.

Finally, Drake looked to his right again and to Lord Skybreak... Sky. He'd avoided trying to catch her gaze so far, fearing she'd still be standoffish. Instead, as he looked to her box, she looked to his. Their gazes met. He suspected she was waiting for something.

It was tempting to wink or grin, but Drake suspected either gesture would only add fuel to the rumors that Sky was crazy about him. Which would further piss her off. So Drake offered nothing but a firm, respectful nod, one manor lord to another.

Sky nodded back. As her gaze returned to the room, she looked more comfortable than she had previously. A bit of visible tension left her shoulders.

Having now gauged the room, Drake leaned over to speak quietly with Lark. "How are you enjoying your first cabal?"

None of the other manor lords could hear what they were saying even if they had a rarity that gave them super hearing—Samuel had assured Drake the magical protection on these boxes included ways to thwart that—but it was important his enemies see him consulting with "Lydia." Assuming today went as he suspected it might.

"It is certainly different from my other engagements, lord," Lark said just as quietly. "This is the first time any manor lord has invited me to a cabal."

That suggested Lark had previously been engaged by other manor lords. Drake was tempted to ask which ones, but he decided that would be hopelessly rude. Not to mention he doubted Lark would answer. He didn't want to put her in an awkward bind.

Drake turned to Fox. "And you? Anything to report?"

"Only that I am still somewhat overwhelmed, lord," Fox said quietly.

"I get that. Just sit there and look like you're brooding over some important matter. That's what Samuel does most of the time anyway."

"Of course, lord."

Drake looked now to Viktoria. "Anything else you want to tell me while we wait?"

Viktoria kept her gaze straight ahead, and her easygoing posture and manner were a sharp contrast to the low warning in her voice. "You brought consorts to this cabal?"

"I did." She'd picked up on that fast. "I also have a good reason."

"Had you asked me, as your advisor, if this was advisable, I would have advised you not to do this."

"I understand," Drake said. "But they're here now, so what else would you advise?"

Viktoria swept the room with her eyes. "First, I must know your consorts will not spread word of our conversation to others. Have you obtained that promise from them?"

Drake assumed Lydia had obtained a promise of discretion, but it wouldn't hurt to verify. He looked to Lark and leaned close like he was asking Lydia an important question. "Can we trust you won't share anything you see or hear here with anyone else?"

"Discretion is how we survive, lord," Lark said quietly. "I would never repeat anything you said or which I saw while you had me commissioned to another living soul. To break my promise of discretion would not only endanger me, but also endanger Lark House."

She was likely right about that. As confident as Lark might seem, she was still a courtesan in a world where manor lords could torture or kill just about anyone with impunity or, at worst, a small tithe. Drake wasn't pleased Lark worried he might kill her if she blabbed, but he was glad he didn't have to threaten her. He wasn't sure how convincing he could be.

He looked to Fox as if getting a second opinion from Samuel.

"I agree with everything Lark said, lord," Fox said. "No word of anything I hear or see during this cabal will leave my lips."

Drake looked to Viktoria. "Satisfied?"

She nodded. "Lord Proudglade is eager to get this cabal started and be done with you. He's confident he has already beaten you, which does cause me concern."

"He's an overconfident prick," Drake said. "I'm going to remind him of that today."

"Lord Ashwind is concerned and angry about something," Viktoria continued. "I've known him long enough to know that particular vexed look. He has learned something recently that angers or upsets him, something he feels will become trouble in today's cabal."

Drake was glad once again he'd asked for Viktoria as his advisor. "You can tell all that just from his face?"

"That, and what reports I have from my spies. Reports of Lord Ashwind's thralls looking dour and upset. Having now seen a man I've known for years, Lord Ashwind has recently received bad news. News I would be more comfortable if I had received as well."

"Got it. What's your take on Lord Redbow?"

"He, too, is confident he can beat you, but he still believes this cabal may go either way. That is the reason he looks so pleased. An enemy who cannot wound him does not interest him. Only prey that could genuinely harm him gets him out of bed these days."

"That's certainly comforting," Drake agreed wryly. "So why aren't the others here? Lords Brightwater, Blackmane, and Frostlight?"

"Lord Frostlight had a hunt this morning. She never misses her hunts."

"There's game she can hunt outside the capital?"

"There are people." Viktoria grimaced. "My spies also informed me this morning's hunt was a success. That means she likely spent some time preparing her latest trophy."

Drake took a breath before he asked his next question. "She hunts *people?*"

"They volunteer."

"Who volunteers to be hunted by a manor lord?"

"Whether they survive or die, she awards their families a large sum of coin after the hunt. Those desperate enough to aid their families or foolish enough to believe they can defeat Lord Frostlight volunteer to be hunted. Only one person has ever escaped her, and only because she was called away on urgent business before she could complete her hunt."

"That's..." Drake stopped himself before he could offer his opinion on Lord Frostlight's murderous hobby. Samuel had warned him disrespect to other manor lords could spread like sparks in dry grass. He knew Lark and Fox wouldn't blab, but he also had only what he'd read in books to assure him the other manor lords couldn't hear him.

"...certainly an interesting fact." He kept his tone neutral. "What of the others?"

"My spies only know that unrest continues to plague Blackmane Manor. Though it is unconfirmed, it is possible a new blood thrall may now be involved. I suspect the negotiations as to who would sit in Lord Blackmane's box today are going long."

Drake groaned quietly. "So there's *three* spurned lovers now?"

"Only two. As of my reports from last night, Lord Blackmane and the third thrall remain together. I do not know why he ended his relationship with the second woman."

Lord Blackmane simply couldn't keep it in his pants. He *had* to be the manor lord Proudglade had bribed or blackmailed. Given one of his prospective allies was a sullen ass and the other an undisciplined lothario, Drake was all the more glad he'd managed to get Sky to the cabal. She was now the only competent ally he had in the room.

The southern doors directly behind Lord Proudglade creaked open, a signal that another manor lord was finally arriving. Drake stared across the central circle as a muscular woman with long black hair strode into the room like she owned it. That woman's gaze swept the boxes and found him, and when their eyes met, Drake felt all the hairs on his arms stand on end. This must be Lord Frostlight, and she must already be planning to hunt him too.

If nothing else, that would certainly make for an interesting day.

37
WHY DO I FIND YOUR CONFIDENCE UNNERVING?

Lord Frostlight wore a dark cloak over a black silverweave shirt and an assortment of golden collars and necklaces, but she didn't wear them the way a rich person might wear them. She wore them like trophies, like a hunter might wear the skins of animals she'd killed. Drake suspected these were the prized treasures of those she had assassinated.

This was a former assassin who hunted *people* for fun. Her stone-cold expression would rival Valentia's on a bad day, except Drake had never sensed true malice from Valentia... at least not directed at him. Lord Frostlight, by comparison, looked like malice incarnate.

Frostlight held his gaze just long enough to ensure he knew she was already thinking of a dozen ways she could carve him up with her wind-slicing rarity... while he was still alive. She then continued down the aisle, past Lord Proudglade, and through the empty box beside Proudglade to her own. Though her thralls were dressed like warriors, in dark leather armor or robes, all walked like people terrified an axe would fall at any moment.

Drake wondered how many of those folks were the blood thralls of the former Lord Frostlight and how many she had taken by force since. Either way, Drake now knew he was looking at what Gloomwood Manor might have looked like had Suck succeeded in killing him before he altered the blood pact to protect his people.

Two manor lords remained. How much longer would he have to wait? The question was answered when the western doors opened, only to be almost simultaneously joined by those to the east. The last two manor lords for this cabal walked in at the same time, and Drake resisted the urge to quickly glance between them like a dumbstruck fan at a concert venue.

As he finally laid eyes on Lord Blackmane, it was all Drake could do not to groan. The dark-haired manor lord looked like the lead singer of a hair metal band, with lustrous raven hair that fell across his muscular shoulders. He was also at least as old as Viktoria, likely mid to late forties, which made the blonde blood thrall on his arm even more inappropriate.

Her silverweave had an actual *cleavage window*, and she looked to be about the same age as Olivia: eighteen. She was obviously Lord Blackmane's date. Given her figure, Drake could easily imagine why Lord Blackmane had recruited her... which might not be for her rarity. Then again, Olivia was even less dangerous looking than this, and she could summon *chainfire*.

Still, the fact that a woman young enough to be Lord Blackmane's daughter was the third blood thrall he'd fucked this month meant at least one manor lord in this world was intent on starting his own harem. Which made Lord Blackmane a piece of shit. Drake now suspected he knew how Sky felt when she was forced to ally with the old Lord Gloomwood.

Lord Blackmane caught Drake looking his way and offered the most confident grin Drake could imagine. He looked so impossibly pleased with himself. It made Drake long to walk over and punch him repeatedly in his larger-than-average nose.

Last but not least, Drake took in the last manor lord to arrive, Lord Brightwater: the undecided manor lord who would tilt the table if she agreed to join Lord Proudglade and his three muskadicks. She was the woman he needed to win over if he wanted to stay alive.

Drake was relieved to find Lord Brightwater didn't look nearly so much like a psycho as the rest of them. Her features were unadorned and pleasant, and she had a no-nonsense look about her that he appreciated after seeing everyone else. In comparison to the others, Lord Brightwater looked like a *reasonable* individual, which meant he had a chance to convince her not to become his enemy.

Brightwater's dark hair looked even messier than his, but given how stiff it was, Drake suspected she'd done it up that way on purpose. A cultural thing? She wore unadorned dark-green robes and had a single medallion about the diameter of a baseball hanging off a thin necklace. The medallion reminded Drake of a cresting wave.

The men with Lord Brightwater—and all five of her thralls were men, which was unusual for manor lords, given how women usually got the most powerful rarities—all looked as no-nonsense as Lord Brightwater, thralls who weren't here to fight but would absolutely throw down if anyone so much as threatened their manor lord. They dressed in light cloth and leather.

These five men reminded Drake of Sky's people. Perhaps they didn't serve Lord Brightwater because of the blood pact or because they were afraid of being murdered. Perhaps they served her because they trusted and respected her. This was a woman he'd love as an ally... if he and Sky could convince her to alter her blood pact like they already had. If only a former Lord Gloomwood hadn't assassinated one of her predecessors.

"Lord Brightwater has brought her own crew to the cabal," Viktoria said softly. "I suspected she might make such a gesture. This is a good sign for us."

"Oh?" Drake was glad to finally get some good news. "How so?"

"Those men are her blood thralls, but many of them don't have rarities. They are, however, the most competent sailors you will ever encounter on the sea. By bringing them as her entourage, she intends to make a point that rarities aren't the only value of worth."

Drake nodded eagerly and motioned for Viktoria to continue.

"Given how many people inhabit her manor, Lord Brightwater could not staff her ships or ports purely with those with divine blood. While immigration is discouraged and difficult, those fortunate enough to be born in Brightwater Manor's territory without a rarity have it better than most. Sailing or working the docks is safer than mercenary work."

Drake remembered the story Valentia had told him about her father, a sailor who had died in Brightwater. Still, perhaps he had been the exception and not the rule. The fact that Lord Brightwater seemed to respect people for their skills rather than their rarities was another huge point in her favor... for him.

Drake went back over all he'd learned about the seas around this realm. "You said she has lots of ships. Doesn't that mean she's often in conflict with the kromians?" Those were the merpeople who had to be appeased before any ship could travel from this realm to the other two land masses in this world.

"Lord Brightwater's manor includes a number of island chains, all of which produce experienced sailors. The kromian empire allows free passage between those islands and along the shallow waters riding our coasts. For that reason, most commerce now travels by sea. Without Lord Brightwater's fleet of commercial ships, commerce would grind to a halt."

"Which is why Lord Proudglade desperately wants her as his next ally," Drake agreed. "If he can recruit her, he can ask her to enforce trade blockades against anyone who opposes what would then be the big five. Choke his allies without even starting a siege."

"You are correct in that. My daughter's manor is self-sufficient, and most commerce to yours comes across land. But Ashwind Manor is entirely dependent on commerce from the sea for food and medicine, and Blackmane Manor relies heavily on the sea trade as well. If Lord Brightwater joins Lord Proudglade's alliance, Ashwind and Blackmane will have no choice but to surrender or fall in line."

"Which means the other four are free to wipe the floor with me and Lord Skybreak," Drake agreed. "Fortunately, today, that's not going to happen."

Viktoria glanced his way for the first time. "Why do I find your confidence unnerving?"

"Everyone does at first," Drake assured her. "Then they learn I can back up my words."

"You did rescue both me and my daughter from a situation I thought would be our doom." Viktoria was referring to when he teleported them and their blood thralls safely out of Fort Graystone. "I can only hope you will prove equally impressive today."

Drake again resisted the urge to wink. He definitely didn't need rumors about him being with Lady Skybreak joining those about Sky. "Keep me advised like you have and I will be."

A loud, clear bell rang through the chamber, one that immediately drew Drake's attention to the central stage. The Judge sat now with a placid yet terrifying expression that reminded Drake of a particular teacher he'd had in high school, the one old enough to be close to retirement and mean enough to get you expelled if you messed with her.

There was no doubt in his mind. The Judge was the teacher he'd had in school who absolutely no kid dared fuck with. No one wanted that kind of trouble to come down on their heads, so he could only hope this Judge would be as impartial as Samuel had claimed.

Because Drake suspected, if everything went down as he anticipated it might, the Judge wouldn't be all that happy with his antics today. He'd simply have to convince her he wasn't disrespecting her or her noble court. Even so, he was as prepared for this as he could be.

Time to go big or go home dead.

"As Judge, I call this cabal to order!" The Judge spoke with absolute and booming authority. "Nine manor lords were summoned! Who has come?"

Drake knew the procedure because he'd memorized it, along with the rest of the stuff he'd need to know. Long ago, at one of the first cabals, the manor lords had voted on the order they would announce themselves at each subsequent cabal. It went by how long each manor had existed, meaning the oldest manor went first. That was Mistvale Manor.

Lord Mistvale rose and swept aside his pointless cape. "I am Lord Mistvale. I have come as summoned to honor the wishes of the noble court." His voice was as prim and proper as the snootiest vampires Drake had ever seen on TV.

The other manor lords rose in turn. Proudglade came next, followed by Brightwater. Then it was Drake's turn—Gloomwood Manor was the fourth manor to be founded, with Skybreak right after—followed by Frostlight, Ashwind, Blackmane, and lastly, Redbow.

Drake had already known Redbow Manor was the last manor to be founded. He also knew a bit about their history. They'd actually started a manor devoted to hunting beasts and honoring archers. That, of course, had only lasted a decade or so.

In the first few decades after the manors began to jockey for power, countless assassins were hired by competing manor lords. Few succeeded in killing their targets, but eventually they formed their own guilds. And when one particularly clever assassin seized a blood pact by assassinating Lord Redbow during his hunt, she took over his manor herself.

With her own manor, the new Lord Redbow gathered up all her assassin friends and officially went into the killing-for-hire business. That was how Redbow Manor went from hunting animals to people. It was also rumored the Gilded Blades, the group of super assassins that had included Suck, were part of Redbow Manor, though they were officially independent.

Plausible deniability. With manor lords and their psycho system of blaming all lords for the actions of the lords who'd come before, it all came down to plausible deniability. All Samuel could tell him for certain was that no Lord Redbow had ever been assassinated by a Gilded Blade.

Once the introductions were out of the way, the Judge spoke again. Drake had read how the cabal would go in the books Samuel offered, but it was still nerve-wracking to see it all in action. He should have brought notes, but he'd been afraid another manor lord might see him reading them and take his reliance on notes as a sign of weakness.

"Lord Proudglade called for this cabal," the Judge said calmly. "Five manor lords have joined him. I now call upon these lords to stand."

Lords Proudglade, Mistvale, Frostlight, and Redbow all stood as expected. Lord Brightwater, however, did not. So she wasn't fully on board with Lord Proudglade's machinations. This was good news... until Lord Ashwind stood in Lord Brightwater's place.

Drake cursed mentally. He had been all but certain Lord Blackmane was the one who'd betrayed him, which would have left him with a sullen but marginally competent ally in Lord Ashwind. Instead, it looked like Lord Proudglade had won over Lord Ashwind with a carrot or a stick, which meant he now had only two allies in this room. Sky... and Lord Haremhunter.

Keeping his title today going to be more difficult than he'd expected.

38
HE IS NOT FROM OUR REALM

"Be seated," the Judge stated loudly.

Everyone standing sat down. Lord Ashwind kept his gaze fixed firmly on the Judge. He was likely afraid Drake was glaring at him... which he was. Glaringly.

"The cabal is called," the Judge stated loudly. "Before our official business begins, I will hear a call for announcements. Stand if you have an announcement."

Drake had known how this would go. Still, he waited to see if Lord Mistvale, Proudglade, or Brightwater would stand first. As with the order they had announced their arrival at the cabal, they would also speak of new business in the order their manors were founded.

No one else stood. Drake stood before the Judge could move on, followed by Lord Skybreak. She'd been waiting for his move and they remained on the same page. Good.

Though manor lords were given unlimited powers over their lands, blood thralls, and subjects, here in Korhaurbauten the rules were different. Here, the noble court held absolute authority on behalf of the Eidolons. That authority now resided in the Judge.

Each manor lord would be allowed only one announcement

before the official business of the cabal began. Drake was confident he knew what Sky would announce for hers. Now, he had to get the unpleasant business of sucking up to the Judge out of the way first.

"Speak," the Judge said firmly. There was no question she directed that at him.

"I am now the new Lord Gloomwood." Drake worked to project his voice without shouting and was pleased with the results. "As the new Lord Gloomwood, I present myself to the noble court and my fellow manor lords." Samuel had insisted he must do this.

"You took your title weeks ago," the Judge said calmly. "Why have you delayed in presenting yourself to us?" The Judge spoke for the entire noble court.

No excuse he made about being hunted, teleported, and repeatedly almost killed would satisfy the noble court and the Judge. Nothing would except obedience. As much as it stuck in his craw, he'd play their game to keep everyone in his manor safe.

"I have no excuse," Drake said calmly. "Today, I offer a tithe to the noble court in exchange for my tardiness." He stated the amount Samuel had suggested.

"The tithe is accepted," the Judge said. "Please be prompt in the future."

If no one is trying to assassinate me, sure, Drake snarked silently. Aloud, he said nothing. He suspected Lydia would be proud of him for that.

With Drake's business obviously concluded, the Judge looked to Sky next. "Speak."

"As Lord Skybreak, I wish to officially announce that I have formed an alliance with Lord Gloomwood." Sky spoke loudly and with confidence which made Drake proud to be her ally. "Our manors now stand as one. Anyone who comes for either of us will face us both."

Drake liked the sound of Sky's vow. He also knew she was only required to announce their alliance, not add anything else. The fact that she'd made it clear she and Drake had now united their forces would hopefully give the other manor lords pause.

Even a large force would be at a disadvantage in Sky's land against her rangers, who could ambush attackers and melt into the country like ghosts. Meanwhile, Drake's silverwood trees could bring a whole army to a halt. Hacking through even one tree would take a determined army half a day, and he knew from his wargaming with Lydia and Emily that his smaller force could make an enemy army absolutely miserable inside his borders.

Still, not a manor lord in the room batted an eye at Sky's announcement of their alliance. Lord Proudglade had already known about it through Robby the creepy surveillance doll, and he must have told the others. As for the rest of the manor lords, even an idiot could figure out Drake and Sky were allied when they arrived in Korhaurbauten together.

"This alliance between Lords Gloomwood and Skybreak is acknowledged by the noble court," the Judge said. "You are now free to trade in all respects, including magical artifacts. As agreed upon in the first cabals, you will continue to report all discoveries and trades."

Drake simply hoped the noble court wouldn't learn that Lords Gloomwood and Skybreak had been trading magical artifacts before they officially announced their alliance, and *without* informing the noble court of this fact. He'd already paid a good chunk of coin for his tardiness tithe. He didn't need to bankrupt his manor with a possible manor war on the horizon.

The Judge waited just long enough to ensure there were no other announcements, then spoke again. "With announcements concluded, we now move on to the cabal's business. Lord Proudglade? As he who called the cabal, stand and announce its purpose to those gathered."

Lord Proudglade stood and fixed Drake with a confident glare. "I have called this cabal to discuss the dismissal of the latest Lord

Gloomwood from his manor and blood pact. He has dishonored the title of manor lord and insulted the noble court."

The man was as blunt as Drake had expected. It was almost a relief to know Lord Proudglade had called this cabal simply in hopes of getting Drake thrown out of the manor lord club because he came from another world. He was prepared to combat *that* argument.

"State your grievance with Lord Gloomwood," the Judge said.

"He is not from our land," Lord Proudglade stated coldly. "He is not even from our world. He is an abomination summoned here by the former Lord Gloomwood. While I held no love for the old lord, his replacement is nothing more than a feral beast who escaped his cage and murdered his better. This beast dishonors us all by claiming the title of manor lord."

So Drake was a beast? A feral beast? He grinned in Proudglade's direction. He'd certainly been a beast the night he ripped through Captain Ro and all his soldiers as a wererat. It would be fun to tear this guy's smug head clean off.

"State your proof," the Judge said calmly.

Drake maintained his silence. If he spoke before the Judge called on him, he could be censured. The noble court had its own rules even a manor lord could not defy... if they wanted to remain a manor lord in the noble court.

"My fourth son, Westin, personally witnessed the arrival of this man from a realm beyond our own," Lord Proudglade said coldly. "He witnessed this because Lord Gloomwood abducted him and intended to use both him and this man for a ritual sacrifice."

Once again, Lord Proudglade was talking about Lord Crow, the old Lord Gloomwood. And once again, it didn't matter. In cabal matters, the name "Lord Gloomwood" simultaneously represented Drake and all the Lords Gloomwood who'd come before them.

Their victories were the same. Their crimes were the same. Sky was absolutely right that it was a stupid way to think about things, but again, he had to play the game by the game's rules. And given how confident Lord Proudglade looked, Drake couldn't wait to disappoint him.

"No rules of the noble court state a manor lord must be from our realm," the Judge said.

"That is because an outworlder has never defeated a manor lord," Lord Proudglade said. "Therefore, I call for a vote to change the rules of the noble court. I say that only those who were born in our realm and worship the Eidolons may become manor lords."

Drake almost spoke up right then. Yet as difficult as it was to remain silent, he had to trust to the Judge's impartiality and the specifics of procedure he'd read about in Samuel's rules. He had to do this by the book.

"Lord Gloomwood," the Judge said. "What have you to say in your defense?"

Finally! He'd been half afraid the Judge would simply call the vote before he could get a word in edgewise, but apparently Lord Proudglade hadn't found a way to bribe this woman like he'd bribed or intimidated Lord Ashwind. Drake still had a chance to turn this around, and with the Judge's impartiality confirmed, he could now do that.

He focused on the Judge. Procedure demanded he make his case to her, though his words were meant for another in the room. "As you have stated, a manor lord need only have divine blood. I do. That means the Eidolons believe I am worthy to fill the role of manor lord." He took a breath. "There are no requirements that I be born in this realm or this world. Even if we change that rule today, it should not be applied retroactively."

"Is this your only defense?" the Judge asked calmly.

"With respect, Judge, I don't need a defense, because Lord Proudglade's request for a vote to change who can become a manor lord is not in the best interest of the noble court. It is obviously in his own best interest."

Lord Proudglade's glower increased, which absolutely thrilled Drake.

"Explain your words," the Judge ordered.

"The former Lord Gloomwood was focused on his own goals and machinations." Drake knew better than to openly disparage Lord Crow, but he suspected his statement would creep up on the edge without going over. "While he was opposed to Lord Proudglade in abstract, he was not a threat to Lord Proudglade's four-manor alliance. I, by comparison, am a threat to everything Lord Proudglade hopes to accomplish... because if he keeps sending assassins after me and threatening my people, I am going to ruin him."

He heard Lark's soft gasp from his side. At least his bold pronouncement had impressed someone. It had evidently only angered the other manor lords, though Lord Brightwater, at least, was now watching him cautiously. That was good. He needed her attention.

"What is your proof?" the Judge asked.

Proof? That he was a threat to Lord Proudglade? Drake could offer that.

"The former Lord Gloomwood refused an alliance with Lords Skybreak, Ashwind, and Blackmane." He might be revealing more than the other manor lords were comfortable with by saying that, but it was true, and he'd already lost Lord Ashwind. "Yet since I became lord, I have allied with Lord Skybreak. I am willing to ally with Blackmane and Ashwind as well. That would bring us to an alliance of four manors, one equal in power to Lord Proudglade's alliance."

Drake looked to Lord Blackmane, who looked thrilled by this news, and Lord Ashwind, who still looked sullen. Drake was also thrilled the Judge didn't challenge him. While making such an open statement of his intent might seem reckless on its face, it was also a chance for Drake to slip an open call for allies and an open threat to his enemies into the procedure.

"Lord Proudglade's only intent with this request is to tilt the table in favor of his alliance, a goal I am now fully capable of thwarting," Drake added. He made sure to make it clear he considered Lord Proudglade the de facto leader of the big four, which might rankle the other manor lords. "Changing our rules is the only way he can stop me from stopping him."

Now Lord Frostlight was watching him with interest as well. Rather than a woman looking forward to hunting him, she looked more like a predator sizing up a smaller but still dangerous predator. And Lord Redbow, surprisingly, was grinning like a fool.

"What is your proof?" the Judge demanded again.

She was still letting him speak. "Lord Proudglade's forces alone are too weak to take my manor in battle, and his many assassins have failed to kill me. Therefore, he wishes to *use* the noble court to change the rules and remove a threat to his power. By placing his lust for power above the welfare of the noble court, Lord Proudglade is the one who shows you disrespect."

"Well done," Viktoria said softly at his side.

Drake didn't look down or acknowledge her because the others might notice. Still, he appreciated her vote of confidence. Only his voice would carry outside his magical box.

As for Lord Proudglade, his glower was all gone. In its place was an implacable and icy hatred that would have made Drake uncomfortable if he didn't already know the man wanted him dead. Now, at least, his enemy seemed aware his survival wasn't simply due to luck.

He simply had to hope his talk of Lord Proudglade's lust for power and his use of assassins had reached Lord Brightwater. She was the true audience for his speech, not the Judge. She considered using assassins dishonorable and had no real interest in a tilted table. If he failed to convince her, he and Sky were as good as doomed.

"Do you have anything else to add in your defense?" the Judge asked.

"I do not," Drake said.

"Lord Proudglade?" The Judge looked to him.

Proudglade scowled. "I seek only to protect the noble court from pollution by the blood of outworld savages. Once again, I call for a vote to change the rules. One must be born in our realm to become a manor lord." He glared at Drake. "Applied retroactively."

"The vote is called," the Judge said. "Six manor lords must agree to change the rules of the noble court. If six votes are found, the matter will be moved into ratification. Manor lords, if you agree to this rule change, stand and vote."

There was nothing more Drake could do to sway the other lords. Nothing to do but wait for the votes. Even so, if they tried to remove him... he knew his people would resist. The fact that his people would fight to serve him *willingly* was a welcome comfort.

Lords Mistvale, Frostlight, and Redbow all stood with Lord Proudglade. After a moment of looking around for guidance, a scowling Lord Ashwind stood as well. He really was a fucking traitor. Lord Proudglade must have already formed a secret alliance with him.

Lord Blackmane didn't stand with the others. Instead, he offered Drake a smug grin. At least he'd won over Mister Haremhunter. At least the man was good for something.

Sky, naturally, remained in her seat. With the vote now five to three, all eyes turned to Lord Brightwater. Her eyes remained fixed on Drake.

He met her gaze but offered nothing further. Samuel had assured him she was a fair woman with a fair mind, and he'd made a fair case. Even so, his heart hammered so hard he suspected everyone in his box heard it. And maybe in the next box over.

"Lord Brightwater?" the Judge asked.

Lord Brightwater looked to the judge. "I abstain."

The moment of incandescent rage that danced across Lord Proudglade's features vanished almost the moment it arrived, but it was all Drake could do not to pump his fist in triumph. Today, he'd defeated the first of Lord Proudglade's devious ploys.

Now, he just had to dodge all the other grenades the man intended to lob.

39
I'M A SPY FOR LORD REDBOW!

"The vote to change the rules of the noble court fails five to three, with one abstaining," the Judge announced calmly. "Lord Proudglade, move on to your next order of business."

Drake had just thwarted one of Lord Proudglade's plans to defeat him. It was also one of the only attacks he could easily anticipate. As much as he wanted to believe he'd knocked the wind out of Proudglade's sails by convincing Brightwater to abstain, he knew it wouldn't be nearly that easy. At least he finally knew which manor lord had betrayed him.

He was *not* going to invite Lord Ashwind to the Christmas party.

"In this matter, I defer to Lord Redbow," Lord Proudglade said coldly. He sat down.

So, Lord Proudglade was tagging out to lick his wounds. Good.

Still wearing his creepy-ass grin, Lord Redbow rose and inclined his head to the Judge. "Thank you, Lord Proudglade." He had the voice of a snake-oil salesman, one that oozed false sincerity and hinted at the metaphorical knife he held behind his back.

"What business do you bring before the noble court today?" the Judge asked.

"The real reason Lord Proudglade wishes Lord Gloomwood removed from his role as manor lord." Lord Redbow's eager gaze fell upon Drake. "This man can defy even the Eidolons."

Drake inwardly groaned as he remembered Samuel's words from the night he'd told the man he could lie. That was the reason Samuel wasn't as the cabal today. Samuel couldn't lie.

"It means you speak with the confidence of a madman."

It seemed Lord Redbow and Samuel had read some of the same books.

"Explain your words," the Judge said firmly.

Drake didn't miss the change in her tone and posture. The very idea of someone who could lie obviously offended her, though she hid it well. This wasn't a good sign.

"Sadly, I can only speak to what I have personally witnessed," Lord Redbow said smoothly. "Weeks ago, I extended an invitation for a parley to Lord Gloomwood."

So the bastard was just going to come right out and admit he'd had Captain Ro use Anna to abduct Drake from his own manor. Drake wondered if he could use that against Lord Redbow. He suspected, given the way the court worked, it wouldn't matter to anyone. Fortunately, this was also an attack he'd prepared for. He hoped.

"One of my trusted hunters invited Lord Gloomwood to a summit on my behalf," Lord Redbow continued. "When he arrived, Lord Gloomwood gave his word to my man that he would remain in our camp and not harm my hunters until I arrived. That night, Lord Gloomwood stole my property, left the camp, and murdered every last man I sent." Lord Redbow paused for dramatic effect. "After assuring my hunter he would not do this."

"Explain your words," the Judge said again.

The implication was obvious to everyone in the room, but the Judge seemed intent on forcing Lord Redbow to spell it out anyway. Again, Drake could only watch and listen as he mentally prepared his defense. Possible lies whirred in his head as he struggled to find a way out. It didn't matter how Lord Redbow knew about Captain Ro, only that he did.

"I believe," Lord Redbow said with great aplomb, "that because he was born on a world outside the reach of the Eidolons, Lord Gloomwood can speak words he does not believe."

Several audible gasps filled the auditorium. That pissed Drake off. Still, he had known this might come up and planned for it. And already, as he replayed the events after Anna teleported him to Captain Ro's camp, he knew how he would answer.

As the Judge turned to Drake, there was no doubt at least some of her impartiality was gone. She looked like she was about to bring the hammer down. Rather than looking calm, Drake thought back on every unfair challenge he'd faced since he was brought here. Looking *pissed* was exactly how a manor lord who couldn't lie would react.

"Lord Gloomwood, how do you explain your actions?"

Drake didn't just have to explain. Now that Lord Redbow had directly accused him of a crime, a direct attack of one manor lord on another, he had the right to demand further clarification and evidence. He didn't just have to sit back and take it.

"Before I answer," Drake said, "I demand to know why Lord Redbow believes this. I imagine the court would like to know that as well, given he wasn't *there*."

He couldn't deny what Lord Redbow had said was "true," because truth and lie didn't exist in this world or this court. There was only what people believed, and Lord Redbow obviously *believed* this. So he simply had to find some way to explain why Lord Redbow was mistaken, some nuance to the situation he'd missed or misinterpreted.

"Lord Redbow?" the Judge asked.

"Revealing that information compromises my manor's security," Lord Redbow said.

Drake had expected exactly that answer. He also knew now was the time to pounce.

"Don't bother," Drake told Lord Redbow coldly. "I withdraw the question, because I already know how you know about my meeting with the mercenary captain you paid to abduct me. I also know how you're mistaken."

Lord Redbow raised an eyebrow, intrigued.

"Judge." Drake looked to her. "I have brought evidence I wish to show the noble court."

"Present it," she ordered flatly.

Drake looked to Lark. "See that bag at your feet? Open it and hand me what's inside."

She complied immediately, opening the bag and hesitating only a moment before pulling out Robby. Drake had told Anna Robby would be coming to the cabal today. Anna had been thrilled, though she had been a bit disappointed he wouldn't come to see the city.

Drake sat the creepy doll on the wooden riser ahead of him, green eyes and all. The reactions were as he expected. Lord Redbow grinned in obvious delight, Lord Proudglade's scowl deepened, and Lords Mistvale and Frostlight appeared intrigued.

"This is the doll Lord Redbow's employer, a man who called himself Captain Ro, gave to the underage child he kept in a cage. He repeatedly forced her to abduct his enemies using threats of violence against her father. His name is Robby. Say hello, Robby." He raised the doll's hand in a tiny wave and pitched his voice up. "Hi there, everybody! I'm a spy for Lord Redbow!"

Beside him, he could swear he heard Viktoria huff in disbelief. Didn't matter. The way Lord Proudglade's left eye literally twitched was worth it.

"Lord Gloomwood," the Judge demanded. "Make your point."

He'd pushed her far enough. "You see the green eyes on this doll? They are actually gems that allow a distant user to see and hear anything the doll sees. After Captain Ro's soldiers attacked me under a flag of truce, Captain Ro reported this fact to Lord Redbow."

The Judge pivoted to Drake's enemy. "Lord Redbow? Is this how you learned the information you presented? About Lord Gloomwood's words to your Captain Ro?"

The Judge didn't ask if it was true. There was no lying in this world. But people could be mistaken and truly believe things that were not correct.

Lord Redbow frowned. "Answering that question would compromise my manor's—"

"You will answer the question," the Judge said firmly. "You made the accusation. You must satisfy the noble court to its veracity. Did you receive your information through this doll?"

Drake again grinned... mentally. By bringing this accusation directly against Drake, Lord Redbow had forfeited any claim to protecting his manor's security. He could simply say the doll wasn't how he knew about what went down in Captain Ro's camp, which would allow him to keep his secrets... but Drake already knew that wasn't the case.

Lord Redbow's grin faded. "It is, Judge."

The Judge pivoted back to Drake. "You stand accused of speaking words you do not believe. This is not possible without defying the Eidolons. You claim Lord Redbow is mistaken?"

Thank you for summing that up so eloquently, Drake said silently. "I do. Now, with your permission, I will tell the noble court what *actually* took place that night in Captain Ro's camp."

It wasn't time to lie his ass off. Not yet. The truth would serve him for now.

"Proceed," the Judge said.

"As I mentioned, Captain Ro, at the behest of Lord Redbow, caged and tormented an underage child he forced to abduct people by threatening to feed her father to the dogs." That statement was specifically to incite Lord Brightwater. "This child, Anna, came to my manor under the guise of requesting my help to save her father. Her rarity allows her to teleport people, and she teleported me leagues across the realm to Captain Ro's camp without asking. She *abducted* me on Captain Ro's orders, and worse, Lord Redbow offered no invitation to any *summit*. I fully believed I had been abducted to be killed."

"My apologies, Lord Gloomwood," Lord Redbow said at once. "I had no idea Captain Ro was so sparing in his explanation. I made it clear I wished him to extend my invitation to open negotiations with you peacefully. That a misunderstanding occurred is unfortunate."

Just like I suggested *Samuel switch our route to the Merchant's Roadway,* Drake thought silently. Lord Redbow, like all manor lords, relied on unspoken orders for his dirty work.

The Judge pivoted to Lord Redbow. "Is Lord Gloomwood mistaken in his words?"

Lord Redbow raised his hands. "Until today, I had no idea Captain Ro had failed to clearly convey my invitation for a summit between our manors. I also did not know he was treating my thrall so egregiously. Had I known, I would never have let him borrow her."

Plausible deniability. That was like how Lord Redbow handled all of his matters with his lesser assassins. Drake would remember this and take it into account in the future.

"She wasn't your thrall," Drake reminded the court. "She's *ten*."

"Of course," Lord Redbow concluded smoothly. "Now that I know Captain Ro was treating the child so poorly, I would never allow the man to borrow her again. Of course, since Lord Gloomwood assassinated Captain Ro after swearing not to do so, the matter is moot."

The Judge pivoted back to Lord Gloomwood. "How do you explain the actions Lord Redbow reported? Did you murder Captain Ro and his soldiers after swearing not to do so?"

"Lord Redbow doesn't have all the facts," Drake said. *Now* it was time to lie his ass off. "He only knows what Captain Ro told him, through the doll, after his men attacked me."

Lord Redbow pounced. "You gave Captain Ro your guarantee you would not harm him or his men or leave his camp. Are these more words you do not believe, Lord Gloomwood?"

"I said I wouldn't attempt to harm him if he didn't attempt to harm *me*," Drake reminded everyone in the room.

"And yet I know he clearly stated he would not," Redbow said triumphantly.

"You're right about one thing," Drake said. "Captain Ro did give such orders to the men in his camp, but here's the thing. He didn't give the order to the man who rode in *after*."

Lord Redbow's features went disturbingly flat.

"That's right," Drake told those gathered. "That is how Lord Redbow instructed Captain Ro to assassinate me. By having a man who was *not* in the camp when we agreed to a truce attack me."

"I gave no such order," Lord Redbow said.

"Be *silent*." The Judge glared at Lord Redbow. "If you speak again before I address you, you will be censured. You have made your accusation. Lord Gloomwood will defend himself."

Drake was liking this old lady more and more. She might be a hardass, but she was looking more and more like an impartial hardass. He could work with this.

"Perhaps Captain Ro acted without Lord Redbow's direct order," Drake amended, simply to smooth things over with the other manor lords. "Regardless, that is why Captain Ro and his soldiers are dead. Ro didn't attack me first. The men in his camp also didn't attack me first. But the man who rode into his camp after we agreed not to harm each other *did* attack me in my tent, and once I knew Ro had used doublespeak to break our truce, I defended myself." He smiled his most hungry smile. "With prejudice."

Lord Redbow was not smiling now. He looked incensed, and Drake mentally dared him to speak up again.

Go ahead, asshole. Get yourself censured right now.

40
I'M SO PROUD OF YOU!

The Judge pivoted to Lord Redbow. "Did you order Captain Ro to assassinate Lord Gloomwood under cover of truce?"

"I did not," Lord Redbow said smoothly. "Nor did I have any part in this supposed plot to assassinate him. As I have already stated, I only wished to arrange a summit to discuss our shared interests. Anything else Captain Ro did or did not do was done without my instruction."

The Judge turned back to Drake. "Did you kill Captain Ro and his men as Lord Redbow claims?"

"I did." As powerful as his ability to lie was… or rather, to speak words he didn't believe… it would work better when blanketed inside truths. It was obvious having his ability to lie known would get him removed from his post as manor lord, or worse. Fortunately, he'd always been mentally quick on his feet.

"After the assassin Captain Ro brought to the camp failed to kill me, it became clear to me that Ro had no intention of honoring our agreement. I left under cover of night and attempted to free the young girl Ro had imprisoned. Unfortunately, I was unable to open the manacles restraining her father, and Anna wouldn't leave without him." He glanced at Lord Redbow once more, hoping Lord Brightwater would see his disgust. "I fled the camp fully intending to return for Anna and her father when I could, but Captain Ro tracked me down."

Lord Redbow offered nothing in response. He simply watched Drake with cold eyes.

"Continue," the Judge ordered.

"Given what I now know Captain Ro told Lord Redbow through this creepy doll, I now believe he only told Lord Redbow I had left the camp after swearing not to. He didn't mention he had a man not sworn to our truce attack me beforehand, thus breaking our deal."

The Judge pivoted to Lord Redbow. "Do you dispute any of this?"

Redbow remained silent. The man was obviously running the same scenarios Drake already had. Drake now knew this manor lord operated on plausible deniability. That meant Redbow's subordinates only told him the bare minimum about what they were doing. This allowed Redbow to "believe" he didn't know they had undertaken underhanded actions.

In other words, if Lord Redbow wanted to clear himself of this so-called assassination attempt, he had no choice but to back up Drake's suggestion. He had to accept that Captain Ro had gone after Drake without telling him. He had no way to prove otherwise.

"Captain Ro told me Lord Gloomwood left his camp after swearing not to do so," Lord Redbow finally admitted calmly, as he turned back to the Judge. "I cannot speak to the veracity of these other claims."

Drake had him beat. Now, all he had to do was stick the landing. He waited until the Judge returned her gaze to him.

"What happened next?" she asked.

"As I said, Captain Ro and his soldiers followed me into the woods after I tried to leave and attacked me." Drake swept his eyes across his enemies. "Ro had perhaps twenty soldiers in addition to himself. The night they betrayed me, I singlehandedly killed every last one of them."

That was no lie, and it was a bold claim. Drake also knew it would give the other manor lords pause as they considered how powerful he was. Lord Redbow might know Drake shifted into a dire rat and torn apart Captain Ro's camp, but the others might not. In fact, judging from the way Lord Frostlight was now eying him—with keen interest—she might not have known.

The Judge pivoted back to Lord Redbow. "Lord Gloomwood has answered your accusation. Do you have anything to add?"

Lord Redbow shook his head. "This is a man capable of speaking words he does not believe. He could make up any story to explain away his blasphemy."

"Do you have anything to add?" the Judge said again. She was more forceful this time.

"Only that I demand we hear from Lord Gloomwood's own thralls on the matter," Lord Redbow said smoothly. "Starting with the testimony of his steward, Lydia Estoria. If anyone can speak to Lord Gloomwood's blasphemous abilities, it is his steward."

"Do you call Steward Lydia Estoria as your first witness?" the Judge asked.

"Yes," Lord Redbow said smugly. "And I call his spymaster, Samuel the Rope Tree, as my second witness. If anyone can speak to the veracity of Lord Gloomwood's words, it is them."

This was what Drake had been preparing for since last night. Without rules, manor lords could call endless thralls and keep a cabal going forever. They could compel all sorts of embarrassing secrets from other manor lords. Therefore, the rules stated that each manor lord could only call two thralls to testify at any cabal, either their own or others.

The Judge turned to Drake. "Lord Gloomwood, send Lydia Estoria to the witness stand."

Drake gave it a beat before responding. "I'm sorry, Judge. I can't do that."

Her glare was immediate and sphincter-clenching. "You defy the noble court?"

Drake inclined his head. "Never, Judge. I am simply incapable of answering Lord Redbow's summons. My steward, Lydia, is not in the cabal. I don't know where she is today. In addition, my butler, Samuel, is also off on other matters."

Lord Redbow now looked absolutely thrilled. "You dare speak what you do not believe in front of the court?"

Drake offered the man a cool gaze. "You know I can't do that."

"Your steward is sitting right next to you!"

Drake looked to Lark. "Please stand and remove your veil."

The courtesan stood smoothly and, without hesitation, pulled back her veil.

Lord Redbow's eyes narrowed as his lips pressed together in a hard line. Lord Proudglade looked disgusted as he realized what Drake had done, and Lord Frostlight gasped and smiled in delight. Human hunting aside, at least she appreciated a good joke.

Drake looked to Fox. "Stand and remove your hood."

Much more hesitantly, the male courtesan did so. In the full light of the cabal, the charcoal that made up his fake beard looked ridiculous. Still, it had to be done.

Beside him, Viktoria spoke softly. "You are playing a very dangerous game."

"*Lord Gloomwood.*" There was no question, now, that the Judge was truly pissed. "Did you come here today intending to make a mockery of the noble court?"

"Never, Judge!" Drake assured her as sincerely as he could. "May I explain my actions?"

"Yes," the Judge said coldly. "Explain why you invited two *courtesans* to this holy cabal in the guise of your steward and spymaster."

Oh yeah. She was definitely pissed at him. Still... Drake hadn't broken any laws, and Lord Redbow *had* just blown his only two witness calls just as Drake hoped. Moreover, Lord Redbow had also tipped his hand. He believed Lydia and Samuel could implicate Drake.

Now, all Drake had to do was figure out why Lord Redbow thought that.

"Judge, I simply didn't expect anyone to call upon my steward or butler to testify today," Drake lied. "I had no idea Lord Redbow would level this ridiculous accusation, but I also knew I couldn't appear weak before the other lords at my first cabal."

"That does not explain why you invited courtesans to our holy meeting."

"The prior Lord Gloomwood left my manor and blood thralls in a less than ideal state. Lydia spent many stressful years keeping my manor from falling apart. Moreover, the prior Lord Gloomwood also abused Samuel in ways that left him practically a rotting corpse."

A murmur went through the court. It seemed even these people frowned upon that.

"Given the many traumas Lydia and Samuel endured under my predecessor, and the fervent loyalty they have shown me since I became Lord Gloomwood, I decided they should enjoy a day of leisure in your fine city. Though I know not all manor lords agree with me, my thralls are people too. Lydia and Samuel have supported me through every trial I have faced. I believed they earned a day of leisure for their good work. I still do."

That, he hoped, would win him another point with Lord Brightwater. She cared for her thralls as well. The fact that he also sincerely believed this was beside the point. He really had wanted to give Lydia and Samuel a break from murder politics for one fine day.

"However," Drake continued, "this is my first cabal as a manor lord. I feared that the other manor lords would treat the absences of my steward and spymaster as an invitation to attack me. Therefore, I asked these courtesans to accompany me today to present strength."

"So you intended to deceive the noble court," the Judge said coldly.

"Never, Judge." Drake inclined his head again. "Had you asked who was with me today, I would, of course, have identified them." He'd also known she wouldn't ask, since there was generally no need *to* ask, but there was no need to say that. He moved on quickly.

"I must also point out that the manor lords assembled here today, many of whom take their orders from Lord Proudglade, have already tried to assassinate me multiple times. I also already knew they had called this cabal to discuss *me,* specifically. I didn't know what they were up to, but I did know I had to prepare for anything."

Another murmur passed through the gallery. Drake wondered if he'd made a mistake by revealing his spymaster had uncovered the purpose of the cabal ahead of time, but he didn't see how. It would likely just make the other manor lords even more wary of Samuel.

Drake held the judge's hard gaze as he moved in for the close. "I couldn't appear weak today. But if my ploy to defend myself, my manor, and my thralls offends the noble court, I apologize for any offense I have given. Disrespecting the noble court was never my intent. I only sought to protect myself and my manor. Protecting *them* is *my* responsibility as a manor lord."

The Judge watched him for a dangerously long moment. She still didn't look pleased about his latest ploy, but she also didn't look quite so keen on censuring him. He hoped. She was so stern and unforgiving it was hard to tell what she might truly be thinking.

"Lord Redbow has called your thralls to testify," the Judge said calmly. "They *will* testify today. Where did you send them?"

"I don't know exactly where they are," Drake said truthfully. "I only told them to take a tour of the city and to enjoy themselves. "

"And how do you contact them?"

"I don't have a way to contact them today, Judge, since I didn't know their presence would be required at the cabal." This was still the truth, but also doublespeak. Sky was the only one who could contact Samuel and Lydia, on the magic mirror she still had in her possession.

The Judge looked to the capital guards stationed behind Drake. "Put out a call across the city. The guard is to detain Steward Lydia Estoria and citizen Samuel Marcos and deliver them to this court to testify." The Judge frowned. "Until they arrive, we will move to other business."

Except the Judge wasn't stating aloud what Drake already knew. The cabal was one day only. It ended at sundown. A new cabal would have to be called before any further announcements, accusations, or grievances could be aired, and a minimum of three months had to pass between cabals... unless six manor lords voted to change the rules.

So if Lydia and Samuel remained out of sight today—as Drake suspected they would—they couldn't testify. And judging from the look on Lord Redbow's face, he was fully aware of this. Now that he'd expended his witness calls, he also couldn't call anyone else.

"Is there other business?" the Judge asked. "Or shall we adjourn for lunch?"

Was it time for lunch already? It seemed like Drake had only just arrived, but with all the waiting and ceremony, perhaps time had gone faster than he perceived. Or the Judge was simply so annoyed by how this cabal had gone she needed some time to cool off.

No manor lord presented new business. Lord Proudglade was already talking quietly with Westin, his youngest son, likely trying to dig up ammo for his next barrage. Lord Redbow sat among his trained assassins and idly stroked his goatee. He was plotting as well.

"Let it be known that the manor lords have no more morning

business," the Judge declared. "The cabal is suspended until this afternoon. We will resume at fourth bell."

Drake glanced to Sky's box to find her watching him with a faint grin. She obviously wanted to strategize now, and there was no reason he couldn't take lunch to speak with an allied manor. That was one advantage of making an alliance official in the noble court.

"Emily, will you lead us out?" Drake asked.

"At once, lord!" Emily walked to the gate of the box. "Oh, and lord?"

"Yes?"

"You verbally pummeled them today." Her grin was infectious. "I'm so proud of you!"

Drake snorted despite his best efforts to remain dignified. "Thanks."

As Viktoria rose, Drake turned to her. "Lady Skybreak, given we have some time before we resume, could you extend a lunch invitation to Lord Skybreak? Given the developments in the cabal, I think we should strategize before we resume."

"I feel the same," Viktoria said. "Except Lord Skybreak already instructed me this morning to invite you to take lunch with us."

"Great," Drake said. "We'll do that then."

41
THEN PERHAPS A SIX

Escorted by several capital guards and Valentia, Drake arrived at the manor lord chambers set aside for Lord Skybreak about half an hour (by his judgment) after the cabal broke for lunch. To him, the break felt like two boxers had just gone a round in the ring. Both had taken blows, tired themselves out, and gone to the corners to recharge.

So both could come out swinging once the break was over.

Still, Drake remained pleased with his performance today. He'd already thwarted what he suspected was Lord Proudglade's greatest hope—to remove him as a manor lord by changing the rules—and while he hadn't expected Lord Redbow to straight up accuse him of being able to lie, at least he knew what his enemies knew about him... or what they suspected.

It was possible Lord Redbow had only limited information from Captain Ro. Perhaps the man had combined that with information from whatever book on Earth Samuel had also read. The best case was that Redbow had taken a high-risk gamble with low odds and lost.

The less-best case was that Lord Redbow *did* know that Drake could lie, somehow, and simply had no way to prove it. Not without compelling testimony from Lydia and Samuel, both of whom knew Drake's secret. In retrospect, he wondered if he should have kept his ability a secret from those two as well... but he didn't see how he could have gotten this far without revealing it.

He shouldn't be alive. Not without taking big risks and without a great deal of luck. The choices he'd made to get to this cabal couldn't be changed. So if Lord Redbow did know he could lie, Drake would deal with that later. For now, he had another idea to pitch.

With Lord Proudglade and his allies finally on the back foot, it felt like a good time to go on the offensive. The only problem would be convincing Sky and her mother it was a good idea. He suspected Samuel would speak up against his idea as well... but Samuel wasn't here today.

The capital guards stopped within sight of the doors to Lord Skybreak's chambers and took up position on each side of the hall. There was nowhere for anyone to hide in the narrow hall leading to the closed double doors (unless you were Nicole) yet even so, Valentia quickly took the lead. Drake let her, if only to make her more comfortable.

Valentia rapped on the door once they arrived. Since they were expected, the doors opened not long after. A woman stood in red silverweave—Ali, if he remembered properly—and she looked them both over like he'd expect his battle maids to do. Never could be too careful when guarding your manor lord, even if you could shift into a demon.

Ali nodded and stepped inside, holding the door open. "You are expected."

Valentia strode in calmly to take in the room beyond. Drake walked in behind her. Ali closed the door and stood by it, which was probably where she planned to remain for the rest of the lunch. Drake hoped she'd gotten something to eat before they arrived.

These chambers looked identical to his own. There was the same big main room he'd been using to meet with his thralls, along with open-air archways leading out to a balcony overlooking the capital below. To the right would be the bedroom reserved for the manor lord, while to the left was the kitchen and the dormitories reserved for a manor lord's staff.

Now that he saw how similar the layout of Lord Skybreak's chambers was to his own, Drake suspected there were twelve sets of rooms just like this arranged around in the same way as in the Chamber of Council. Given Sky's chambers seemed to be located relatively close to his, it was possible they were right next door... though a thick wall separated them.

Such a layout also explained the odd route he'd taken here. He'd had to walk down an almost straight hallway to the center of the temple, and then he'd made almost a complete 180 and walked up another long hallway to get here. The hallways must run parallel without being connected. Otherwise, he supposed, it would be too easy for one chamber to invade another.

He was also pleased to see that Lord Skybreak's thralls had set up a long wooden table that had actual food on it. Drake's stomach rumbled as he took in all sorts of fruit, including luscious-looking grapes, as well as steamed meat that was likely venison, boar, or whatever else her rangers had hunted up. After his light breakfast, he could definitely eat.

Valentia completed one more visual sweep of the room before she glanced at him and offered a nod. He'd considered bringing Emily as his second instead, mainly because she would likely be far more chill, but he needed Valentia here to make sure she wasn't surprised by his latest nefarious plot. Assuming Sky even went for it. Which she might not.

Another woman in red-and-black silverweave emerged from the kitchens. Given the rapier she wore on her belt, Drake pegged her as Kari: the woman with a rarity that made her blows as heavy as those from a much larger sword. That meant Mary, the thrall who could make you bleed from every pore in your body, was elsewhere.

"Please help yourself to anything you like," Kari said. "Lord and Lady Skybreak are currently in chambers. They will join you as soon as they are free."

Drake suspected Sky must be having yet another big argument with her mother outside of where their thralls or allies could hear. He hoped those two managed to sort it out sooner rather than later. They both had such strong wills he doubted it would be so easy.

In the meantime, however, there was delicious meat just begging to be eaten.

Drake helped himself to a plate of food and some of Sky's delicious Moonberry mead, though he sipped instead of chugged. The stuff was mild, but he didn't need a buzz going into the afternoon cabal. He suspected the Judge remained on the verge of censuring him for his trick... but he couldn't stop grinning as he remembered the look on Lord Redbow's face.

He glanced at Valentia, who stood with her hands clasped at her back. She hadn't touched anything on the table. "Hey, Val? You can eat."

She offered a small shrug. "I'm not hungry."

"You should still eat," Drake said. "You need your strength for this afternoon."

She glanced his way. "Is that an order, lord?"

When she called him lord, he knew he was pushing it with her. "Just a suggestion from a friend. One who wants to make sure you don't faint in the afternoon cabal."

It surprised him when Valentia smiled, though perhaps it shouldn't have. She seemed far more willing to trust him now... and to give him the benefit of the doubt.

"When the air is this warm, it makes me nauseous. That is why I have no appetite. However, with Nicole's help, I did manage to eat last night once it cooled down. I will be fine."

In other words, Drake thought, *I appreciate your concern, but you don't need to worry about me.* That was reasonable. She must be miserable here.

"Understood," Drake said. She was handling the heat like a champ.

Meanwhile, Sky and her mother must still be going at it. He didn't hear any shouting, but Kari, who stood guard at the door Drake knew from his own rooms led into the manor lord's bedroom, was looking increasingly uncomfortable. She hadn't expected this delay.

Drake considered getting up and pacing, but that could make him look nervous. So he sat. Valentia chose to remain standing. He finished a full plate of meat and was just thinking about grabbing a second when Sky finally marched from the hall leading to her bedroom.

Her gaze met his immediately. Instead of remarking on the way he was lounging in a chair by an empty plate, she merely inclined her head. "I apologize for keeping you waiting. I was having a difficult conversation."

Drake belatedly scrambled for a napkin to wipe what he expected might be meat juice from his chin. "It's fine. You put out a nice spread. I always appreciate a nice spread."

Sky strode right to where several cups of mead waited. She picked one up, chugged it like she'd just lost a whole game of beer pong, and then grabbed the second. She chugged that one as well, then set the empty cup down as Drake looked on in surprise.

Kari, standing by her bedroom, was looking increasingly embarrassed by her manor lord.

Having satiated what was apparently an *incredible* thirst, Sky grabbed a third cup of mead, slid a chair out from the table with one boot, and sat down. She then picked up a knife and cut into a slash of venison with force Drake would charitably describe as *intense.*

What the hell had she and her mother been arguing about in there?

The door to the room Sky had emerged from open again, but it was not Lady Skybreak who emerged. It was Karth, and he was dressed in what looked like noble clothing. As he noticed Drake, his eyes widened noticeably.

"Lord Gloomwood?" The man's greeting sounded almost accusatory.

Drake eyed him up and down. "Hey, Karth. Looking good."

"What are you doing here?" Karth demanded.

Drake grabbed another grape. "Having lunch. You?" He popped it into his mouth.

Lady Skybreak—Viktoria—emerged from the hall not long after, looking as composed as she had looked at today's cabal. At least one of them looked composed. Still, as Viktoria's gaze swept first to Karth and then her daughter, her composure *flexed*.

"Karth," she asked, "don't you have a patrol to complete?"

The seasoned ranger flinched like he'd been struck and glanced back at Viktoria. "Yes. Of course. I'll go do that right away." He looked to Sky again, features tense, but she was still staring at the table as if she intended to burn it to ash with her eyes.

"Right." Karth met Drake's gaze. "Good to see you again, Lord Gloomwood."

Drake simply nodded. "You too, man."

Inwardly, he was wondering what all of this was about. Sky, Karth, and Viktoria all seemed involved now, and something between them was *awkward*. Had Karth screwed up some matter during his brief time as Lord Skybreak, and now the three of them were trying to find a way to fix it? That seemed plausible. If so, Drake pitied the man.

Once Karth was gone, Viktoria smoothed down her dress and smiled at him. "Welcome, Lord Gloomwood. I apologize for the delay. We needed to resolve an internal matter."

Sky ripped off a piece of venison and popped it in her mouth.

She said nothing in response. Drake decided to let her get some lunch in her before revealing the latest plot he'd cooked up after the cabal. He just hoped he hadn't had a plotting look while he did so. Every one of his battle maids (and Sachi) had warned him he had a plotting look.

"Not a problem," Drake assured them both. "So, on a scale of one to ten, how do you think things went this morning?"

"Is a ten good or bad?" Viktoria asked.

"Uh... we'll say good."

"Then perhaps a six."

Drake was disappointed with that result. "Really?"

"You did well to counter the gambits of Lord Proudglade and Lord Redbow," Viktoria said. "Yet your use of those courtesans to trick Lord Redbow into calling your steward and spymaster has greatly agitated the Judge. She will be harsh on you this afternoon."

Drake had been afraid of that. "How harsh?"

"She will not rule against you simply out of malice. The Judge will always remain impartial. However, any consideration she might have afforded you due to you recently taking your title is now gone. Do they have leashes on Earth? Ones used to lead animals?"

"We have those," Drake agreed cautiously.

"Then you may understand this metaphor. You, Lord Gloomwood, will now be on an exceedingly short leash."

Drake grabbed his cup of delicious mead. "I get it."

"Be careful the leash does not choke you," Viktoria added calmly.

Sky thumped a fist on the table. "Oh, come off it, Mother!"

Drake blinked at the force of her words. Sky really was pissed.

Viktoria merely frowned. "Lord Skybreak—"

"Lord Gloomwood's ploy was clever," Sky said calmly. "Ensuring those who knew my most intimate secrets were not available to testify is exactly the approach I would have taken had I been advised the cabal was called about me. The fact that he forced Lord Redbow to waste his witness calls on people who weren't in the room only makes the victory sweeter."

Drake knew better than to grin at Sky's words. He didn't want to seem like he was taking sides between her and her mother. Still, he was pleased Sky appreciated the art behind his ploy, even if the Judge and the other manor lords didn't.

He also appreciated Viktoria's warning about the Judge. He had suspected the Judge might be annoyed with his antics this morning, but he'd decided the risk worth it to force his enemies to show their hands. Still, he'd play it by the book this afternoon.

Assuming Sky didn't jump at his new plan to blow the roof off the place instead.

"Should we eat first?" Drake asked. "I mean... I've eaten. Val's going light. Sky, you obviously need some food. Is this a manor lord lunch, or something more casual?"

"I am eating," Sky informed him calmly. "We have time before the cabal resumes. But if you and my mother have more to discuss, please, don't let me stop you." She glared at her mother. "Lady Skybreak has exceedingly clear ideas about how I should run *my* manor."

Drake decided to take her words at face value. "Lady Skybreak? Care to join us?"

Viktoria nodded and took a seat at the end of the table, on Sky's side but as far from her daughter as she could be. Drake suspected that was more Viktoria being cautious of Sky's foul mood than anything more. He was truly curious about what they kept arguing about. He also knew better than to butt in and risk having his head ripped off by both of them.

Once she sat down, Viktoria grabbed a small plate and then snapped off a portion of grapes. She placed those delicately on her plate and reached for a cup of mead. She took one sip, set it aside, and popped a grape in her mouth. She, too, was going light.

Sky and Viktoria ate in awkward silence as Drake pondered

grabbing another hunk of meat. He decided to hold off for now. He wasn't that hungry, and he didn't want to be caught awkwardly in mid-chew when Sky or her mother abruptly decided to rejoin the conversation.

Sky finished her venison first, then glanced at Drake. "So?"

Drake eyed her cautiously. "Yes?"

"Why did you invite me to lunch?"

He grinned at her. "Actually, you invited me."

Her smile barely reached her eyes. "I suppose I did, didn't I? Very well. I'll start." She took a deep breath. "Do you or do you not want to get married?"

Drake was very glad he hadn't grabbed a second helping of meat.

Otherwise, he might have choked on it.

42
I UNDERSTOOD THAT METAPHOR!

Sky's exceedingly intense gaze remained locked with his. She obviously expected an answer to her unexpected marriage proposal, and the longer he took to give one, the more annoyed he suspected she might be. Was she... really?

"Lord Skybreak," Viktoria said quietly, "now may not be the time—"

"No," Drake said. "I'm not ready to marry anyone, at least not right now."

Sky's intense posture incrementally relaxed. It seemed he had chosen the correct answer, though... damn. He had also spoken honestly, no matter how much sense Samuel and Lydia and probably Viktoria thought a marriage between them might make. He wasn't ready, she wasn't ready, and there was no need to rush into anything.

"Obviously, I understand the strategic advantage of such an arrangement," Drake continued cautiously. "Both Samuel and Lydia have briefed me on all the benefits."

"As my mother has with me," Sky said. "As if I wasn't already *well aware.*"

Was a marriage what they'd been arguing about? It might be.

Yet it also simply didn't feel big enough. Perhaps this had only been one part of their argument and there were others they were still trying to resolve. Drake would focus on the prospective marriage first.

"So, Lord Skybreak—"

"Sky," she interrupted. "We've faced both battle and a cabal together, so we're past the formalities. Unless you wish to remain formal over meals?"

Drake smiled again. "No. And if we're just going to discuss this possibility of marriage openly, I'll also say I haven't ruled out the possibility. I would be a fool to discount the benefits to our manors. After we have a better understanding of how we each run things and have both taken time to consider what *we* believe we should do, we may speak of it again."

Sky eyed him with obvious approval. "So you believe now is a time for new ideas?" It was obvious what she was talking about. Changing or removing all the blood pacts.

"I do." Drake then glanced at Viktoria. "Not that I will ever discount your council, Viktoria. I am very grateful I have your experiences to rely upon, just as I appreciate the counsel from my steward, my spymaster, and my thralls. Even Val there."

Valentia glanced at him and raised an eyebrow.

"We don't even agree on who to kill half the time, but I still value everything she says."

His battle maid offered a small smile before returning her gaze to the doors.

"To be clear," Viktoria said, "we were only discussing a marriage abstractly."

"No you weren't," Sky said crossly. "Anyway, you have heard Lord Gloomwood's answer. The noble court's ink is barely dry on our alliance. This is a first step and a good one, but I plan to proceed cautiously until matters have settled. Do you agree?"

Drake nodded. "I do."

"Then is there anything else we have to talk about? Because

otherwise, I'm inclined to take a nap before the afternoon cabal. The Judge might take exception to me falling asleep."

"Rough night?" Drake asked sympathetically.

Sky shrugged. "It will be better once I can name a new steward. I have it handled."

"I'm not worried," Drake assured her. "Though, if we're done talking marriage, there is one more important matter I wanted to discuss. An attack on our enemies."

Sky leaned forward. "An attack?" She sounded absolutely hungry for one.

"One that will come with a big cost," Drake said. "Actually, I'm not even sure how expensive it's going to be for us, which is why I wanted to consult with you both before launching it." Drake winced. "Oh, and also, I need to borrow your magic mirror for tonight."

Sky smiled a predatory smile. "You gave yours to Lydia."

Drake grinned back. "Why in the realm would I do that?"

She now looked amused, which was better than annoyed. "Even if you can't defy the will of the Eidolons, you certainly tweak their noses well enough."

It was dangerous to ask her more about this topic, but he decided now was the best time to risk it. "So you don't believe Lord Redbow's ridiculous claim?"

"Why would I? No one can defy the Eidolons."

Drake hid his relief. "Of course not. Still... why do you suppose he brought it up?" He paused. "And why do you think he really wanted to interrogate Lydia and Samuel?"

"Any number of reasons," Sky said. "Mother? Now is the time to offer your counsel."

Viktoria visibly held back her sigh. "As Sky has already said, there are any number of reasons Lord Redbow might have wished to interrogate your steward and spymaster. The simplest is that he was shooting into a stream hoping to spear a fish."

"I understood that metaphor!" Drake said excitedly.

"So you know what it means." Viktoria watched him calmly. "While I wish I could believe that's all there was to it, Lord Redbow rarely acts so carelessly. While he expends his lower-level assassins recklessly, his own hunts are usually far more methodical."

"So what was he fishing for?"

"That is what I must ask you. What *was* he fishing for?"

Drake sat back and considered what to say. "It's possible that how I defeated Captain Ro may not be the only time I gave him the impression I could speak things I don't believe."

"So what else might have led to this... belief?" Viktoria asked.

Drake then explained the ploy he'd used to prove that someone was spying on him with Robby. Except this time, he left out the fact that he'd berated Samuel about not following his orders to change their route the next morning. Instead, he suggested he and Samuel had come up with the ploy together once Samuel raised his suspicions about the doll.

"Clever," Viktoria agreed. "I would expect no less from the Rope Tree."

"That's such a cool name," Drake said enviously. "When can I get one?"

Sky eyed him with new interest. "You wish us to give you a nickname?"

"Only if it sounds fucking metal."

Her brow furrowed. "Your world's slang really is odd."

"Still, if you come up with a cool nickname for me, run it by me before you start spreading it around. Now. Shall we discuss my attack strategy for this afternoon?"

Viktoria took another, much longer sip of her mead. Then, she set down an empty cup. "What is this attack, and why are you so worried about its cost?"

"I'll start with my understanding of this morning," Drake said. "Feel free to tell me if I'm wrong. First, while I'm pleased I managed to get Lord Brightwater to abstain from today's vote to remove me as a manor lord, I can't believe that was Lord

Proudglade's only play. He's been at this too long to rely on any one vote, even one he thought he'd rigged."

"With Lord Ashwind," Viktoria agreed. "Rest assured, my spies will now be fervently researching whatever leverage Lord Proudglade has found on him."

"As will mine," Sky added. "And you're right about something else, Clint. He'll come at us again this afternoon, as might the others. So your suggestion is to hit them first?"

"And we hit them so hard we knock them out before they can throw another punch," Drake agreed. "To do that... both our manors may have to pay a rather large tithe."

Viktoria frowned. "For what?"

He told them.

Sky eyed him cautiously. "How is *that* an attack?"

"Viktoria, tell me if I'm wrong here." Drake looked to her. "This morning, watching the other manor lords, I got the impression they don't fully trust each other. They're obviously all in on their alliance, and they're willing to accept Lord Proudglade as its leader. But it also seems like they aren't sharing information as much as they could."

"What gave you that impression?" Viktoria asked.

"Lord Frostlight," Drake said. "When I revealed I tore through Captain Ro and twenty of his men, I'm fairly certain I watched her opinion of me change from dismissive to impressed in real time. I'd bet good money she didn't know I'd taken out Ro and his crew of not-so-merry men, which means Lord Redbow didn't tell her. Even though I'm a possible threat to her."

"Interesting," Viktoria said. "And what else did you observe this morning?"

"Lord Proudglade's eye twitched when I pulled out Robby," Drake said. "At first, I thought it was because I'd shoved his prize doll in front of him. But now... I wonder if it was something else. Would you both agree Lord Proudglade despises deception?"

"He may claim to," Viktoria said. "That doesn't mean he won't use it."

"I agree, and ever since I learned Lord Proudglade sent the bloodsucking assassin after me, I assumed he was the one watching through Robby's eyes as well. But what if he wasn't?" Drake paused to let them get there with him. "What if Lord Redbow was watching instead?"

"Why does it matter who was spying on you?" Sky asked curiously.

"Because it's possible Lord Proudglade may have been relying on Lord Redbow for intelligence, but not have been aware of how Redbow was gathering it," Drake said. "In fact, given how much I've seen those manor lords rely on plausible deniability, it would make more sense for Lord Proudglade to stay intentionally ignorant of the plots of his subordinates."

"I agree," Viktoria said. "By specifying their target but keeping their methods and attacks isolated to their own manors, they minimize the risk that blood thralls they cannot swear to silence may reveal their plans. Lord Frostlight's thralls may be of particular concern to the other manor lords, since they are not forbidden to speak of plots besides hers."

"Because many of them still hate the woman who assassinated the old lord," Drake said. "I never want that to happen to my people."

"Nor I," Sky said fervently. "I will *never* let that happen to my manor."

Sky didn't mention that she had already solved that little problem. Did her mother not know? Of course she did. Viktoria had to know. Sky was simply being cautious about saying anything regarding her decision in Korhaurbauten, where the noble court had ears everywhere.

Drake would remember to do the same. "Anyway, to sum up my impressions from this morning, I got the feeling that while the big four are allied, they're working independently. Maybe not even as closely as you and me, Sky."

"That would make sense," Sky agreed. "The interests of Lords Proudglade and Mistvale have always remained aligned, but Lord Redbow's allegiance has forever remained to himself. Moreover, the former Lord Frostlight had no interest in an alliance with the others. It was only once the new one took over that this changed."

"That implies they might even have sent the current Lord Frostlight to kill him," Drake said. "Or Lord Redbow did that on his own. As hard as it is to admit, I also get the impression Lord Proudglade may not be fully comfortable with Lord Redbow or Lord Frostlight as allies. That suggests he's selectively sharing intelligence with them. As you said, he'll use any advantage available, but I swear he looked pained when I spoke about Anna's conditions."

"Lord Proudglade does have a soft spot for children," Viktoria agreed. "He makes a fierce enemy and is rigid in his ways, but his people also benefit from his strong rule, and most in his territory consider him fair. He also takes matters of manor debt more seriously than any lord I know, which is why he remains so intensely set against you, Clint."

"Because of the bad breakup," Drake agreed. "Zuri told me all about it."

"What did she tell you?" Sky asked. She sounded genuinely curious.

"I'd say about... twenty-five years ago?... a former Lord Proudglade and a former Lord Gloomwood planned to get married and join houses. Then Lord Gloomwood cheated on Lord Proudglade with one of her battle maids, who was a dude, and shortly after that, the blood thrall killed Lord Proudglade. That's a longstanding grudge if I've ever heard one."

"We've all heard the story," Sky agreed. "Such a debt is heavy indeed."

"You've set the stage," Viktoria said. "I understand why you wish to hit them before they hit us again. But why does it require revealing what you suggest?"

"It's because they don't trust each other that this attack may work," Drake said. "Viktoria, you should really scoot down here. We need to talk quietly."

She rose and walked over to sit beside her daughter without a word. Sky also seemed to have no objection. He leaned close to both women, lowered his voice, and explained his plan.

Sky thumped her fist on the table. "So we turn them against each other."

"That's right." Of course she'd immediately see his goal. "If they aren't sharing information, this might be just enough to damage their alliance, or at least weaken it."

"We should do it," Sky said. "No matter what it costs, it is time for us to hit *back*." She looked to Viktoria. "So, Mother? Just how much will this cost?"

Viktoria sat back and rubbed her temples. "More than I care to think about."

"But we're still doing it," Drake pressed.

She nodded... reluctantly. "Given the case you have just made, I think we must."

43
WHAT RITUAL IS THIS?

The afternoon cabal began much the same way as the first, with the ringing of the fourth bell followed by a capital guard escort to the Chamber of Council. Drake had long since returned to his borrowed chambers with his new plan of action in place. He had passed the remaining time making sure Nicole wasn't being too rough with the new thralls.

Robin, naturally, was taking to Nicole's training regimen like a champ, while Gaby could barely keep up and Carl had the stamina but not the strength. Drake was also relieved Nicole had them doing more than running laps, though everything beyond that seemed to revolve around them trying, and failing, not to get smacked with a blunt wooden knife.

Still, every time Nicole "killed" one of them, he hoped it would make it a little less likely they'd get killed if he ever put them in the field. He still wasn't completely sure about whether he'd be willing to send the equivalent of three high school kids off to fight for him, but to be fair, his battle maids weren't that much older. Age was just accelerated on this world.

That was why he was going to continue to call 43-year-old Samuel "old man" until the old man either stopped being annoyed by it or got so pissed he couldn't focus on his work. Either would be amusing. For today, he was pleased Samuel and Lydia remained unfound. Even with Anna along with them, the capital guard had yet to find Lord Redbow's witnesses.

Once Drake was once again in his manor lord box, he noted with approval that Sky had brought a thrall to the cabal she hadn't brought this morning: Oswell, the only surviving member of Steward Rodney's bodyguard detail. The other manor lords had likely failed to miss that detail, so the only question was if any of them would have any idea what was coming.

Drake sincerely hoped they did not.

Once the last manor lord arrived—this time, Lord Ashwind was the one who took the longest—the Judge's booming voice once more filled the chamber.

"As Judge, I call this cabal to order. First, an update. The capital guard continues to search the city for Lydia Estoria and Samuel Marcos, who have been called by Lord Redbow as his witnesses today. Once they are found, we will suspend any business and allow Lord Redbow to question his witnesses regarding Lord Gloomwood's questionable actions."

So Drake defending himself from a group of mercenaries who abducted and tried to kill him was "questionable" now? He really had pissed the Judge off with his consort gambit. This time, he'd spared Lark and Fox the trouble of attending the cabal. He'd instructed them to simply chill in his chambers until the day was through.

He'd paid for a full day. He was going to use it, and he suspected they both needed a break. That left him with only three people in his box: Emily, Valentia, and Lady Skybreak.

"Until then, we will resume our business," the Judge continued. "I will now open the floor to grievances."

Lord Proudglade stood at the same as Drake and Sky. The man glared across the chamber at Drake, obviously annoyed to see

Drake standing. Drake glared back and allowed himself a small smirk. *That's right, motherfucker. I'm coming for you now.*

"Lord Proudglade," the Judge said. "Air your grievance."

Unfortunately, the Judge letting Lord Proudglade go first wasn't her punishing Drake for this morning. As with the orders manors did announcements, the order in which they were allowed to present grievances was also based on the founding order of the manors. Proudglade Manor had been founded before Gloomwood Manor, so Lord Proudglade got the first shot.

"I have a grievance with Lord Gloomwood," Lord Proudglade said coldly. "Several weeks ago, he abducted my youngest son and attempted to sacrifice him in a sadistic ritual. I will not tolerate attacks on my family, nor will I abide blood sacrifice."

"What reprisal do you claim?" the Judge asked.

"I demand recompense in blood. A duel between thralls."

In other words, Lord Proudglade wanted Drake to choose someone from his manor to fight someone from Lord Proudglade's manor in a battle to the death. That wasn't happening. As much as Drake wanted to hurt Lord Proudglade, murdering the man's thralls simply to prove a point wasn't the direction he wanted to go... though he wouldn't hesitate to do so if forced.

Drake said nothing for now. He still wasn't allowed to speak, but if Lord Proudglade was going to go this route, perhaps the man really was out of ammunition. This felt more like a Hail Mary pass than something Lord Proudglade had planned in advance.

The Judge turned on Drake. "Lord Gloomwood, what do you say to this accusation?"

"Lord Proudglade is mistaken," Drake said calmly.

The man glowered but didn't speak.

"Explain your words," the Judge ordered.

"It is true that the former Lord Gloomwood—"

"You are Lord Gloomwood," the Judge interrupted coldly. "You bear all Lord Gloomwood's debts. You will cease denying your title in this holy court."

Wow. The Judge really was pissed off at him. He'd make due. Anyone who didn't buy into this nonsense that each new manor lord was responsible for the crimes of the old one would understand what he meant. If he was honest with himself, he was just being picky.

"I apologize if I misspoke," Drake said. "It is true Lord Gloomwood abducted Lord Proudglade's youngest son and held him at my manor for a few days. However, Lord Gloomwood did not attempt to ritually sacrifice Westin. That was Lord Crow."

"This is your last warning," the Judge said.

"I'm not defying your order, Judge," Drake said calmly. "I am correcting a misunderstanding held by Lord Proudglade. Before he abducted me from my realm, the former Lord Gloomwood, Lord Crow, passed his title and blood pact onto me. *Before* I arrived in your realm. That means, Judge, that Lord Gloomwood did *not* attempt to ritually sacrifice Westin."

The chamber went completely silent as Drake repeated his bold lie from weeks ago.

"Instead, it is I, Lord Gloomwood, who *saved* Westin from being ritually sacrificed by Lord Crow, a man who had previously passed his blood pact to me. I also prevented Lord Crow from sacrificing me in the same ritual. As the lord of Gloomwood Manor, I defended *myself* from an assassin and saved Lord Proudglade's son."

Lord Proudglade's gaze and glower went completely flat. Had he not known? How could he not have known? Westin must have told him, right?

"What ritual was this?" the Judge demanded.

Now to really put them on their back feet. "Lord Crow believed he could use the divine blood possessed by Westin and myself to summon and control a leviathan from the underside."

Audible gasps filled the chamber, some even coming from his fellow manor lords. Lord Blackmane had gone pale, seemingly unaware his eighteen-year-old blood thrall/grooming victim now clutched his arm for dear life. Lord Ashwind's standard glower had been replaced with a slightly more surprised glower. Even Lady Skybreak gasped quietly.

Drake realized now that he'd never told Viktoria or Sky. He hoped they'd roll with it.

"You say Lord Crow attempted to summon a leviathan," the Judge said quietly. Even with her voice so much softer, the silence in the room made it loud.

"Yes, Judge," Drake said. "And I stopped him. I, Lord Gloomwood, did not simply save Westin, Lord Proudglade's son, when I defeated Lord Crow in battle. I also thwarted his attempt to summon that leviathan. I saved this realm from the consequences that might result when I, Lord Gloomwood, executed a man who committed an unforgivable crime."

No one spoke. Not even the Judge. Drake let them chew on what they'd begged for and kept his face calm. This was not the time to look smug. His words had already expressed everything he wanted to express.

The Judge finally spoke. "The noble court will launch an investigation into the unforgivable crime you report. When our inquisitor arrives at your manor, we will expect full cooperation from you and your blood thralls. We will be interviewing everyone."

"Of course, Judge," Drake said. "I have only one request."

The Judge's eyes narrowed. "As a manor lord, that is your right." She left unsaid that she was warning him not to ask for anything big.

"I ask only that the inquisitor's interrogation of my blood thralls be confined to matters relating to Lord Crow's attempted leviathan summoning," Drake said. "I trust my thralls and share many secrets with those in my manor. So I would only be comfortable allowing your inquisitor to interview them if all questions remain focused on the summoning attempt."

Even Lydia didn't know the exact circumstances of what had

happened in the ritual chamber that first day. Drake had made sure of that. No one could betray this particular lie.

"The investigation will take place as you request," the Judge said, as Drake could almost hear her snarkily adding, *Obviously.* "Is that your only request?"

"It is." Drake inclined his head. "I want this matter cleared up as much as you do."

"It will be," the Judge assured him grimly. She looked back to Lord Proudglade. "Lord Gloomwood has offered a different account of events than yours. Do you dispute his words?"

"I request a moment to confer with my advisors," Lord Proudglade said stiffly.

"You have five minutes," the Judge said. "Be prompt."

As Lord Proudglade glanced at his son, Drake could see Westin hunkered down in his seat. He looked as uncomfortable as if he'd just been caught trying to sneak out while grounded. So he really had kept this news from his dad.

What had happened after Drake freed Westin and lied to him about the ritual? Westin really hadn't told his father about Drake saving him? Or was Lord Proudglade putting on an act because he hadn't expected Drake to just bring up an unforgivable crime?

An act didn't feel like Lord Proudglade. He seemed far too blunt and "honorable" to resort to playacting in the cabal. Why would Westin keep their discussion from his father? Hadn't Westin known it could get his father in trouble if he brought it up in the cabal?

No matter. Drake remembered one of the favorite pieces of military advice he'd ever heard in school. *Never interrupt your enemy when he is making a mistake.*

Lord Proudglade's short conference with Westin and his other thralls took far less time than five minutes. Drake mentally counted. When Lord Proudglade returned his attention to the judge, he looked resigned. "I do not dispute Lord Gloomwood's account of events. But in recompense for Lord Gloomwood's abduction of my son Westin, I demand a tithe."

The Judge turned back to Drake. "Do you agree?"

"I call for a vote from my peers as to whether we should pay a tithe or dismiss the matter," Drake said. That was his right as a manor lord. "I also demand we consider that I saved Westin's life and stopped a demon summoning."

"The record is clear," the Judge said coolly. "Does any manor lord second the vote?"

"I second," Sky said. There was no reason to expect enough manor lords would vote with them to keep Drake from paying a tithe, but they could still try.

"The vote is called," the Judge said. "If you agree the grievance between Lord Proudglade and Lord Gloomwood should be resolved with a tithe, raise your hand. Otherwise, stay your hands and we will consider the matter settled without recompense."

The results weren't surprising. Neither Sky nor Lord Blackmane raised their hands—questionable dating decisions aside, at least Drake could count on Lord Blackmane for his vote—but everyone else, including Lord Brightwater, raised their hands. He'd tried.

"The vote is six to three. The noble court decrees Lord Gloomwood must pay Lord Proudglade a tithe to compensate him for abducting his son, Westin."

Drake inclined his head. "Then I will resolve the matter with Lord Proudglade when we are both available to do so." He was going to make this fucker fight for every cent.

"Do you have other grievances to air before this court?" the Judge asked Lord Proudglade.

"I do," the man said stiffly.

"You may air your next grievance after Lord Gloomwood and Lord Skybreak have offered their grievances." She remained tough but fair. "Lord Gloomwood." The Judge turned to face him once more. "What grievance do you bring before the noble court today?"

"I have a grievance with Lord Proudglade, Lord Mistvale, Lord Frostlight, and Lord Redbow. One of them attempted to falsely bring me and my ally, Lord Skybreak, to war."

"Against which lord to you claim grievance?" the Judge asked.

"All of them." Drake swept his gaze across his enemies box by box. "But if one of you wants to speak up, I'll narrow it down."

None of the four he'd named confessed on the spot. After he'd given everyone in the room time to process their hesitance, Drake nodded. "I have witnesses to testify as to how I have been wronged by the manor lords I've just named. I wish to call my first witness."

"Name them," the Judge said.

"I call Lord Skybreak's thrall, Oswell, to speak before the noble court."

44
EXPLAIN YOUR WORDS

It was immediately obvious to Drake that none of the enemy manor lords had expected him to call this *particular* thrall. Lord Frostlight looked disappointed, Lord Proudglade looked annoyed, and Lord Brightwater actually looked intrigued.

They must all be wondering why he'd call a witness from his allied manor. Given he and Sky could interview each other's thralls at any time, this meant something juicy was coming. Something Drake wanted to air before the entire noble court.

"He may approach," the Judge said.

Oswell stood stiffly, using the arms of his seat to help. Another man—Karth, of course—handed Oswell his crutches and then slid an arm underneath the man's shoulders.

Sky spoke up. "My thrall, Oswell, lost his lower leg in an ambush by mercenaries. I request permission for my thrall, Karth, to assist him in reaching the stage."

"Both may approach," the Judge assured them calmly.

Drake waited as Karth helped Oswell walk down the stairs to the stage in the center. Drake also couldn't be sure, but he suspected Oswell was milking the chamber's sympathy for everything he was worth. Sky must have instructed him to look particularly pathetic. In this case, that might play to the sympathies of Lord Brightwater.

Once Karth helped Oswell to the wooden stool between two scribes and beneath the Judge, he turned to face her. Drake knew from reading that a thrall had to give all testimony directly to the Judge, even if they were technically answering the question of a manor lord.

He didn't envy Oswell this task. The Judge remained intimidating as fuck. However... as she looked down on Oswell, Drake actually saw a bit of kindness in her eyes.

He hoped.

"Lord Gloomwood, ask your questions," the Judge ordered.

Drake focused on Oswell. "Please tell the noble court everything that happened the day Lord Skybreak's steward, Rodney, was assassinated in the mercenary ambush south of Skybreak Manor... exactly as you remember it." That last bit was *particularly* important.

Still facing the Judge, Oswell once again offered his chilling account of death and betrayal. Along with other thralls who served as Steward Rodney's personal bodyguards, Oswell left Skybreak Manor to meet with battle maids from Gloomwood Manor. Once they met on the edge of a lake, mercenaries ambushed them.

Then Valentia, Lord Gloomwood's blood thrall, betrayed them by freezing Steward Rodney's bodyguards and stabbing Rodney himself through the chest with a sword of ice.

Drake didn't watch Oswell's testimony. He watched the room. Lord Frostlight seemed bored at first, but as Oswell's account revealed the betrayal, she grew visibly more intrigued. So unless she was a good actor, which he wouldn't put past her, she hadn't known any of this.

Lord Proudglade simply glowered in annoyance. He was now consistently so pissed off it was impossible to tell if he'd known or not. Lord Mistvale remained an unreadable elder vampire, and

Lord Redbow's trademark creepy grin was gone for the first time in the cabal.

That was interesting.

As for Lord Brightwater, she actually looked a bit ill as Oswell recounted the cold-blooded murder of Rodney, the others, and Valentia's betrayal. When she looked Drake's way, he saw her sizing him up once more. He hoped she'd defer judgment for now.

Once Oswell finished his account, including how he survived by using his rarity, *coagulation*, to stop his blood loss after losing his lower leg, the Judge looked at Drake. He might be imagining it, but he thought he saw a hint of incredulity on her face. As if she wanted to ask *"Why in the fuck would you incriminate your own battle maid?"*

Instead, the Judge asked, "Do you have any other questions?"

Drake took a breath. The other manor lords would be able to ask questions of Oswell after Drake got done. They would inevitably ask why Steward Rodney had been meeting with Drake's battle maids, and the man would be forced to answer. Now that he'd left Oswell exposed, Lord Gloomwood and Lord Skybreak's crime of exchanging magical items in secret, while they weren't allied, was going to come out no matter what he did.

But the penalty might be less severe if Drake *confessed* voluntarily.

"Oswell, why was Steward Rodney meeting secretly with my battle maids outside of both your manors, at the lake, where they could be ambushed?"

Oswell said nothing.

"You will answer Lord Gloomwood," the Judge ordered firmly.

"Answer his question," Sky called. "It's fine, Oswell."

Drake realized something then. While Oswell could answer the Judge's question any time he wished, since Sky's blood pact had no power over him, he had waited until Sky audibly gave the order. Otherwise, the other manor lords would have realized something was off. Sky's thralls had been pretending to be compelled for quite some time.

Oswell took a breath. "On orders from Lord Skybreak, I escorted Steward Rodney to meet with Valentia and Nicole, Lord Gloomwood's battle maids, to pass on a magical artifact from our treasury."

The silence that followed was deafening.

The Judge spent a beat watching Oswell before she looked to Drake, and this time, she looked truly vexed. "Lord Gloomwood."

"Yes, Judge?"

"You are aware that, until just after this morning's announcement, your manor was not officially allied with Skybreak Manor?"

"I am aware of that."

"And are you also aware that secretly exchanging magical items between manors that are not officially allied is not allowed by rules of the noble court?"

"I am, Judge."

"Then, understand, I ask this next question because I am beginning to worry you may be mentally unwell. Do you understand that by calling this witness and asking that question, you have just implicated your manor in a crime?"

"I do, Judge. Lord Skybreak and I both agreed we should not remain bound by the decisions of our predecessors. We regret this crime and confess it as a gesture of good faith."

He could swear he saw the Judge mentally facepalm before she looked to Sky. "Do you wish to dispute your blood thralls' accounting of events?"

"No, Judge," Sky said. "Everything Oswell just said is true... as far as he believes."

"Explain your words," the Judge said immediately.

"With respect, I believe a full accounting of the events surrounding my steward's assassination would best come from Lord Gloomwood and his witnesses."

Lord Redbow was sweating now. The man was actually sweating. He wiped his brow with a handkerchief and then leaned over to whisper something to a thrall. Drake could barely hold back his grin as he watched the man wriggle in his seat.

The Judge seemed on the verge of asking Sky to explain herself, but finally, she looked to the court at large. "Do the other lords have any questions for this witness?"

No manor lord spoke up. They appeared truly at a loss. Nothing they could ask Oswell would do more damage to Drake's manor than Drake had already done to it himself... but by revealing this before the other manor lords could cross-examine Oswell, he'd left them no way to seize the momentum for themselves.

Drake also ignored Lord Blackmane, who was currently staring at his box and trying to catch his eyes. Probably to ask if he was actually insane.

"The witness is dismissed," the Judge said. As Karth helped Oswell back to his box, the Judge continued to glare at them both.

"Lord Gloomwood. Lord Skybreak. Based on this witness's testimony, this court judges you both guilty of secretly and illegally trading magical artifacts against the rules of the noble court. You will tithe for this crime, and you will both be censured. Do you understand?"

Drake certainly did. Being censured meant he would no longer be able to take any actions at this cabal. He could still answer to the grievances of other manor lords and defend himself, but he could not make announcements, air grievances, or do anything, really.

But since his current grievance was already in motion, he could still complete it. Sky could also complete hers if they needed it, because she'd stood and claimed her grievance *before* they both got themselves censured. He had made sure to quiz Viktoria all about that.

"Call your last thrall," the Judge said.

Drake stood once more. "I call Valentia Vincano as my next witness."

Again the Judge narrowed her eyes. "You do know you only get two witnesses?"

At this point, he wasn't sure if the Judge was trying to help him out or fuck with him. Either was more amusing than annoying. "I do, Judge. I wish to call Valentia Vincano."

The Judge all but sighed. "She may approach."

Valentia stood, nodded Drake's way, and walked out of the box as Emily opened the door. She strode down the stairs with every bit of self-assured poise Drake would expect from one of Gloomwood Manor's most experienced and dangerous battle maids. When Drake glanced at Lord Blackmane, he found the man watching Valentia like a wolf in heat.

Drake scowled. If he didn't need the other manor lord's vote to keep himself and Sky alive, he'd call a grievance on Lord Blackmane simply for being an irredeemable horndog. Lord Blackmane's current lady friend was *right there*, and it was obvious from her frown she knew exactly whose ass her lord was ogling.

Valentia sat herself on the stool and stared up at the judge. Unlike Oswell, he suspected Valentia was directing every bit of her ice queen calm at the older woman.

"Lord Gloomwood," the Judge said, almost as if she was dreading what colossal mistake he might make next. "Ask your first question."

"Valentia," Drake said. "Would you describe everything that happened when and after you met Steward Rodney and his bodyguards to receive a magical item? As you remember it?"

One of Lord Redbow's thralls rose and stepped out of his box. Drake watched with keen interest as the man hurried out the double oak doors. Where exactly was he going? It looked like turning on the lights was already scaring the rats.

With a cold and remorseless fervor that kept Drake's ears glued to her account, Valentia described everything that happened the day Steward Rodney died. Including that she did *not* stab him with an icy sword. Including that she and Nicole were both taken *alive* by the mercenaries who murdered Steward Rodney after *not* betraying him.

When she finished, the Judged actually looked pale. Drake suspected he might have taken a year off her life with today's testimony. He hoped she could afford that. Finally, the Judge's eyes met his once more.

"What is this?" she asked softly.

Drake hadn't rehearsed for that question. "I don't understand the question."

"Why did you call these witnesses?" the Judge asked. "What is your goal here today?"

The fact that she'd gone straight to the heart of this matter was a good sign. "Judge, I think it should be obvious to everyone here that Oswell and Valentia remember entirely different accounts of Steward Rodney's assassination."

"*That* is obvious to everyone," the Judge said sardonically. "How does this relate to your grievance with Lords Proudglade, Mistvale, Frostlight, and Redbow?"

Drake took a breath for dramatic effect. "Judge, the fact that Oswell and Valentia remember entirely different versions of events was intended to trick Lord Skybreak into demanding the execution of Valentia, my battle maid. Had we not uncovered the fact that they remembered differently, our bad blood would have destroyed any chance of our alliance."

The Judge waited silently. He took that as permission to continue.

"Neither I nor any of my thralls hired those mercenaries to murder Steward Rodney and abduct my battle maids. We do, however, now know the mercenaries were connected to Lord Redbow." Drake glanced at the man to find him visibly placid once more. "Oswell was tricked into giving the account he gave... into seeing the betrayal he saw... by enemies of our manors who hoped to prevent Lord Skybreak and I from formalizing our alliance."

Drake looked to the other manor lords. "Our enemies, right

now, are Lords Proudglade, Mistvale, Frostlight, and Redbow. At least one and maybe more have already tried to assassinate me multiple times, which means it was almost certainly one of them who was behind this effort to drive a wedge between my manor and Lord Skybreak's."

"What is your proof?" the Judge demanded.

Now for the kill shot. "I have secured letters from Captain Ro, the man Lord Redbow has already admitted worked directly for him earlier today, with instructions leading Ro to his targets. We already know from today's earlier testimony that Captain Ro worked for Lord Redbow... by Lord Redbow's own admission... and Valentia has verified the men who ambushed her also worked for Captain Ro. That means Lord Redbow was also behind the attack on Steward Rodney, unless Captain Ro once again did it without his knowledge."

Lord Redbow said nothing. He simply sat silently in his box.

"Yet Oswell saw your battle maids murder Rodney," the Judge reminded everyone in the room. "How do you explain this?"

Was she setting him up to make his point? It felt like she'd just tossed him the easiest softball ever, and she was now expecting him to hit it out of the park. He'd oblige her.

"This strongly suggests Lord Redbow or one of his allied manors has a blood thrall, or has contracted a blood thrall, who has a rarity that changes what people see. That thrall can make anyone see anything, which means any testimony anyone gives to this noble court could be mistaken." Drake paused. "This suggests not only that one of the lords I named sought to start a war between me and my ally, but that this lord *also* sought to deceive the noble court."

That was his bombshell. Attempting to deceive the noble court was, other than a demon summoning, one of the only unforgivable crimes a manor lord could commit. Even though it wasn't supposed to be possible, since no one could lie, manor lords had occasionally attempted to deceive the court through doublespeak or other methods.

Drake had just suggested that one of the four manor lords allied against him had committed an unforgivable crime... and neither the Judge nor anyone else had contradicted him. Drake took the utter silence in the chamber as permission to lob one final bomb at his off-balance enemies.

"I would also ask my fellow manor lords to consider everything they and their thralls remember about the circumstances leading to their alliance with Lord Proudglade with fresh eyes. Because it now seems possible, to me, that some among you may *also* have been tricked into allying with Lord Proudglade. Because he could make you see things that didn't happen."

Lord Proudglade stood. "As the manor lord who called this cabal, I call for it to end."

45
I CALL FOR AN INQUISITION

Drake couldn't believe the old man would give up so easily. Just like that? Lord Proudglade was going to roll over and play dead?

Still, Drake allowed himself a very small, very satisfied smile. When he glanced at Sky, he saw her grinning his way unabashedly. He was starting to like her grin quite a lot.

"On what grounds do you wish to end this cabal?" the Judge asked Lord Proudglade.

Drake knew just how unusual Proudglade's request was. Calling a cabal was a huge deal. It required the consent of four other manor lords and a considerable investment of time and resources from the noble court, who had to rearrange their schedules and the schedule of the entire capital city to accommodate nine incoming manor lords on their entourages.

No manor lord was foolish enough to call a cabal and then *cancel* it halfway through. That suggested they had called it frivolously and without proper foresight. Or rather... no manor lord was foolish enough to call a cabal, cancel it, and be allowed to call one *again*.

"Lord Gloomwood's claims are unprecedented, disturbing, and

possibly intended to confuse and mislead us all," Lord Proudglade said. "Therefore, I call for this cabal to end before any more of it can be tainted by his possibly deceptive testimony."

Drake's smile disappeared. If the man was going to be a sore loser, that was fine. Even censured, he was still allowed to defend himself.

"We have no proof Lord Gloomwood can say things he does not believe," the Judge reminded everyone in the room.

"Because today he ensured any who could reveal his crimes could not be interviewed!" Lord Proudglade threw one hand out in frustration. "It is quite possible that he has now used his ability to speak that which he does not believe to sow discord and confusion among this noble court. He is an outworlder. We have no idea what he's capable of."

And you're a sore loser, Drake thought silently. *With no fucking proof.*

"Lord Proudglade." The Judge's face went placid. "I will offer this warning once. We do not have any testimony supporting Lord Redbow's claim that Lord Gloomwood can speak that which he does not believe. Lord Gloomwood himself has provided an account of the events the night he left Captain Ro's camp, one Lord Redbow has not challenged. You remain a friend of this noble court, but you will not repeat unproven claims in this cabal."

Lord Proudglade sighed heavily. "Forgive me, Judge. I spoke rashly."

Drake glanced at Sky to find her still standing with a fierce expression on her face. She looked like she was on the verge of yelling at the Judge for attention. Fortunately for both of them, the Judge turned to Sky at last.

"Lord Skybreak. You remain censured for the crime of illegally exchanging magical items. However, as you raised your grievance before you were censured, you may air it in a moment." The Judge turned back to Lord Proudglade. "And it is only after we have resolved all the noble court's current business that we will allow a vote on ending the cabal."

Lord Proudglade bowed his head.

"Lord Skybreak?" the Judge said. "Air your grievance."

Sky stood straight and tall, and her voice immediately commanded the chamber. "Through all the testimony brought before the court today, it is now clear Captain Ro's mercenaries, who were working directly for Lord Redbow, assassinated my steward. Whether or not they also attempted to turn my strongest ally against me remains to be proven by further testimony, but I now have no doubt Lord Redbow was behind this crime."

The Judge looked to the accused. "Lord Redbow? Your defense?"

The man simply sighed. "I am aware Captain Ro took a contract to assassinate Steward Rodney as described in the accounts given today." He looked to Sky and Drake. "However, I did not order the assassination of Rodney. For that contract, Ro was employed by someone else."

Redbow was telling the truth. He could do nothing but tell the truth. As much as his earlier successes thrilled him, Drake was taken aback by this new information. If Redbow hadn't murdered Steward Rodney and tried to pit him and Sky against each other... who the fuck had?

"I demand to know who offered the contract on my steward," Sky said coldly.

"I do not know that information," Lord Redbow replied smoothly. "Captain Ro never told me who had hired him, only that he had taken the contract."

"Then I will have an answer from your thralls!"

"Unfortunately, Lord Skybreak, I believe your allied manor lord murdered Captain Ro and every single man in his mercenary party.... as Lord Gloomwood himself has stated. However, I do wish you luck in finding the culprit. Perhaps it will be in Ro's letters?"

"I will find out who murdered my steward," Sky growled. "You can be assured I will."

Lucien, Sky's pattern-recognizing thrall, would translate Ro's letters sooner or later. This was a setback, but it wasn't going to stop them from finding the culprit. They just had to be patient.

"Lord Skybreak?" the Judge asked. "Do you have anything to dispute, or do you acknowledge that Lord Redbow did not order the assassination of your steward?"

"It seems I have no choice but to acknowledge that, for now," Sky said. "But when I learn who was behind the contract on my steward, I reserve the right to air this grievance again." She glowered at Lord Redbow. "And to punish the culprit myself."

The Judge turned to Lord Proudglade. "You called this cabal. You swore to the noble court that the matters you wished to discuss were worth requiring eight other manor lords to make the long trip here. Is this no longer your belief?"

Lord Proudglade looked as pained as if he were trying to piss out a kidney stone. "As I said, Judge, I simply believe that after all the testimony given today, continuing this cabal for the purpose it was called will not yield the desired result."

The Judge's tone became noticeably stern. "Whether the cabal will result in an outcome you *favor* has no bearing on whether it should continue."

Lord Proudglade simply shook his head. "My concern is that any outcome would remain suspect. If Lord Gloomwood can speak that which he does not believe... which I am only saying is now a possibility... then all the testimony he gave today is meaningless."

Before Drake could interject, Proudglade continued.

"However, if he is correct that there is a person with a rarity that can change what people see, then none of us can trust anything we believe. Anyone of us could be... mistaken... about the beliefs they bring to this cabal. We must first investigate his claim."

"And this, in your mind, justifies calling a premature end to this cabal?"

"It does, Judge."

"Seconds?"

"I second!" Lord Redbow said immediately.

Drake would take this win. His enemies were retreating in poor order, scrambling away with their tails between their legs after he'd slammed them to the mats. He was still bothered that Lord Redbow actually wasn't behind everything that went on with Steward Rodney and this person who was changing what people could see, but that could wait.

"I now call for a vote," the Judge declared. "Five lords must vote together to call a cabal. Five must also vote to end it. If you wish this cabal to end now, raise your hands."

Drake glanced at Lord Blackmane, who had started to tentatively raise his hand. *"Don't you dare,"* Drake mouthed.

Blackmane lowered his hand at once. He even looked properly abashed.

Proudglade, Redbow, and Mistvale all raised their hands. Shortly after, Lord Ashwind did as well, but only after a stern glare from Lord Proudglade. What did the man have on him?

Lord Brightwater did not raise her hand. Neither did Lord Frostlight. The former was expected, but the latter was a surprise. Lord Proudglade's alliance was already fracturing.

It seemed, murderous people-hunting habits aside, Lord Frostlight was no more pleased by the idea that she might have been manipulated into an alliance than any normal person would be. Busting up Lord Proudglade's party was going better than Drake had hoped.

"Lord Frostlight?" Lord Mistvale said quietly. "We should evaluate the veracity of these odd and disturbing claims before we proceed."

"Or we could simply find out who's playing us all for fools

right now," Frostlight replied coldly. "Vote however you like. I, however, am not ready to end this cabal."

Drake wanted to cheer her on. Maybe she wasn't so bad after all. No, she hunted people for fun, murdered them, and made trophies out of their corpses. She was *definitely* still bad. Still, he could respect her for taking no shit from her so-called allies.

"The vote is four to five," the Judge said. "This cabal will continue. Lords Gloomwood and Skybreak remained censured for their crime, and we await testimony from Lydia Estoria and Samuel Marcos regarding Lord Redbow's—"

"I withdraw my grievance," Lord Redbow said.

The Judge offered him such a hard glare even Drake was taken aback. "You *what?*"

She was, it seemed, entirely done with today's nonsense.

Lord Redbow nervously adjusted his stupid-looking hat. "As Lord Proudglade has said, in light of this new information about the possibility that someone has a thrall who can change what people see, I am no longer fully confident my accusation has merit."

"You aired your grievance before the noble court."

"And I did so before this disturbing news came to light," Lord Redbow said smoothly. "I apologize for the imposition, but Lord Gloomwood's... testimony... offers new possibilities."

"Yes, we're all very much aware of that." The Judge now sounded about as snarky as she'd been all day. She sighed in exasperation. "Very well. Lord Redbow, your grievance against Lord Gloomwood is withdrawn, as is the order to seize Lydia Estoria and Samuel Marcos." She turned to the other manor lords. "Are there any other grievances?"

Lord Frostlight stood.

"Don't," Lord Mistvale said firmly.

"Lord Mistvale!" the Judge shouted. "Speak out of order in this court again, and I will censure you for this cabal and the next!"

The goddamned elder vampire immediately clammed up.

The Judge looked to Lord Frostlight. "Air your grievance."

Lord Frostlight smiled what could only be a predatory smile. "Based on Lord Gloomwood's testimony, it now seems possible I have been misled in one or more matters. This is unacceptable no matter *who* is responsible." Her raptor-like gaze passed across all those in the chamber, including her so-called allies. "I call for an inquisition. I say every manor lord now standing in this court must answer whether they know of, or have employed, any person who can change how people perceive events."

Drake could barely believe his luck. When Lord Frostlight thought she was being fucked over, she went straight for the throat. Which was no surprise, given she was an assassin.

An inquisition was very different from asking for testimony from blood thralls. It was also extremely rare. Few manor lords ever called for an inquisition because an inquisition, in the noble court, meant that manor lords themselves all had to answer the question posed.

That included the manor lord who called for the inquisition itself.

Drake had been excited by the possibilities an inquisition offered when he'd first read about it, but unfortunately he could think of no way to convince five manor lords to agree to call an inquisition without first revealing that someone had a thrall who could change what people saw... which would get him censured. As a result, he'd discounted the possibility.

Now, however, Lord Frostlight was calling for an inquisition herself. But would anyone second it? Drake and Sky couldn't second the inquisition since they remained censured, so would Lord Blackmane...?

"I second," Lord Brightwater said. "I also wish to know the answer to this question."

"The inquisition is seconded," the Judge said. "I now call for a vote. If you wish this inquisition to occur, raise your hands. I will remind each of you that five must vote in favor of this inquisition, and that all of you must answer the question if this motion passes."

"Which, if you are not involved in this business of deceiving the noble court, you will all happily do," Lord Frostlight added.

The Judge merely glared at her. "The vote is called. Raise your hands."

Drake immediately raised his hand, as did Sky, Lord Brightwater, Lord Blackmane, and Lord Frostlight. He couldn't believe it. They hadn't just put their enemies on their heels today. They might actually unravel this whole damn conspiracy before supper!

"The inquisition is called," the Judge said. "Lord Proudglade? I will put the question to you first. Do you know of, or have you employed, any person who can change how people perceive events?"

Before Lord Proudglade would answer, Lord Blackmane's manor lord box exploded in a shower of frothing water and wildly flopping fish people.

46
THIS IS WHY I CARRY A CROSSBOW

"The fuck?" was all Drake managed before the fish people attacked.

Or rather... a whole bunch of blue-skinned humanoids that were probably people. Who had flippers instead of feet. So fish people. Who also immediately started stabbing anyone nearby with silver spears, including all three blood thralls in Lord Blackmane's box.

Two unarmed women and one armed man died quickly, throwing their bodies between fish people spears and their manor lord. The next person the fish people tried to stab after they literally fell out of the fucking sky was Lord Blackmane himself... who evaded them by tossing his blonde blood thrall at the monsters. He then leapt over the wall of his box.

The shocked young woman got one spear through her stomach and another through her chest before she collapsed, stone dead, with the others. Meanwhile, Lord Blackmane sprinted for the doors as he ran for his very stupid life. What an incomprehensible asshole!

Rather than shooting Lord Blackmane in the back, which was

sorely tempting, Drake raised Magnum and pointed it at whatever the fuck these were. "Emily, go!"

His murdermaid charged the thrashing spear-wielding fish people with her glowing spectral axe. Since these fish people had appeared in Lord Blackmane's box, that sandwiched the invaders between the entourages of Lord Gloomwood and Lord Ashwind. With Blackmane's thralls all dead, the fish people were going to be Drake's problem next if his people didn't handle them right now.

As the first fish person leapt out of the box, Drake fired Magnum. That took the enemy down with a bolt through the chest. It wore a loin cloth and a bunch of beads on strings and had a little golden tiara on its head, but it had no armor. Good.

Drake took another enemy down with his next shot, which taught the rest to crouch inside the armored box... until Lord Ashwind's giant blood thrall arrived.

One fish person immediately stabbed the big man in the chest with a spear, a stab the huge man entirely ignored. With a deafening roar, he sliced three blue-skinned warriors apart with a single swing of his axe. The fish people bled blue, and a *lot* of blue spattered the box in the wake of the big man's axe. He didn't even glance at the spear straight through his torso.

Two other fish people leapt out of the box on Drake's side and then froze before he could shoot them. Each fell and shattered. Behind him, Valentia stepped to Drake's side. Meanwhile, Emily finally reached the rest of the surviving and wildly milling fish people. They now had glowing shields of light in their hands, and those seemed solid enough to block strikes.

One of the blue-skinned humanoids bellowed something in an indecipherable language Drake had no hope of understanding. His fish people allies collapsed into a tight group in the center of the box, shields locked to ward off any attack. They now numbered six in all, and they'd formed a seemingly impenetrable phalanx.

A visibly undeterred Emily leapt over the wall of Lord Blackmane's box, dodged past the slash of the nearest fish person, and swung her spectral battle axe. It first went *through* the light shields of the fish people and then *through* their flesh. The sounds they made as her spectral axe chopped their souls were the oddest, saddest sounds Drake had ever heard, like a dolphin being clubbed to death underwater.

Four died.

The two that survived only did so by diving backward to avoid Emily's soul-chopping slash. That put them in a perfect position to get curb stomped, shields and all, by the berserker giant thrall of Lord Ashwind, which he did. With his giant boots.

Once the huge man was done stomping the last two fish people into blue-colored fish people paste, he ripped the spear out of his torso and beat his chest with fists. He really was a berserker. Still, one soul chop from Emily would put him down if they got in a fight.

It was over. The... attack?... was over. And only then, as the shock and adrenaline and sheer *what the fuck is this now* began to fade, Drake remembered what these were called.

Kromians. These blue-skinned fish people were kromians. That's what Zuri and Lydia had both called them, and that left only two questions in his mind. Had these kromians known they were going to be summoned into a kill-or-be-killed murderfest before they arrived?

And how, exactly, had Lord Redbow summoned them here?

As Drake turned to see Redbow still standing in his box with his five remaining blood thrall assassins arrayed around him in defensive positions, the man looked to Drake and offered the faintest hint of a wink. Nothing else. Nothing that would prove anything.

The doors all burst open at once. A deluge of capital guards in gleaming black ferrocite came sprinting into the room, brandishing long spears and big shields. There was more than a bit of shouting and confusion as Drake wisely cautioned his people to stay in their box.

Emily sauntered back, quite visibly pleased with herself. Why wouldn't she be? She'd finally gotten to kill herself some assassins.

Still... the eyes of the pile of now-dead kromians haphazardly strewn about Lord Blackmane's box were as wide of those as his dead blood thralls. These didn't look like trained assassins. Rather, they looked like a bunch of very surprised and now very dead fish people.

"Clint!" Sky hissed at his side. "Are you hurt?"

Drake glanced at her in surprise to find Sky, Kari, Karth, and Ali all now standing in his box with him, along with Valentia and Viktoria. Sky, in particular, was standing surprisingly close. That was nice, actually.

"What?" He frowned. "I'm fine. They're all over there. This is why I carry a crossbow."

"Guards!" the Judge bellowed in a voice that shook the entire room. "Secure these chambers! Lords! Remain in your boxes! No one is leaving until we secure the room!"

Drake abruptly sat down in his box. "I sure didn't see that coming." He glanced at Viktoria, whose gaze was even now sweeping the room. "Does this mean the cabal is over?"

Emily dropped on her ass beside him and punched him in the arm. "And just when it was getting interesting! I really want to find out who's changing what people see."

He glanced at her. "Nothing ever fazes you, does it?"

"I'm not entirely sure what that means, lord. But I'm going with a no."

Valentia knelt at his other side. "Lord Blackmane is dead."

"What?" Drake sat up straight. "No, he's fine. He ran off? Right?"

"Gods." Sky stared out of the box. "Was it the kromians? How did they manage to kill him all the way up there?"

Drake sat up just enough to look over the top of the box in the direction Sky was looking. He grimaced as his stomach sank. Lord

Blackmane had fallen flat in front of the doors, atop the steps. The two capital guards kneeling beside him looked grim.

Lord Blackmane wasn't moving. Not one bit.

"Fuck," Drake whispered. "One of Redbow's thralls left before the attack. Did he take down Lord Blackmane in all this? Was the fish people explosion a distraction?"

"I saw the man leave as well," Viktoria agreed quietly. "If Kuzo is the thrall who left, we may be meeting the new lord of Blackmane Manor very soon."

Drake glanced at her in alarm. "Who's Kuzo?"

"Kuzo Turano is one of Lord Redbow's most successful assassins," Viktoria said. "The fact that he is now widely known is why he no longer takes many contracts. His rarity allows him to grab the heart of his target. If they move before he lets go, their heart ruptures."

"Wow," Drake said quietly. "Fuck that guy."

As Drake glanced at Lord Blackmane again, and as he acknowledged the man was dead, he couldn't feel too bad about it. Blackmane had tossed an eighteen-year-old girl at the kromians to save himself, and while Drake knew the reasons for it, logically—if a manor lord died, the whole manor and every blood thrall in it could be enslaved by a far more evil lord—it still bothered him that Lord Blackmane hadn't even hesitated.

Drake glanced at his thralls to get their opinions. "Wouldn't Blackmane's silverweave protect him from magic heart-grabbing guy? Like how it blocks Valentia's *flashfreeze*?"

"It should have," Viktoria said grimly. "All we have now is speculation. For the moment, I would suggest everyone remain alert. If kromians have somehow gained the ability to teleport right into the Temple of the Eidolons, they could pop up anywhere."

"That shouldn't be possible," Kari said. "Not with the temple's wards."

This was the first time Drake could remember Sky's blood

thrall, the one with the *my sword hits you very hard* rarity, speaking since lunch. "Yeah? How do those work?"

Kari glanced at him, visibly annoyed, but then Sky cleared her throat and Kari suddenly got a lot more friendly. "The temple has magical wards around it created by the Eidolons themselves. They forbid hostile magic from entering or exiting the temple."

"So what defines magic as hostile?" Drake asked. "Is teleporting hostile?"

"We don't know that much about kromian magic," Kari admitted. "I suppose it's also possible that some sort of totem, fetish, or magical artifact was involved."

"Like a magical artifact placed in Lord Blackmane's box that summoned them?"

Kari shrugged. "Anything is possible, Lord Gloomwood. I don't know how anyone could slip a magical item into a secured box in the Chamber of Council, but those kromians were certainly summoned here somehow."

"Sure," Drake agreed. "Sorry. Speculating about whatever magical bullshit is messing with me on a given day keeps me from freaking out any more than I have."

Kari's expression softened. "I forget you are not from our world. I see now why you might not know some of this, despite your position."

"So you thought I was... what? Mocking your expertise?"

Kari looked away. "Let's focus on remaining alert for more attacks."

Right. Kari wasn't his blood thrall, and he really didn't care how she felt about him so long as she was ready to kill kromians. Assuming Emily didn't kill them all first.

After a boring, grueling delay where an unseemly number of capital guards swept every bench and box in the room for anything out of the ordinary, the Judge finally spoke.

"The cabal is ended. Manor lords! You will be escorted to your chambers one by one, where an inquisitor will speak to you. You will not speak of the events of the cabal to anyone outside your manor. Lord Proudglade! You first."

The cabal was ending after all... just like Lords Proudglade and Redbow had intended. This fish people attack had to be the doing of one or the other. Drake had no proof, and he couldn't know exactly how either man had done it, but it made perfect sense.

Through this attack—however they had executed it—Proudglade and Redbow had stopped Lord Frostlight's inquisition, which would have revealed whoever employed a thrall that could alter what people saw. They had also, in a two-for-one coup, assassinated Lord Blackmane, the only other manor lord Drake could trust for votes besides Lord Skybreak.

Finally, it would now be three months before anyone could call another cabal.

Drake knew what would happen with Blackmane Manor now. He thought he did. But he'd better check. "Did Lord Blackmane have a successor?"

"He did," Viktoria said. "The last blood thrall he took to his bed before the one he brought with him today. She, however, killed herself shortly after lunch by jumping off the balcony." Viktoria grimaced. "Or that is the story being told."

"Fucking hell," Drake whispered.

He hadn't heard anything about this. But then again, since Lydia and Samuel would have been the ones who'd told him, and they'd both been on vacation today, it was unsurprising he was out of the loop. The "suicide" must have occurred after they ended their lunch.

Had this blood thrall killed herself because Lord Blackmane tossed her aside for the blonde girl? Or had Lord Redbow or one of his assassins gotten to her first? Had they made it look like she'd tossed herself off a balcony in preparation for today's attack?

"Does Blackmane have any other successors?" Drake asked.

If Lord Blackmane didn't have another successor, and this Kuzo assassin guy working for Lord Redbow had killed him... that made Kuzo the new lord of Blackmane Manor. Which meant Lord Proudglade's alliance of four manors had just hopped up to five.

"This speculation accomplishes little," Viktoria reminded him. "You are up next."

"Lord Gloomwood!" the Judge bellowed. "Now is your time to leave!"

As Emily waved at four very serious-looking capital guards who had just arrived at their box, Drake acknowledged Viktoria's point. "Right, talk later. My chambers or yours?"

"You come to us," Sky said. "For tonight."

She meant they had to get in touch with Samuel and Lydia using her magic mirror. Now that the cabal was over, Drake could once more rely on the council of his steward and spymaster without worrying they would be called to testify that he could lie.

Setting aside all the people and *fish* people who'd died today, this cabal hadn't gone half bad for Drake. In many ways, he'd actually won.

Go Team Gloomwood.

47
LEAVE, STAY, IT'S FINE

Once he and his blood thralls arrived safely back in his chambers, an inquisitor was, in fact, waiting. It was a man about Samuel's age with short salt-and-pepper hair, a crisp gold-and-blue uniform, and an expression that told Drake he would not appreciate being fucked with.

Which, naturally, made Drake want to fuck with the man all the more.

For the sake of his people and his manor, he refrained. Perhaps in compensation for all the bullshit he'd endured today, Drake's first inquisition was short.

"Lord Gloomwood, did you summon the kromians?"

"No."

"Do you know who summoned the kromians?"

"Not a clue."

"Did you order a blood thrall or anyone else in your employ to summon the kromians?"

"I did not."

"Did you assassinate Lord Blackmane, order a blood thrall to assassinate him, or contract an independent to assassinate him under the truce flag of a cabal?"

"I did not do any of those things. I don't know who killed Lord Blackmane."

Those questions were expected. The last question, however, was not.

"Have you ever had any contact with, or do you know of, any person with a rarity that allows them to change what people see?"

So the inquisition was proceeding despite the fish people interruption. Perhaps Drake would get his answer after all. If he did, Lord Redbow and his manor might be razed or dissolved without another word from him. *That* was an exciting possibility.

"I've never met or spoken with any thrall who can change what people see," Drake said. "But I know one's out there, somewhere, so keep looking. You can do it!"

After the inquisitor finished asking these same basic questions of Valentia and Emily, who were the only two blood thralls who'd been at the cabal today, he bowed once, rose, and left Drake's chambers without another word.

Drake glanced at Emily. "Are all inquisitor interrogations that quick?"

"I have no idea, lord." She grinned. "But today was fun! You got to beat up on the other manor lords, with words, and I got to beat up on a bunch of kromians, with Chopper!"

"Sure," he agreed. "Fun is one word for it."

Valentia, who was sitting beside him, abruptly jumped in her chair, then sighed. "*Now* is not the time to sneak up on me."

Nicole melted into view with her arms wrapped around Valentia's waist from behind, then lightly kissed the top of her head. "You were attacked today."

"They were just kromians. I froze them."

"You were *attacked* today." Nicole hugged her tighter. "Now hug."

Drake glanced at her. "You know, I was attacked today too."

Nicole, arms still wrapped around Valentia, smiled at him. "So you were!"

"Would you like me to hug you, lord?" Emily asked from his other side.

"I'm fine, thanks." He leaned back in his chair and closed his eyes. "Fuck," he added. "What a day." It wasn't even past sunset yet.

Eventually, after he felt somewhat sane again, Drake opened his eyes and looked around. "Anyone need a drink? I could use a drink."

Emily hopped up so fast her chair skidded backward. "Be right back, lord!"

As Emily hurried off to the kitchen, Drake glanced at Nicole, unsurprised to see her now sitting in a somewhat-grumpy-but-also-content Valentia's lap. "So? How was your day?"

"Robin is an excellent archer and shows promise with a blade," Nicole said. "I do not trust Gabriel to wield a spoon at supper. Carl gets faint at the sight of blood."

"Seriously?" Drake asked. "Who was bleeding?"

Nicole *tsk*ed. "Everyone bleeds, Lord Gloomwood." As she belatedly realized he wasn't going to stop staring menacingly, she sighed.

"But in this case, little Gaby tripped while attempting to evade me and smashed her head on the tile."

Drake straightened in his seat. "Is she all right?"

Nicole wiggled her fingers in one of her white gloves. "Healing magic. I am not cruel."

"Sure, right. I knew that." Drake frowned. "So you're not letting them use rarities?"

"Rarities only work until you're too tired to use them. Then you die." For once, Nicole sounded quite serious. "They know how to use rarities. They don't know how to not die. Today, I attempted to make them better at not dying."

As he remembered how easily he, Lydia, and Valentia had taken down his JV team outside Fort Graystone, Drake nodded.

"That's a good approach. You know... you might have a knack for teaching newbies."

She frowned. "I don't intend to make a habit of this."

"Oh, is that so?"

Her expression turned surprisingly sober. "Please don't make me make a habit of this."

"I'll consider it," Drake said. "But I'm not mocking you. Your training methods make sense, and it does seem like you'd be a good teacher. I think if those kids got a few more sessions with you, they could stay alive. So... what I'm saying is, you did a good job today."

Nicole eyed him like she'd eyed a strange bug. "You get odder every day."

Valentia squeezed her. "Shush now. Have you eaten?"

"I have eaten *some*."

"Then no mead for you," Valentia said.

"But, Val," Nicole whined.

"You know what?" Drake said. "You two take a break."

Valentia glanced at him. For once, she didn't ask if that was an order.

"I'm fine here," Drake said. "Emily will be back in a moment, the whole capital is on high alert for a fish people invasion, and I'm not going to step out on the balcony. So, Val, you get some food into Nicole, and Nicole, you get some rest after all your hard work today." He waved them off. "You two are both dismissed until this evening. Go."

Nicole hopped up at once. "You heard the lord, Val! We must go now."

Valentia stood as well, then glanced guiltily at Drake. "Are you certain?"

He nodded. "Oh, and you did good today too."

"I know." She offered a faint smile before yelping as Nicole grabbed her by both hands, then literally dragged her off in the direction of the servant's quarters.

Drake hoped they'd find someplace to *relax*. The sound of wooden cups bumping the table announced the arrival of more mead and Emily, but more importantly, he discovered both Lark and Fox standing behind her.

He had completely forgotten about the courtesans. He actually felt bad about that. Still, they got paid either way.

"Sit!" Emily said. "Lord Gloomwood needs drinking companions."

"Of course," Lark said softly. She had changed out of her fake battle maid uniform and now wore loose, silky clothes that were cut in all the right places. It was honestly unfair just how attractive she was right now.

Lark sat, gracefully, across from Drake on the other side of the table. Her resemblance to Lydia remained uncanny, which made Drake's heart flutter just a bit as the afternoon sun lit her features. What was that about? He'd just had an adrenaline-filled day.

Fox sat beside her and grabbed a cup of mead. Yet he hesitated before drinking, looking to Drake for permission. The poor guy still looked a bit spooked.

"Drink," Drake said. "You've already done everything I asked of you today, and I appreciate your hard work. So if either of you want to leave early, you can. That's fine."

"I have no other engagements," Lark said. "But I will leave now if you wish."

"No, you can stay! You can both stay. Leave, stay, it's fine."

Emily elbowed him meaningfully. "You know, you have at least one free hour before anyone will bother you. For anything." She also whispered that more than loud enough for both Fox and Lark to hear.

"I'm *done* for today," Drake reminded her. "Now, are we drinking or chatting?"

"I'll drink." Fox raised his cup to the group, then took a long swig of his mead.

Lark lifted her mug to her lips and took a tiny sip, then stared at Drake across the top of her mug. "And to what are we drinking this afternoon, Lord Gloomwood?"

Drake was tempted to say *"To not getting killed by fish people"* but that would reveal what had happened in the cabal today, which the Judge had explicitly said not to do to anyone outside his manor. He thought a moment, then raised his mug. "To not being dead."

Emily slammed her mug into Drake's so hard mead sloshed all over the table. "I will drink to that!" She then chugged with ferocity that made Fox stare... and immediately poured herself another mug.

With nothing else to do until the sun set and no one trying to kill him, Drake decided it was time to just stop thinking and enjoy a good buzz. It occurred to him, for the first time, that he hadn't even blinked before killing the fish people. They were people too... sort of.

So he'd killed two people today and ordered his thralls to kill a bunch more, which was pretty much the same as killing them himself. He'd also seen four people killed today... no, five, counting Lord Blackmane. Four women and one man had been butchered right before his eyes by kromian spears, and then Lord Blackmane's heart had apparently exploded. Or something.

And Drake felt... what?

Not horror or sadness. If he felt anything, he felt the satisfaction of a long day where he'd succeeded in more tasks than he'd failed. He was alive, his people were alive, and he'd pretty much won the cabal today... even if it ended before he could land the finishing blow.

There was no doubt in his mind. This title, or this blood pact, or something in the very fabric of this fucked-up fantasy world... it was making him more and more immune to the concerns he'd had back on Earth. People died. He even killed them. That happened here.

So long as they weren't *his* people, even if they were *good* people, he could simply look past it and get on with his day. If he got too hung up on grief over random deaths and guilt over killing his enemies and all that useless crap, he'd fail every person in his manor who now depended on him to keep them safe. He wasn't about to fail any of them.

"Lord Gloomwood?" Lark asked softly. "Are you all right?"

Drake snapped out of his reverie to realize he'd been staring at the table holding a half-empty drink. He looked up to find Emily nowhere in sight. Fox was gone as well.

He scrambled for a remotely intelligent question. "Uh... where's Emily?"

"She rose a moment ago to fetch more mead. Fox also excused himself after taking you up on your offer to leave early. I believe today was difficult for him."

Drake remembered he'd asked them to attend a manor lord cabal today. That must have been terrifying for them. "Was it okay for you?"

She smiled again. "I am fine, lord. Thank you for asking. And thank you for everything you did for me today."

He blinked. "What did I do for you?"

"You gave me an experience I've never had and one few outside of a noble manor have ever had. I attended a manor lord cabal." Lark's soft smile only grew more intoxicating with each moment. "You also agreed to interview my brother for a position in your manor, a generous gesture I truly appreciate. And finally, you were kind to me. That is appreciated. So... if there is anything I can do for you before I depart, I would be glad to do it."

Wow. He was obviously buzzed, and that wasn't good at all. Him being drunk and lonely with *her* looking like that, and also being sworn to do anything he asked, and also eager and *willing* to do anything he asked... was not a combination he felt safe experimenting with right now. Even if no one would care.

Emily had done this on purpose. She was actually trying to get him laid! Drake wouldn't be surprised to find her listening from the kitchen, silently hoping he'd score.

That thought alone managed to keep him from giving in to temptation. However... that didn't mean Lark couldn't help him in other ways. Ways his own people couldn't, at least since Lydia wasn't here. Lydia was the only person he could talk to after he watched people die.

Yet Lark was a capital courtesan, sworn to secrecy in regards to everything they said or did. She wouldn't repeat his doubts to anyone. And after today, he'd likely never see her again.

So perhaps there was another way she could make him feel better.

48
WHAT IF WE SIMPLY KILLED HIM?

"Lark... I'm going to ask you something now, and I'd like you to answer it as best you can. I promise, no matter how you answer, I won't be upset. I just need a friendly ear."

Her smile once again made his heart flutter, which was both hot and annoying. "I have had a number of strange requests in my time, lord. Ask anything you wish."

"In your opinion. Based on what you've seen in your time. If I can kill people and not feel guilty about it, and I can see people die and not feel sad about it, is that normal?"

"Were these people whom you killed trying to hurt you or those you care about?"

She hadn't so much as batted an eye at his question. "Yes, I suppose. The people I've killed were trying to kill me or others I wanted to protect."

"And these people you saw die, how well did you know them?"

"Not that well. Not at all, mostly. Except a few."

"And would you say the deaths of those you knew personally hurt more, or less, than those you do not know?"

Drake considered how he felt about Thak, the zarovian Suck

had killed. A zarovian who loved hitting things, and a loyal soldier who'd served him and died protecting him. "It hurts more. But still... I'm doing all right. More than all right. Should I be?"

She shrugged. "Could I suggest, Lord Gloomwood, that you are simply overwhelmed?"

He was immediately intrigued. "What does that mean?"

"A person in your position lives every moment under the threat of assassination and with the weight of protecting a manor full of people always in his thoughts. The situations you encounter every day are disturbingly intense. You see far more death than most."

"And that makes it okay to not feel sad about it?"

"It means you simply may have so many intense experiences washing over you at once that you may not be capable of feeling... well, much of anything in any moment. Or perhaps too much. I have only known you for a day, so please forgive me if I speculate."

"You're forgiven," Drake said quickly. "And please speculate."

"After seeing how you treat your thralls, I suspect you are simply too focused on protecting them and yourself in this current storm to worry about anyone outside your manor. I have spoken with many who face intense situations every day. Sailors. Soldiers. Mercenaries. Some have expressed similar concerns to yours, and they do not face all you face."

Drake considered her words in silence for a moment. He appreciated that she didn't add any others. He swirled his drink and looked into what remained. "So you're saying it's normal that I don't necessarily feel sad when I see innocent people get murdered in front of me, or guilty after I kill people trying to hurt me or my people."

"I am suggesting you cannot process such emotions due to the weight of your position and the frequency of these events. I would suggest you not worry about the intensity of your emotions until you enjoy a period of relative calm, one where you can reflect and think without the constant worry of protecting yourself, your manor, and your thralls."

Drake managed a chuckle, downed the rest of his drink, and put the empty mug down on the table. "I don't think that's happening any time soon."

"Then I would not trouble yourself. I would suggest how you feel today is as normal as anyone can feel when forced to deal, every day, with the situations you encounter."

Drake sighed and smiled. "That actually does make me feel better."

"Then... I am very glad I could be of service." She raised her mug to her lips once more, her eyes never leaving his.

A heavy knock sounded on the door to his chambers. With a curse, Emily stumbled out of the kitchen, then glanced his way in obvious alarm. "There's a knock!"

Drake stared at her. "I heard." So she *had* been listening the whole time.

"Shall I get the door, lord?" Emily asked innocently.

He scowled at her. "Yes. Why don't you go do that."

As Emily walked to the door, Drake sighed and glanced at Lark. "Sorry about her. Anyway... it's almost sunset. You're been great, and, um..."

"You may call upon my services at any time," Lark said softly. "For any reason."

He couldn't help but grin as he basked in her warm smile. "I just might."

Emily returned wearing an annoyed expression. "It was simply a courier from the royal court, lord. She had a message."

Drake nodded. He waited a beat. When Emily said nothing else, he added, "What was the message?"

"It was a message for you, lord."

Lark rose immediately. "I shall take my leave."

Oh. Right. It wouldn't be great for Emily to repeat a secret manor lord message in front of Drake's currently employed courtesan, even if she was sworn to secrecy and all that. He *was* buzzed. Still, it was awful late for a young woman to travel home alone.

"Can I send an escort with you?" Drake asked.

Lark smiled at him. "I will be fine, lord. Thank you for asking, but I know this city well."

"Okay, cool. So... thanks again."

She offered a half bow, rose, nodded to Emily, and headed for the door. After she closed it behind her, Emily glanced at him and shook her head in visible disappointment.

"That, lord, is what I would call a missed opportunity."

"Thanks for sharing," Drake said. "What was the message?"

"The cabal is now officially canceled. However, the royal court requests that all manor lords remain in the capital until the inquisitors charged with investigating today's incident are satisfied they have both apprehended the culprit and confident it cannot happen again."

"In other words, don't leave town until we know who summoned all those fish people." Drake sighed. "I wish they could just go arrest Lord Redbow."

Emily perked up. "You have proof it was Lord Redbow?"

"All I have is a cocky and annoying wink, which is the problem. That sneaky fuck probably had whatever magic or artifact he used to summon those fishmen and murder Lord Blackmane ready to go long before the cabal started, but I don't know how we could prove that. All I'm certain of right now is he did it to stop the inquisition, which means he's almost certainly the one with the thrall who can change what people see."

Emily nodded as if all of that made perfect sense. "What if we simply killed him?"

Drake was buzzed, but not *that* buzzed. This sounded a bit less crazy than Emily's normal suggestions. "Wouldn't we get arrested for doing that?"

"If we attacked him in the capital while the royal court said not to attack him, then yes, of course they would be upset," Emily said calmly. "But once this business is concluded, we could ambush him on the road out of the capital. I bet you could even use the blood you got from that assassin to suck his blood out through silverweave!"

Was she right? When Suck had used his blood-sucking rarity, it had been powerful enough to drop a person even through silverweave. Since Drake burnished rarities, that suggested that if he were to absorb Suck's power, he would be even more powerful. If he could get close enough to Lord Redbow, he could straight up murder the man.

But what then? Would the noble court censure him? He'd have to ask Samuel, but he suspected a direct attack would be frowned upon. Lord Proudglade could use his *shock spear* rarity to blow Drake to smithereens if he wanted, but he hadn't. He'd sent assassins instead.

Also, if Redbow died at Drake's hands, whoever he had chosen as his successor... if he had one... could be an even more dangerous assassin with even more reason to kill him. That meant killing Lord Redbow might not even solve anything. The next lord could be worse.

Finally, thanks to the stupid way debts passed on here, he'd saddle his successor... who might be Samuel... with the "Lord Gloomwood killed Lord Redbow!" debt. As much as he liked annoying Samuel in casual conversation, he didn't want to fuck the man over in that way.

Drake needed to confirm the details with Samuel, but it seemed like manor lords didn't directly fight other manor lords except in specific cases, like an honor duel. What if he challenged Lord Redbow to one? Could that resolve it? Another question for his spymaster.

A man who Drake wouldn't see until he told him it was okay to return.

Drake rose. "Emily? We're going out."

"Of course, lord!" She smiled. "We can still catch Lark if we move quickly."

Drake rolled his eyes. "We're not going to get me laid. We're going to speak with Lord Skybreak, and then we're going to use the mirror I gave her to contact Lydia and Samuel."

Emily nodded thoughtfully. "I suppose that's also important."

He'd already given Nicole and Valentia the rest of the night off. With the capital guards on high alert due to the fish people incident, he doubted he'd need an escort at all. Still, Emily would be upset if he left without her, and Lydia would be really upset if she found out. So Drake grabbed his cloak, adjusted his silverweave, and headed out the door.

With Emily walking close at his side like a very nervous mother hen... with a giant axe... they passed a number of capital guards either patrolling the hallways of the building or standing at attention at various doors and cross tunnels. The Judge really had stepped up security. The guard population had been noticeably thinner before now.

Fortunately, Drake knew the way to Lady Skybreak's chambers since he'd traveled them before. They had to go all the way to the center of the building. There, even more capital guards were stationed. They traveled around a curved hallway and then back up a parallel hall. It wasn't a short path, but it was at least straightforward.

Once they got within sight of the door to Lord Skybreak's chambers, Drake spotted several men and women in leather armor in addition to the capital guards. So Sky wasn't trusting purely to the capital's security force to keep her safe. Having some of his own people outside as well was a good idea. He'd give that order as soon as he got back.

The capital guards in the hall didn't challenge him, but the leather-armor-clad man and woman outside the door did. Both carried long blades, which made sense given the close quarters. A blade would be better than a bow and arrow in here.

"Halt!" the woman ordered. "State your business!"

"Lord Gloomwood here to see Lord Skybreak," Drake said. "We talked about this."

"Wait here," the man ordered. He knocked on the door, a pattern of three knocks.

The door opened just a bit. The man spoke quietly with someone on the other side but did not enter. The door shut again. The man resumed his post.

Lord Skybreak's people really were paranoid after the cabal. Drake would make sure his people were equally paranoid when he returned. He glanced at Emily to see if *she* looked paranoid, but she was simply humming quietly to herself.

His blissfully zen murdermaid always looked like she was having the time of her life. Maybe he'd feel the same if he could chop the soul of anyone who darkened his day. Either way, Emily's calm helped him remain calm. She was a good friend.

The door opened once more, and then another ranger stepped out. "You may enter."

"Thanks," Drake said. "Also, my battle maid's entering as well." He didn't want Emily throwing a fit if he tried to leave her outside… or chopping someone.

"That's acceptable," the man said.

Drake slipped in through the door with Emily practically on his heels. They entered to find that Sky's chambers were now organized differently than he had been at lunch. The common room now had a large table in the middle of it with a big map laid out on that table. Drake looked it over and realized it appeared to be a map of the whole realm.

The map matched what he'd seen before in Samuel's books. This realm was a mostly circular mass of land with a few noticeable bays and inlets. Korhaubauten rested on the center east of the mass, facing the sea, with the manor territories arranged around it. There was an island chain off the west coast that added to Lord Brightwater's territory.

He also spotted colorful markers like those he'd made for his diorama map at home placed on the map. A number of blue markers were clustered along the border between Skybreak and Redbow territory, facing a number of red markers.

Perhaps they were gaming out some sort of military encounter. Perhaps Sky was worried about Lord Redbow's forces invading her lands. Was she working out what would happen if Redbow tried to invade her territory? He'd ask her when he saw her.

"This way, Lord Gloomwood," the man who'd invited them inside said.

Drake didn't recognize anyone in these chambers. He didn't see Karth or Head Ranger Cask or Lady Skybreak. The reason why became obvious when he reached the balcony. All four of them were out there talking in quiet tones. Sky looked up when he arrived.

"Lord Skybreak," Drake said. "Am I interrupting?"

"Yes," she told him.

Oh. Well then.

"But I know you wouldn't have done so if it wasn't important," she added. She glanced at Cask. "Can you and Karth excuse us a moment?"

"Of course, lord," Cask said.

Karth glanced at Drake again. When he did so, Drake caught an odd look. Karth didn't exactly look angry with him, but he certainly didn't look happy. While he hid it, Drake had the distinct impression Karth was annoyed by his arrival. He'd ask about that later.

Once they'd exited, which he hadn't asked for but was absolutely willing to allow, he approached Sky and her mother. "Sorry to bother you, but I need another favor."

"Does this favor involve us being censured by the noble court?" Viktoria asked.

"Not this time." Drake grinned. "But I do need to call my steward and spymaster."

"I suppose their counsel might be useful," Sky agreed. "I'll go get my mirror."

49
TIME TO FIND OUT HOW MUCH I CAN SUCK

Fortunately, a brief exchange over Sky's magic mirror assured Drake that Lydia, Anna, and Samuel had simply had a lovely day exploring the city. They did not get attacked by assassins, nor were they ambushed by a horde of fish people. They simply had a nice time walking, seeing the sights, and enjoying some snacks.

There was one minor incident where Anna almost choked on a pastry she'd tried to eat far too fast, but Samuel was there to help her recover. Even in this world they had the Heimlich maneuver... though obviously, they didn't call it that.

After he'd given Lydia and his people the all clear to return to his chambers, Drake spoke with Sky and Viktoria long enough to form a game plan for their immediate future. They both agreed Lord Redbow had summoned the fish people to stop the inquisition before he could be forced to speak about it. Since no one could leave the capital until the Judge proved that (or found another culprit), they would continue to meet once a night and compare notes.

Viktoria assured them both that the Judge couldn't detain them forever. Pressure would grow from all quarters if the investigation continued with no leads or progress, and she suspected, perhaps within a week, that the manor lords would be free to return to their manors if no one had been implicated. The delay wasn't great, but at least Drake could go home.

He once again pondered Emily's suggestion for ambushing Lord Redbow on the way home and just straight up murdering the old fucker. It wasn't exactly noble or legal, but it could get him some breathing room between all the assassination attempts... if he could pull it off without getting censured. The biggest problem was Lord Redbow's cadre of assassins, who were at least as deadly as Drake's battle maids. And they had numbers.

He already knew one: Kuzo, the thrall who could grab your heart and crush it if you took a step. Redbow no doubt had many others like him, and as much as Drake wanted the man dead, he didn't want to lose his people in a straight-up battle. Hiring a Gilded Blade would be too expensive (they really did cost an absurd amount of coin) and even if they could afford it, the rumors remained that the Gilded Blades were secretly associated with Redbow Manor.

Any Gilded Blade he hired might warn Lord Redbow or even refuse the contract. If that happened, Redbow would go on even higher alert. So Drake needed another, better plan. And fortunately, he had a few days to come up with one. He did not, however, mention his thoughts or plan to Sky or Viktoria.

Plausible deniability. That was how you handled your business as a manor lord. If not for the damned blood pact and Lord Redbow's use of it, Drake could have hired one of Redbow's people to turn against him and seize the manor. He'd find another way.

Drake returned to his chambers and didn't sleep until Lydia, Samuel, and Anna all safely returned home. Seeing them back unharmed was a massive relief, and Anna immediately started chattering about the amazing time she'd had today. Even Lydia looked flushed and satisfied by the day's activities, and only Samuel looked as dour as he usually did.

Lydia and Anna were also a bit reddened from the sun, though Samuel looked the same as always. His regeneration rarity, most likely. Once everyone was settled down, Drake decided it was finally time to get some sleep himself. He didn't have anything big to do tomorrow, but it was dark, his people were all asleep or working, and he had finished a busy day.

He had almost drifted off when there was a sharp rapping at his chamber door.

"Lord Gloomwood?" Lydia called. "Lark has returned. We have a problem."

Drake sighed heavily, pushed up in his bed, and reached for his boots. "Here we fucking go again." He got dressed just enough to be respectable and emerged from his chamber expecting to find his battle maids and Samuel assembled.

They were all there, and as Lydia had said, Lark was with them. She also had one hell of a black eye... not to mention her split lip, bruised cheek, and some once-nice clothes that looked like they'd been torn on a fence line. They'd even been stained with blood.

As Lark saw him emerge, her eyes widened in what looked like relief. "Lord Gloomwood. Thank you for seeing me."

It was all he could do not to rush to her. He walked at a hurried pace instead. There was only one question on his mind as she looked around the room. "What happened?"

"It's Darion," Lark said. "My brother." She took a breath. "Lord Redbow's people abducted him this evening. I believe they intend to force him to take the Redbow blood pact."

Drake glowered. "Like hell they will."

So with the cabal now at a close, Lord Redbow was moving on to other matters in the city. Lark had mentioned Redbow was interested in Darion and his flesh-mending rarity, but Drake had assumed that since Darion had promised to join his blood pact instead, he wouldn't need to protect the man so soon. He should have known better.

"Who did this to you?" Drake demanded. "Was it Redbow's thugs?"

"Local mercenaries, lord," Lark said. "They abducted Darion and me at the same time and placed me in protective custody."

"Doesn't look like they were that protective."

"Their orders were to hold me until Darion took the blood pact and the matter was concluded," Lark said. "However, I managed to escape."

"How?"

"I would prefer not to discuss the details."

Drake wanted to leave it there, but he'd encountered too much doublespeak and barely avoided falling into too many traps. "I'm sorry, but that's simply not acceptable right now."

She wilted a little under his hard gaze. "How do you mean?"

"I've been played too many times." Drake considered carefully. "I need you to answer *all* my questions before I agree to help you. First, do you serve Lord Redbow in any capacity?"

"No," Lark said firmly.

"Have you served him in the past?"

"Once, for the services I generally provide."

Drake hated that he had to ask this question. "You mean sex."

She took a breath. "Yes."

"And only sex?"

"Yes."

Moving on, then. "Are you under any sort of duress?"

"No."

"Is anyone forcing you to be here or to ask me to rescue your brother?"

"No."

"And is there anything else about this abduction or your reasons for being here tonight that you aren't telling me?"

"No, lord," Lark said again, so quietly and pitifully it made his heart ache.

Still, this wasn't enough. "Do you have any plans to betray me in any manner? Or betray anyone who works for me? Or do anything other than ask me to go get your brother?"

"I have no plans to betray you or anyone in your manor, lord," Lark said quietly. "I have no association with Lord Redbow. My only purpose in coming here tonight was to beg you to rescue my brother from the mercenaries who took him so they could force him to join Lord Redbow's blood pact."

Drake glanced at Samuel. "Anything I missed?"

Samuel brushed his chin beard. "Nothing that cannot wait."

Good enough. He felt like he'd just kicked a puppy. "Lydia?"

"I sense no deception, lord."

"Good." Drake looked to his people. "Here's what's going to happen next. We're going to get a crew together, and then we're going to find the mercenaries who gave Lark a black eye and took her brother away. Then, if they don't give Darion back to us, we are going to fuck them beyond recognition... and bring him home."

Lark bowed her head. "Thank you, lord."

"This isn't benevolence," he sternly reminded everyone in the room. "It's business. Darion has a healer's rarity, and it sounds like a powerful one. He's already said he wanted to serve me, not Lord Redbow. I want his rarity in my manor. I'm not letting Redbow steal him."

"Agreed," Samuel said. "Still, we must approach this matter cautiously."

Drake resisted the urge to say "*Duh*." He looked to Lark instead. "Do you know where they're holding your brother?"

"On the docks," Lark said firmly. "I managed to get that much out of one of the men who was tasked with holding me. The mercenaries make their home in a heavily armored skiff that moors often in the harbor. It has cells inside. That must be where they have Darion."

"And you're sure Lord Redbow hasn't forced him to take the blood pact yet?"

Lark grimaced. "I... cannot be certain of that, lord."

"But you still came to me. You still think we have a chance to free him. Why?"

"The mercenaries who took me had enough supplies in the building where they took me to last many days. This suggested they did not intend to go out again. Also, because they had orders to imprison me for three days, that suggests Lord Redbow cannot immediately meet with Darion and force him to take the blood pact. He needed me contained."

Lark continued to impress him with her judgment, smarts, and capabilities. She might not have a rarity, but it looked increasingly like she might not need one. Drake was already starting to think she might make an excellent spy, but that was a question for later.

"The Judge is watching all of us closely," Samuel said thoughtfully. "All the manors."

Drake nodded. "Which means Lord Redbow might not want her to see him traipsing down to the dock to pick up a guy his mercenaries just illegally abducted so he can torture him into joining a blood pact." He glanced at Valentia. "You once told me it's illegal for manor lords to snatch people off the streets and hurt them in Korhaurbauten. That's still the case?"

Valentia simply nodded.

"So Lord Redbow might need some time to arrange a way to meet Darion in private. That means we have time to rescue him before he can force Darion to submit." He considered Lark's story. "What about the men who held you captive? Will they warn the others?"

"No," Lark said. "I was forced to kill them during my escape."

Holy shit! Lark really could handle herself. His respect for this woman, which had already been at a decent level, spiked by a considerable degree.

He looked to Nicole. "Find Sachi. Find this boat. Scout it out and tell me everything you can about it. I want to know how many guards they have and if anyone's hidden on the docks."

Nicole frowned at him. "You mean right now?"

He stared at her in stone-faced silence.

"Right," she agreed. "Off I go!" She hurried off to find Sachi.

"The capital guard also patrols the docks of Korhaurbauten," Samuel said. "Thus far, we have only Lark's testimony against the two who abducted her. They are now deceased. We have nothing tying the mercenaries on the boat to Darion's abduction."

Drake eyed him in annoyance. "Other than he's literally sitting in a cell in their boat?"

"We can't know for certain they are still holding Darion in their boat," Samuel reminded him... which was a good point. "They could have him hidden elsewhere. They could even murder him the moment we attack, then destroy his body before witnesses arrive."

The way Lark paled at Samuel's words made it obvious how much they pained her, but Drake didn't have time to worry about her feelings right now. Samuel was right. Lord Redbow could have given his mercs orders to kill Darion if it seemed like he might escape... and if they had someone who could destroy bodies, they could also destroy the *evidence.*

"So what you're saying, Samuel, is we can't just roll up and beat the shit out of them. Not until we know they actually have Darion, and that we can get him out of there alive."

Samuel nodded. "Regardless of whatever legal resolution eventually emerged, attacking those who have violated no laws on the docks would violate local laws. So if we start a conflict on the docks in front of the capital guards, we would be held liable by the noble court."

Drake considered. "Is there any way we could tie Lord Redbow to this? Capture the mercenary leader, maybe, and make her testify?"

"It is possible, but arranging a trial and testimony could take days or even weeks. As harsh as it may sound, this is a minor matter in the court's eyes. I doubt the Judge will spare time to resolve this minor dispute. Her inquisitors remain focused on today's other matter."

Everything Samuel had just said made Drake's decision all the easier. "So we'll handle it ourselves. Just like I planned."

"And how," Samuel asked cautiously, "will we be handling it? Need I remind you of the question raised in today's inquisition?"

Right. There was a thrall out there who could alter what people saw. So was it possible Lark had seen Redbow's mercs abduct Darion when it hadn't happened? That this was all some sort of elaborate trap to make Drake commit a crime?

It was *possible*, but so were a lot of other things. Drake couldn't let his fears about misdirection paralyze him. He had to take *action*, for better or worse, and he would only do whatever he did once he was certain he wasn't being played.

"We won't attack anyone until we know what we're dealing with. Once Nicole and Sachi get back with the details, we'll all brainstorm a plan to rescue Darion, one that won't get us in trouble with the capital guards or censured by the noble court if we start a fight. I don't know what that plan will be, but if we all put our heads together, we can find one."

Drake looked around for arguments or suggestions. No one said anything. That worried him. "Anyone disagree?" he asked finally.

No one shook their heads. Lydia spoke up. "This seems like a fine course of action, lord."

Really? Maybe he was finally getting the hang of this manor lord thing. "Good. Samuel, while we're waiting for intel, go talk to your spies and see if any of them witnessed Darion and Lark's abduction. We need independent verification. Witness testimony."

Samuel nodded and strode off.

"Everyone who's not doing something I already said, I want in a team meeting in ten minutes. I want to hear all ideas for rescuing Darion, no matter how odd." He glanced at Emily. "Go haul the JV team out of bed. I want them in on this too."

Emily smiled at him. "Does everyone include the zarovians, lord?"

Drake considered a moment. There wasn't enough room for all his zarovians, so their leader would be enough. "We could use Cresh. He can speak for the zarovians and whatever they might offer to this, right?" Also, the dude was massive. If he wanted someone to intimidate some mercenaries, Cresh seemed like the right... lizard guy... for the job.

He glanced at Valentia. "You mind heading down to the temporary barracks and bringing Cresh back up here?" The zarovians were bunked with other soldiers below.

Valentia briefly inclined her head and strode off. His advisors were decreasing by the moment, but no one seemed to mind. Meanwhile, Emily darted off to route Robin, Gaby, and Carl out of bed, likely through some traumatizing method he'd prefer not to know about.

He looked around at who was left. What did he still need? Time was of the essence now.

"And me, lord?" Lark asked. "How can I aid you?"

Lark really was impossibly brave given all she'd been through, but she'd also had a hell of a night. "*You* can go see my shaman, who's going to look at those cuts, wounds, and bruises and make sure there's no other injuries. I'd ask my battle maids to heal you, but they'll need their blood for whatever happens next." He spotted Tamara watching from the edge of the room and snapped his fingers at her. "Tamara? Show Lark to Raylan."

"Yes, lord." Tamara touched Lark's arm. "This way, please. I'll make you some tea."

As the two of them strode off together, Lark glanced back at him with wide eyes. "Thank you, lord! If you need anything else, you need only ask!"

Drake looked to at rest of his people, most of whom he now knew by name. "The rest of you, get everything together we'll need to pull this off. Weapons, medical supplies, whatever. When we figure out our plan and decide to move, I want to move right then. Now get to it."

Everyone walked off in all directions with determined expressions, bound to follow his orders and willing to do so. It was odd he hadn't expected that. Maybe it was about time he should. As he headed to his bedroom again, Lydia fell into step at his side.

As he opened the door, he glanced at her. "Keeping an eye on me?"

"Always," she said firmly.

Once he closed the door behind them, Lydia took up position beside it. As he rummaged through his belongings by the bed, Lydia spoke again.

"Regeneration may still be the best rarity for you, lord. Especially if we're going to go up against others with rarities."

"It's the best defensive rarity, but these mercenaries sound dangerous. They'll probably be wearing silverweave or ferrocite. If we get in a fight, I need to be ready to take them out."

Lydia gasped quietly. "So… it's time for *that* vial?"

"I think so." Drake pulled out a vial of blood he'd drained from a man he'd strapped to a chair and shot through the chest. "Time to find out how much I can suck."

50
LET'S GO SAY HELLO TO THE ACID LADY

By the time midnight rolled around, Drake had all the information his people could obtain about the mercenaries who'd abducted Darion, the boat where they were holding him, and the (visible) defenses they'd erected. A few hours after that, after a spirited and illuminating strategy session with his people, he had an actual plan to rescue Darion without getting his people killed or causing enough damage he'd get censured by the noble court.

They might actually pull this off after all.

It took another hour to get permission from the temple guards to leave the temple and "take a nighttime tour of the city," but eventually, either the guards had run out of excuses or they had people shadowing him from the rooftops to keep an eye on him. Drake suspected both, but he was fine with that. The more witnesses who said he hadn't started this, the better.

An hour after that, he was crouching on the docks of Korhaurbauten. Street traffic had been light and the sunrise remained a few hours off, which made it possible that at least some of these mercenaries might be asleep when they arrived. Drake doubted it.

His luck wasn't that good, and they'd be on high alert until Lord Redbow showed up to retrieve his prize.

Waiting any longer hadn't been an option. These mercenaries would be stupid to not check on the crew who'd been holding Lark hostage every few hours, and since Lark had killed the mercenaries holding her hostage, the enemy mercenaries would know she was free and had gone for help. They'd be on high alert and ready for any attack, but the less time Drake gave them to prepare, the less time they'd have to ready themselves for battle.

Or get additional mercenary reinforcements from Lord Redbow.

Drake's new plan was a bit risky, but what plan wasn't? The most important part of it was that it put his people at less risk than if they confronted the mercenaries directly. He wasn't dealing with amateurs any longer. Every person in this mercenary group was a seasoned warrior with a powerful rarity and absolutely no reason not to kill those who crossed them.

Drake knew that confronting these mercenaries directly would be dangerous because, thanks to intelligence gathered by Nicole, Sachi, and Samuel, he now knew who led them. She was a real piece of work that one of his people had a personal grudge against.

The leader of this merry mercenary band was the Asp, the ruthless acid-throwing lady who Robin desperately wanted to kill. She'd served Lord Redbow by entering Fort Graystone and waiting there until he posted his fake bounty. In retrospect, it shouldn't have surprised Drake that a powerful mercenary devoid of scruples would abduct people for Redbow as well.

The Asp had also slaughtered Robin's entire village, which had naturally caused a bit of a ruckus when Robin learned the woman was right here in the city. He'd been glad he'd already made the decision to confront the Asp and free Darion, because if he hadn't, he might not have been able to stop Robin. Yet as much as Robin had pleaded for Drake to just murder the Asp in cold blood the moment she showed her face, he couldn't do that.

At least, not if he struck *first*.

If Drake attacked the Asp without cause, he would be committing assault and possibly murder. While manor lords could murder whoever they liked in their own territory with impunity, their authority was limited in the capital city. Keeping manor lords from simply killing anyone they liked inside the capital's walls was the only way to maintain the city's neutrality.

Still, the laws of the city only forbid him from attacking the Asp *first*. If she attacked him, she would be striking directly at a manor lord. The noble court wouldn't stand for that, and Drake would be fully within his rights to murder her ass... or, more likely, to order his cadre of powerful battle maids to murder her ass for him.

Still, if all went well with his brilliant plan, no one would get murdered today. The Asp's mercenary company would get pissed off and humiliated, and be out a good bit of money, but hopefully they'd take their financial losses as a sign not to fuck with Lord Gloomwood in the future. They'd move on. If they didn't, well... he already had no shortage of enemies in this world. It wasn't like one more band of mercenaries gunning for him would change things.

The salty smell of the bay joined the gentle lapping sounds of waves as Drake paused in the shadow of a large warehouse on the docks. This was the closest warehouse to the stretch of dock leading out to where the Asp's battle boat was tied up and moored. It was a low-slung, sleek-looking vessel with an armored hull and glistening metal doors leading to the cabin. The only way to reach it was to walk down an open dock with no cover for fifty paces or more.

A tall main mast led to a crow's nest in which a single shadowed figure sat motionless with a clear view of the entire docks. The gently bobbing boat sported no cannons—gunpowder wasn't something they had in this world yet, fortunately—but it did have four prominent crossbow turrets mounted at the fore, aft, left, and right. Those crossbows were big enough Drake suspected they could send a bolt clean through a zarovian.

While those weapons were intended to kill people, Drake suspected a big enough bolt fired at the right portion of a boat could also cause it to start sinking. He didn't see any other weapons besides the crossbow turrets, but the Asp wouldn't need those. Samuel had told him she could fling her acid a good ways, almost as far as Carl would throw his meteor kabooms.

Then, of course, there were the Asp's mercenaries, which the intelligence his people had gathered told him numbered at least eight... each with a rarity comparable in power to that of his battle maids. While Samuel hadn't been able to find out what all of them could do, at least one was a shifter and another could shoot fire-bolts from his fingers. All bad.

Finally, these mercenaries would, of course, be fully equipped with silverweave outfits over which they would wear ferrocite armor. Most rarities and weapons would have very little effect on them. So if it came to a fight between them, Drake would just have to hope his "uniquely targeted rarity"—Suck's rarity—could bypass their defenses and drain their blood.

At least he knew Suck's rarity was now functioning. He knew because every time he looked at someone, he saw a brilliant yellow glow embedded inside their head. He could *feel* blood pumping inside whoever he looked at. It was the creepiest feeling ever.

Also, like with Anna's rarity, he instinctively understood how Suck's rarity would work. If he mentally concentrated on the glow inside someone else's head, he'd start sucking their blood out through their eyes and mouth. He hadn't dared test this new rarity on any of his people. Suck had killed Thak the zarovian quickly even when his rarity *wasn't* burnished.

So, he had the burnished rarity of a now-dead Gilded Blade. He had Magnum strapped to his back and loaded with a full quartet of bolts. And he had some very powerful people on his side. He was confident he and his people could give a good accounting of themselves if it came to battle... but not that some of his people wouldn't die.

Which was why they were doing this the clever way.

He glanced back at the crew he'd chosen to act as the decoy team. Lydia and Emily were present, of course, but Valentia and Nicole weren't. They had other jobs to do. Gaby and Carl *were* here, for offense and defense, and both looked somewhere between thrilled and terrified to be on their first official mission as Gloomwood Manor thralls.

Finally, six zarovians in ferrocite armor were with him as well, including Korrag. They formed a sizable vanguard that looked like they could beat the shit out of anyone who crossed him. They were here for their skill in battle, their intimidation factor, and to make the Asp think she knew where his zarovians were... so she wouldn't wonder where Cresh and the rest were hiding.

Robin (with Sachi to keep her in check) would even now be creeping across the rooftops of the warehouses on the dock to get a good angle on the mercenary boat. Sadly, even having two talented archers on the high ground wouldn't improve their chances against the Asp's crew in a straight-up brawl. Arrows couldn't penetrate ferrocite, but at least he'd have eyes up there to warn him if Lord Redbow's people came at him from behind.

Finally, Raylan was with Drake's party as well. The man looked more than a bit nervous to be out in the field in a place where he could get murdered, but with an acid-throwing lady in play and all her other powerful mercenaries with her, Drake needed at least one healer close on hand. His battle maids would be too busy fighting for their lives to heal others.

Samuel, naturally, was stuck back in the temple. If Drake's entire party got wiped out today, the title of Lord Gloomwood would pass to Samuel instead of the Asp. The manor would remain in good hands. That was a comfort on a night when not much else was comforting.

He had his people. He had his plan. And he had to move out and rescue Darion before Lord Redbow reinforced the Asp or came himself. Drake knew he could defend himself from random mercenaries and kill them if they attacked him, but directly attacking Lord Redbow or his blood thralls was a different matter entirely. He still hoped to avoid that.

"Any questions about the plan?" Drake asked. "Last chance."

No one spoke. They'd gone over the plan and accepted it. He appreciated his people's faith in him. It was time to go be a fucking manor lord.

"Form up," Drake said. "Let's go say hello to the acid lady."

Drake rose as Korrag led two zarovians around the group and out of the shadows. Drake fell into step right behind the wall of muscle and armor they formed with Lydia on one side and Emily on the other. Gaby was right behind him, followed by Carl and Raylan. The last three zarovians formed a loose wedge around them, completely encircling the group.

In that way, Drake and his vanguard walked straight down the middle of the docks in full view of the waiting boat. A piercing whistle told him the lookout in the crow's nest atop the main mast had warned the others. The lookout didn't descend from his position, which suggested he either had a rarity that worked from up high or was keeping an eye out for others.

By the time Drake's vanguard stopped about ten paces from one of the two tall posts around which ropes attached to the Asp's boat were moored, her gangplank was already up and most of her crew was already on deck. He counted six visible figures plus the one in the nest. That made seven. So was that all of them? He glanced at Emily.

"Three remain below, lord," she said quietly. "Two are moving. One is not."

The soul who wasn't moving was likely Darion in his cell. The two moving souls would be patrolling mercenaries in reserve in the cabin. They were the people Drake needed to get up here on deck before his plan would work. He had to force the Asp to call for reinforcements.

Worse, unless he wanted everyone in Korhaurbauten to know

he could speak words he didn't believe—exactly what Lord Redbow had accused him of doing earlier today—he couldn't use his ability to lie. He had to use doublespeak and good old-fashioned guile. Even if he killed the Asp and everyone with her after, his own people would know he'd lied.

A tall woman with a flowing red hood and robe under a patchwork of ferrocite and feathersteel armor sauntered into view. She placed one boot on the low-slung railing of her boat and leaned dangerously over the edge, arms crossed. This must be the Asp. Her hood shadowed her face, revealing only her narrow, brown chin and her bared white teeth.

The five figures on deck with her were dressed in similar garb, silverweave overlaid with armor. All wore hoods as well. Drake could see a faint-yellow glow in each of their heads even through their silverweave, but that didn't mean he could suck them dry. Also, all of them appeared entirely unconcerned by his arrival. He hoped that was an act.

"Lord Gloomwood!" the Asp called from her boat. "Are you in need of my services? If you are, you should know that I and my people don't work cheap!"

Drake wasn't surprised she'd recognized him despite the full suit of feathersteel he wore and the silverweave beneath it. He had, after all, shown up with two battle maids and a vanguard of zarovians. That was kind of Lord Gloomwood's thing.

So now all he had to do was bullshit her long enough to steal Darion away.

51
IS YOUR BOAT OKAY?

Drake pulled back his hood to reveal his face. That was dangerous and reckless since it left him open to an arrow through his eyes, but it was his first shot at getting the opening he needed. It would also suggest he wasn't scared of the people arrayed against him.

"And you'd be the Asp!" he shouted back. "Any reason you're hiding your face from me? Got some old battle scars? Are you shy, maybe?"

If he could get the Asp to pull her hood back, he would have a clean shot at sucking her blood out of her eyes. He could still see the yellow glow he saw inside the heads of other people, though on her the glow was much more faint. Muffled, but still present.

"I'm afraid the sight of my great beauty costs more than you've offered!" the Asp shouted back. "Now state your purpose here. If I like your job, I just might take it!"

She wasn't pulling back her silverweave hood. He also wondered if she was referring to an offer he might make her… or his job as manor lord. Either would be what she believed. She was already taunting him with doublespeak.

"I'm not here to hire you!" Drake called back. "I'm also not here for a fight! I'm here because you have someone who belongs to me!"

Drake had no intention of fighting the Asp and her mercenaries. That was true enough. It didn't mean he wouldn't if she forced the issue.

"You're most likely mistaken, lord!" the Asp called back. "We have not abducted any of your blood thralls, nor do any of my people have any open contracts with you!"

Most likely mistaken. Clever. It wasn't a lie, because the Asp could conceivably believe he *might* be mistaken about this. She didn't know who he was here for yet. He filed her ploy away under "weird shit he could say in the future" and moved on with his plan.

"Then I'll make this real easy for you!" Drake called. "You're holding a man named Darion Bressos in the belly of your boat there! He's already agreed to join my manor and become my blood thrall! So if you'll simply return my property, you can go about your day!"

"Has this man signed an official contract to join your manor?" the Asp called.

Of course she'd asked that, and of course he hadn't. "He said he wished to join me! My thralls heard it too!"

"And did this man speak to you directly?" the Asp called tauntingly. "Or did you hear about his uncommitted musings from another source? A woman, perhaps? His sister?"

Damn, she was good. Drake would have almost liked the Asp if she hadn't ruthlessly melted an entire village because they pissed her off. He knew from his chat with Samuel that even a direct conversation with a person where they agreed to join a manor wasn't ironclad. They had to sign an actual paper contract or be inducted into a blood pact to be off limits.

Yet the Asp had also slipped up just now, at least if he'd heard her right. It was easily possible that she could know Lark had called for help simply by the fact he was here, but she couldn't know that Darion hadn't spoken to him directly about joining his manor. Not unless Darion had told her that, which he'd only do if she'd tortured him.

Drake hoped Darion wasn't going to be all burned up and scarred after whatever the Asp and her people had done to him. That was a horrible fate he wouldn't wish upon anyone... except maybe Lord Redbow. That fucker could melt in a vat of acid.

"Still two below, lord," Emily said softly. "Along with the third one."

Time to escalate. "We had a verbal agreement! Darion Bressos intends to join my manor, which means you, lady, are holding one of my blood thralls hostage! I'm fully in my rights to retrieve him! So if you want to keep this boat and your lives, get him up here!"

The Asp straightened and stepped back from the railing of her vessel. When she spoke again, loud enough to echo across the docks, her voice contained a clear note of feigned offense. "Are you threatening us, Lord Gloomwood? In the middle of Korhaurbauten?"

He'd keep playing his role. "It's not a threat! It's a promise!"

"But we've done nothing to you, and you've already admitted that you have no legal claim on this man! Do you intend to order your people to illegally attack a licensed mercenary company legally fulfilling a contract? In sight of these witnesses?"

Drake glanced around for eyes on them. There were already people gathering on the other docks and onlookers gathering by the rails of other boats. Even if the noble court didn't have spies here, he had plenty of witnesses. So far, so good.

"Last chance!" Drake called. "Return my thrall or face the consequences!"

"He's not your thrall!" the Asp said confidently. "Now step back!"

Even as she spoke her previously relaxed mercenaries leapt into motion. Two hopped up and gripped the handles on the crossbow turrets on the aft and side of the boat facing his people. A moment later he had two huge crossbows pointed at him.

Drake glanced at Gaby. "Ready up."

She bit her lip, visibly tense, and nodded at him. She then raised one hand toward the boat and focused her attention on the space between them. If the mercenaries did fire, they'd all find out if Gaby's *fullstop* rarity could stop crossbow bolts as well as flutter-stepping Lydias.

It made sense that Gaby could stop those hurtling bolts. He suspected she could. But if she couldn't, that was why he had a wall of armored zarovians holding big spears and bigger shields gathered in front of him. They were, quite literally, meat shields.

And zarovians had a *lot* of meat on their bones.

A single armored mercenary leapt off the boat like a ninja, easily leaping what had to be fifteen feet across open ocean. He landed smoothly on the dock. As he went to untie the ropes binding the boat to the docks, Drake whistled loudly.

Ice crackled around the post that contained the rope. The nimble mercenary recoiled as a layer of ice overtook the post, freezing the rope there and making it impossible to unwind. A moment later the other post abruptly iced over as well. Then, ice crackled all the way up both ropes to freeze the rings on the boat to which they were tied.

Drake fired a grin over his shoulder at the single cloaked figure standing on the next dock beyond this one. She was just within range of the docking posts. *Flashfreeze* might not be able to do much against silverweave and ferrocite, but that didn't make it worthless in a fight.

"Return!" the Asp ordered.

The armored ninja bent, flexed, and then leapt into the air like a pole vaulter who didn't need a pole. He easily cleared the distance between the docks and boat with multiple feet to spare and landed smoothly. So his rarity was probably something like "super jump."

Whatever. Lydia and Robin both did it better. This guy was basically a giant frog.

"You have no right to detain us!" the Asp shouted. "Release my boat!"

"Release my man and you can go!" Drake shouted back.

"I already told you, he isn't yours!" The Asp, finally, sounded a little frustrated. "And the person who owns him is more terrifying than you are, so all you're doing is wasting my time!"

Ouch. That actually hurt a little. Still no one new had joined the Asp on deck, and he still couldn't execute his brilliant plan. Time to pull out the big guns... or in this case, the big vanguard. Drake whistled again, then made a circling up motion with one hand.

Armored shadows emerged from the warehouses and stomped down the docks in a loose group. More zarovians—almost his entire contingent—had been waiting in the shadows this whole time. They formed up around Korrag and the others and his people. Once the armored march finished, Drake stood on the docks with five thralls and twelve zarovians.

Drake now had the Asp outnumbered two to one. "One last question for you!" Drake called up to the boat. "How many zarovians can you take in a fight?"

"We've done nothing to you!" the Asp shouted for her witnesses. "We've offered no offense and haven't assaulted you in any way! But if you harm us, we will defend ourselves!"

"They're moving, lord!" Emily said excitedly, followed by an "Aww."

"What aw?" Drake asked quietly.

"Just one is moving. The other is staying below."

Drake shrugged. "Guess that guy is fucked, then."

One of the mercenaries who wasn't manning the crossbow turrets, standing in the crow's nest, or staring him down expertly rotated a large valve-looking ring on the outside of a metal door on the side of the boat. The hinged door opened. It looked heavy. One additional mercenary dressed the same as the others hurried out.

Eight above. One below, plus the prisoner. It was the best he was going to get. Drake glanced at Carl. "Meteor kaboom time."

Carl sighed heavily. As those on the boat watched in increasing alarm, Carl spun his hands. Molten rock manifested as he did so, forming a large molten ball that spun rapidly as burned with flame. It was an intimidating display.

"Hold!" the Asp shouted to her people. "Lord Gloomwood, stop! This is madness!"

Her people tensed across the boat. They couldn't unload their crossbow turrets and rarities on Drake's people until they attacked first, but Drake suspected they'd go full bore the moment Carl tossed his flaming projectile at their boat. Worse, since he'd ordered his thrall to blast their boat with meteor kaboom, he would have struck first and committed a crime.

Fortunately, that wasn't his plan at all.

Carl shouted and tossed his meteor… straight up. It rocketed into the air almost directly above Drake's people and their zarovian vanguard. Once it was at least eight stories above the docks, it exploded in a brilliant shower of rock, flame, and embers. It was completely harmless… but everyone across the entire docks and beyond had seen that explosion.

It wasn't an attack. It was a signal. Only one enemy now waited in the belly of that boat, guarding Darion. He wasn't going to be nearly enough.

Now to stall, Drake thought silently.

"Hey!" he shouted up to the Asp. "I have another question for you!"

She stepped forward and spread her hands. As she did so, glimmering globs of hissing acid manifested there. She must be immune to acid. That was a pretty cool trick.

"What is this mummery?" the Asp shouted. "Will you flee, or fight?"

"I think I'll just keep wasting your time instead!" Drake shouted. He looked to his people. "Zarovians! Drum show!"

In unison, his zarovians started banging their spears against their shields with deafening clangs. They were as perfectly choreographed as a marching band, and Drake wasn't the first person to wince and resist the urge to put his hands against his ears. He might have some serious tinnitus after this scheme... but that was better than having arrow-in-ear-itus.

It would also prevent the mercenaries on the boat from hearing the sound of Cresh and the others literally *chomping* through the hull from below. Zarovian jaws were stronger than alligators from back home, and Cresh was stronger than the average zarovian. The drum show would also hide any urgent, desperate shouts from the single mercenary in the belly before Cresh and the three zarovians with him ate that guy.

That was the problem with using a boat as a home base. The cell bars might be iron, but the boat's hull was still mostly made of wood. The only reason that hadn't worried the Asp was likely because most of her enemies couldn't *chew through the bottom of her boat*.

Still, they'd have to hope Darion was in a condition where he could hold his breath long enough for Cresh and the other zarovians to haul him out from beneath the boat, *through* the water, and back to a part of the Korhaurbauten docks not patrolled by the Asp's people.

Lark had been confident Darion could do it. Drake was confident in Lark. And it wasn't like Cresh and the zarovians who'd swam out to assault the boat from below would give him a choice. It would be literally sink or swim... or, in Darion's case, be dragged.

As he, his people, and the mercenaries on the boat all watched in increasing confusion, his zarovians slammed their shields together and beat their feet on the dock with a rhythm that almost made Drake want to dance. The deafening clamor was audible across the docks and maybe in the city. Their hissing joined the drumming and became white noise that filled in the gaps.

Drake stood tall and endured a full song. All the while he stood braced for an attack that never came as those on the Asp's armored boat did the same. He'd commit a crime if one of his people freaked out and struck first. She'd commit a crime if hers did.

Finally, the last spear hit the last shield. His zarovians unleashed one last loud "Huh!" that shook the docks, then stomped their tails in unison in their version of applause. Finally, they fell back into formation with shields raised.

Ears ringing in the aftermath, Drake rubbed at one. That had certainly been loud enough to cover the sound of Cresh and his chosen zarovians bashing in the hull of the boat from below. That was one great thing about zarovian soldiers. While they couldn't actually breathe underwater, they could hold their breath for a very, very long time.

Emily shouted something at him. He glanced at her and leaned close. She shouted again.

"What?" he shouted over the ringing in his ears.

"He's out!" she shouted back.

Drake barely heard the words, but he'd heard enough to grin. Emily's rarity allowed her to see that Darion's soul was no longer inside the boat. Cresh and the others had rescued him and gotten out clean... other than the one mercenary who'd likely been eaten alive.

This victory wasn't as satisfying as draining the blood out of the Asp's eyes and mouth, setting her boat on fire, and sinking it into the bay, but it was also a victory no one in the bay had seen. No one could *prove* he'd done anything. Darion was simply not in the boat now.

"We're done here!" Drake shouted to his people. "Roll out!"

At his orders, the zarovians nearest the docks marched off. He and his people fell into close formation behind them as the other zarovians formed a wall blocking off the boat. Surrounded by his large vanguard, Drake marched away from the docks and the boat. They left the now angry and befuddled mercenaries tracking them with crossbow turrets.

"Lord Gloomwood!" a woman bellowed across the docks.

Drake winced at the volume. That woman had a set of lungs. Too bad she couldn't see souls through the hull of a solid boat. Otherwise, she might have seen this coming.

"All you are is bluster!" the Asp shouted. "You stand like a child in the boots of a manor lord!"

And you're a real bitch, Drake thought without a glance back. *But I'm not going to jail for killing you. Humiliating you is enough for now.*

He doubted simply humiliating the Asp would be enough for Robin, but who knew? Maybe the Asp wouldn't forgive him for what he'd done to her and she'd come after him with her folks. In that case, Drake would happily kill all of them... or let Robin do it.

"All who stand here now saw you flee in cowardice!" the Asp shouted. "Remember that, people of Korhaurbauten! Remember how Lord Gloomwood fled like a rat!"

Drake chuckled at an inside joke. They were now far enough away that he had no fear that their rarities could reach them, and they'd see the bolts coming a mile away. He turned around and stepped back just enough for him to see her head.

"Just one more question for you!" he shouted. "Then I'm done!"

She glared across the distance between them.

"Is your boat okay?"

Her eyes widened.

"Because from where I'm standing, it looks like it might be sinking!"

Though he couldn't hear her curse or the others as the boat listed, now visibly lower in the water, he could easily imagine them. He imagined the water flooding the belly of the boat, their desperation as they realized bailing was pointless, and their panic as they realized their home base was rapidly sinking to the bottom of the Alicean Bay.

That was fun.

52
THAT'S TERRIBLE

They'd made it all the way to the city when Sachi dropped down from atop a nearby building. "Darion is safe, lord. Raylan is tending to him while Nicole and Valentia stand guard. Cresh and a small vanguard now escort them back to the temple."

"Fan-fucking-tastic," Drake said. "Are they being pursued?"

"No." Sachi tauntingly bared her sharp teeth. "But you are."

So his plan to work as a decoy had worked better than he'd hoped. "Figured that might happen. How many are after us?"

"Four mercenaries led by the Asp."

Only four? The rest of her mercenaries must have cut and run instead of tangling with a manor lord and his zarovian army. That was good since it gave him numbers, but also bad, because these four were likely the Asp's most committed followers.

The Asp hadn't been willing to cut her losses after all. On another day Drake would have relished the chance to teach her about a sunk-cost fallacy, but today, he'd be happy just to suck her blood out through her eyes and leave her twitching in the street.

Drake looked around and found someone missing. "Where's Robin?"

The young woman came into view at that moment, hopping "down" from the rooftop with three well-placed air jumps. She landed in front of him. "You can't let her escape!"

"Not letting anyone do anything," Drake said. "I just sank her boat."

Robin gripped his bow and stepped forward, eyes desperate. "Let me kill her."

"Not yet."

"I can beat her!"

Drake stared at her. "Real talk, Robin, and I don't want you to disappoint me here. What's more important to you? Killing the Asp? Or seeing her brought to justice?"

She frowned. "Is there a difference?"

"Do you *need* to kill her yourself? Or will you simply be happy if she gets arrested for what she did to the people in your village?"

She stared coldly. "I will not rest until the Asp no longer draws breath."

He'd been afraid of that. Still, he'd play this encounter by ear. He raised a fist to halt his vanguard and then turned to face his pursuers. "You told me you wouldn't fight her yet."

"That was then! This is now!"

"Let me handle it," Drake ordered. "If I fail, you'll get your chance to take her out."

He still had no plans to actually *kill* the Asp, and not because he didn't want to. She was an asshole. Yet killing her would just lead to endless complications, and he didn't need more complications with everything else he was dealing with right now.

If he murdered their leader in front of them, the Asp's mercenaries might never stop coming after him. Especially if they were in love with her or some bullshit like that. Worse, her mercenaries wouldn't simply target him.

These were the type of folks who'd take any opportunity they could to kill his blood thralls, or even his thrall's families, to get to him. Simply murdering the Asp in the street would lead to someone murdering one of his people in revenge, but defeating her and sparing her life? That would teach them some manners.

Word would get around that Lord Gloomwood had defeated one of the most feared mercenaries in the land. His reputation would grow. Some would call him weak for sparing her, but not all of them. And as for Drake... he would simply call it funny.

His zarovians formed a wall of armor at the same time a whole contingent of capital guards in ferrocite marched from the alleys on either side of the street. So the noble court *had* been watching the confrontation. There were only eight of them, but eight people in full ferrocite were intimidating even without the weight of the court and Judge at their backs.

"Halt!" the leader shouted... but not toward Drake. She was a tall woman, and she directed the order at the Asp and her people. "There will be no bloodshed in this city!"

"He sank my boat!" the Asp roared. "He stole my property!"

"If you have a complaint against a manor lord, you may lodge it with a clerk at the city center," the female captain said calmly. "You will not assault Lord Gloomwood on the streets of Korhaurbauten. Do so, and you will face the noble court."

"Lord Gloomwood!" the Asp yelled over the guards. "In sight of all of Korhaurbauten, I call you an enfeebled coward! I demand satisfaction! I challenge you to a duel!"

Drake wanted to chuckle at this lady's naked desperation to fight him, but he wasn't going to turn her down. A manor lord was under no obligation to accept a duel from anyone, especially a powerful mercenary. Few ever did unless they were brash and stupid.

Drake wasn't sure which one of those he fell under. He did know the Asp needed a good thrashing before she'd back off. Her mercenaries needed a clear sign to back off as well, and it just so happened he had a rarity that would give them all pause.

As he turned around, Lydia gripped his arm. "Lord," she said warningly. "This is not a good idea."

He grinned at her. "When has that ever stopped me?" He brushed off her hand and walked to his clustered zarovians.

"Okay!" he shouted over the crowd.

The armored female captain turned to him in alarm. "Lord Gloomwood?"

"I said okay!" Drake shouted. "I'll duel the Asp right now!"

The way the noble court captain stared at him was almost... pleading. "You are under no obligation to do this." Her eyes practically screamed *Please don't do this*. Drake doubted it was because she liked him. She almost certainly didn't want to handle the paperwork.

"Captain! Clear a path!" Drake ordered. "The rest of you! Back off unless you want my zarovians to shove their pikes up your asses! And Asp? You and me need to talk first."

Drake glanced back to find Lydia watching him with a visibly pained expression. Emily also looked ready to charge into the fray and chop everyone in the vicinity. Yet none of them would attack until he ordered it. They'd all grudgingly agreed to let him try this his way.

If the Asp was using doublespeak to draw him into an ambush, she would be killed by the capital guards, knifed in the back by a flutterstepping Lydia, and clawed to pieces by a snarling Sachi. If this was a trick, the Asp and her people would pay for it.

Ahead of him, still muffled by her silverweave hood but visible, the light inside the Asp's head—evidence that Suck's burnished rarity could still target her even through silverweave—glowed. Her mercenaries backed off as the capital guard captain, who was still clearly not on board with this idea, had her soldiers push back the onlookers to form an open ring.

The Asp stepped right into the ring of capital guards. Drake stepped in from the other side. And as she raised both hands and summoned globs of acid, he raised a palm straight up.

"Hold up. I said talk first. I need something before we duel."

The Asp glared from across the ring as the globs of acid on her hands fell to the ground. Tile hissed and burned as they melted through rock and dirt. That was powerful acid.

"Now you beg for your life?" the Asp demanded. "You are craven and a fool."

"I'm not begging. I'm negotiating. You asked for this, so I'll duel you under one condition. If I defeat you in this duel, your mercenaries can't ever come after me or my people. And to show you I'm serious, I'll say the same for my people." He looked back to his soldiers. "If the Asp defeats me, none of you will seek reprisals against her or her people! That is my order!"

His orders didn't compel his people, but they couldn't reveal that without raising questions. He also wouldn't need them to avenge him. Given how *hungry* Suck's rarity felt at the thought of battle, he was fairly confident of that.

He looked back to the Asp. "I told mine. Now tell yours. Or the duel's off."

To her credit, the Asp didn't even hesitate. "After I kill Lord Gloomwood or he kills me, you will not seek reprisals against him or his thralls! That is my order! Agreed?"

A chorus of assents came from her gathered mercenaries. Drake glanced at the capital guard captain. "So you heard all that, right? No reprisals on either side? We duel, someone loses, and everyone moves on with their lives?"

"I did hear it," the guard admitted. "But dueling in the streets of our city is frowned upon, Lord Gloomwood, even for manor lords. I must tell the Judge about this."

"That's fine," Drake said. "You do that. And remember, the Asp challenged *me*." He turned to the evil acid lady. "Your move, assface."

She bared her teeth as acid once more gathered around her hands. Before she could toss it at him, Drake raised his own hand... and focused intently on the glow inside her head.

Her stance wobbled. Her hands dropped as her acid balls slid off and once more slapped into the earth. They hissed loudly as they burned up the street. Meanwhile, the Asp stumbled on her feet like a drunk, visibly trembling. All of that was great, but she didn't bleed.

Drake ground his teeth and increased his focus, but her blood wouldn't come. What was he doing wrong? Why wasn't he sucking blood out of her eyes and mouth? Suck had done it through silverweave, so he could do it through silverweave. He'd absorbed the rarity from Suck's blood and burnished it. The glow assured him of that.

He just had to suck enough blood out of her to drop her. He wouldn't kill her, but he'd leave her anemic and famished. Yet the blood... wouldn't... come!

The tableau held like that for another moment until Drake heard a loud, wet *pop*. It sounded like a watermelon exploding in a microwave. A huge glob of warmth hit Drake directly between the eyes. It splattered across his face and blinded him as wetness flooded his nose.

As he stumbled backward, clawing at his eyes and coughing like he'd just inhaled a whole shaker of pepper, he was pummeled by what felt like a storm of wet hot chunks of Jello. Was that acid? Was he dead now? It didn't burn. It was just... warm.

"Gods," someone whispered. "Gods!" It was the capital guard captain, and Drake heard several people audibly retching nearby. Had she poisoned them?

"Lord, stop thrashing!" Lydia shouted. "You've won the duel! Let us... clean you!"

Drake trusted Lydia. He listened to her. He stopped thrashing, and he felt arms on his side and then hands and what might be handkerchiefs cleaning off the... hot, wet Jello. Finally, he felt like he could pop open one eye. He glanced down at himself and gasped.

He was absolutely covered in blood, and worse. Brown chunks, gray chunks, and... oh, fuck. That was an eyeball. There was a fucking *eyeball* dangling off the gunk on his chest. It was halfway embedded in what looked to be a piece of rolled-up intestines dripping with brown. He reflexively peeled it off his chest and noticed a lot more intestine came with it.

When Drake looked to the Asp to see how she was faring, he didn't see her. What he saw, instead, was the bottom two-thirds of a corpse in bloody silverweave. She still had legs, and hips, and most of her stomach. He could see the remains of part of her ribcage. A couple of arms severed below the shoulders sat in pools of blood on either side of the mess.

But her chest? Her head? The rest? That was apparently glued to his hair, face, and body like sticky mud splashed up from a big puddle. Drake *urk*ed loudly and fought the urge to lose his lunch in front of witnesses. That wouldn't be very intimidating.

So, he hadn't just defeated the Asp using Suck's burnished rarity. He was *wearing* her.

"Ugh," Drake managed as his stomach burned. "That smell. It's bad!"

Lydia shook her head as she continued to dab at the carnage. "You're going to need a bath, lord. Or... several of them." She glanced at the half-blown-up corpse in the street and then at the space beyond the capital guards. The Asp's mercenaries were long gone.

Drake dabbed futilely at his eyes with the back of his wrist, taking shallow breaths to minimize the stench. "Anyone got eyes on her buddies?"

"Sachi does." Lydia's expression remained solemn. "I doubt we'll have any more trouble from that quarter. Still, I wish you hadn't risked yourself."

Drake wiped gunk off his chin. "And I wish I didn't have brains up my nose." He sneezed. "Consider this a win. None of those assholes will ever bother us again, and Robin must be happy now that her evil enemy is... all that." He looked around. "Where is Robin?"

"She left the moment you defeated the Asp, lord. I didn't see where she went." Lydia grimaced. "Shall I order someone to pursue her?"

Drake considered and immediately discarded the idea. "No. Let her roam. Killing the Asp was a real big deal for her. A walk will clear her head."

"Of course, lord."

"Also, I know what I'm going to call this rarity now."

As Lydia led him back to his people, he ignored the squelching sounds from his now disgustingly red boots. She focused her eyes on the road ahead instead of glancing back at him. "What name have you chosen?"

Drake picked something gray and squishy out of his hair and tossed it on the road nearby. "Given the results of today's duel, we're going to call this one *mindblow*."

"That's terrible," Lydia said.

Drake sneezed again. "Isn't it?"

After *that* horrifying conversation, all that remained was to return to the Temple of the Eidolons with his people. Drake spent the rest of the morning in several successive baths as he waited for Raylan to help Darion heal from the acid wounds he'd received. He also worked to scrub the feeling of having brain up his nostrils from his short-term memory.

Mindblow was powerful. That was true. But it was also fucking gross, and Drake didn't want to end every battle covered in the brains, bowels, and eyeballs of his enemies. Once had been enough for the time being, and with the cabal ended, the Asp dead, and all her mercenaries terrified of him, he'd likely get a break from assassination attempts.

Still, better safe than sorry. He had Samuel give him a vial of blood and mixed it with his own as he lounged in the bath. He'd considered trying to collect the Asp's blood, but given all the other stuff it was mixed with—her bowels *had* exploded—he'd decided he didn't want that in his body. Plus, if he dropped a burnished acid glob on accident, it might burn a new well.

He still had at least six more treatments of *mindblow* left in the vial if he wanted to use it again... but it was going to remain his last resort. And if he used it again, he'd be sure to wear a mask or a full-face helmet or... something. Maybe a poncho. A really big, thick poncho.

Yet Darion was alive, and with Raylan's help, he'd recover from his acid torture with rest and regeneration. Word from Lydia had assured him that Lark was safe as well, thrilled and grateful, which was fine and not something he was going to let go to his head.

Or any other parts. He still wasn't *that* kind of manor lord.

By the time morning rolled around, Drake was already over making a woman explode... on accident. Darion was safe, his people were alive, and he was clean, relaxed, and satisfied with how the day had gone. He'd fucked over Lord Redbow, he had a new healing thrall for his manor, and the mercenaries who'd challenged him would spread the tale of his victory.

All in all, he'd had worse days as a manor lord.

53
SO THIS MIGHT BE A GOOD THING

After all his baths Drake managed a few hours of sleep, which meant he actually slept until just before lunch. He had no cabal today, and no other business to attend to so long as the noble court continued to investigate the fish people attack. He'd had a late night and deserved a little rest. So when the knock came at his door past noon, he almost didn't answer.

But he did anyway.

"I'm awake!" he called.

"Darion is up now!" Nicole called through the door. "Do you wish to induct him today, or do want to wait until after another lord abducts him?"

Drake sat up, yawned, and looked at the door. "Out soon!"

Once he'd dressed in his manor lord best and mashed down his stubborn hair as best he could—he was still convinced there were some bits of brain or flesh hidden in there—he knocked on his own door. Nicole opened it. He stepped outside to join her.

"How's he looking?" Drake asked quietly. "Is he horribly disfigured? Are we going to have to get him a mask or something?"

"He's looking just fine, lord," Nicole said coyly. "More than fine, by Emily's standards."

Drake eyed her. "What does that mean?"

"You'll find out soon enough."

He obviously wasn't going to get any more than that out of her, and he wasn't in the mood to try. "Fine. Where is he now?"

"Last I saw, he was standing in the common room."

The sound of laughter, and lots of it, came from that direction. It was all female laughter too. Was Emily trying to balance plates on her head again?

Drake hoped not. Last time she'd tried that, they'd lost half the cabinet. As he walked that direction, he glanced back at Nicole. "Are you coming?"

"It's my turn to guard the door!" she called. "Plus, I just don't want to."

He looked ahead. "Just be careful out there."

"When am I not?" she asked irritably.

The common room was about twice the size of his master bedroom, with two narrow doors leading out onto the balcony. It included chairs scattered all around its edges as well as several tables in the center and a number of long, comfortable benches. Visitors could drink, eat, play games, and so on.

He entered it to find a scene he didn't expect. Darion—and it must be Darion, since he was a tall, dark-haired, and unusually handsome young man Drake didn't know, dressed in fine clothes—stood between several tables surrounded by four of Drake's current staff, including Tamara. All women. All were also laughing in delight.

The only woman not standing in the pack around Darion was Lydia. She glanced at him as he entered, and the smile that immediately lightened her face felt good. She looked away before he could smile back, so he'd take that as relief he wasn't covered in blood and brains.

Emily was there as well, standing *much* closer to Darion than the man was likely comfortable with. She was grinning the way she grinned when she knew she'd made someone uncomfortable, except Darion didn't look uncomfortable at all. Also, Emily was visibly more flushed than normal. Which was weird.

In fact, every woman currently in Darion's confident, smiling orbit displayed some variation of a blush, doe eyes, or a besotted grin as they clustered around him... save Lydia. And as the man glanced his way and stood at attention, Drake understood why.

There was no trace of damage to his face, and he had a fine face. Darion offered a thousand-watt smile that would have been right at home on a Hollywood boardwalk. Yet it wasn't a smile that immediately made Drake dislike him, or a smile like some snooty noble who thought he was too good for everyone else.

Rather, it was a warm, confident, and genuine smile. Drake couldn't explain why, but Darion struck him as a genuinely nice guy rather than a smug asshole. Given how attractive Lark was, it was no surprise her brother could turn heads as well. Darion was, Drake could confidently say without feeling weird about it, a good-looking man.

As he approached the group, Drake then began to wonder if adding Darion to his manor was going to provide his manor staff with more benefits than he'd planned. The ratio of women to men in his manor remained two-to-one. After he added Darion, the man might find himself busy with a lot more than simply stitching people's flesh back together.

Drake just hoped he didn't end up with another Lord Blackmane, though Darion, at least, wouldn't be in charge of other thralls. There was no messy power differential to contend with here. So long as everyone was a consenting adult, Drake wasn't going to get involved.

"There he is now!" Emily said excitedly. "Darion, this is our lord."

Darion ignored the grinning red-haired battle maid who was currently watching him like she wanted to jump his bones. He bowed smoothly at the waist, which gave Emily a great opportunity to stare at his backside. Which she took, shamelessly.

Drake hoped jealousy wouldn't become a problem with any of the staff. "Rise," he said as he approached. "My thralls don't bow to me."

"Forgive me, Lord Gloomwood," Darion said smoothly. "I misunderstood Emily."

"No you didn't," Emily said. "I just wanted to see you bend over."

Was this sexual harassment? Did they even have a concept of sexual harassment in this world? Either way, Darion didn't seem to mind all the female attention, so if Emily become a problem for him, he'd talk to her. Regardless, Drake decided to give the man some peace.

He looked at his people. "I imagine it's about time to prepare lunch?"

Tamara inclined her head and then turned on the others. "Let's get busy, everyone." She shooed the other maids away, all of whom immediately complied... though one or two offered longing glances at the new thrall as they scurried away.

Lydia stayed. As for Emily, she moved far enough away to give Darion space, but still remained close enough that a few steps would bring her back. She also seemed absolutely unabashed about hungrily staring at him, even if he wasn't looking her direction.

"I don't know how I can ever repay you, lord," Darion said softly. "You saved my life last night and, more importantly, you protected my sister. Even swearing my lifelong loyalty seems like a poor recompense for all you've done."

"It's fine." Drake shrugged. "Your rarity will serve me well."

"As will I, lord. After last night, I will die for you if I have to."

"Great." This man couldn't lie. "Do you know what's involved in becoming my blood thrall?"

"Only that I must say the words you provide. And please, Lord Gloomwood, allow me to say just how honored I am to be allowed to serve you."

"You came highly recommended," Drake said. "However, I also don't need you to blow smoke up my ass."

Darion frowned for the first time. "Blow... smoke up your...?"

"Sorry." Drake raised a hand. "It's an expression from my world. You don't need to constantly remind me how awesome I am. I'm not that type of manor lord. All I need you to do is do your job and protect me, my manor, and my people. Can you do that?"

"With my life, lord!"

"Great." Drake nodded. "Now, you ready to do the thing?"

"You mean... to be inducted in your blood pact?"

Drake couldn't blame the man for checking. "Yes."

Darion offered his arm, palm up. "I'm ready."

Behind him, Drake didn't miss as Emily pumped her fist. He had no idea how forceful Emily got during sex, but given how forceful she got about everything *else*, he had his suspicions. She hoped she wasn't too rough with Darion the first time.

Drake pulled his handy letter opener—which was really more of a body opener at this point—from his pocket. "Just so you're aware, I heal quickly. So I'm going to make a far larger incision than normal. You'll need to slap your hand atop mine and not dawdle."

"I understand, lord. However, I don't have anything with which to cut my..."

He trailed off as Emily eagerly shoved a small knife into his hand.

"Here you go!" she said happily.

At this moment, Darion's life was likely now in more danger than it had been when he was a prisoner of the Asp. If he made any move toward Drake with that knife, it would be a toss up as to whether Emily soul chopped him before Lydia flutterstepped over and cut his throat. Yet Drake could regenerate, and he sensed no malice or trickery from this man.

Darion opened his palm and sliced it, then grimaced. "Oh!"

Emily was now standing practically on top of him. "First time?"

Drake eyed her. "Could you give our new thrall some space?"

"I just want to protect you, lord!" She did, however, back up. Incrementally.

Drake jammed his letter opener into his own palm, then gritted his teeth as he tore his flesh open and continued to do so. He was getting better at enduring this sort of pain, but it still hurt like hell. He offered his bloody hand. Darion clasped it tightly.

"Once I'm done inviting you, say the words 'Beneath the eyes of the Eidolons, I swear undying loyalty to you, Lord Gloomwood. I will serve as your blood thrall.' Got it?"

Darion nodded.

"As Lord of Gloomwood, I ask you to join my blood pact."

Darion repeated the words he'd been given as smoothly as if he'd rehearsed them a dozen times. Drake felt a faint tug inside his body and a brief rush of warmth as the magic pact sealed, and then he released Darion's hand. It was done.

The man drew his hand back to his chest, keeping his bloody palm up, and then touched the fingers of his other hand to it. His flesh knitted together before Drake's eyes, which assured him the man hadn't lied about his *fleshbind* rarity. Not that he could lie. Still... useful skill.

"Oh!" Emily already had a handkerchief out. "I was going to wrap that hand for you!"

"No need," Darion assured her confidently, and looked to Drake. "Lord? I can heal your palm as well."

Drake showed the man his palm, which had already healed on its own. "I've got it."

Darion's eyes widened. "That's very impressive."

"Our lord is very impressive," Emily agreed. "And welcome to Gloomwood Manor!"

Nicole chose that moment to wander back into the room for

some reason. "Make sure you let him settle in before you break him in."

Darion looked between them, visibly unsure for the first time. "Is there some sort of initiation ritual?"

"There could be," Emily said hungrily.

Lydia cleared her throat. "Emily, aren't you needed in the kitchen?"

"No."

Lydia watched her for a long moment.

"Oh!" Emily said. "Perhaps they could use help in the kitchen." She slapped Darion on the arm hard enough the man wobbled. "I look forward to working with you!"

Darion smiled grandly. "Oh! Uh... same!"

A loud knock came on the door to the chamber.

Lydia glanced at Nicole and frowned, visibly irritated. "I told you to watch the door."

"I am watching it," she said. "I can see it from right here."

"I'll get it!" Emily shouted. She hurried to the door.

Drake sighed and turned back to Darion. "So. You've met the maids and probably every other woman in my manor. Before you head off to get... settled in... there's one more decree I need to make. And I warn you, it's a weird one."

Darion nodded gravely. "I am yours to command, Lord Gloomwood."

For the next few seconds, anyway. "So, as your manor lord—"

"Hey!" Emily shouted angrily. "You all stop right there!"

Drake looked to the door to find Emily standing with her feet spread in a battle stance, and more importantly, with her spectral battle axe glowing in one hand. Goddammit. Was this about him making the Asp explode in the middle of the street yesterday morning?

Drake left Darion to gawk and hurried to the door. "The fuck is this now?"

It took him but a moment to recognize that the people

standing outside his door weren't kromians, or assassins, or any of the types of people who usually tried to kill him. They looked to be capital guards. The wore the same black ferrocite all the capital guards wore.

The inquisitor he remembered from earlier today stepped from within the ranks. "Lord Gloomwood! On orders of the noble court, I order you to order your thrall to stand down!"

"You are not coming in here!" Emily said. "Try it and you're getting soul chopped!"

"Emily, let's not kill any capital guards." *At least not until I know why they're banging on my door with... just how many of them are out there?*

As Lydia hurried to his side, Drake touched the arm in which Emily wasn't holding a soul-chopping battle axe. "Stand down."

"But, lord—"

"That's an order," Drake said. "But if they try to hurt me, you can still chop them."

She grumbled as her axe disappeared. "You bet I will."

Drake turned to the mass of armored soldiers gathered outside. "What's this about? Do you have another question about the fish people?"

There were at least eight capital guards with the inquisitor. Maybe even more. It was a narrow hall. There could be a full platoon standing back there.

"No," the inquisitor said. "We do, however, request that you come with us."

"Fine," Emily said petulantly. "But we're all going with him."

"We request that *you*, Lord Gloomwood, come with us. Alone. The capital guard will see to your security. You will order your thralls to remain here in your chambers."

Drake glanced at Emily, then at Lydia. Then, he glanced back at the inquisitor. "Yeah, I don't think that's happening. Not until you tell me what this is all about."

The inquisitor scowled. "Are you refusing an order from the noble court?"

"I haven't decided yet. Who sent you?"

The inquisitor sighed. "I was sent here by the Judge."

"And the men behind you? She sent them too?"

"No, but all of them serve me and are also sworn not to harm you, lord. And since I asked for them to accompany me, *I* sent them. And I, Inquisitor Grayson, am not here to harm you. I am simply here to escort you to a meeting with the Judge at her request."

"As in the lady who runs the noble court?" Drake asked.

"The Judge *administrates* it," Grayson corrected. "Which you, as a manor lord, must know. So please, let us dispense with your mockery. We have all had a very stressful day."

Drake offered him an intentionally sardonic smile. "No shit, you too?"

Lydia gripped his forearm. "Do not do this, lord. You cannot go with them alone."

He glanced at her. "Yeah? What's the alternative?"

"I chop them," Emily added from his other side.

Drake chuckled and glanced at her. "No, Emily. That's not going to work this time." He looked to the inquisitor again. "Have you come to imprison me? Is that your plan?"

"No," Grayson said. "You have been invited to a private meeting with the Judge. We will not detain you once that meeting concludes. You will remain free to leave at any time."

"So I can leave this meeting with the Judge whenever I like?"

"That is what I just stated." Grayson grimaced. "This is an *invitation*."

"And if I turn that invitation down?"

"The Judge would be... offended."

He looked to Lydia again. "How bad is an offended Judge?"

She looked physically uncomfortable. "Very bad, lord. I do not like the idea of you visiting with her alone, but I also know it is very unusual for her to ask to meet with a manor lord in private. Such meetings happen rarely to avoid any appearance of impropriety."

In other words, if she met privately with manor lords during a cabal, it could be easy to think she was taking a bribe. If she was willing to risk *that* sort of gossip, this must be important. "So this might be a good thing."

"I cannot say." Lydia sighed heavily. "I do not want to let you do this, but I also do not know that we can refuse. Not if we wish to retain the favor of the noble court."

It would be bad to lose that. Drake saw no way around this. These did look to be capital guards, and the inquisitor's statements were straightforward. His new and healthy paranoia suggested that going anywhere without his battle maids and sworn blood thralls to protect him was always a bad idea, but he also couldn't hide in his chambers forever.

"Hey," Drake said. "Remember what you said about those little crabs?"

Lydia's lips pressed together.

"At some point, I have to come out and play."

A private meeting with the Judge where he could air his accusations about Lord Redbow and his wink back before the attack might be a very good opportunity to further make his case that the other manor lords were at fault for... well, everything. If he could bend the Judge's ear in private, perhaps he could even get some money shaved off his tithe for the prior lord's habit of illegally exchanging magical artifacts. Or something.

By comparison, if he refused to accept the Judge's invitation or, worse, ordered Emily to chop the souls of a bunch of capital guards, the noble court was going to order every other manor lord to get together, execute him, and burn his manor the ground.

Not much of a choice. Also, there were ways he could spin this to his advantage. Sometimes, he was going to have to step out of his little hole in the sand.

"I'll go with you," Drake told the inquisitor outside.

Emily still looked on the verge of chopping them all anyway. Drake gently touched her arm. That caused her to stare at him in surprise.

"I'll be just fine," he told her. "But I do have an order for you."

She looked on the verge of chopping everyone anyway. "What is your order, lord?"

"If I'm not back by an hour or so after sunset, I want you to take a message to Lord Skybreak in her chambers. Tell her I was unable to meet with her tonight and where I've gone. You are the only person I can trust with this message."

He trusted Lydia, too, but he'd need her to run his manor while he was chatting with the Judge. Plus, getting Emily away from Darion would let the man get settled in before she pushed him into a broom closet and fucked his brains out. He needed time to prepare.

"I will go, lord," Emily said. "Though I still think it would be better if I went with you."

"Just make sure everyone else knows where I've gone, including Lord Skybreak. Also, these are capital guards. What's the worst that could happen?"

"They could all die screaming in a wave of ferrocite-melting acid tossed by a group of evil assassins, after which you would be burned alive with a fire that scorches your flesh off until your eyeballs burst and your limbs shrivel down to husks. And then you would die, lord."

Fuck. She had an *imagination*. "Well... let's hope that doesn't happen."

"If it does, I am chopping everyone responsible."

"Thanks." Drake looked to Grayson. "All right. Let's go."

Inquisitor Grayson stepped back, visibly relieved to finally have compliance, then looked to his soldiers. Drake willingly stepped into the hall. Behind him, Darion shouted grandly.

"Safe journey, Lord Gloomwood!"

From his maids, he heard not a thing.

This was fine. Despite his antics yesterday, the Judge was willing to listen to him. Perhaps that was why she wanted to talk. She wanted to hear more about his thoughts on this thrall who could change what people saw, or how he knew Lord Redbow had summoned those fish people. Or she wanted to berate him for blowing up a woman in the middle of the street.

Right now, Drake figured the odds were 50/50.

54
YOU'RE NOT HUNTING ME

Ringed by Inquisitor Grayson and ten different capital guards (he'd counted), Drake walked the halls of the Temple of the Eidolons for much longer than he had when he walked from his chambers to Sky's. They descended multiple floors and, he suspected, were getting ever closer to the center of the temple. There certainly weren't any windows down here.

They also passed multiple checkpoints, or what he assumed were checkpoints. They were narrow portals in hard stone blocked by multiple capital guards. Grayson flashed some papers at each one of them. They must be going into a truly secure part of the temple.

After descending his sixth flight of stairs, Drake also knew he was now underground. He hadn't known the temple went underground. Still... why wouldn't it? The Eidolons—this world's six-legged My Little Ponies—had created this temple, supposedly, and gods who could create a *world* and *people* wouldn't have trouble digging through a little bedrock.

Eventually, they emerged from another spiral staircase and

entered a wide, arched hall that looked similar to the main halls upstairs. Once they entered that hall, all but two of the capital guards dispersed, leaving him with Inquisitor Grayson and two soldiers. Grayson led the way to a set of closed oak doors at the end of the hall, then knocked.

The doors opened to reveal a set of desks with a number of people doing what looked to be clerical work—they had quills, scrolls, and inkwells—and Grayson motioned him inside.

Drake frowned at him. "You're not going with me?"

"This is as far as I go, Lord Gloomwood," Grayson said. "The chambers beyond are the most secure in the temple. No one will harm you inside. Atticus, one of the Judge's clerks, will direct you to her chambers from here. But first, I must have your assurance you will harm no one inside."

"I won't harm anyone inside," Drake said. "Unless they try to harm me first."

Grayson sighed. "You manor lords are a paranoid lot."

"You did see what happened in the cabal last afternoon, right?"

Grayson scowled. "We will not allow anything like that to happen again."

Drake eyed him. "I believe *you* believe that."

Grayson motioned for him to head inside. "Please, head inside."

"Thanks," Drake said. "Hope the rest of your day is less of a shit show."

Once inside, Drake looked around at twenty people or more busy scribbling on or pouring over scrolls. What were they doing in here? Probably recordkeeping of some sort, or possibly copying official decrees or notices. This world didn't have photocopiers, so people would have to make copies of public notices by hand, just like in the old days on Earth.

A man in a truly ornate white-and-gold uniform approached from across the room. It had big shoulder pads and tassels. All sorts of tassels. He looked kind of like an old-style train conductor, and even had a little train conductor hat. But there were no trains here.

"You Atticus?" Drake asked.

"Lord Gloomwood." The man inclined his head. "If you would, please follow me."

"Sure," Drake said. "Why not?" He was being passed off like a baton.

He followed Atticus across the room and past whoever these people were, one or two of whom looked up, eyed him a moment, and went back to their work. The rest didn't seem to care about his presence. They probably saw all sorts of weird shit down here.

Drake followed Atticus the sort-of-a-train-conductor down another hall to a single closed door, again formed of heavy wood with reinforced metal, then stopped when the man raised a hand.

"One moment," Atticus said. He knocked, delicately, on the door.

"Enter," the Judge called from inside.

Atticus grabbed the door handle and pulled with visible effort. The heavy door came open to reveal what looked to be a small private office inside, as well as two people. The Judge he recognized, sitting behind a large oak desk. The other was Lord Frostlight, who wore her dark-blue silverweave and a large furry cloak with a clasp that looked like crossed axes.

The enemy manor lord looked rather amused to see him.

"What's she doing here?" Drake asked everyone in the room.

"Peace, Lord Gloomwood," the Judge said. "Lord Frostlight has already promised not to harm anyone in these chambers, including you."

"Unless you try to harm me," Lord Frostlight said with a wolfish grin.

"Please," the Judge said. "Join us."

"Right," Drake said. "So..." He glanced at Atticus, who

motioned him inside. He was here. He didn't even know how to leave. And he could physically regenerate if necessary.

He stepped into the small office with one woman who could slice him apart with her *windshear* rarity and another woman who could probably do even worse with whatever *ultimatum* did, since she was the Judge of the noble court. The door closed.

The Judge motioned at one of the two empty chairs ahead of her desk. "Take a seat."

"Lord Frostlight isn't sitting."

"That is because she won't let me turn the chairs to face the door," Lord Frostlight said.

"I'm going with standing as well," Drake said. "Because your city is currently suffering from explosions of angry fish people."

Drake leaned against the wall to the left of the desk and crossed his arms. That put Lord Frostlight straight ahead, the Judge to his left, and the door to his right. He could keep an eye on all of them from here, but wow, did he miss Magnum. Heavy as it was, his repeating crossbow sure did make it easy to kill people. Or fish people.

The Judge sat back in her chair. "The kromians who invaded the chamber yesterday were summoned there through a sea gate. It is a rare kromian teleportation artifact we discovered in Lord Blackmane's box, cloaked in a spell of illusion whose origin we have been unable to discover. Unfortunately, despite a valiant effort by my guards and inquisitors, we have been unable to prove Lord Redbow was responsible for placing it there."

Drake felt relieved. "So you believe Lord Redbow was behind that nonsense."

"What I believe means nothing without proof, which we do not have. Based on your evidence, my inquisitors have asked Lord Redbow if he has employed or knows of any person who can change what people see. He and all other lords had stated they do not."

That was annoying. Lord Redbow must have had one of his

flunkies interact with the illusion-summoning thrall for him. "So do you know who killed Lord Blackmane?"

"After a thorough examination by my people and an interrogation of his thralls by my inquisitors, I do not believe anyone killed Lord Blackmane. He simply had a weak heart."

Drake watched her cautiously. "You're saying he had a heart attack?"

"His heart gave out during the attack."

"And you *believe* that?"

"There is cause for it. Interviews with his thralls revealed that Lord Blackmane's activities over the past few years have included a heavy diet of red meat and intoxicants, combined with multiple dangerous pleasure drugs that are known to weaken the organs. He was also having frequent intercourse with his blood thralls, often multiple times a day."

So basically, Lord Blackmane had spent the last few years eating poorly, snorting cocaine, downing Viagra, and fucking his brains out. And when a bunch of fish people fell on him, he got so terrified he ran off and had a heart attack. Was that really all there was to it?

It didn't matter. It sounded like there wouldn't be a new Lord Blackmane joining Lord Proudglade's alliance. The title would simply come up for a vote.

"Now, to the reason you are here," the Judge said. "Lord Frostlight has brought me an interesting proposition. One that requires your participation."

Drake frowned at her. "You're not hunting me."

The dark-haired manor lord chuckled. "Don't be so quick to discount the idea. It might be quite fun."

"For you, maybe."

The Judge glanced at Frostlight. "Make your offer."

Drake frowned. What offer was this?

Frostlight smiled at him. "Would you be interested in a temporary alliance?"

Drake looked to the Judge. "Are we running our own private cabal now?"

"Outside of a cabal, you keep your own counsel," the Judge said. "I am here because Lord Frostlight's offer is one part of a multi-part scheme she has suggested to reveal the culprit behind yesterday's attack, one which I have, reluctantly, agreed to indulge. However, it requires you to agree to participate. Otherwise, I will end this meeting and send you both away."

Drake eyed Lord Frostlight. "Before I listen to your scheme, I want to know why you're even scheming with us. You're part of Lord Proudglade's alliance."

"Your testimony yesterday made me rethink my current loyalties," Lord Frostlight said. "Naturally, I have been aware that Lord Proudglade is dissatisfied with my dominion over Frostlight Manor for some time, even though I have killed only disloyal blood thralls."

Did she know something he didn't? "I can't say I blame your blood thralls for being disloyal, since you murdered their former master and seized his manor."

"Loyalty to a former lord is admirable," Lord Frostlight agreed. "Stupidity is not. I am loyal to those who are loyal to me, and anyone foolish enough not to recognize my authority would soon die anyway. My leadership style is not what I am here to discuss. I wish to continue as the Lord of Frostlight Manor, and now, I do not believe I will do so if I stay my course."

"So you think Lord Redbow's going to assassinate you?"

Frostlight grinned dangerously. "It would certainly be interesting if he tried. But instead, I believe it is Lord Proudglade who seeks to remove me, especially after I stood for my interests during the cabal today. Lord Redbow, after all, is the one who gave me the information and means I used to defeat the former Lord Frostlight and claim his manor."

Drake glanced at the Judge. "And this is just all cool with you?"

"I am the keeper of the noble court," the Judge said calmly.

"My responsibility is to protect the Eidolons and our capital. I have no stake in the conflicts and disputes between the manors and their lords, who, as I have already said, keep their own counsel, *unless* those manor lords threaten the noble court. I believe the ability of this mysterious thrall does just that."

So the Judge was now involved because she didn't want the noble court being tricked by false testimony—or testimony people believed was true, because they'd been tricked. He'd won that much through his testimony in the cabal. It was good progress.

Lost Frostlight looked genuinely disappointed in him. "You would look down upon me because I killed a lord and seized his manor? Didn't you kill a man who offered you his title voluntarily? That seems far more ruthless."

Drake paused mentally to make sure he kept his story straight. "I killed him because he tried to ritually sacrifice me afterward. I defended myself."

"And I eliminated a weak, spineless fool who was doddering into old age and who allowed his finances, thralls, and lands to languish as he spent his time painting landscapes. *I* will restore Frostlight Manor to its former glory, but only if I continue as its lord. The old lord's former thralls and subjects are far better off with me in charge."

"At least those who are still alive."

Lord Frostlight frowned. "Given what I'd heard of your accomplishments thus far, I'd expected a stronger stomach. You present surprisingly inconvenient moral scruples. Didn't you blast a woman's head off her body last night?"

"She made the mistake of coming after me and my people," Drake said. "So are you willing to tell me *why* you believe Lord Proudglade is looking to get rid of you?"

"Likely the same reasons you would," Lord Frostlight. "Inconvenient moral scruples. The moment he finds a thrall with the power to defeat me, he could slip them into my manor and gain a Lord Frostlight more willing to dance to his tune."

"So if you don't want allied lords who have moral scruples, why ask to ally with me?"

"Because I believe you can help me, and I don't believe you can kill me."

Drake chuckled. He couldn't truly dislike this woman, no matter how ruthless she was. Her people hunting was reprehensible, but her prey did volunteer, and she did toss money at their families. He could never endorse or be okay with that, but he also couldn't save everyone.

His primary duty remained to safeguard himself, his manor, and his people. "I'll listen to your scheme," Drake said. "But dubiously."

"First, I will tell you why your testimony worried me," Frostlight said. "When I assassinated Lord Frostlight, I was able to do so because his own thrall admitted me to his manor. He admitted me through his lord's private passageway."

Drake felt suddenly cold. His former employee, Arno, had admitted four assassins to his own manor a couple of weeks ago. Drake and his advisors had never been able to find an obedience fetish on the man, so he still had no explanation for why Arno had done that.

"Do you have any idea how this blood thrall was able to do that?"

"Naturally, I was curious! So before I killed him, I asked why he admitted me. Confused, he said Lord Frostlight had ordered him to admit me. I was expected for our summit upstairs."

"But Lord Frostlight didn't order him to do that," Drake said quietly. "His thrall just *thought* he had."

Lord Frostlight smiled her predatory smile. "Now you see why your testimony worried me today. If Lord Proudglade or someone in his employ has a thrall who can make others see anything they wish, our blood pacts no longer protect us. Our thralls could believe anything."

If this was true... if the current Lord Frostlight was correct about how she had been admitted to the former Lord Frostlight's manor to kill him... then it was possible that despite Drake's vetting of his people, any one of them could unwittingly betray him at any time.

Which, given his blood pact no longer prevented his people from harming him, was going to make his life even *more* difficult.

55
LOOK, I AM CHARMING

Drake silently considered Lord Frostlight's motivations and claims as he debated how to handle her offer. One thing he would give this world was that knowing people could only say what they believed made decisions like this a lot less complicated. Unless Lord Frostlight herself had been tricked.

Yet why would her allies have tricked her in regards to killing the old Lord Frostlight? They'd wanted exactly what they had right now—a Lord Frostlight as part of their alliance—and until today, this former assassin had no reason to sell out her allies. Until today, she'd had no idea they could trick blood thralls into unwittingly betraying their lords.

Yet now that Drake had revealed there was a blood thrall who could alter what people saw, Lord Frostlight knew she, too, was vulnerable. So it made sense she'd seize on Drake's implication that the big four were also trying to deceive the noble court and run with it. She'd hopped onto the train he'd started in order to survive.

So now… the question was whether he'd cooperate with Lord Frostlight or continue to try to handle this with Sky. The first part of figuring that out would be hearing her plan.

"You've convinced me to listen," Drake said. "So let's hear your plan and why you need me for it."

Frostlight smiled. "To start, Lord Gloomwood, you will agree to be arrested."

"I'm out," Drake said.

"Please hear her out before you decide," the Judge said crossly. "And this would be *protective custody*." Her glare at Lord Frostlight made the woman's smile fade.

Drake glanced at the Judge. "In my world, those are pretty much the same thing."

The Judge watched him calmly. "I told you my inquisitors have no proof Lord Redbow was responsible for placing the sea gate that summoned those kromians into the Chamber of Council. We do, however, have testimony stating you were involved."

Drake pondered smashing the door open and making a break for it. Even if he managed to regenerate through Lord Frostlight's *windshear* and whatever magical bullshit the Judge's *ultimatum* was capable of, he'd never make it. Also, fleeing would make him look guilty.

"Testimony from a thrall?" Drake asked. "Who we now know could be mistaken?"

"That is the only reason I have not already ordered you arrested," the Judge said. "That, and the fact that you willingly confessed your crime of trading magical artifacts with Lord Skybreak despite knowing it would lead to you being censured. I believe, perhaps foolishly, that you genuinely wish to atone for your crimes and improve your standing with the noble court."

"They weren't my crimes." Drake raised one hand as the Judge tried to correct him. "But we're arguing semantics. So, you're asking me to let myself be arrested?"

"I'm trusting that you are the manor lord you claim to be. A lord who saved the son of his sworn enemy despite it being easier to allow him to die. A lord who risked his life to stop a demon summoning. And a lord who would never seek to deceive the noble court."

That last one was dangerously close to getting him executed for an unforgivable crime. The Judge didn't know he could lie. She could *never* know. But it was reassuring to hear she still trusted him. So how long would she continue to trust him if he refused to cooperate?

"I didn't place that gate there, nor did Lydia," Drake said. "Also, it would have been *stupid* of me to place that gate there, since the arrival of those kromians led to the death of my only ally in the chamber other than Lord Skybreak." Even if Blackmane had been a lecher. "It also ended a cabal where I was this close to getting answers as to who was behind all this."

"*We* were this close," Lord Frostlight corrected with a dangerous smile.

"That is another reason you are not under arrest," the Judge said. "Now that I know it is possible to fool our people, I am hesitant to trust any testimony we receive without further verification. By allowing my inquisitors to so easily find evidence that you were behind the sea gate, your enemy has taken one step too many. I believe it is possible for you to be mentally unwell, but I have trouble believing you are *this* mentally unwell."

"Check back with me after a couple more weeks of this bullshit," Drake said. "So you know I didn't summon fish people because it would be the stupidest thing I could possibly do, and our grand plan starts with me being taken into protective custody. Then what?"

"We will announce to the other manor lords that we have testimony implicating you in placing the sea gate in Lord Blackmane's box," the Judge said.

And she did have that testimony. She wouldn't be lying. The Judge had been playing this game a long time.

"However, we will also announce that due to the possibility that the guard who observed your entry into the chamber during lunch could have been deceived, we need more evidence. We have simply chosen to detain you until we know more."

"So how does telling the other lords..." Drake paused as he immediately sussed it out. "Oh, hell. You want to use me as bait."

Lord Frostlight grinned at him. "Your enemies do seem remarkably determined to kill you. They will want to do so before the noble court decides you are correct in your assertion that they can change what people see. Even so, it is exceedingly difficult to reach and assassinate someone in the noble court's chambers... unless you can make the guards see anything."

"So your plan is to put me in a nice guest prison, make it known to every manor lord that I'm there, and then... arrest whatever assassin comes to kill me?"

"I knew you would see it my way," Lord Frostlight said.

"Except that if you fail, I die."

"You seem far too resourceful for that," Lord Frostlight said. "But if you die, I will help the noble court expose your enemies and whoever is behind this plot."

"That'll be real comforting when I'm dead." He frowned. "But so far, this sounds like the whole plot is executed by the Judge. How are you involved?"

"I am the one who will catch your killer," Lord Frostlight said. "Or rather, my thrall. I have a thrall who maintains a bubble of awareness that can detect any living soul that enters it. I will station this thrall inside a locked room with me off the only hallway leading to the chamber where you will be kept. And when your assassin arrives, I will take them alive."

"And what will the capital guards be doing while I'm trusting my life to you?"

The Judge sighed. "If this dangerous and reckless plan is to work, I cannot allow the capital guards to know our plan. We have hundreds of people, all of whom talk, and every manor lord has many talented spies. The only way this plan has the slightest chance of working is if you, me, and Lord Frostlight are the only ones who know what is going on."

"Which is why you insisted I come here alone." Drake frowned. "You don't want even my own people knowing we're doing this, if we do this, to stop spies." He looked at Lord Frostlight. "So what about your bubble-awareness thrall? What if he blabs?"

"I tell my thralls nothing they do not need to know," Frostlight said. "And they obey."

Drake believed that. "So your thrall will know to alert you when she detects someone coming to kill me, but not know why you want her to tell you or what you plan to do."

Frostlight nodded. "If you wish, I will also offer you lessons on how best to manage your blood thralls. From what I know of your current techniques, you could be more efficient."

"I'll pass," Drake said.

"On my plan to finally unmask and destroy your enemies for you, or my guidance in efficiently leading your thralls?"

"The last one. I'm still considering this halfway crazy plan. I can't say I'm thrilled by the idea of placing my life in the hands of someone allied with Lord Proudglade—"

"Not anymore," Lord Frostlight reminded him.

"—but I imagine you're going to make me feel better about that. Aren't you?"

Lord Frostlight nodded. "Lord Gloomwood, if you agree to my plan, I will not harm you. I will forbid my thralls from harming you. And until we discover who is trying to kill you, I will protect you as if we were allied manor lords... but only if you can say the same to me."

If Drake had any of his own people protect him, which the Judge had no reason to allow, the other manor lords might figure out this was a trick. His thralls had to remain exactly where they were if there was going to be any chance his enemies would fall for this. Which meant he had to have someone protecting him they *wouldn't* expect.

"There is one other matter on which I must be clear," the Judge said. "As much as Lord Frostlight would wish it otherwise, I will not launch this plot unless you agree. If you choose not to participate, I do not plan to take you into custody for the sea gate incident... yet."

That was a considerable olive branch. The Judge could have threatened to arrest him if he didn't go along with this plan and had instead offered him a way out. That made him all the more inclined to trust her... and she, having been at this so long, must know that.

Also, there was another consideration. The noble court had, thus far, done jack shit to find evidence against Lord Redbow. The other manor lords would continue to press for them to name the guilty party and let everyone get on with their lives. If the noble court couldn't find any new evidence, they might be forced to resort to the evidence they did have.

Drake had to act, and soon, and now he had a plot before him that actually had some chance of success. It wasn't his plot, but he could understand it.

Also... he was simply tired of countering his enemy's moves after the fact. Whoever had been fucking with him since he arrived was going to come at him again. At least if he went along with this, he'd know *how* they planned to come at him... and could hit back.

"I need some assurances first," he said.

The Judge nodded. "Name them."

"First, I need to know I can leave protective custody whenever I want."

"That will be difficult without informing my guards you are not in protective custody."

"So give them a safe word," Drake said.

The Judge raised one eyebrow. "What does that mean?"

"Like... tell your guards to listen for a phrase. Tell them that if I say that phrase, they should come directly to you for further instructions. They don't have to know what the phrase means or what you're going to do when I say it, only that they should immediately report to you that I've said it when I say it. And if they tell you I've said it, you have to let me go."

"That seems clever enough," the Judge agreed. "What phrase do you wish to use?"

Drake pondered but a moment. "This is some bullshit."

The Judge might have smiled. He couldn't be sure. "Very well, Lord Gloomwood."

"Also, after I'm taken into custody, you need to allow my steward to speak to me wherever I'm imprisoned, and as often as she likes. I need to speak to her to keep up with my manor's business while I'm staying as your guest. And unless I tell Lydia, myself, why I'm doing this, she won't stand for it."

Lord Frostlight eyed him curiously. "For a man who is so gentle and light-handed with his thralls, you have remarkable confidence in their loyalty."

"It's because they *want* to serve me that I trust them to have my back," Drake said. "So if you like, I can give you a few lessons about that."

Frostlight's laugh was far more pleasant than he expected, given she was an assassin who hunted people for fun. "I have no objection to allowing your steward to visit you, and I do believe it would be in all our interests. I wouldn't want your Lydia doing anything rash."

Drake nodded. "I might be just about willing to go along with this."

"And what of Lord Skybreak?" Frostlight asked coyly. "Rumors say she is quite enamored with her new ally."

"She's not in love with me," Drake assured them both. "But I will have Lydia clue her into our scheme. It would seem suspicious if you let Lord Skybreak visit me." He considered. "Lord Skybreak also knows better than to piss off the noble court, especially if I'm in no immediate danger. She and Lady Skybreak will instead focus on proving my innocence."

Lord Frostlight eyed him curiously. "Tell me, Lord Gloomwood. Is there any woman with whom you are involved who you have not ensnared with your charms?"

Drake frowned at her. "Look, I am charming. But I've also turned out to be rather fucking good at this, and the trust I've earned goes both ways. You should try it sometime."

"Would that I had anyone I could trust," Lord Frostlight said wistfully.

That gave Drake pause. Did she mean that? She must mean that... which meant being Lord Frostlight sounded rather lonely. Still, he wasn't about to go soft on her now. And he was, dammit all, actually on board with this half-assed plan.

Every self-preserving instinct in his body urged him not to risk himself, but if he wanted to finally end the threat to him, his people, and his manor, he *had* to risk himself. There was no one else who could draw his enemies into doing something so reckless as trying to assassinate a manor lord in the protective custody of the noble court. He had to bait them into it.

So Drake would allow the Judge and her capital guards to put him in a nice cell. He would place his life in the hands of a ruthless manor lord who yesterday had been his enemy. He would face anyone who made it past Lord Frostlight unarmed and without his protectors.

This decision was almost certainly going to bite him in the ass. It always did. But doing *something* was better than waiting around for his enemies to launch their next attack. At least now he would be *choosing* to get fucked over and be ready when it happened.

"Any chance I could bring my crossbow with me into protective custody?" he asked.

"No," the Judge said. "But I will see that a sharp sword is placed in your room."

Drake glared. "The fuck am I going to do with a sword?"

Lord Frostlight frowned at him. "Generally, Lord Gloomwood, one stabs people with it."

"Right, but shooting them from fifty paces is way safer."

"If we are to do this, we must do it now," the Judge said. "No one will believe I intended to take you into protective custody if I release you now. That is another reason I approached you as I did. Your thralls will assume I requested you come alone so I could arrest you."

"Right, sure." Drake sighed. "Guess we better get on with it." The sooner he put this crazy plan into motion, the less chance he'd chicken out and change his mind.

Preparations were quick. Lord Frostlight left soon after, and then the Judge ushered him out of her office and back to Atticus the train conductor. As Atticus escorted him past the people making copies, Drake was surprised to spot *Westin* walking toward him.

He stopped. "Westin?"

"Lord Gloomwood!" The blond man stared at him in surprise. "What are you doing down here?"

"I'm not sure I'm supposed to tell you that. You?"

He grimaced. "I have been summoned."

"Ah." So the Judge was continuing to interview people about the sea gate incident. "Any idea who made those fish people appear?"

Westin grimaced. "I cannot discuss my suspicions with anyone but the Judge."

"But you have suspicions."

"Lord Gloomwood," Atticus said. "We should be on our way."

"Right, sure." As they passed, Drake nodded. "See you later, man."

"Yes," Westin said softly as he walked away. "See you."

56
ROOM SERVICE!

Hours later, shortly after night fell, Drake was officially in "protective custody."

His new chamber wasn't bad at all. He had a full room to himself, one even bigger than his private manor lord bedroom back in his old chambers. While it didn't include a massive four-post bed like the one back there, the bed in here was big and fluffy.

He had a reading desk, two chairs, a selection of books, some board games he had no idea how to play, and even a selection of fresh fruit and his own barrel of mead in the corner with a shiny spigot and a table of wine glasses. He also had a private bathroom, though it was small. They hadn't put him down with the rats.

But still, he was alone in here, and he had only Lord Frostlight and her thrall to stop him from being killed. He would never fully trust that woman... but he did need her.

Lydia wouldn't do anything foolish until she knew more. He also knew that the Judge would allow Lydia to visit him in his new chamber as his steward, where he could relay the new plan. So now, all he had to do was kill a few hours and fall asleep.

That proved far more difficult than he expected.

However, despite his boredom, lack of people to talk to, and his endless paranoia about someone getting into his locked and guarded room and stabbing him in the throat, he eventually dozed off. He snapped awake the next morning when a knock sounded on his door.

"I have breakfast!" a woman called.

That was the oldest trick in the book. "Leave it outside!" Drake shouted. If she was an assassin back in his world, she might as well have shouted "*Room service!*"

"Yes, lord!" the woman responded. "Good day, lord!"

Drake heard footsteps moving away. He mentally debated, then walked to the locked and reinforced door leading to the single hallway outside. It was the only way back to the wider temple. He slid the tiny slot in the door open to see the hallway unchanged.

The hall was well-lit with torches, two alert capital guards stood at attention at the end of it, and a woman dressed in the white and gold of the capital was departing without looking back. Drake realized then that she could have just slid his breakfast through the slot at the bottom of the reinforced door. She likely hadn't because he'd ordered her not to.

Dammit. That smelled like bacon and eggs out there. The woman was gone.

"Hey!" he shouted down the hall. "Can one of you guys push my food tray in here?"

The capital guards ignored him.

Drake slid the slot closed to block out that delicious smell. He could open the door himself, but that would require opening the locks to his door, opening the door, and stepping outside. Which would be a great way to get killed by some bullshit rarity.

So it looked like he'd be going hungry this morning.

With nothing else to do, he paced the room and even tried doing a few pushups to keep himself from getting bored. He stopped when that made his stomach grumble even more. He didn't need to burn calories. He needed to preserve them.

Still, eventually, he got bored enough that he picked up his borrowed sword. The Judge, true to her word, had placed one in his chambers, though she'd advised him to keep it out of sight of the guards. Since Drake was in protective custody and not a prisoner, he was allowed to remain in his "guest chamber" unobserved. He took a few experimental stabs with the blade.

Nope. He wasn't feeling it. Shooting people was so much better. Still... if someone got past Lord Frostlight and her thrall, at least he'd have a way to defend himself. And since he still carried Samuel's burnished *regrowth* rarity, he could probably win a sword fight even if he got slashed a dozen times by his opponent simply because he was so hard to kill.

Drake kept at it. He had even started feeling somewhat comfortable with his thrusting technique when another loud knock came on his door.

"Lord Gloomwood!" That was definitely Lydia. "May I enter?"

She'd gotten his message. The Judge hadn't arrested her. She'd kept her word to allow his steward to visit... but of course the Judge had kept her word, since she couldn't lie. And here Drake was, waving a sword around like a kid playing musketeer.

This was not a good look. "One second!" Drake called.

He debated as he looked around the room, then rushed over to stash the sword under his pillow on the bed. That seemed the best place for it. He then ran his hands through his increasingly shaggy hair, took a breath, and walked to the door. He slid the tiny slot in the door open that would allow him to see outside.

Lydia stood outside in her battle maid best, staring with a mixture of worry and anger.

"Hey," Drake said. "Just in case you're Lydia's evil twin, what did I say you were to me when we were alone in my carriage? The night I asked you if I could trust Samuel?"

Her eyes widened slightly. "You said I was your rock."

"Damn, it's good to see you." Drake closed the slot and unlocked the several locks on his reinforced door. As a guest in protective custody, he controlled his own locks. The moment he opened the door, Lydia stepped inside, kicked the door shut with her heel, and immediately hugged him. Her head only came up to his chest.

That surprised him. "Good morning."

Having Lydia hug him like this wasn't weird. Not weird at all. She'd probably been somewhat concerned about him. That was understandable, wasn't it?

Lydia released him and stepped back. "I'm sorry, lord, but... you *worried* me. You worried us all a great deal. I barely stopped Emily from going down to the noble guard barracks and soul chopping them. Why did the Judge arrest you?"

"Let's talk about that over bacon and eggs."

"You mean the meal outside? It looked shriveled and cold. Is she punishing you?"

"No, that one's my fault." He locked all the locks and motioned for her to follow him. "Let's go sit down over here. I have chairs. There's more to this."

"Well..." Lydia frowned. "It is good they gave you chairs."

Once they were sitting close enough to speak quietly well away from the doors, Drake quietly explained the plan he'd agreed to last night. When he finished explaining, Lydia clenched her fists. "I could slap you right now.

Drake grinned. "You can, can't you?" Because he'd changed the blood pact.

"You should have demanded we be allowed to protect you."

"Our enemies are watching you," Drake said. "They're watching all my people. If even one of you isn't where you're supposed to be, they'll know this is a trick. They're also watching Sky's people, which means we can't have any of them protecting me either."

Lydia glared at him. "So you trust an assassin with your life?"

"Former assassin," Drake corrected. "And to be clear, I don't trust her, like, at all. But I do believe, until we've found out who's changing what people see, our interests remain aligned. She wants to keep her manor, and we both want to stop the assholes coming after us."

"Lord Frostlight could still find out who's doing this after she lets you die!"

"Point," Drake said. "But I have a sword now." He pointed at his bed. "It's right over there. I'm actually getting good with it."

As Lydia stared at him with real desperation in her gaze, he felt guilty for agreeing to this. For worrying her. Still, he needed to make a move, and there hadn't been a lot of moves available. At least with this move, he knew the risks.

"I do not like this," Lydia said finally.

Drake nodded.

"I would have advised *against* this."

"Yeah, I know."

"But as it seems you must do this, then... as always, lord, you have my support."

He tilted his head. "Why?"

She huffed. "Because I trust you. Right now, I hate that I do... but I trust you, lord."

He swallowed an unexpected lump. He was genuinely touched by her seemingly unshakable faith in him. "Thanks, Lydia."

"But I'm still inclined to slap you."

Drake leaned forward and turned his cheek. "If it'll make you feel better."

Lydia sighed and looked around the room. "So... what else can I do while we wait?"

"Tell me how everyone else is doing. Getting you in to see me wasn't just a ploy to tell you the plan. I do need to know what's going on in my manor."

"Other than the frantic scramble to keep your thralls from going to war with the noble court last night, everyone remains safe. Anna was beside herself when she heard you'd been arrested, but I managed to comfort her. Samuel has disappeared once more, likely meeting with every spy he has in the city in hopes of proving your innocence."

"And the other maids?"

"Emily got very drunk, so we are allowing her to sleep this morning. Valentia and Nicole are... well, as you'd expect. Also, Lark came to speak with you again this morning, but I wasn't around to receive her. She didn't say what it was about."

"Interesting," Drake said. "I wonder what that was about."

"You didn't ask her to return to conclude your prior engagement?"

"My..." Drake got it, then made a face. "No. Obviously."

"Then I do not know why she would have come to visit you. Perhaps she wished to speak to her brother?"

"Maybe." Drake put it from his mind. "What about what went down with the Asp? Any blowback on that?"

"Samuel's contacts have confirmed that all the mercenaries who worked for the Asp have left the city," Lydia said. "That supports their decision to cut their losses."

"Good. They better. And Robin's come back by now? She didn't desert, did she?"

"She returned last night," Lydia said. "She was also distraught to hear you had been taken into custody. Gaby and Carl seem quite upset as well. Nicole is keeping them busy with training, but I will not spare the details, lord. Your manor is in an uproar at how you have been treated. If your deception continues much longer, even I may not be able to hold them off."

"Aww." Drake felt a rush of warm fuzzies. "I'll try to get almost murdered quickly."

Lydia sighed heavily. "Other than what I have already told you, I have little else to report. Everyone who came here from your manor is either busying themselves with their daily tasks or looking for ways to get you freed. And I can't tell them why you're really here."

"You don't believe they can keep it a secret?"

"You've already made it clear our enemy can make our thralls see anything. I can't watch them all. Any of them could be touched by this powerful rarity at any moment and see you order them to confess this plot. In the matter of keeping the true purpose of your incarceration to a chosen few, your instincts are correct."

"So what's Sky going to do about it?"

"For now, she has registered an official grievance against the noble court."

Drake whistled softly. "We can do that?"

"Not if one wishes to stay in the noble court's good graces," Lydia said grimly. "Lady Skybreak advised against it, but Lord Skybreak would not be swayed. I do like her, lord."

So did Drake. "Well, the Judge knows the truth, so once we capture who's behind all this and expose them, I'm sure we can get all that forgiven."

"I should hope so," Lydia said firmly. "So... what are your orders while we wait?"

He could still communicate with his manor, so he wasn't isolated. So what should he have them doing, other than trying to prove his innocence, while he acted as bait?

"Find Lark. Make sure she's not in trouble. Lord Redbow might be done pursuing Darion, but he could still go after Lark for her part in what went down on the docks. After all this, I'd feel bad if we got her killed because Redbow wanted to make a point."

Lydia nodded a determined nod. "I will find her, lord."

"Not you," Drake said. "You can't go into the city, because you know the secret plan."

She opened her mouth to argue, then sighed. "I will order Valentia to do it."

"Not Emily?"

Lydia offered the tiniest chuckle. "Gods no."

"I'm sorry I made her drunk. Let her know that, all right?"

"It won't help. But I will assure everyone you are comfortable here."

"But not safe?"

"I cannot speak that which I do not believe."

She was right, of course. So what else did he need her to do while he was bait?

"Also, invite Sky to our chambers. Reveal my plan to her and her alone. She's going to be mad I did this without consulting her, but she's the only other person I feel comfortable bringing in on the secret. And since she's my allied manor lord, I feel like I should."

"I will, lord. What else?"

Drake pondered. "I think that's it for now. You should have free access to visit me if something comes up, but make sure you always have an escort. You can't ever be alone. Just pretend you're me."

"Yes, lord. Then... do you require anything more before I return to the others?"

"One more thing." Drake glanced at the shelf and the boxes on it. "Can you teach me how to play one of those board games before you leave? I'm going out of my mind in here."

He needed something to do in here, alone. Waiting to be assassinated was *boring*.

57
I'M STILL A MANOR LORD

The rest of the day passed in solitude. While the board game Lydia had taught him the basics of before she left was intriguing—it reminded him a little of chess, except the movements each piece was allowed to make were different—playing it against himself wasn't all that entertaining, especially after the eighth repetition.

With his chair to the wall and his face to the door, he tried reading some of the books provided for his entertainment, but they were all simply historical accounts of real events. Since people in this world couldn't lie, it seemed that did even extend to writing fiction. Some of the stories were interesting, especially the one involving an account of some well-known explorers' short visit to a kromian city, but Drake was too anxious to concentrate on enjoying them.

Why couldn't someone just try to kill him already? Someone had tried to kill him almost every day since he arrived. Now, now when he actually *wanted* someone to try and kill him, they were jerking off in a corner somewhere? He couldn't catch a break.

Lunch arrived, which Drake, this time, wisely ordered be slipped through the slot beneath his door. He doubted it could be poisoned, but even if it was, his burnished regeneration rarity should take care of any problems. At least the food was good. The noble court had chefs who were almost as good at seasoning meat as Meryl.

As time marched on, he alternated practicing with his sword and reading non-fictional accounts of weird shit. He even felt like he was starting to get the hang of the weird chess-like game enough that he could play someone in it. Yet none of this was what he wished to do.

His second night in protective custody arrived with no word from the Judge and no updates on any thwarted assassination attempts. He hoped Lord Frostlight was as bored as he was. She better not be taking a break or sleeping on the job. While it took Drake some time to get to sleep, he did sleep... lightly.

He was dreaming about being a pizza delivery driver back on Earth—a job he'd never actually done—and was annoyed that he kept getting the address to deliver the pizza wrong when a loud, firm knock on his door snapped him awake.

"Lord Gloomwood!" A cold voice came through the door. "Your steward is here to speak with you!"

Drake fumbled his palm across the tile on the wall, which would turn on the lights. He had no idea if it was the next day, but it didn't feel like the next day. He was groggy and felt like he'd only been asleep a few hours, but adrenaline woke him up fast.

His steward? If Lydia was here to talk with him, why not simply announce herself? Had the enemy lords made one of the capital guards think Lydia was outside, but it was instead the assassin sent to kill him? Was it finally time to spring their trap?

He snatched his sword from beneath the pillow beside him and padded to the door on bare feet. The knock sounded again, which told him whoever was outside was impatient. He wasn't about to open the slot until he had a better idea who was out there.

"If she's out there, have my steward announce herself!"

"Lydia," the man's cold voice said. "Announce yourself to your lord."

A soft voice followed. "I am here, Lord Gloomwood."

That did sound like Lydia, but she sounded... depressed? Forlorn? Was he being tricked by this rarity that forced him to see things? How could he be sure?

Drake slipped open the door slot against his better judgment and peered out. He made sure to keep his borrowed sword down far enough none of them could see it through the slot. Three capital guards in ferrocite stood outside, frowning with hard eyes. Lydia stood between two of them, and it took Drake only a moment to process two legitimately disturbing sights.

First, Lydia's wrists were bound in metal shackles connected with a chain. She was wearing a long-sleeved button-down shirt and pants instead of her battle maid uniform. Second, the top of a small, black, glowing disc resting just below her collarbone, visible where the first few buttons of her shirt sat undone. Drake knew what that disc was.

Lydia was wearing an obedience fetish.

Drake gripped the sword tightly enough to hurt his palm. "The fuck is this?"

"Lydia," one of the guards ordered. "Explain to your lord why you are here."

Lydia shuddered visibly as if in pain before she spoke again. "Lord Gloomwood, I have come to learn whom you wish to name as your successor."

Drake glared at the guards outside. "You stuck an obedience fetish on my *steward?*" He was sorely tempted to open the door, step out with his sword, and stab them all. "I am in protective custody, and this was never part of our arrangement! Where's the Judge?"

"You won't be speaking to her," the guard said coldly.

"And who told you that, numb nuts?"

"The Judge."

So these guards had seen a fake vision of the Judge ordering them to stick an obedience fetish on Lydia and bring him here? Why would she even allow that to happen? Where was Lord Frostlight? How could the Judge even double-cross him when she couldn't lie? Even if the Judge saw something she couldn't explain, she should know not to trust it.

"Lydia," the guard said. "Tell your lord what is to be his fate."

Again Lydia trembled, teeth bared as she ground them and tried to resist. With a gasp, she almost fell. The only reason she didn't collapse was because the guards caught her by the arms. They lifted her as she continued trembling. Finally, through gritted teeth, she spoke.

"Lord Gloomwood, you are to be executed on this coming morning for the crime of attempting to deceive the noble court."

Something had gone horrifically wrong somewhere in the plan he'd conceived with the Judge and Lord Frostlight, but he couldn't figure out exactly what had happened and how to stop it right now. Not with Lydia practically killing herself to resist the compulsions of an obedience fetish.

"I will talk to my steward alone, right now," Drake growled.

The guard shrugged. "Lydia, you will not attempt to free your lord from this room. You will not take any action but to speak once you are inside."

Lydia shuddered again, then bared her teeth. "Lord Gloomwood... open the door."

"Oh, we'll also be taking your sword as well," the guard said. "Unless you want to take your chances with all three of us and watch your steward die."

"You think I'd let you kill her?" Drake challenged.

"Lydia," the guard said. "Tell your lord the order I gave you."

Lydia ground her teeth before she spoke again. "Lord Gloomwood, if you attempt to harm these men, remove this fetish, or stop them from searching your room... they have ordered me to die."

His blood ran cold as he understood just what a fetish could do. "Just like that?"

"Just like that," the guard said smugly.

Drake frowned at the man. "Just so you know, I've never killed a capital guard."

"What does that have to do with anything?"

"If I have to, I'm going to start with you."

The man chuckled. "My understanding is you can speak words you do not believe. That grievous crime against the Eidolons is just one reason you are soon to be executed by the noble court. So forgive me if your threat doesn't inspire the fear you hoped."

So it seemed, somehow, the Judge had been convinced Drake could do what Lord Redbow accused him of. Lie. And now, the noble court was going to execute him for it.

Time to use his safe word.

"Guard?" he said. "This is some bullshit."

The guard frowned at him.

"Did you hear me? Guard? This is some bullshit."

"Open the door," the guard said.

"This is some *bull shit*." Drake stressed each word.

The guards glanced at each other. One shrugged. The other sighed and pointed back down the hall. Without another word, that guard left, hopefully to go speak to the Judge.

Now, Drake had to speak to his steward. "I need your word you won't harm me if I open this door."

"None of us will harm you," the guard said. "We will, however, search your room and seize any weapons you might have in there. Your execution is for the royal court."

Drake unlocked the locks as Lydia stared outside, forlorn and lost. She must have allowed them to slap that obedience fetish on her because it was the only way the Judge would allow her to speak to him now that he was to be executed. It made no sense otherwise.

Once the door opened, Drake stepped back as two men walked

inside. He considered bolting, but he couldn't without Lydia. One man took his sword while the other walked around and calmly tossed the room. Pillows, blankets, books, and everything else ended up on the floor as the man efficiently searched every nook and cranny for weapons.

Once Drake's once nice guest room was thoroughly disheveled, the guard rose and turned to his fellow. "No other weapons."

The first guard nodded. "Lydia, step inside the room and stop inside the door."

Lydia stumbled forward, grimacing, and stopped just inside the door.

"Lydia, don't move from that spot until we return," the guard said.

"I demand privacy," Drake said. "No listening outside my door. We will speak in private."

The guard frowned. "And what makes you think you have any right to ask that?"

Drake stepped forward and glared. "Because I'm still a fucking manor lord. Until I die tomorrow, I have the right to speak to my steward in private, even in the capital. Or did you not read the same laws I did?" He couldn't believe he was finally grateful for all those boring lessons from Samuel.

The guard shrugged. "We will stand at the end of the hallway. We will not be leaving, and there is no way you can escape." He motioned to the other guard. "Let's step outside and give the soon-to-be-executed Lord Gloomwood some privacy. You have ten minutes."

After the guards all stepped out, Drake slammed the door behind them and locked it. Finally, he turned to Lydia. She stood facing away from him at the same spot where she entered the room. She couldn't even turn around. That fetish had absolute control.

Drake hurried around in front of her and gently touched her

arm. She was trembling, and it physically hurt him to see her like this. "Are you okay?"

She blinked fiercely. "I have no intention of allowing them to execute you."

"I know that. But first, do you have any idea how this happened?"

"I do. But first, you should know the noble court executed Lord Frostlight last afternoon for the same crime they plan to execute you for this morning."

"Fuck!" Drake kicked the floor with one boot. *"How?"*

"The Judge and the noble court revealed Lord Frostlight conspired with you to deceive them regarding placing that sea gate in the Chamber of Council. Moreover, when they placed an obedience fetish on her and compelled her testimony... she confessed her crime before the noble court and all the gathered manor lords."

Drake stared a moment. "She did *what?*"

"When the Judge compelled her to say if she had placed the sea gate in the Chamber of Council, she said the two of you did it together. You told the guards on the chamber that day the Judge had ordered them to check the doors on the other side, speaking words you did not believe, and then she slipped inside and placed the sea gate before they returned."

"None of that ever happened!" Drake said angrily. "Also, how could anyone make anyone believe that happened? I talked to the Judge before we set this all up, and she mentioned none of this. She specifically said she knew I wasn't responsible!"

Lydia shuddered. "I do not know, lord. I only know that we must free you."

"And do you have an idea on that?"

She stared with new determination. *"Flutterstep."*

He frowned as he saw the same possibility she did. "How would that help?"

"The courtyard where the noble court handles executions is outdoors. The walls around it are at least as tall as our manor and staffed by archers, however, I can flutterstep up to the top of our manor from the ground if I put my effort into it."

She was serious about this. "So—"

"You burnish any rarity you absorb," Lydia said. "I am confident that if I allow you to once again absorb *flutterstep*, you could step to the top of that wall and back off again without injury, before any archers could feather you. Just beyond the wall, you should see a single house with a wolf banner atop it. Samuel will be waiting with Anna inside that house. You need only reach it, and she will teleport you out of the capital to safety."

"And then what? Wouldn't the whole manor just be hunted down by the noble court?"

"Not immediately," Lydia said. "It will take time for them to organize their army and over a week for them to reach Gloomwood Manor. We can hold a large force for weeks. Once we save you, you will flee to Gloomwood Manor and, from there, figure out our next move. But first, we must save you from execution."

Drake stared at her. "But Lydia, that's insane!"

She breathed deeply and focused on him with determination in her eyes. "Your manor is of one mind. Either we will save you, lord... or we will all fall beside you."

58
I HAVE COMMITTED NO CRIME

"Samuel can't have agreed to this," Drake said.

"Samuel helped me come up with this plan. He denied your call to make him your successor. That is how I was able to speak to you despite the gravity of your so-called crime. Even when a manor lord is to be executed, they are still allowed to name their successor."

All of this was sinking in, finally. He couldn't deny it any longer. "But you had to agree to be shackled and accept an obedience fetish."

"It was the only way to provide you the opportunity to absorb *flutterstep*, lord."

His people really were fully committed to saving his life. He only wished he could thank all of them right now. But for the moment... what was he going to do?

None of this made any sense. None of this should be possible. His enemy had a rarity that could make people see things that weren't real, but they couldn't retroactively change what people *saw*. The Judge had told Drake she knew he wasn't responsible for the sea gate.

And Lord Frostlight? She never would have confessed to a

crime she hadn't committed, especially one that would get her executed... and she had also told the Judge she hadn't been involved in planting that sea gate in their private council. How could she change her story?

As Drake racked his brain for what he'd missed, his very first conversation with Sky in the central chamber of her manor all flooded back at once.

Her eyes narrowed once more. "Are you always this random?"

"Only when I'm taking a victory lap." Still, there was no benefit to rubbing her face in the fact that he'd been right about Valentia's innocence, and it also wouldn't be very diplomatic. "But now that we can speak privately, I'd like to know what you think now that you have more information. Why did Oswell see Valentia murder Rodney when she didn't?"

"One possibility would be you have found some way to change the memories of your blood thralls so they remember events differently than they occurred."

Drake ground his teeth. *Fucking fuckballs.*

Sky had been right all along. She had to be right. The thrall they were facing couldn't just change what people *saw*. They could change what people *remembered*.

Every time Drake knew where this dangerous rarity had been used before now, he and all his allies had assumed those people had seen an illusion. A trick. But instead, each of them had their memories of events changed after the fact.

That also explained how his enemies had managed to finally kill Lord Frostlight. They had *changed Lord Frostlight's own memories* so she remembered placing that sea gate inside the Chamber of Council... and made sure she implicated him in the attack as well. After the noble court compelled her testimony through an obedience fetish. When forced to tell the "truth," Lord Frostlight had given the *false* testimony she *remembered*.

This was the only possibility that accounted for all the ways he'd just been fucked. And now he was stuck in a room he couldn't escape, with the entire noble court and even the Judge determined to execute him tomorrow for a crime he hadn't committed, because they all remembered a reality that was different than what had actually occurred.

"Lydia?" Drake said. "I was wrong."

When he told her what he'd just figured out, she looked faint. "You're right, lord. This is the only thing that makes sense."

"So can you tell the Judge that?"

"I am not allowed to see her. After we speak today, I will not see her again until your execution. Only I will be allowed in the courtyard for your execution. None of your other blood thralls may attend, and I will still be wearing this obedience fetish. That means I will not be able to speak, move, or do anything but later testify your execution was humane."

He blinked at her. "Humane?"

"You will be beheaded."

Which was the only way he could die while he had Samuel's physical regeneration rarity. His enemies really had thought of anything. He was going to kill them so hard after he escaped.

"So how will you escape?" Drake asked.

"I won't."

Drake scowled. "No."

"There is no way for me to escape, lord."

"I'm not leaving you behind to be executed."

"They will not execute me," Lydia said. "Not immediately. I have committed no crime."

"But once they see me flutterstep to freedom, you can bet they're going to put two and two together and figure out you gave me your rarity. And once they know that's possible, they'll compel you to confess what you did with the obedience fetish."

She smiled bravely. "Then you need simply prove my innocence before they come to a decision as to what to do with me."

"And what if I can't?"

"Then I will gladly die to protect you and our manor. The only way any of us will be safe is if you survive long enough to prove your innocence."

"But I don't *need* to stay alive to protect our manor! You'll be fine without me! I can just... pass the title onto Samuel and go become a hermit somewhere!" Or look for a way back to his own realm.

"No," Lydia said firmly. "We wish you to be our lord. No other. None of us is willing to accept that you must die, least of all me."

She really meant that. Lydia truly would die for him, and while he had understood that concept abstractly since she'd flutter-stepped in front of three crossbow bolts to save his life, it was always disorienting to be reminded of her loyalty. He wasn't about to let her die, either.

But he also didn't want to have his head cut off.

Drake hated the necessity of leaving Lydia behind while he ran off more than anything he'd had to do since he arrived in this world. But he also wasn't going to question her decision to freely risk herself to protect him. He'd do the same for her, and refusing to let her risk herself like this... of her own free will... would make him a massive hypocrite.

"I'm not letting them execute you," Drake said firmly. "I'm going to find a way to prove this rarity exists, that the noble court was tricked, and then I'm going to get you released."

She smiled again, a warm smile that actually melted his heart a little. "I know you will, lord. These are words I believe."

She was being too sincere right now. He couldn't bear it. He glanced at the door. "We don't have long. Better get this over with."

"Then you will need to open my shirt, lord," Lydia said.

Drake blinked. "Say what?"

"I am wearing a shift beneath this shirt. You will not compromise my modesty," Lydia assured him. "However, I cannot take any action other than stand here. That is another compulsion that guard gave me through this fetish. You will have to open my shirt for me."

"But..." Drake stared. "Why are we doing that?"

"We have hidden a small steel shard inside a bandage on my upper arm. Do you have any other way to cut your flesh or mine? To share blood?"

"No...?"

"Then please, lord." She was looking increasingly desperate. "I recognize that this may be awkward for you, but we have little time."

Still feeling like he was as much of a lecher as Lord Blackmane, and entirely uncertain about any of this, Drake carefully unbuttoned Lydia's shirt about halfway down, revealing her bare upper arms. He was relieved to see she was, indeed, wearing a gray shift underneath, which, by this world's fashion standards, was about the same as a sleeveless undershirt.

"Look to my left arm, lord. Samuel wound a bandage there. Remove it, but carefully."

Drake saw it then. There was gauze wrapped around Lydia's upper arm, hidden by the long sleeves of her outer shirt. He barely held back a grin, and only because he was worried Lydia might misinterpret the reason he was grinning.

That was clever, old man. Real clever.

Drake took a firm grip on the end of the gauze, an end that had obviously been left for him to find, and unwound the gauze. He gasped as he peeled it back to reveal a small but open wound. She was bleeding! Why was she bleeding?

"You will find a small metal shiv tucked inside the bandage," Lydia said. "That should be sufficient to open your palm."

So she had literally stuck a shiv in her own arm and walked around with it all this time. While she surrendered. While they put the fetish on her. While they marched her to his cell. The whole time she'd had a *shiv* in her arm, and she hadn't even winced.

"You and Samuel really did think of everything," Drake said

quietly... and with no small trace of awe. The guards had likely searched Lydia for weapons, but not *in her own arm*. And since this little piece of steel wasn't a weapon, not really, she could say she didn't have any.

"Please, lord. Hurry."

Drake found the shiv, a tiny sharpened stick of steel. A trickle of blood was even now coursing down Lydia's arm, and he prayed her shirt would hide it. He jammed the shiv into his palm and grimaced at the pain, but he tore a nice big hole. He slapped his hand on her wound. Hopefully, he wouldn't regenerate that quickly.

As he held his bleeding hand against her bleeding arm, he once again pondered all the ways he'd screwed this up. "I'm sorry."

"Lord, this is..." She firmed her stance. "I am glad to do it."

"Still, I should have anticipated this. I should never have left us in this situation."

"I do not know how anyone could anticipate *this*, but you have proven ever nimble in the face of your opponent's attacks. You will do so again."

Drake had nowhere to look but her. He also had his bleeding palm resting on her bleeding arm, and that was going to feel weird and awkward no matter what happened. It wasn't even sexy, just... not something he should be doing with his steward.

"Okay," Drake said finally. "We've definitely mixed blood. So what do I do now?"

"Wrap the shiv in the bandage, then wrap the bandage back around my arm."

Right. That made sense. He could do that. He was still doing his best to finish wrapping the bandage securely when a loud, firm knock rattled the door.

"Open up!" a guard bellowed.

"We're still talking!" Drake wrenched the bandage tight, then grimaced as Lydia sucked in her breath. "Sorry!"

"My shirt, lord. You must button my shirt."

"Shit! Right!"

The door rattled again as the guards forcefully banged on it. "Open this door! Now!"

"One second!" Drake shouted. "Hold your fucking horses!"

He was still fumbling with Lydia's hopelessly complicated shirt—stupid buttons—when, to his shock, the first of the bolts in the door slid back on its own accord. Magic? Then another bolt, then another. He was never going to get this done in time. They were going to get busted!

"Kiss me," Lydia ordered fiercely.

"What?" Drake yelped.

"I give you my consent to kiss me!" A lock slammed open. "They will think—"

Drake kissed her just as the door flew open, and the moment their lips touched was far more electric than he expected. This wasn't right! She was his steward, he was her manor lord, and he wasn't supposed to—

"Stop that right now," the guard said with disgust.

Drake broke their impromptu kiss and glared at the man. He didn't have to fake his anger. Nor, in retrospect, was he surprised at the anger on the guard's face. What must he think, seeing Drake like this with a woman bound in place with her shirt half open?

The guard marched forward, face twisted with concern. "Did he—"

"Nothing my lord has done was done without my consent," Lydia interrupted angrily. "Tend to your own business."

The guard paused in surprise, then glowered at them both. He didn't come closer. His steward, bless her, had stumbled upon the one situation that would make the guards feel too awkward to investigate more closely. At least Lord Blackmane was good for something.

Setting absurdly low expectations for the average manor lord.

Drake numbly finished buttoning up Lydia's shirt and then stepped back. The guard immediately approached and patted her down, respectfully. He wasn't so embarrassed he wouldn't search her for hidden weapons.

Yet there was no weapon for the guard to find, and the gauze blended in with the rest of Lydia's shirt. The guard's scowl made Drake feel like a lecher, but at least the man didn't question him. After seeing this, he couldn't blame this guard for thinking he was a prick.

"What did you discuss?" the guard demanded.

"Samuel is my successor," Drake told Lydia. "Tell him I haven't changed my mind."

"I will tell him, lord," Lydia said quietly.

"What else did you discuss?" the guard demanded. "Lydia, tell me all that you discussed with your manor lord while we were gone."

"I compel you not to do that," Drake said.

Lydia gasped. She ground her teeth and trembled in place. She was *choosing* to obey his blood pact compulsion, which was just powerful enough to let her resist the obedience fetish... but it was hurting her. It might even be killing her. It was killing him to watch her suffer.

Yet Drake kept his face calm and cruel. He smirked at the guard. "That is my business."

The guard glared in obvious fury, glancing between a trembling, suffering Lydia and a smug-looking Drake. The man's disgust was evident... disgust Drake now felt about himself.

"Do you have orders to torture and kill my steward?" Drake asked. "Because otherwise, you're going far beyond the call of duty here."

"Order her to speak of your counsel," the man demanded.

"No," Drake said. "Withdraw your order."

Lydia coughed. Drool ran down her chin as her legs wobbled. He belatedly reached out to grab her before she fell. She was trembling so hard it made him want to scream.

"You're not getting this out of her," Drake said coldly. "I'll let her die first."

Lydia said nothing. She didn't look to be *aware* of them at the moment. Drake only wished he could bear this pain in her place... but he couldn't break first. Everyone in his manor, and even Lydia, needed him to be cruel now.

"Lydia," the guard said coldly. "I withdraw my prior order."

She gasped and collapsed. Drake caught her, supported her, and helped her back to her feet. "Talk to me," he said quietly. "Can you hear me? Are you hurt?"

Still trembling, she offered a fierce smile. "I will live, lord."

Drake could only stare at her in close-mouthed awe. Lydia wasn't just his steward or his friend. She was... special. She was the most loyal and determined person he'd ever met.

"Lydia, step outside," the guard ordered.

She stumbled outside without another word.

The guard looked him over with distaste that was even greater than it had been before. "Your execution will take place in a few hours. Normally we'd place an obedience fetish on you, but since you can speak words you do not believe, including your own name, the Judge suspects it might not work. We won't be depending on it."

"I wouldn't," Drake agreed.

"We will, however, arrive with a small army capable of killing you a dozen times over. We will execute you right inside this room if you do not agree to meet your end with dignity."

"Oh *no*," Drake said. "I sure would hate to be *executed*."

The guard scowled. "If you have any honor at all, you should think of your manor. The Judge has accepted that they were not involved in this foul business, and Samuel Marcos is known far and wide as a fair man. Lord Frostlight swore to that before she died. So when Samuel becomes Lord Gloomwood, they will finally have a manor lord *worthy* of the title."

So the Judge had offered that, at least. If he fucked up his escape despite all the help he'd been given, Samuel and his manor would survive. That actually made Drake feel better about this whole situation. It took the pressure off.

"Also," the guard added, "if you do resist your lawful execution, the Judge will give the order to raze your manor to the ground. Along with everyone inside it."

So *that* was why the Judge had offered to leave his manor unharmed. To the noble court and everyone else, she appeared benevolent, but she was also literally holding Drake's whole manor hostage in hopes it would compel him to let himself be executed peacefully.

She was a hardass... but it was a good play. He could respect it. "I won't resist."

"I wish I could believe you believed that." The guard stepped backward out the door. "There is one last matter before I leave. Despite your crimes, you are entitled to a last meal."

Drake chuckled darkly. "Of course I am."

"So what shall I have our cooks prepare you?"

"I'll take steamed crabs from The Swollen Net." That was the best seafood place in Korhaurbauten, according to Samuel. "And some of those pastries from the bakery outside the capital. Sweeney's, I believe it's called?" He hadn't gotten to eat any pastries.

The guard nodded. "I will have them delivered to your room in an hour or so. Enjoy your last morning, Lord Gloomwood."

Drake offered his most predatory smile. "Hey, you too."

59
DON'T THROW UP

An hour later, Drake got his steamed crabs and pastries, hot and fresh. He ate hearty. He was going to need all his energy for his dramatic escape today. Especially after he rose from the table where he was eating in private, focused on the door, and stepped to it.

In a shower of spectral purple butterflies.

He could no longer regenerate. That was the bad news. He could, however, instantly teleport a good distance simply by focusing on where he wanted to go and taking a step. That was the good news, and the trick that might just keep his enemies from winning today.

Lydia's fierce loyalty and keen mind had come through for him once again.

Drake spent the next hour alternating between fluttersteps and shuffling slowly around with his eyes on his feet. It did seem that this time, so long as he kept his eyes focused on his own feet, he did not flutterstep. He also managed to get better at stepping back and forth across the room, though each teleport still dizzied him and made him slightly nauseous.

Still, he wasn't about to let himself be executed.

A firm knock sounded on his door. The guards had come to take him to the courtyard. What if he just refused to open the door? Could they even get in here?

The sound of the locks unlocking themselves once more answered his question. They must have someone with a rarity capable of unlocking locks from the other side of the door. The door swung open before seven capital guards all walked inside.

Four carried crossbows, all pointed at him. Two carried swords. The last carried heavy manacles, but he wasn't the man who had given Drake so much shit earlier today.

Instead, the guards were led by Inquisitor Grayson. The man who'd spoken to him after the kromians appeared in the cabal. Drake knew this man might listen to him.

"You escorted me to meet the Judge two days ago," Drake said. "She asked specifically to see me because she wanted my help. The Judge also told me, in that meeting, that she knew I had nothing to do with the sea gate. You remember bringing me to see her, don't you?"

Grayson shrugged. "I am going to shackle you now, Lord Gloomwood."

"Dammit, Grayson, I just told you the Judge said I wasn't responsible for the sea gate. She's been tricked! There's a thrall out there who can change what people remember!"

"You can speak words you don't believe," Grayson said calmly. "No nonsense you spew today will change your fate. However, I have no intention of offering you anything but the courtesy and respect afforded a manor lord... but only if you cooperate with us."

If he didn't cooperate, the Judge would raze his manor, and this time, he couldn't just shift into a dire rat and eat everyone in the room. Plus, he already had a plan to escape. He couldn't risk getting his knees broken. That would make it a lot more difficult to flutterstep.

Drake extended his wrists. "I did not plant the sea gate in the chamber. I did not send those guards away. I'm in here because the

Judge offered to place me in protective custody so she could bait our true enemies into trying to kill me. Lord Frostlight was my protector."

Grayson scoffed. "A manor lord outside your alliance agreed to cooperate with and protect you?" He snapped the heavy metal manacles on Drake's wrists, linked by a thick chain. "If you intend to plead your case with nonsense, you should come up with better nonsense."

"Ask Lord Frostlight's blood thrall! The one who can create a bubble of awareness that tells them when someone's nearby! That person will remember."

"Lord Frostlight refused to name a successor before her execution." Grayson pulled another pair of shackles off his belt. "Therefore, her former thralls have left for Frostlight Manor, where they will remain until the cabal chooses a successor."

"Then ask Lord Skybreak! She knows about the plot as well!"

"Lord Skybreak has now been twice censured, first for the crime of illegally trading weapons and again for the crime of challenging the noble court," Grayson said. "She is a good woman, and your words have done great harm to her. That I cannot forgive."

"Dammit, Grayson, you're being played!"

The man eyed him calmly. "Do I need to have my men pin you to the floor while I attach the leg shackles, or will you allow me to do it without a fuss?"

He scowled. "I said I wouldn't resist, but I'm not dying in shackles."

"We will remove your shackles before you take the stage," the man said. "That much we can offer. Your dignity. We will also have ten crossbows pointed at you at all times."

Drake pointed. "Fine. Get it over with."

This was too perfect. While Samuel would inherit Gloomwood Manor, Lords Proudglade, Mistvale, and Redbow would now have a majority when it came to choosing the new manor lords. They'd choose the new Lord Frostlight and then the new Lord Blackmane.

Only Sky would stand against them... since they still had Lord Ashwind in their pocket.

Moreover, now that the allied lords had shown they could defeat Lord Gloomwood, Lord Frostlight, and soon Lord Skybreak in short order, Lord Brightwater would have no choice but to side with them if she wanted to keep her own manor safe. That would give them five votes, which would be enough to install any Lord Frostlight and Blackmane they wished.

His enemies really were going to finally tilt the table. They would have control of seven manors, isolating Gloomwood and Skybreak and ensuring they could destroy both anytime they wished. He'd had no idea just how many plots they'd put into motion.

The enemy manor lords had planned for years for the scheme that came together today. They had used a dozen dirty tricks it would have been impossible to anticipate. Even so, there was one problem they could never have anticipated... Lydia and Samuel's desperate and brilliant plan to help their manor lord escape.

No thrall would launch such a risky and desperate plan to save some asshole who enslaved them with blood magic. No sane thrall, anyway. Not without being explicitly ordered to do so, which Drake couldn't do from here.

His people were awesome. If he got out of this alive, he was going to throw the biggest fucking party Gloomwood Manor had ever seen. For everyone. After all the bullshit they'd been through the past few months, and the *years* before that, his people had earned it.

The death march to the courtyard felt like it took forever, likely because it did. Drake kept his eyes focused on his feet. He practically slipped into a meditative trance as he walked the hallways of the Temple of the Eidolons surrounded by alert, armed capital guards.

When a door finally opened to the outside, Drake squinted as the bright morning light flooded the hallway. He'd been inside so long it took his eyes awhile to adjust. Even so, as he was shuffled outside, he verified he was where he expected.

The courtyard for his execution was just as Lydia had described it. It was smaller than the big rectangular courtyard back in the middle of Gloomwood Manor, perhaps as big as a large school auditorium, and had a ground of cobblestone. Stone walls towered over them at all sides. They stood three stories tall, and multiple archers stood on those walls in clear sight.

There was a raised rectangular wooden stage at the end of the courtyard, and on it stood a man with a huge steel axe wearing a dark hood: an executioner. So they didn't have guillotines here, at least not yet. They did old-school beheadings.

In addition to the dozens of capital guards standing around him now, there were at least another two dozen guards around the edges of the courtyard. They clustered by every available door and also stood guard over the wooden seats arranged for those witnessing his execution.

He recognized the enemy manor lords—Proudglade, Mistvale, Redbow—all watching him with confident and spiteful eyes. Each had a second with him, and Proudglade had even brought Westin with him as his second. Interesting choice.

Drake saw Lord Brightwater as well, staring at the stage instead of him. And, of course, Lord Skybreak was in the courtyard as well. She smiled at him as he entered the courtyard.

She seemed unconcerned to see him shackled and on the verge of being executed. That suggested his people had spoken to her, too, and told her how he was going to escape today. Her confidence, in him, buoyed his own. Lady Skybreak was here as her second.

Drake still had Sky and her entire manor on his side as well, in addition to his own people. Every last one of them must know, just like he did, that he hadn't committed the crimes of which he was accused. So unlike Lord Frostlight, who'd had no one, he had all sorts of allies.

It turned out being a manor lord who wasn't a total asshole had advantages after all.

The Judge sat high up in a chair overlooking the courtyard as well. Her box was on a platform attached to the second floor of one of the three-story tall walls, looking down on everyone. As he approached the box, Drake glanced up at her.

"Hey, Judge!"

"Quiet!" the guard ordered.

"Our enemies can change what people remember with their rarity!" Drake called. "They changed your memories to make you think I committed a crime, so before—"

A guard slammed his club into Drake's stomach so hard he doubled over coughing. He dropped to one knee, glared up at the guard, and then rose again. He ignored the burning in his stomach. It would take far more than one hit to keep him down.

He spit on the ground. "What happened to respecting a manor lord?"

The guard glared back. "Disrespect this court again and we'll tear your tongue out."

Having his tongue torn out would be annoying. He wasn't sure it would grow back, not unless he had a regenerating rarity at the time. No more delicious meat.

Drake had said what he needed to say. As he glanced at the gathered manor lords for their reaction to his words, he was unsurprised to see he hadn't gotten much from his last gambit before his escape. Lord Proudglade was still scowling. Lord Mistvale was still solemn. Lord Redbow was still grinning like a lonely prick with an unmarked white van full of candy.

But Westin… Westin?… was staring at him wide-eyed. He looked terrified. A moment later the expression vanished beneath fake calm, and Westin casually looked away as the guards marched him forward. Yet Drake had no doubt as to what he'd just witnessed.

Westin Proudglade had reacted to his shout. Westin knew

something about this rarity that allowed someone to change what others remembered. Drake immediately decided he wasn't about to leave this courtyard alone.

He couldn't take Lydia with him. While he could carry her out of here, he wouldn't put it past the guards to have her obedience fetish kill her if she left the courtyard. But Westin knew something about this rarity, and taking him would also give Drake leverage.

Gods. He wasn't just going to escape. Today, Lord Gloomwood was also going to abduct Lord Westin Proudglade.

Again.

The guards marched him past the other manor lords and then to a step of wooden steps. A guard knelt there and removed his shackles. Otherwise, he couldn't climb the steep steps. That was one problem handled. He'd solve the ten guards pointing crossbows at him from the ground and the archers pointing bows at him from above in a moment.

A guard thumped up the steps and motioned for him to follow. "Up, now."

Drake walked up the steps. His heart was pounding as hard as it had been just before he'd turned into a dire rat and torn apart his captors, but it was good to feel more adrenaline than fear. He was afraid... who wouldn't be?... but he wouldn't let that stop him.

Once he stood on the stage, Drake turned to stare out over the gathered audience. Given he had yet to escape, Sky now looked a bit concerned. Lydia was watching him with clenched lips. Westin wasn't looking at him at all.

"Lord Gloomwood!" the Judge boomed from above. "You have been judged guilty by the noble court of attempting to deceive the noble court! There can be no tithe, and you will pay for your crime with your life! Now, for the sake of your manor, meet your end with dignity."

The guard behind him grabbed his arm. "To the block, prisoner."

Drake glanced at him. "How about you go fuck yourself instead?"

Before the man could reply or strike him in anger, Drake looked back to the gathered manor lords... and took a *step*.

He smashed directly into Lord Proudglade. The two of them went over together as the man's chair tipped backward, and Drake punched the shocked man several times in the face before he scrambled up. He then slammed his shoulder into Westin and flutterstepped again.

Westin slammed into the far wall of the courtyard hard enough to knock the breath out of him, at which point Drake spun with the man braced in one arm. Archers above had already pointed their bows at him, but they couldn't shoot him without hitting Westin.

"Lord Gloomwood!" the Judge roared.

As shocked observers scattered in all directions, Lord Proudglade rose to his feet. A ball of literal lighting appeared in the man's hands. His glare was terrifying.

"Release my son!" Proudglade roared.

"Hey, Westin?" Drake said. "Don't throw up."

He looked up to the far wall, focused on where he wished to be, and stepped.

An instant later he nearly fell off the far edge of the three-story wall, and Westin, who was still too out of breath to struggle, actually did throw up. Drake barely noticed the wide-eyed gazes of the shocked archers on the wall beside him as he scanned the area below.

He immediately spotted a single small house with a banner on it bearing a wolf. The flag Lydia had told him Samuel would place upon its roof. Drake focused on the house as he stepped off the wall with Westin still clenched tightly in his arms.

He flutterstepped into the roof of the house hard enough that he immediately lost his balance. Westin gasped as he tumbled away. They both slid down along with a pile of broken tiles and slammed hard into the earth. That knocked the wind out of Drake as well.

A hooded man stepped from a nearby door and gasped. "You brought *him?*"

"He knows about changing people's minds!" Drake wheezed.

Samuel pulled Drake up, then glanced back into the house. "Get Westin!"

A muscular hooded woman who just had to be Emily rushed out, punched Westin hard enough to make him bend in two, then picked him up and rushed back into the house. Drake heard guards shouting nearby, but unlike him, they couldn't step over a three-story wall.

As he stumbled into the house, Drake managed a chuckle. "Well done, old man."

Anna stood inside, anxious and blinking. "Will you come with me, lord?"

"Not yet," Drake said. "Emily! Sit Westin's ass down."

Emily slammed Westin onto his ass hard enough he threw up again, then grimaced as she pushed him against the wall. She also raised her hand. Her spectral battle axe appeared.

"Don't soul chop him," Drake said. "We need him alive."

"It is time for you to leave," Samuel said warningly.

"I told you, Westin knows something about the rarity that's been fucking with everything. It changes what people remember."

Samuel reached into his robe and pulled out a black disc. "Then use this on him."

Of course the old man had brought an obedience fetish. Samuel always came prepared. As Drake grabbed the disc, Westin managed to get enough breath back to speak.

"Clint, don't—"

"Shut it, asshole. Emily, rip his shirt open."

She did that, forcefully, and then Drake slammed the obedience fetish onto Westin's chest in the exact same spot it had sat the day they first met. The sound of searing flesh sounded as Westin screamed.

Emily peeked out a window covered in boards. "Guards are coming, lord!"

Drake glared at Westin. "Westin, stand up and don't say a fucking word."

Westin stood, blinking. He might even be crying now. Too bad.

"Go now, lord," Samuel said. "The others await you at the recall spot."

Drake glanced at him. "We're all going."

"No," Samuel said. "Anna can only teleport three people. Four will kill her."

"I'm so sorry, lord!" Anna cried. "Order Samuel to let me teleport you all!"

Drake wasn't about to do that. "You and Emily better escape, then."

"I already have a plan for that. But if you don't go now, we will fail."

"Will you come with me?" Anna asked again, more desperately this time.

Drake glared at Westin. "Westin, say yes."

"Yes," Westin said quietly.

Drake looked to Anna. "Yes." He looked to Emily. "Don't die, murdermaid."

She grinned wide. "Not while I'm having this much fun!"

He looked to Samuel. "Don't let her soul chop anyone unless you have to. Once we prove my innocence, we'd still be guilty of murdering capital guards."

Anna stepped through an open doorway leading deeper into the empty house. "Lord!"

"I'm going." Drake looked to Westin. "Westin, walk through that door. After you get to the other side, stand until I tell you to move again."

Westin, visibly miserable, walked to the door and stepped through. He vanished.

The door of the old abandoned house splintered as a mace hit it. Samuel dropped to the floor and pulled open what Drake saw was a trap door. "Go, lord!"

"See you soon." Drake jogged for the open doorway.

The house vanished to be replaced with the interior of his armored carriage. He stumbled over Westin, who he had ordered to stand right where he arrived. Anna crouched on one couch inside. Drake pushed off Westin and pulled back to the curtain to see that they were already on the Noble Road outside Korhaurbauten. His thralls had planned for everything.

The carriage door swung open. Valentia stepped inside to check on Anna, took a look at Westin, and then glanced his way. "We did not know you were bringing a guest."

"Target of opportunity," Drake said. "Are we safe here?"

"Safety is relative. However, no one followed us out of the city. Sachi made sure."

"We're not leaving without Lydia and the others."

"Of course not," Valentia said. "What do you wish me to do with your captive?"

"For now, nothing." Drake glanced at Westin. "We're going to have a little talk."

60
JUSTIFY IT HOWEVER YOU CAN

"Anna?" Drake said. "I need you to leave the wagon."

She nodded immediately. "Yes, lord."

"Val? You stay. You're going to listen to every word this fucker says and make sure you testify to it when I need you."

Anna hopped to the door and left without complaint. She didn't even ask if Valentia was going to hurt Westin. Anna probably already knew the answer.

If she had to.

Valentia, meanwhile, settled beside him. The glower she directed at Westin would have made it difficult for anyone not to piss themselves. Drake was glad she was here.

The rumble of the carriage told him they were on the move, and a glance out the window told him they were moving off the main road. Drake assumed Samuel had ordered the carriage to wait somewhere close to where it could easily get out of sight.

He also assumed the rest of his people were out there walking alongside him. He didn't see why they wouldn't. He normally wouldn't ask Anna to walk, but he didn't need her inside his carriage, watching, if he had to get forceful with Westin today.

Or order Valentia to freeze his balls off.

Now, to find out if Drake's impetuous decision to kidnap the son of another manor lord was going to finally get him out of this mess... or just drop him into another pile of problems.

"Westin, raise your right hand."

The man's right hand popped up. His eyes were still visibly wet.

"Westin, slap yourself on the cheek."

Westin slapped himself, quite forcefully, and then gasped. There was no doubt the obedience fetish was working. Drake had total control of his enemy now.

"Just wanted to make sure the fetish worked." Drake did his level best not to feel guilty. "Now, Westin, tell me exactly how your rarity works."

The man visibly struggled for a moment, teeth bared and fists clenched, before he gasped and slammed against the seat, breathing hard. "I can change what people recall."

Fucking finally! Proof. The proof he needed to save his manor and himself... and Lydia. His impetuous decision to kidnap Westin again during his execution had actually paid off.

"How many people has Lord Proudglade ordered you to use this rarity on?"

Westin grimaced again. "No one, lord."

Westin couldn't even lie normally, and he was under an obedience fetish. So how...

"Does Lord Proudglade even know what your rarity can do?"

This time, Westin struggled almost a full second before he gasped and slammed once more against the back of the carriage. "He does not."

Drake finally understood how all of this was possible. Westin had kept his rarity secret from even his own father, or perhaps Lord Proudglade had never asked. That made even more sense now that he knew more about the noble court.

Lord Proudglade couldn't keep the truth about Westin's rarity secret from the noble court. But he couldn't tell them what he didn't know. That would be what Drake demanded next.

"Westin, how did you trick Lord Proudglade into not knowing your rarity?"

"I altered my own memory before we spoke. I made myself remember that I had no rarity. I even continued to think that for weeks before I found the diary I left for myself in my room."

That was... actually brilliant. Westin might be responsible for every plot he'd faced, and as furious as Drake was with the man right now, he was also an evil genius. Westin had changed his own memories to ensure he could give his father false information about his rarity.

Drake had assumed, all this time, that Lord Proudglade was the man pulling the strings for all the manors arrayed against him and all their plots. But now... he wondered if Westin had been pulling the strings all along. If Westin had been the mastermind behind everything.

This also explained why Westin had been at Drake's execution. Had Lord Proudglade known that his son could alter people's memories, he'd never have put him anywhere near Drake, even if he was certain Drake was to be executed. In this case, it seemed Westin's need to keep his rarity secret from even his own father had finally bitten them both in the ass.

Westin might not have had any choice other than to attend Drake's execution with his father, since he couldn't tell his father of the dangers. This also explained why Lord Proudglade had been so surprised to hear that Drake had become Lord Gloomwood before Lord Crow attempted that demon summoning during the cabal. Westin had kept that from him as well.

"Westin, who else is knowingly working against us on your behalf?"

Westin sighed. "Lord Redbow knows what my rarity can do. He

has been helping me, as was his associate, Captain Ro." He wasn't even trying to fight the fetish any longer.

So there it was. Lord Redbow had been speaking what he believed when he said he knew of no thrall who could change what people see, because, instead, he knew of a thrall who could change what people *remembered*. Drake had been so close. Not close enough.

"Westin, tell me every plot you and Lord Redbow have launched against my manor and Lord Skybreak's. Answer every question I have about them until I tell you to stop."

"First, I contracted Captain Ro to assassinate Lord Skybreak's steward and to escort me to where the assassination occurred. I also ordered him to leave one of her thralls alive. I changed that man's memory so he would remember Valentia murdering the steward."

"And that was Oswell? The thrall I called to testify in the cabal?"

"Yes."

"So why let Valentia and Nicole live?"

"I believed Lord Skybreak would need someone to execute in order to ensure bad blood arose between your manors, on both sides. After she executed your battle maids, whom Captain Ro's mercenaries would deliver, for a crime Lord Gloomwood knew they did not commit, it would ensure you never trusted each other."

"And why not change Valentia and Nicole's memory as well?"

"I cannot. Changing even one person's memory exhausts me for a full day."

So that was how it was. Westin's rarity did have some limits. Otherwise, Drake suspected Westin would simply change the memory of everyone he met and never get caught.

"Westin, who put that sea gate in the Chamber of Council?"

"I do not know," Westin said. "I also did not know they

planned to do that. I would never have agreed to that. I only sought to defeat those who threatened my father."

Westin certainly believed that. And... maybe he was right. Still, he was going to pay.

"Still," Drake said to confirm it for himself, "the reason Lord Redbow summoned those kromians and stopped the cabal was because he was worried we'd keep the inquisitions going until we asked the right question. He had to stop it before he was forced to confess that he was working with you."

Westin nodded. "I can only assume that was his reason. As I said, I was not involved in the decision to use the sea gate ambush to stop the cabal."

"But did you make Lord Frostlight remember placing it there?"

"I did. It was the only way I could stop her from becoming a threat to my father."

"So you intended to have Lord Frostlight executed. You murdered her."

"I did," Westin agreed calmly. "She was an assassin by trade, a woman who hunted desperate peasants for enjoyment and killed them all in brutal ways. She was no soft flower, and she had already begun to conspire against Proudglade Manor with you, Lord Gloomwood."

No soft flower must be how they talked about *innocents* or *saints*. Drake actually agreed with Westin—about Lord Frostlight—but still, the fact that Westin had tricked a manor lord into confessing to her own execution was ruthless. He had also tried to kill Drake many times.

There was still more he needed to know. "Westin, how did Lord Gloomwood capture you?" That was where they had first met, after all. In Lord Gloomwood's torture dungeon.

"That was a mistake." Westin grimaced. "As the final step of my plot against Lord Gloomwood, I planned to meet with him and change his memory so he remembered Lord Skybreak killing his thralls. I asked to meet him to trade information about my manor."

"And the old fucker really believed that?"

"I intended to tell him some of our manor's secrets to gain his trust, though I was going to make him forget them all afterward. But he simply ordered his zarovians to knock me out the moment I arrived, then restrained me in his dungeon where he could force it out of me."

Now Drake was curious about something else. "How do you use your rarity?"

"I must touch someone. I must also maintain contact for a few seconds."

And once Westin got knocked out and woke up chained to a standing wooden X, he'd been helpless to use his rarity. Moreso after Lord Gloomwood slapped an obedience fetish on him. It seemed Westin was right. He'd been clever, but he'd gotten too ambitious.

And, finally, one last memory clicked. The day he'd agreed to go into protective custody, as he'd left the Judge's office, Westin had been coming in to speak with her.

"So after we ran into each other a few days ago, you changed the Judge's memory? By telling her you had information about who had placed the sea gate in the chamber?"

"Yes," Westin said quietly.

So, by saving Westin from Lord Crow the first day he arrived, Drake had put himself in a world of pain. Not all good deeds, it seemed, were rewarded. Shit happened.

"Lord Gloomwood," Westin said, "may I ask you one favor before you turn me over to the capital guards?"

Drake chuckled darkly. "That's rich. You tried to kill me, like, a dozen times."

"I did."

"You directly threatened my people and even got some of them killed. You very nearly killed everyone in my manor. Why the fuck would I do you a favor?"

"Because I never wished to be your enemy. Once we had

control of your manor, I knew my father would appoint someone who would treat your thralls properly." Westin sighed again. "That is my favor. May I tell you, Lord Gloomwood, why I did all this?"

Drake frowned. "You think I'll care?"

"I would like you to understand."

"I'm not going to keep anything you did secret. I'm not going to let you go. I'm going to take you to the capital and use that fetish to make you confess every last one of these crimes to the court. Then, they're going to execute you just like they executed Lord Frostlight."

"I know all this. I am resigned to my fate and will confess my crimes to the court. But before I die, I still wish to tell you why I did all this... Clint."

Drake simply couldn't understand the sudden sincerity in Westin's voice. "Why?"

"Because now that you have defeated me, I wish to apologize."

That was not what Drake had been expecting to hear. Yet Westin was under multiple compulsions that prevented him from lying. Was Westin actually this deluded? Drake was actually curious to find out.

"All right, Westin. Tell me why you did all this. Justify it however you can."

"All I ever wanted to do was bring peace to our realm."

Drake glanced at Valentia, who looked no more convinced than he did. Then, he turned back to Westin. "So tell me how you planned to do that."

"Manor lords have fought for dominance and killed each other for centuries. This was the realm into which I was born, and it is not just manor lords who die. Many of their thralls suffer as well, tortured or executed for trivial slights. Countless peasants also suffer every day beneath ruthless manor lords. My father protects his people, but others still hurt theirs."

Drake remembered Robin's quest to kill the Asp, the mercenary with the rarity that allowed her to melt people with acid. That woman alone had slaughtered half a town, and many of the others had done worse. He could only imagine how many they'd hurt.

He also remembered Anna and her father, forced into slavery by Captain Ro and Lord Redbow. There must be so many others out there. So many innocents hurt or killed.

"The last Lord Gloomwood was among the worst of our lords," Westin said quietly. "He tormented his thralls, hurting and executing anyone he believed disloyal or weak. He even attempted to summon a leviathan. You saw it as I did."

Drake couldn't deny that.

"When I put my plan into motion to ensure Skybreak Manor and Gloomwood Manor would never ally, I aimed my attack at Lord Crow. He was the man I wished to defeat, not you. Crow's thralls suffered so much at his hands. I couldn't stand by and let them all suffer."

Still Westin wasn't lying, and he wasn't wrong. In his own bizarre way, Westin had actually set out to *save* Gloomwood Manor... and all the people Drake now protected... from their evil overlord. Drake didn't have to agree with Westin to understand his purpose.

"I had no idea Lord Crow would summon you, nor that you would somehow defeat him and take his place. I also had no idea you would be... this."

"What, Westin?"

"Noble." Westin smiled sadly. "Even kind. You have been ruthless when you had to be, but only to protect those close to you. You trust your thralls and treat them well. Had I known a man like you would seize Gloomwood Manor, I would never have launched my plot... but I launched it before you arrived. I was committed, but still, I wish to apologize for my actions."

Drake stared in disbelief.

"The die that made me your enemy was cast before you arrived in our realm," Westin continued. "My intent was always to stop the suffering of thralls abused by their manor lord and bring peace to my realm. I set out to eliminate the former Lord Gloomwood, the evil manor lord who would doom the world for his own power... and when you killed him for me, to my eternal shame, I could not prevent you from bearing the brunt of my plots in his place."

61
HE RAN OFF, DIDN'T HE?

"You can't really believe that," Drake said incredulously.

Yet Westin did believe it. The man couldn't lie, now more than ever. Westin really did believe he had been doing good... in his own fucked up way.

What if he was right?

"I'm sorry for everything," Westin said. An actual *tear* rolled down the stubborn man's stubborn face. "For killing Steward Rodney. For harming your battle maids. For making the Judge believe you were responsible for the sea gate. None of these actions were moral, and all grieve me, but I knew no other way to protect my family and manor after all I had done."

"You expect me to forgive you?"

"Never." Westin took one shuddering breath. "I have injured you too grievously. Yet once you began to tear my plans apart one after the other, I had to protect my father. I did all I could to talk him out of calling this cabal to unseat you, but he would not listen to me. He coddles me, but he does not take my council. And as I stated, he knew none of this."

Drake grimaced. He really wanted to blame Lord Proudglade

for his part in all this, but it sounded like, now, Lord Proudglade had been played, like everyone else Westin touched.

"My father sought only to defeat an evil manor lord, which, thanks to my machinations, he thought you were. If you must hate someone, hate me. My father was only doing what he thought was necessary to protect our manor and our world."

None of this changed that Drake would turn Westin over and make him confess. None of it changed the fact that once the Judge knew what Westin had done, she would execute him. Westin had hurt too many people and caused too much havoc to go free.

But, dammit, now that Drake knew the man had done it all to save the people of Gloomwood Manor and bring peace to his realm, turning Westin over to be executed was going to feel like shit. He couldn't even celebrate by pissing on the grave of his defeated enemy. Unlike Lord Crow, Lord Westin Proudglade wasn't a man he could completely hate.

He looked to Valentia. "Turn this carriage around."

She watched him carefully. "And do what?"

"We're calling a peace summit. We need to get this all out in the open before they execute Lydia, or they find Samuel and Emily and she soul chops forty capital guards."

"And what if the capital guards and manor lords won't agree to hear us out?"

"They will," Drake said. "Because you're also going to tell them if they don't accept my summit and allow me to tell them the truth about all that happened, I'll execute Westin."

Even if Westin died, Valentia could still testify to everything he'd said... eventually. And she, just like everyone else in this world other than him, couldn't lie.

After the carriage was back on the road and Valentia had left to arrange a summit with the capital, Drake turned to Westin. "I will execute you if I have to." They were alone now.

"I know. I also understand why."

"But I'll make one last deal with you. I actually do believe your only goal was to protect your realm and your people, so while you fucked me over, I'm still willing to help you protect your family... but only if you help me clean up your mess."

"I will do anything you ask. I owe you that and more. What would you ask of me?"

Drake told him.

———

The parlay Drake had requested took place outside Korhaurbauten near a forest where he could hide Sachi, Robin, and every ranger Sky brought to the party. In the time it took Valentia to enter the city and arrange it, Drake was able to set up his entire zarovian army, Sky's rangers, and Nicole to defend him during the negotiations for his "surrender."

Sachi was out scouting now, and Sky Skybreak once again stood at his side. So long as she did so, her *void* rarity would ensure no magic could harm him or anyone near her. So even if Lord Proudglade tossed a lightning bolt at them, it would dissipate as it arrived.

After his escape, Sky, Lady Skybreak, and their thralls had reinforced Drake's vanguard with every one they had, just like allied manors did for each other. Sky had even clasped arms with him again she arrived. That still felt good.

After he told her what he'd uncovered about Westin's plotting, she shook her head ruefully. "You have the Eidolons' own luck." She chuckled. "And perhaps a curse as well."

The representatives from the capital arrived at mid-afternoon, escorted by capital guards and, unsurprising, Lord Proudglade's golden knights. Lord Proudglade himself also arrived, flanked by a young man a bit older than Westin in the same ornate armor. He looked like an older Westin, so he must be Westin's elder brother. The similarity was striking.

Drake saw no sign of Lord Mistvale or Lord Redbow. The Judge also was not present. Inquisitor Grayson was here, however, and Drake assumed he was here on the Judge's behalf.

Also, they had Lydia. Of course they had Lydia. She was shackled in nothing but loose peasant clothes, not silverweave. Lord Proudglade's nights marched her forward.

A hostage for a hostage. Drake hated it, but it made sense. The fact that he saw no sign of Samuel and Emily also suggested they had avoided capture. The Rope Tree sure was slippery when he meant to be. He likely had a dozen hideaways inside Korhaurbauten.

Lord Proudglade took the lead of his vanguard, which seemed foolish on its face, yet he was flanked by his armored son, four of his golden knights, and at least twenty capital guards in full ferrocite. Even Drake's zarovian army would have trouble cutting through that, and ferrocite was also resistant to magic, which meant Valentia couldn't freeze them.

Valentia walked with the capital's entourage as well, but not as a prisoner. Lord Proudglade retained his honor. Drake had sent Valentia to the capital as his representative to arrange this summit. It would be dishonorable for Proudglade to take her prisoner.

The first thing he was going to do after he got Lydia back was get that obedience fetish off her and get her some nice tea. She loved tea. He owed her his life, again.

Lord Proudglade stopped at Drake's perimeter, staring angrily at Cresh. The huge zarovian still towered over his fellows and made an intimidating sight. His fellow zarovians, including Korrag and Xutag, all stood ready for battle, and Drake knew Sachi and Robin were in the trees ready to commit a dozen arrow-based assassinations.

Even with his vanguard and Sky's, Drake wasn't sure if he could win a fight against Proudglade's private army. The man could toss balls of explosive lightning. Fortunately, today, he didn't have to defeat this man and his army of thralls in battle.

He was going to defeat him by revealing the crimes of his own son.

"Lord Gloomwood!" Proudglade called angrily. "Show me my son!"

Drake snapped his fingers at Nicole, who opened the door to his carriage. "Westin?" Drake ordered. "Step outside and stand beside me."

Westin emerged from the armored carriage. Proudglade's eyes visibly narrowed when he spotted the obedience fetish on his son, but it wasn't like he could call foul. He'd placed the same horrific item on Lydia.

"My thralls will admit you, your second, and Inquisitor Grayson for our summit!" Drake called. "I will not harm you, or order my thralls to harm you, unless you attempt to harm us!"

"You can speak words you do not believe!" Proudglade shouted angrily. "Why should we believe anything you say?"

"I actually can't do that!" Drake lied. "You've been deceived by Lord Redbow and others, including your own son! I committed no crime! Westin is behind everything!"

"Preposterous!" Lord Gloomwood shouted. "Now surrender him or Lydia dies!"

"You kill her, I kill him, and we all kill each other! That seems like a shitty summit!" Drake looked to Westin, and then said his next words very loudly. "Westin, speak freely."

"Father, Lord Gloomwood is correct!" Westin yelled. "I tricked you! I tricked everyone! Lord Frostlight and Lord Gloomwood did not place the sea gate in the Chamber of Council! I believe that was Lord Redbow! Moreover, it is I who deceived the noble court!"

Lord Proudglade had gone from a man whose glower could kickstart a sun to a man who looked to be as horrified as someone walking in on his murdered dog.

"He's tricked you!" Proudglade shouted angrily. "He is an outworlder!"

"He is an outworlder, but he has not tricked me!" Westin

shouted back. "He saved me from Lord Crow! He stopped a demon summoning! He did *not* summon those kromians!"

Inquisitor Grayson approached Lord Proudglade and spoke with him quietly. The man glared and trembled, and for a moment Drake was afraid that Proudglade would simply blow Grayson to cinders. Would this man take them all to war to save his youngest son?

Yet Lord Proudglade wouldn't start a war simply to hide the truth. Westin had assured him when they talked. Even if it meant sacrificing his own son, if Westin was truly guilty and Drake was truly innocent, Lord Proudglade would not take them to war out of spite or love.

The cursedly pompous man truly had too much honor for that.

"Lord Gloomwood!" Inquisitor Grayson called. "We will listen to what you have to say, but you must meet us in neutral territory! Step out of your lines! We will step out of ours!"

Drake considered. "Agreed! Now back your people the fuck up! And bring Lydia!"

Grayson turned to his capital guards and gave a number of orders too quietly for Drake to hear. Though all of them looked annoyed and angry about it, they backed up a good distance. They were still all in crossbow range, but so were Sachi, Robin, and Sky's rangers. His zarovians could also take dozens of crossbow bolts in the time it took them to reach the capital guard lines and beat those ferrocite-clad pansies into bloody paste.

Drake looked to his people. "Westin, with me. Nicole? Melt in case we have to fight. And if we do fight, I want you to stab Lord Proudglade first, preferably in the balls." He looked to Sky. "Could you accompany me as well?"

She smiled warmly. "I will always stand at your side."

Nicole went invisible as Drake strode forward with Westin on one side and Sky on the other. As they walked, Drake leaned close to Sky and spoke. "Who's his second?" The blond, armored man standing beside Lord Proudglade looked to be in his late twenties.

"That is Lord Felix Proudglade," Sky replied just as quietly. "His rarity, *dissolve*, allows him to melt any substance with a touch of his hand."

Including flesh. Yikes. He wasn't about to let that man touch him.

"Felix is actually quite nice," Sky added. "He and I met often as children, and I would almost consider him a distant brother. He is not so buried in tradition as his father."

Drake grimaced. "Let's hope he stays that way when she finds out what his little brother's been doing. And that he's gonna' die."

Drake, Sky, and Westin met Lord Proudglade, Felix Proudglade, Inquisitor Grayson, Valentia, and Lydia in the open ground between their two armies. Drake couldn't feel calm, despite the fact that he knew he had everything under control.

So many things had gone wrong since he arrived. So many things could still go wrong. Once they were all gathered closely enough to speak, Drake looked to Westin.

"Westin, I order you to tell Lord Proudglade and Inquisitor Grayson everything you told me. Leave nothing out. That is how you save your manor and your family."

Westin quietly repeated his entire confession in front of an increasingly pale Lord Proudglade, an increasingly incredulous Felix, and an increasingly concerned Inquisitor Grayson. Drake listened closely, prepared to compel Westin to testify again if he left nothing out, but the man was thorough. He revealed everything he'd done.

Westin's only concern remained ensuring his family didn't suffer for his crimes. That the crime was his alone, the crime of a lowly thrall rather than a haughty manor lord. Because if not... it was possible the Judge could order Proudglade Manor razed.

When he finished, Lord Proudglade trembled as he started at Drake. "You did this."

"I did nothing except put a stop to your son's schemes."

"It is you who can change people's memories! You tricked him somehow!"

"Father." Felix gently touched his arm. "I hate this as well, but we must consider it."

"No! I will not! This must be some other scheme from Lord Gloomwood!"

"Hey," Drake said. "Question. Where's Lord Redbow?"

Lord Proudglade's desperate glower shattered as his face fell.

"He ran off, didn't he?" Drake asked angrily. "He took off as soon as I grabbed Westin during my execution, because he knew I could force Westin to implicate him in these crimes. Redbow's already left the capital, hasn't he? You idiots just let him get away!"

Grayson now looked visibly uncomfortable. "We had no proof Lord Redbow was involved in any of this. We had no reason to prevent him from leaving with his thralls. With an answer to who had sabotaged the cabal, we had no reason to detain anyone."

"Well you do now, so fucking go after him! Oh, and Proudglade?"

The man bared his teeth.

"Take that obedience fetish off my steward. Right now."

62
NOW ARREST THIS CRIMINAL!

"I will not," Lord Proudglade said angrily. "You have deceived us all, and I will prove to everyone gathered here today." He glanced at Lydia. "Lydia! I command you to tell us if your lord can speak words he does not believe!"

Lydia trembled hard as the obedience fetish tortured her, and Drake immediately knew why. She was *choosing* to obey the compulsion he'd given her earlier—the one that prevented her from divulging his secrets—to resist the obedience fetish. That must be agonizing.

"She cannot answer!" Lord Proudglade bellowed. "That is all the proof we need!"

Drake rushed forward and grabbed Lydia before she could hurt herself any further. "Lydia, I know you believe I can say things I don't believe, but I can't! Westin changed your memories to make you think that. Tell them what you remember. It'll be okay!"

Still Lydia suffered, trembling as tears streamed down her cheeks and the fetish tortured her. How could he stop this? He couldn't compel her to do anything. He'd given up that power over her the day they met, and now she was dying because of it.

There was only one way to save them. He looked to Westin. "Tell them what you did to her! Right now!"

Proudglade turned to his son. "Silence!"

Westin ignored him. "I made Lydia remember Lord Gloomwood telling her he can speak words which he does not believe. I changed Lydia's memories so she would remember that."

"You hear that?" Drake shouted at Lydia. "It's fine! Answer him! It's just a trick!"

Lydia gasped, trembled in his arms, and fell against him. He clutched her close to keep her from collapsing. She had just endured an unthinkable amount of pain attempting to protect him... but she didn't have to protect him right now.

"Lord Gloomwood can say words he does not believe," Lydia whispered.

She felt so faint and fragile in his arms. His desire to keep her safe intensified a hundredfold. He'd done such a shitty job of that so far.

Lord Proudglade turned to Grayson. "Arrest this criminal."

"No," Drake said with a scowl. "You heard Westin. She remembers it wrong."

Lydia stared up at him in disbelief, pale and visibly exhausted. "Lord? Are my memories compromised?" She swallowed and blinked. "He changed what I remember?"

"Yes," Drake lied softly. He'd known that, one day, he might have to lie to her again, and he doubted this deception would work longer than it took for her to remember everything else he'd done that he shouldn't be able to do. For now, temporarily confusing her was enough.

"I can't speak words I don't believe, so you didn't betray me. You'd never betray me, and you're safe now. The manor is safe. Everyone's going to be fine."

Except Westin, he supposed.

Lydia pressed close once more. Everyone in his manor had

saved his life, but Lydia most of all. It didn't matter whether this looked appropriate to the others or not. His loyal and amazing steward needed his support right now, and he was *not* going to let her fall.

He glanced to Sky to see her smiling with relief. Valentia looked calm as well. With one last assist from Westin, he'd finally covered up his ability to lie... for now.

This was the last deal he had made with Westin. The deal that earned the man the right to justify his crimes and minimize the damage to his family. At Drake's request, Westin had changed his own memories so he believed he had made Lydia falsely believe Drake could lie.

Drake still wasn't sure when he would tell Lydia the truth about his abilities. Definitely not until they were back safe in his manor. Yet he couldn't keep it from her forever. They'd been through too much together for her to fully accept that *all* those memories were a lie.

For now, he'd be satisfied that they'd deceived the noble court.

Negotiations continued for some time after Drake finally proved his innocence to Inquisitor Grayson, and through him, to the noble court. As much as Lydia obviously wanted to be a part of the negotiations to clear his name, she'd endured so much just to get here. Drake asked Valentia to escort her back to his carriage and get her some tea, and Valentia made it clear to everyone she intended to do just that.

Drake was in no danger from his enemies any longer, at least not those gathered here. Inquisitor Grayson was apologetic. Lord Proudglade looked... broken. And so it was Felix Proudglade, Westin's older brother, who ended up doing most of the negotiations with Drake.

Sky and Inquisitor Grayson would go on ahead to clear the way and inform the Judge of what they had learned. Westin would remain in the joint custody of Drake and Felix until he presented his testimony to the noble court, at which point the Proudglade family would surrender Westin to face the noble court's justice.

Finally, to make up for all the assassination attempts, Lord Proudglade would allow Orson, his best golden knight, to duel Cresh, Drake's champion, for possession of Blood Woe, Cresh's enchanted axe. The duel was to be unarmed wrestling. Orson was going to get his mustachio'd ass handed to him, but that was kinder than what Cresh wanted to do to him.

Orson lived, Cresh got his axe back, and Drake forgave Proudglade Manor just a bit of their dickishness. Cresh bared all his teeth when the deal was finalized and thumped his tail in satisfaction. He even nodded at Drake. The big lizard might actually respect him now.

A little.

As for Felix and his father, he couldn't imagine what it must feel like to send your own brother or your own son to be executed, even if you understood their crimes were technically unforgivable. Fortunately, he wasn't the one who had to do that. Sucked for them.

A day later, it was all official. Drake's innocence was announced to everyone in the noble court and the capital at large. Lord Redbow was now an enemy of the noble court, with multiple manors soon to be called to go after him and remove him from power... after they decided who would be the next Lord Blackmane and Frostlight.

Lord Proudglade's alliance was shattered. Lord Mistvale still stood with Proudglade, as he always had, but Lord Frostlight was dead and Lord Redbow no longer had a vote. Finally, Lord Brightwater had made it clear she was no longer considering an alliance with anyone.

That made Drake and Sky the strongest manor alliance in Korhaurbauten, especially after they finally found out the truth about Lord Ashwind. After Lord Redbow fled, Lord Ashwind begged to join Drake's alliance as well... to ask for his help.

Lord Redbow, without Lord Proudglade's knowledge, had secretly kidnapped Lord Ashwind's only son. That son now remained a hostage of the fugitive Lord Redbow. Getting the son back alive still might not be possible... but Drake said he would try.

Drake also understood, a little better, why Lord Ashwind had betrayed him. Everyone in this fucked up world wanted to protect their family, just like back home. If he did manage to get back Lord Ashwind's son, Drake would get some free ferrocite and another loyal ally.

The trial took but a day. Westin denied nothing. Drake attended to ensure that Westin left nothing out and changed nothing in his story, but he took no joy in the task.

He couldn't. Not now that he knew Westin's reasons for launching his plots to try to save as many people as he could. He was simply glad it was finally over.

The noble court announced their decision that night. Lord Proudglade would be censured at the next cabal and pay a heavy tithe, but since he had truly been unaware of his son's actions, his manor and the rest of his family would be spared a worse judgment.

Protecting his family was the last goal Westin sought. That was the last deal Drake had made with him. The deal that finally assured the noble court and the Judge he couldn't lie.

The time for Westin's execution came the following morning. It was a warm, clear day with excellent weather and a gentle breeze. It was a chance for Drake to watch as the man responsible for almost every problem he experienced since coming here lost his head.

Yet though he was invited to the execution, Drake did not attend.

With Lydia at his side, now rested and much recovered from her grueling ordeal, Drake strode down the hallway leading to the Judge's private office with her at his side. Lydia was the only person with him today (Samuel, after all, still knew he could lie), but despite the Judge recently trying to execute him, he felt safer now than he had in a long time.

For the first time in weeks, he could truly feel comfortable no one was trying to murder him. Not even Lord Proudglade. The man was too busy burying his dead and noble son.

Atticus the train conductor met them in the room with all the scribes and record keepers, who were all still hard at work. "This way, please."

Soon after, Drake and Lydia stood in the Judge's private office. This time, there was no one in here but the three of them. Drake stood silent and waited for her to speak.

"Thank you for agreeing to meet with me," the Judge said. "I know you are both eager to return to your manor and your own affairs."

"You're the noble court," Drake said evenly. "I didn't think we could refuse you."

"That doesn't mean I don't appreciate all that you have done for us. Particularly you, Lord Gloomwood. If not for your bravery and cleverness, I would have allowed my entire court and capital to be forever fooled by one incredibly ambitious young man."

"Westin was only interested in making things better for people and putting an end to evil manor lords," Drake said. "Have you thought about how you can do that?"

"Every day," the Judge said quietly. "But the fact that you even now speak up for a man who caused you much harm shows me I was right to place my faith in you."

"You tried to execute me."

"But before that, and before my memories were changed, I trusted you and even worked with you to try to uncover the people who'd gathered against you. That has to count for something, doesn't it? I was your ally." She smiled as if she expected him to say yes.

Drake sighed. "Judge, can I ask why you asked us to come speak with you?"

"Of course," she agreed. "First, Steward Lydia, I wished to personally apologize for handing you over to Lord Proudglade. Your valor is commendable and your bravery without question. You are a woman I would love to have on my own staff."

"Thank you, Judge," Lydia said graciously. "But I am where I intend to stay."

"I understand," the Judge said. "But your part in saving the noble court from this unprecedented attempt at treachery still deserves recognition. Tomorrow, I will announce that you are now a friend of the noble court."

Lydia bowed. "Thank you, Judge. That is generous."

"It is only what you have earned."

Drake had no idea what a "friend of the noble court" meant. If he was able to choose Lydia's reward, he'd simply tell the judge to pay her a ton of money. But still, he wasn't going to interrupt their moment. Lydia, at least, seemed tremendously pleased.

"As for you, Lord Gloomwood, the noble court must also offer you recompense."

Drake simply raised an eyebrow. Could *he* ask for a ton of money?

"As Judge, I pardon you for the crime of exchanging magical artifacts with Skybreak Manor. You need pay no tithe. It is now as if that crime never occurred."

So the Judge was offering not to stupidly blame him for a former manor lord's stupid actions. How noble of her. Also, completely fucking useless so far as he was concerned.

"In addition, I offer you a token of the court's favor," she added.

Drake had no idea what that was.

Lydia leaned close and spoke quietly. "That means you can ask the noble court for anything. To grant you a boon. To forgive a crime, if that crime is forgivable. To summon a cabal. You should discuss your options with Samuel and Zuri when we return home, but know even one token is incredibly valuable. Manor lords would kill for them."

"But they can't actually," Drake said. "Right? I'm not going to get killed over this."

"No," the Judge assured him. "Only you can spend the token."

Drake nodded. "Thank you, Judge." He wasn't going to blame everything on her. She'd been tricked just like the others, and staying on her good side was good for his manor. "But since we're talking about how you can thank me, I have one other request outside of a token."

The Judge raised one slim, gray eyebrow. "What is it?"

"I ask that you also forgive Lord Skybreak's tithe and crime regarding the exchange of magical artifacts. She, like me, was not the lord who started that, and she also agreed we should confess and end it. So if I'm forgiven for that crime, she should be forgiven too."

"Done," the Judge said. "I had assumed you would ask that, but am pleased you did."

"Just don't tell her before I do."

"When do you wish to tell her?"

"After we leave. This afternoon should be fine for the official announcement. I want to see the look on her face when I tell her what else I pulled off today."

The Judge actually smiled. "Understood, Lord Gloomwood."

Silence fell between them. Drake glanced at Lydia, who said nothing, then back at the Judge. "Is there any other business you wish to discuss before I return home?"

"There is one other matter," the Judge said. "One that, before I discuss it with you, I need you to assure me you will keep secret from all save Lord Skybreak."

That sounded suspicious. "Why?"

"Understand that I am not the one making this request. A visitor for whom I have great respect has come to the capital to see you, and it is they who have requested this secrecy. They wish only to offer you counsel, yet they also wish to keep their arrival and alliance with your manor secret for now. If you can agree to all that, I will introduce you."

Who was this person? Why was the Judge willing to bend so far for them? Yet if they were this important, it sounded like it would be worth at least meeting with them. Even if he had to keep it secret from everyone but Sky.

"Very well," Drake said. "Introduce me to this advisor. I will not tell anyone outside my manor, other than Lord Skybreak, that we've met with them."

The Judge nodded, then looked past him. "Atticus?" She was speaking to the man in the train conductor outfit standing outside the door. "Send Lady Gloomwood in!"

Drake turned around as the door opened and caught his breath. A *Lady* Gloomwood? That wasn't possible. He was the only Lord Gloomwood in this world now.

The door opened, and an older, dark-haired woman Drake judged to be about the same age as his mother stepped into the office. The door closed behind her. She wore a fine green silver-weave tunic and pants, and dark boots that looked made for travel.

This so-called "Lady Gloomwood" was about his mother's height as well, with her same short dark hair and coy smile. She also, oddly enough, shared his mother's narrow nose and piercing blue eyes. Also, wait a minute. She had his mother's build too, which was...

No. This wasn't possible. He was seeing things. *What in the actual fuck.*

"Hello... son." The woman he'd known only as Marissa Hughes —or Mom—now stood in the office of the Judge in the fucked up fantasy world where he'd been sent by dark magic on a dark night in the New Mexico desert. His mother was here now, somehow.

Did that mean he could actually get home?

"I'm sorry it took me so long to find you," Marissa said. "It was a long and stressful trip. However, I am tremendously pleased to find you are still alive." She looked to the Judge, to Lydia, and then back to Drake. "It's time we had a talk."

The rise of the Lord of Gloomwood Manor will continue in book 3.

THANK YOU FOR READING THE RISE OF A MANOR LORD 2

We hope you enjoyed it as much as we enjoyed bringing it to you. We just wanted to take a moment to encourage you to review the book. Follow this link: The Rise of a Manor Lord 2 to be directed to the book's Amazon product page to leave your review.

Every review helps further the author's reach and, ultimately, helps them continue writing fantastic books for us all to enjoy.

Also in series:
The Rise of a Manor Lord 1
The Rise of a Manor Lord 2
The Rise of a Manor Lord 3

Want to discuss our books with other readers and even the authors? Join our Discord server today and be a part of the Aethon community.

Facebook | Instagram | Twitter | Website

You can also join our non-spam mailing list by visiting www.subscribepage.com/AethonReadersGroup and never miss out on future releases. You'll also receive three full books completely Free as our thanks to you.

Looking for more great books?

Magic school isn't cheap. To be a Mage, he must work smart and learn fast. *Fate dealt Nox the Alchemist unfavorable cards, but he has learnt to compensate for his shortcomings with scholarly pursuits, tenacity, and sheer grit. Fortunately, for him Woodson University and their scouts are always seeking individuals with his work ethic. The Department of Dungeon Studies sees the value of the mind and its ability to overcome all limitations. After all, they stripped the divine of their titles. The department turned gods into Dungeon Lords and their domains into Dungeons. Now, the department can teach Nox how to use magic to stand strong in a broken world. It will give him the tools to achieve his ambitions and his limitations will force him to the forefront of arcane discovery. Unfortunately, more immediate challenges await Nox, too. He lacks the means to pay the university's ridiculous tuition. Only alchemy and smart business deals will earn him the hundreds of gold coins he needs.* ***Join Nox on his journey from Novice to Archmage in this Arcane Academy LitRPG series from J Pal, bestselling author of*** The Houndsman ***and*** They Called Me Mad. *It features a unique magic system which involves cultivating a solar system in one's core, Detailed spell crafting and alchemy, Dungeon diving, arcane archery, a magic university setting and so much more.*

Get Department of Dungeon Studies Now!

Where others see doom, he sees opportunity. Hell Difficulty? More like a chance to thrive. *Nathaniel's bus ride was supposed to be just another boring commute. Wrong. Now, he, 23 fellow passengers, and a corgi named Biscuit, are stuck in a "Hell Difficulty" Tutorial, battling monsters and leveling up to survive. Easy difficulty, anyone can handle. Normal difficulty, you've got to put up a fight to get by. Hard difficulty is where only the tough ones last. And Hell? That's where you have to be a bit out of your mind! With his terrifying talent for mana manipulation, Nathaniel decides to invest every stat point into mana. Attribute imbalance be damned. It will either kill him before the monsters and his enemies can, or turn him into one of the most powerful beings within the system. Never underestimate the guy who has so much Mana it should kill him...* ***Follow Nathaniel's crazy journey as he takes on nightmarish foes and teams up with a far-from-normal group of bus passengers in this action-packed LitRPG Adventure. He must outsmart the odds, survive, and emerge stronger than anyone else! Perfect for fans of* The Primal Hunter, Defiance of the Fall, *and* Apocalypse: Generic System. *Grab your copy today!***

Get Hell Difficulty Tutorial Now!

The last of humanity will rise again... He will lead them. *The Earth met its end, bathed in holy fire. Rifts spill monsters into our world. Chaos reigns. Now, the Kingdom of Cindrus is the last bastion of humanity. The last vestiges of a broken people clinging to life deep underground. But not all hope is lost. Erec has been blessed by the Goddess. From a line of disgraced nobility, he seeks to reclaim his family's honor and join the prestigious academy – the institution that trains the next generation of Knights. With a power that brings him to an uncontrollable Rage, and an old-world AI aiding him, Erec seeks to reconquer the world with the remains of human-kind.* **Knights Apocalyptica *is an action packed, apocalypse LitRPG from debut author Zach Skye. Loaded with progression, a detailed system, power armor, a magic academy, and so much more, it's perfect for fans of* The Iron Prince, Bastion, *and* 12 Miles Below.** Available on Kindle, Kindle Unlimited, and Audible narrated by the legendary Roger Clark (Arthur Morgan in Red Dead Redemption 2)!

Get Knights Apocalyptica Now!

For all our LitRPG books, visit our website.

MORE FROM TE BAKUTIS

If you'd like to support TE Bakutis and read advance chapters of this story and others, as well as bonus short stories from other characters you've seen in this book, please check out TE's Patreon at https://www.patreon.com/SummaryInferno

If you'd like to read some other books by TE Bakutis, you can view those and read advance chapters from each at https://www.tebakutis.com/.